1984

Contemporary
American
Fiction

Contemporary American Fiction

Edited and introduced
by Douglas Messerli

Sun & Moon Press

Washington, D.C.

1983

© Sun & Moon Press, 1983

Copyrights for individual works:

"Genre Studies: The Textbook," © Mel Freilicher, 1975
"Alphabet of Revelations," © New Directions Anthology, 1980
"What Noni Hubner Did Not Tell the Police about Jesus,"
© Russell Banks, 1981
"The Catalogue," © John Perreault, 1983
"A Jean-Marie Cookbook," © Jeff Weinstein, 1978

Grateful acknowledgement is made to the publishers and editors of the following publishing houses and journals which first printed some of the fictions in this collection: *New Directions Anthology* (for "Alphabet of Revelations"); Houghton-Mifflin (for "What Noni Hubner Did Not Tell the Police about Jesus," in *Trailerpark*); New Directions (for "The Game," in *Seaview*); *The Alternate* (for "Objects in Mirror Are Closer Than They Appear"); and *Crawl Out Your Window* and *Sun & Moon: A Journal of Literature & Art* (for "A Jean-Marie Cookbook").

Library of Congress Cataloging in Publication Data

Contemporary American Fiction.

(Sun & Moon contemporary literature series; no. 18)
1. Short stories, American. 2. American fiction—20th century. I. Messerli, Douglas, 1947-   . II. Series.
PS648.S5C66 1983   813'.01'08   83-9087

ISBN: 0-940650-22-3 (cloth)
ISBN: 0-940650-23-1 (pbk)
10 9 8 7 6 5 4 3 2 1
First Edition

Cover design: Kevin Osborn

This book also is published as *Sun & Moon: A Journal of Literature & Art*, issues nos. 15/16.

Synchronic Fictions

"The map is not the territory."
Ludwig Wittgenstein

Attempting to describe the state of contemporary fiction, one finds oneself in much the same position as the ancient sailors must have felt, tracing the routes laid down by the geographers of the day, who, Plutarch observed, "crowd[ed] into the edges of their maps parts of the world they [did] not know, adding notes in the margins to the effect that beyond [lay] nothing but sandy deserts full of wild beasts and unapproachable bogs."[1] After even a casual reading of current fiction criticism, one suspects that some of today's literary cartographers not only map parts of the terrain "they do not know," but—taking the methods of the early geographers one step further into the absurd—define the unknown less by what they suppose it to be than by what they imagine it is not. Increasingly over the past two decades, contemporary American fiction—plotted by many critics as lying in the deep seas of Postmodernism—has come to be depicted as a sort of *terra incognita*, an unknowable and frightening region that stands apart and against the familiar shores of Modernism, mimesis, the symbol, experimentation, interpretation, moral value, and even, itself."[2] And there is just enough of an atmosphere of parody and nostalgia in the present-day environment to have convinced some of its explorers—most notably, John Barth—that they have strayed into a world of fiction in which the old cannot subsist.[3]

Other critics—Robert Alter, Philip Stevick, and Alan Wilde, among many—argue, more convincingly, that what seems to be an island—if I may extend my metaphor a bit further—is actually a peninsula, linked to literary tradition; that contemporary American fiction basically is a restoration and amplification of pre-realist modes and genres of fiction (Alter and Stevick) or is a new episode in an evolving and reactive pattern of fictional irony (Wilde).[4] Still others, portray the contemporary scene as a vast archipelago, a topographic free-for-all in which self-reflexive, experimental, parodistic, and more classically-structured works coexist with Modernist fiction in a pluralist Eden, so to speak.[5]

In short, where once our literary guides focused their energies on describing specific aspects of the landscapes of current fiction, it now appears that they feel a necessity to map the shape of new fiction in relation to this and other centuries. It is as if suddenly critics of fiction have grown fearful that readers may lose their footing in the morass of contemporary culture; as if they must assure themselves and their fellow readers that new fiction is either "dangerous" or "safe."

This moral imperative, in part, has to do with the fact that many contemporary fictions do not seem to require or reveal much of significance through thematic interpretation; and with the end of that formalist function, several critics have abandoned the study of individual authors and works in preference for investigations of various critical methodologies themselves. For those who continue to write on contemporary fiction it often seems that there is little choice but to turn to literary history in order to establish contexts in which to understand and evaluate new writing. But there is an obvious danger in this; for what begins as an outline has a strange way of becoming the border; what may be understood as charting the course, may ultimately work toward the establishment of a canon as inflexible as that of the formalists. For, surely, whatever else might be said about contemporary fiction, "it" is not an "it," is not a "thing" to be mapped, but rather is process itself. How can one "locate" or "define"—as either friend or foe—a literature that has neither been assimilated by the culture nor finished being written? To speak of contemporary fiction—even a part of it—as a *body* that stands "against," "for," or "post" anything is merely conjecture, is to image its completion, its death.

Ironically, if the contemporary writers—of this collection at least—share anything in common, it is an opposition to these very attempts to historify and exclude or canonize their works. In their baroque embellishment of genre, authors such as Mel Freilicher, Michael Andre, Gilbert Sorrentino, John Ashbery, Tom Ahern, Harrison Fisher, Jeff Weinstein, and Michael Brownstein challenge concepts of cultural necessity and literary destiny. Through the superimposition of numerous traditional and popular forms (drama, catalogue, dialogue, romance, autobiography, literary history, political satire, and textbook—to name only a few), a fiction such as Freilicher's *Genre Studies* implicitly advocates a non-linear, synchronist approach to literature, asserting a structure which permits the contemporary writer to be less anxiety-ridden (to borrow Harold Bloom's expressive description of the condition of today's authors[6]) than enthusiastic about the influence of writers present and past.

Behind this exploitation of genres, no doubt, is the desire to parody formalist fictional techniques. But this same synchronist sensibility also permits a genuine recovery of the

Gogolian comic fable in Ahern's "Chenken and Nartzarzen in Several Days on the Town"; a rediscovery and infusion of new energy into the genre of the masque in Ashbery's "Description of a Masque"; and a transformation from a mere travesty of the academy in Sorrentino's "The Gala Cocktail Party," to a dazzling linguistic anatomy of names and types. This same fascination with structural simultaneity, moreover, is the force behind Leslie Scalapino's and Norma Jean Deak's experimentations with the performative possibilities of fiction that push it beyond text. Indeed, despite the notoriety of explicit parodists such as John Barth, Donald Barthelme, Kurt Vonnegut, and Robert Coover,[7] one is struck by the seriousness of purpose with which many contemporary fictionists explore the potentials of simultaneous structures and styles.

Particularly in the past couple of years, storytellers have begun to re-incorporate chronological narrative, the objective point of view, and even realist characters into their works. To label this as a "return" to Modernist or realist modes of fiction, however, is precisely the kind of misreading fostered by the attempt to *locate* fiction in a particular time and place. Pointing to this misapprehension, Alan Wilde perceptively describes several of these parable-like works as mid fictions, fictions in which the world is perceived "as neither objectively knowable nor as totally opaque. . . ."[8] But by placing such fiction between "the indicative and subjunctive, realism and reflexivity," Wilde, himself, is caught up in the metaphor of the map. Perhaps these works do not lie *between* two extremes as they make use of both. For, like their peers in this anthology, Walter Abish, Richard Padget, Russell Banks, Mark Sacharoff, Toby Olson, Steve Katz, Donald Olson, John Perreault, Joe Ashby Porter, Paul Witherington, Roberta Allen, Corinne

Robins, and Laura Ferguson are engaged, in part, in an attempt to reveal parallel and antipathetic realities.

Walter Abish's "Alphabet of Revelations," for example, is on one level a fairly straight-forward satire of suburban life; its small-minded characters, their gossip, extra-marital affairs, divorces, and meager revelations might equally be at home in a novel by John Cheever or John Updike. But even the incompetent reader cannot help recognizing that there is something rotten on Sustain Drive. For the "reality" that Abish presents is something like that of an old maid schoolmarm's who has watched too many soap-operas over summer vacation. The alphabetization of the character's names (Arlo, Bud, Clem, Donna, Erna, Faye) deflates them from rounded figures with whom the reader might empathize to flat signs that emblematize contemporary society in general. The surprising revelation at story's end, accordingly, belongs less to the characters than to the author, who—turning the tables, so to speak—suggests to the reader that these characters and, by extension, the society are more complex than what meets the eye. Through a combination of conventional and inventive structures and techniques, in other words, Abish undermines what David Antin describes as the "normative-realist" notion of fiction in order to build anew a more complex fictional reality for the reader and himself. By engaging with the reader's expectations, Abish not only parodies the values of middle-class society, but challenges the ways in which it sustains those values in its fictions, in its conceptions of itself.

The fictions by which we define our lives are also the focus of John Perreault's "The Catalogue." Described in painfully objective detail, the sole character of this tale is the consummate consumer, a creature of the Victorian culture confronted with the superabundance of 20th-century artifacts. One by one, her dreams and desires are revealed—in what must be the most extreme use of the objective correlative in all of fiction—by the objects she procures through her mail-order catalogue. The story itself, in fact, becomes a kind of catalogue, not only of this woman's wants and purchases, but of the products by which her culture defines itself. Despite the story's near-absolute objectivism, no reader can miss the irony that Katherine's culture is his culture as well; thus, as the author implies, his character's fate is the fate of all who passively accept the artifacts of society rather than engage in their creation. Ultimately, Perreault's fiction is less a study of an Iowa recluse than it is a guidebook to cultural icons, a dictionary of the culture's dead fictions.

Similarly, Toby Olson's "The Game"—a chapter from his novel, *Seaview*—presents a series of scenes which function in terms of realist plot while simultaneously serving as *tableaux vivants*, which reveal to both characters and readers their psychological and metaphysical conditions. Not since the final chapelhouse scene of Djuna Barnes's *Nightwood*, has an American fiction used such theatrical trappings. Olson's broken-down miniature golf course, replete with dolphin, sea, moon, bird, and snake, is a virtual diorama in which a confrontation between good and evil is enacted.

A more secular struggle between sin and salvation is the subject of Donald Olson's "Objects in Mirror Are Closer Than They Appear." In this work the battle is waged between two sisters against the backdrop of a paranoic dystopia. In fact, in several of the stories of this collection the authors imply that only those whom the society sees as abnormal recognize that good and evil are forces with which to be reckoned. In

"Keeper," Steve Katz leaves the salvation of the race to a man who is convinced that the souls of all human beings are about to be stolen by bats with whom he shares his bedroom. The narrator of Richard Padget's Kafkaesque tale, "A Brief Guide to the Fall Repertory," wakes one morning to find his paranoia confirmed by a cannon aimed at his bedroom window. In short, as Noni Hubner of Russell Banks's "What Noni Hubner Did Not Tell the Police about Jesus" recognizes, in today's society it is often dangerous to reveal one's visions.

Behind the "real" worlds presented in these tales, in other words, there is authorial acknowledgment of other realities which in their very inexplicability are alluring and perilous both. The flat-footed realist, like Mark Sacharoff's plainclothes cop, can never comprehend the world around him, will never be able to answer the questions with which he is obsessed: "Why is everybody behavin' so queer?" "What's happenin'?" Only those who go beyond what they see, beyond the bounds of socialized normalcy, these authors suggest, will experience through the synchronousness of time and space, a revelation.

Certainly such thematics are not original in the history of twentieth-century fiction (one thinks immediately of the search for transcendence in the works of William Faulkner, E. M. Foster, Virginia Woolf, and Eudora Welty); but, then, neither have these concerns been previously expressed in these new ways. And that, in brief, is my argument. Despite the assertions of literary critics and historians, most contemporary writers do not write because they have something to say, I suspect, but because something cannot be said. And it is that effort to express that ineffable "something," I argue, that energizes these works. The reader of this editor's Contemporary Fiction, may have to forego the search for implicit or explicit statements that reveal the author's *position*, in order to participate in the creation of a world not on any map. For it is only as a participant, as an attentive, empathetic, and inquisitive listener, that the reader of these tales—like the character who listens to Fletcher's chillingly mad story in Katz's "Keeper"—can find a way to share the author's perceptions of simultaneity, a mind-expanding sensation described by Katz as taking "seventeen steps away from the tower, twenty-six steps away from the moon."

These stories, accordingly, are not indicative of all the varieties of contemporary fiction nor even fully representative of this kind of contemporary writing. Rather, they are twenty-four of the most exhilarating and inenarrable experiences the editor has participated in during the recent past.

Douglas Messerli
Temple University

NOTES

[1]Plutarch, Bernadette Perrin, trans., *Lives. (Theseus)* (London: W. Heinemann, 1914), p. 3.

[2]Among the most vehement of critics of contemporary fiction are Gerald Graff and John Gardner. Graff's *Literature Against Itself: Literary Ideas in Modern Society* (Chicago: The University of Chicago Press, 1979) and Gardner's *On Moral Fiction* (New York: Basic Books, 1978) are particularly virulent attacks on contemporary literature, viewed from the postmodern perspective.

[3]John Barth, "The Literature of Exhaustion," *Atlantic Monthly*, August 1967, 29.

[4]Robert Alter, "The Inexhaustible Genre," *Partial Magic: The Novel As a Self Conscious Genre* (Berkeley: University of California Press, 1975); Philip Stevick, *Alternative Pleasures: Post-realist Fiction and the Tradition* (Urbana: University of Illinois, 1981); Alan Wilde, *Horizons of Assent: Modernism, Postmodernism, and the Ironic Imagination* (Baltimore: The Johns Hopkins University Press, 1981). I must confess that, despite my advocation of a more experiential approach to contemporary fiction, my own criticism might generally fall into this category. At their best, these critics less "map" the contemporary scene than they "trace" certain of its patterns; and when they succeed at this, I have little criticism of their methods.

[5]See Ihab Hassan's *The Dismemberment of Orpheus: Toward a Postmodern Literature* (New York: Oxford University Press, 1971), Jerome Klinkowitz's *Literary Disruptions: The Makings of a Post-Contemporary Fiction* (Urbana: University of Illinois Press, 1975), and Larry McCaffery's *The Metafictional Muse: The Works of Robert Coover, Donald Barthelme, and William H. Gass* (Pittsburgh: University of Pittsburgh Press, 1982). In the latter work, McCaffery argues that the contemporary scene in general might be characterized as having a "metasensibility."

[6]Harold Bloom, *Figures of Capable Imagination* (New York: Seabury Press, 1976).

[7]A list of other explicit parodists might include Tom Veitch, Steve Katz (in a work such as *The Exaggerations of Peter Prince*), Russell Banks (in *Family Life*), Harry Matthews, and Jaimy Gordon. What is interesting is that, except perhaps for Veitch, the lesser-known group of writers might all have been said to have shifted to fictions that rely less on parody alone.

[8]Wilde, " 'Strange Displacements of the Ordinary': Apple, Elkin, Barthelme, and the Problem of the Excluded Middle," *Boundary 2*, 10 (Winter 1982), 182.

Table of Contents

Tom Ahern

Chenken and Nartzarzen in Several Days on the Town

On the sixth day of spring, 1920, Chenken and Nartzarzen were riding a tram in Budapest.

It was their custom to rendezvous in the city every few weeks, Chenken arriving from her home in Presk, and Nartzarzen from his in Pope. They were at this moment ten minutes into their customary meeting and very few words had been spoken, although both had more than simple thoughts with which to pass the time.

Chenken, Mrs. Chenken, was at that time aged thirty, while Nartzarzen was seventy-five. Mr. Nartzarzen: he was a widower. He had known Chenken from her birth, and he'd known her parents a good long time as well.

The city was half-opened and half-closed, reflecting the times, which were both horribly optimistic and aggressively pessimistic. Who's to know? was a phrase often heard on a tram in Budapest then.

It just so happened that that day the tram's conductor was Fearsome Willie. His reputation had been assembled with great care, of countless insults murmured and flung through the years from his perfectly bow-shaped lips.

Chenken had never seen Willie before. Nartzarzen knew him well enough and disapproved of the man. But it was really the trees that claimed the attentions of these two passengers, trees in colors of new shirts and cars.

Fearsome Willie liked the trees as well as the next one. But he seldom looked at them, preferring in most people's opinions to study the road ahead for a chance to intimidate a presumptuous citizen or ignore someone chasing the tram: he disliked people who were late. He'd intone the streets with the vigor and solemnity of a patriarch, then slide Willifully past the stop if no one stepped forward instantly.

Willie was actually a case of unparalleled emotional exhaustion and ought to have been pitied, which he was occasionally, with evil results.

It happened first on a sunny August Saturday in 1919, and again on a September morning that year, and once more that month: three times altogether, with complaints lodged against Willie and without, but in the days before prices had begun to rise very much, when all Budapest—even the tram conductor—should have been happy. Nartzarzen, for our information, had seen none of these despicable incidents, though they did nothing to improve Willie's reputation, and that Nartzarzen knew plenty about.

I'll skip the last two and proceed directly backwards to the first of the incidents, that August afternoon, a Saturday, hot and bright and unforgiving, though prices were fine and shopping was a nice weekend activity.

An elderly man, pious by the look of him, and dressed substantially and in beautiful fabrics, boarded the tram in front of the Dolshemsky's Bazaar, a least favorite stop of Willie's since it often involved a lot of coming and going and packages. The Bazaar was—is—a department store of great beauty and extent. Anything can be found. Beat our prices if you can and you usually could, but it was convenience they were really selling. Take it or leave it.

This elderly pious fellow was absolutely fortified with packages, inner and outer walls and breastworks of packages, festoons of them outlining his figure, which by the look of it, was a medium one on all counts. And these dangling bundles stabbed and nicked everywhere, even giving Willie a poke.

Naturally, Willie hated this new package, yes: this moving colossus of packages—(certainly except for fingers that were strangled a vivid pink and blue with string, handles and ribbon; and two feet that might or might not belong to the above, it *was* simply a package or a roosting flock of packages that had boarded his tram)—and, for the sake of decency, Willie allowed it that one poke, intending to throw it off instantly the moment it stuck him again.

At that moment, just as Willie had decided on his principles, the pious gentleman emerged, discarding the packages in one brief and cluttered avalanche. Willie's right foot was the only victim.

"My apologies!" said the gent draftily. "You poor man: having to stand here all day and take this!"

Willie the Fearsome turned an unusual shade around the jowls. The color of the smocks of porcelain Dutchboys.

"You poor man! At least you get to travel." The passenger smiled to indicate that he meant it.

"You'll have to find a seat!" stated Willie.

"If *you* have to stand, then I don't mind standing," the man argued comfortably. "We can talk between stops. I have a way to go, don't I? You poor man! Your ear will be half chewed off by the time I'm home!"

17

"Find yourself a seat," scowled Willie.

"There aren't any left," the man said.

"I'm afraid then we're above our legal capacity. Sir, you'll have to debark."

"But, poor fellow, I'm not home yet," the man sighed, adding "I think you mean 'unboard.' "

Willie restated his official opinion with a few stray kicks to the fallen packages.

The man stared dreamily out the window at the passing street. "Anyway, the tram's moving, poor man."

"I'll stop it for you," Willie bowed.

"Don't stop it for me! It's out of the question! Just look at all these packages!" And he gave them one or two kicks himself.

Just then another passenger stood up to get off.

"I'll take her seat," said the old man.

"Get up!" Willie demanded.

"No-no. Now I have a seat. You poor fellow," the gent concluded.

"But these packages! You have too many, for one thing. They're a nuisance to public clearance!"

"Poor fellow. . . Yes, I'm sure. But you know while I was in that store at least fifteen people asked me my opinion of something and at least ten of those wished me to hold a bundle. And they were all aunts and cousins and nephews and nieces; you can't imagine what it's like to have a large family. Well, poor man, I'm sure you can, with your shepherding tramsful. They all hooked and strung one thing or another on me until you see what you see: a human ruin of bundles!"

"You can't come dragging every spare aunt's box onto a public tram. You've only paid one fare!"

The pious fellow let tumble one final paper-wrapped ring case. "My poor poor man,"—with unconcealed anger—"do you think I asked to be mistaken for a pack camel?" And after a moment's hesitation: "Stop the tram, please!"

Willie rang for the tram to stop.

"My stop," confided the man, who again was decked in layers of goods.

Willie blossomed in some lovely shades, many of them an orchid hue.

"Good day," the old gent saluted as he descended the tram's steps, his hands again pinched by string and ribbon, and poking for safety along the nickel rail that led unquestionably downward.

For a second he stood on the sidewalk, as perfectly concealed as in his own house by the boxes about him, then he called to Willie: "I left a box on the floor, I think. One more favor, my poor man. Could you hand it here?"

Willie nudged the box with his polished brown boot, getting everything aligned, then kicked it airborne out of the tram so that it flew right over the fellow's head. The heap of packages collapsed slightly then straightened, having addended the one that had just landed.

It was for incidents such as this that some rode this tram at all, cruelly savoring Willie's apoplexies, while others, such as Nartzarzen, had only the simpler need to get from one place to another and rode this tram because it was the correct tram and Willie's conductorship was of little or no interest to them.

This day, number six of a new spring, twelve persons were aboard, not counting Willie and its driver Georg: Nartzarzen, of course, who endeavored to have no opinion of the conductor, though naturally there were many Nartzarzens in the favored sense and several of these did have opinions, ones they would rather have enjoyed making public if there were no risk; Chenken, who had hardly glanced once at Willie—though Willie was following her with keen interest; and ten others: two matrons, a woman of business, a salesman, two men of business, and a group of four school children. You'll be surprised to hear that Willie liked children. Nartzarzen on this count was of a strict opinion: he despised about every third one he met, and the rest were either placid or unintelligible. Chenken had no children. The other six adults, seven if you include Georg, the driver, were assorted.

The twelve tram patrons were scattered and swaying in unison throughout the vehicle, with the four children grouped in a silent party toward the rear. Willie posted himself near them. Nartzarzen and Chenken sat behind the driver, then moved once to a seat quite near Willie.

That the couple moved even once seemed suspicious to Willie, who was sensitive to these things. When they moved a second time he felt he should investigate, as these were troubled times.

"Are you being bothered by a draft?" he asked, soliciting their reply with a pleasant yet imperious glance.

Nartzarzen looked up, which he'd forbidden himself doing, and shook his head. Chenken nodded stolidly, not really nodding if one were to split hairs, which Willie did from time to time in pursuance of his job.

"Yes?" he inquired a second time, misconstruing or pretending to.

"No," said Chenken. "It's the sun."

Willie looked sympathetically out the wrong window.

"The sun's going down," he observed, poking the back of their seat.

"Thank you for asking," croaked Nartzarzen, who was not at his best when addressing strangers and was particularly nervous when addressing officials of any stripe or authority.

Willie waited nearby.

Nartzarzen, seeing that they weren't now to be left in peace, suggested they get off for coffee which they did at the next corner shop, *Cafe von den vuin Nasn.*

As I haven't mentioned it yet, I should tell you that the business Nartzarzen and Chenken attended to in Budapest was political, political and revolutionary, and destructive by mutual aspiration and agreement. I won't tell you which party they allied themselves with, because right or left didn't matter, and I don't want to prejudice you one way or another.

Chenken and Nartzarzen sat at a table near the windows, talking, a couple among couples. Chenken was tall but not tall enough in her husband's eyes, which were set too far apart in most everyone's opinion—he was back in Presk, looking as if he were trying to stare around both sides of a post. And she was: dark, careful while appearing careless, direct when seeming ironic. A little lighter than dark, too. Nartzarzen was an assortment of things that were not like Chenken. Each of them had ordered coffee and was dissecting a pastry, crumbly with anticipation.

This was the coffee shop you haven't heard of that had shelves of noses, plaster and marble and papier mache and some lovely rare woods, numerous famous noses or obscure noses, noses unfettered by eyes of any cast and as free-floating as the bud of a lily on a drifting pond.

Across the street the School for the Normally Superior was about to disembowel itself and gush forth rank after rank of students. Pleasure seethed in the air. The doors flew open, and Chenken added more sugar to her coffee, while Nartzarzen studied a recently reawakened fly crawling nearby, but not near enough to swat with the paper he soon purchased from the cashier.

And now the School for the Superiorily Normal was letting out for the day, one city block off, and a rush and dance of students, even younger than the ones before, passed the windows where Nartzarzen creased and recreased his paper and Chenken considered a second cup of coffee and the fly had disappeared to be replaced by a wasp.

"Heard. . ." Nartzarzen began, broke off, then ventured: ". . . anything?"

Of course Chenken was very eager to know something herself and was disappointed in this evidence of ignorance on Nartzarzen's part. After all, he was the one with the decades of acquaintanceship among revolutionaries. More from lack of anything to say than the reverse, Chenken announced: "We'll have to do it ourselves. Whatever it turns out to be."

Nartzarzen, a redoubt of hope, only heard the first part, or ignored the second, for his heart warmed noisily to the call for action.

"Take, for example, off the top of my head, that conductor on the tram," Nartzarzen mused. "First, clearly he's an official. His uniform spits that fact in our eye. Second, he's abusive. . ."

Each sipped.

". . . so that his civil authority—which may well be illegitimate in the first case—is abused and rendered obnoxious in the second."

Nartzarzen lit an oily oval cigarette.

"At least I find it obnoxious," he said. "And the reports are none too good."

Chenken took the necessary steps to convince herself that

Nartzarzen was speaking seriously. She squinted, focused and refocused her eyes, counted backwards mentally from five, and attempted, with the relative success she'd lately commanded, to clear her mind of random thoughts. Sweaters, lice, smoke-stacks went, as went a statement on her religion from birth, and her mother's religion. By imagining each of Nartzarzen's statements as propaganda banners slicing through the air like winter cranes, she kept her attention on him.

To reward himself and her grave interest, he sipped fastidiously from his cup, hoping she'd recall his face when she needed courage some day.

"Maybe," she said.

"No," he blistered, "we'd have to assassinate him."

"We could overturn the tram."

"The reason I say I think we should assassinate him . . ."

"Murder him."

"It's as much murder," Nartzarzen said preemptorily, "as my eating this roll is a murder of good wheat. The maw of time is the fate of officials such as Willie. And the maw is a bin for the sustenance of the new order, the refreshed body politic. We have to strike at a level that can go home with the average observor. If a cabinet minister is shot, who cares but other cabinet ministers? And they are all complacent and over-protected anyway."

"Who's going to do it?"

"We are."

"Who besides yourself?"

"We! We are! We can do it," Nartzarzen writhed. "If a tram conductor dies, everyone in the working class who hears about it dies a little, too. And that's a lot of people! And complacency goes out the window with the bath water."

Nartzarzen rested precisely five seconds.

"Furthermore,"—and at this stage of Nartzarzen's argument, a tram clattered past—"we may if we don't do this ever do anything."

"We must take a poll," said Chenken dismally.

"Poll!" Nartzarzen sagged. "Are you serious? Why? Poll *who*?"

"It would be plain murder to kill a man whom you personally don't like, unless it is the demonstrable will of those who would most know whether it is called for or not."

"I think we can act independently in this instance," said Nartzarzen sourly.

"You can."

"But what about secrecy! We can't ask everyone if it's alright to kill Willie-the-tram-conductor."

"I had in mind something more subtle."

"I can't waste time on delays," Nartzarzen said. "I'm too old. And it's getting too late."

"And I," Chenken scrutinized him, "can't waste time on a lunatic."

They sat for a minute or two, as the cafe's clock measured its time across the wooden tables and the conversation of the patrons.

"How?" he inquired distastefully.

"You agree on why?"

"How?" he said.

"We'll ask them. We could say, 'What would you think if someone like Willie was assassinated for political reasons seeing that he's such a prick?' Would they be outraged do they think? Indifferent? Frightened? Pleased? Sympathetic? Would they call the police?"

"Probably the latter."

"We could ask people who ride the tram."

"Well," Nartzarzen said, "we'll have to talk about the weather first."

"Then a complaint or two about the government; everybody has one."

"You mention the unrest; I'll mention the problems."

"Having struck up this thoroughly bland conversation, we will then ask in passing what they'd think if someone like Willie were assassinated."

Chenken reached for one of Nartzarzen's cigarettes.

"You pop the question," she said. "You're older."

Nartzarzen smiled. He picked a flake of tobacco from his lip. "My pleasure."

WHAT HAPPENED

Two weeks later Chenken and Nartzarzen boarded Willie's tram again.

Each of them carried a modest number of parcels.

Nartzarzen had bought several items from a bakery, hoping the odor would disarm those they questioned. Now and then he'd breathe deeply from that particular bag. If worse came to worst—and he had ideas of what the worst might be—he'd give his rolls and pastries away and retire to Pope.

Willie patrolled the tram as usual, greeting some, frowning upon others, a little of one, a little of the other.

After they'd shaken in their seats for a quarter mile or so, Chenken pinched Nartzarzen's nearest knee and directed his attention to a woman sitting alone across the aisle.

"Remarkably fine weather," said Nartzarzen, in a startled and querulous squeak.

The woman stared steadily ahead, bobbing with the tram. But Nartzarzen, who sat nearest her, leaned across and confided, "We've no right to expect weather like this in Budapest."

"The nights are too cold for me," the woman laughed.

"*Some*thing's happening," Chenken added. "If you don't have an umbrella, you don't like the rain. If you're a farmer, you go out and stand in it."

"Those pastries smell delicious," the woman remarked.

"Willie's in top form today. Have you noticed?" said Nartzarzen.

"Willie?"

"The conductor," Chenken said. "Willie-the-conductor."

"I don't ride this one very much," the woman explained. "I heard this was the coldest spring in years," she added. "By the way, where did you buy them?"

"Uncle: may I?" Chenken gently freed the fragrant bag from Nartzarzen, who was not in fact her uncle. "It's still warm," she said. "Can we tempt you?"

The woman refused at first. Chenken passed the bag to Nartzarzen to hand across. "They'll just be thrown away."

The woman selected a roll. Willie raised his head and seemed —Yes!—Nartzarzen was sure of it—to be looking at them with awakening displeasure.

"There he goes," Nartzarzen whispered.

Willie was shaking his head. He shook his head at the woman and her pastry, slapped his hands now on the sleeves of his neither clean nor unclean coat, strolled toward her . . .

But he said nothing. Because after all, it was not against regulations for her to eat on the tram.

"Did you *see*?" Nartzarzen asked the woman. She had picked a delinquent crumb from her blouse.

"What?" she inquired.

"The conductor!" said Chenken.

"That roll was superb," she laughed. "Thank you."

"Did you hear," Nartzarzen interrupted, drawing a great unmanageable breath mid-sentence, "that a conductor was shot down just two weeks ago in Vienna?"

"In cold blood," Chenken said.

"For dereliction of duty," said Nartzarzen. "Of course it was an assassination really, since it was a political killing."

"I'm not surprised," said the woman. Then she added, "Things like that happen in Vienna all the time."

That day Nartzarzen and Chenken interviewed eight persons on Willie's tram. Every so often they'd get off to eat or smoke. By the end of the day Willie was greeting the pair like old friends.

"He recognizes us," Nartzarzen said.

"He likes us," said Chenken.

"He smells a fish."

Of the eight interviewed:

Mr. Vegetable-Garden Face had been conventionally horrified by the thought of a conductor's assassination, though the man had at first misunderstood and thought Nartzarzen meant an assassination *by* a conductor and not *of*.

Mrs. Walnut-Meat-Textured Skin had nothing good to say of it.

Miss Smoke-'em-Ups was in favor of it—and soon, since Willie objected to her smoking.

Mrs. Moles-and-All was silent and reprimanding.

27

Mr. Plow-and-Mules nose was basically indifferent, and his hat was indifferent;

while Mr. Ripe Shoes was a cynic, dismissed as such.

Of the woman who ate a pastry you know, though you don't know her opinion: she thought it was heinous. And there was an eighth person who agreed with her.

"And do you still think you can kill him when virtually all Budapest is against it?" Chenken asked.

Nartzarzen said no and went home to Pope. And Chenken went home to Presk. Most of those with homes went to them. And those without homes went without.

Melvyn Freilicher

from *Genre Studies: The Textbook*

UNIT I DEVELOPMENT

Lenin said, "Dialectics in the proper sense is the study of contradiction in the very essence of objects." Engels said, "Motion itself is a contradiction." Lenin defined the law of the unity of opposites as "the recognition (discovery) of the contradictory, mutually exclusive, *opposite tendencies in all* phenomena and processes of nature *(including* mind and society)." *Her father was a landholding peasant, his mother a devout Buddhist.*
   —Mao Tse Tung

Introduction

ONE SCENARIO (there are an infinite number like snow-flakes): In the Beginning was the Soft Shell. *Paradise* ah yes Paradise that realization, so full & hauntingly beautiful, of the concept: "play." The actual word "play" was coined. Then too, you know, as the young of the species (who were also the kindly, the hermaphroditic and the very old) babbled together in the silky flow of a long moonlit night. All the parts flowed smoothly together in those days; hierarchical organization meshed with no-organization-at-all-only-Pristine Unique-ness (she went to Andrea's high school!) constantly, constantly.

Fig. 3. Andrea de Rouge in what she believes to be Paradise.

In the Beginning, Everybody had very many (& no) "identities" and people talked to themselves blushed out loud juggled selves around with the grace of a crazy young monkey, laughing always laughing and jumping around, keeping company in a dancing sort of way. Each self was many others; the other was each self and so forth into the deeply mustachioed night. In other words, Syncretism was practiced, not just preached. The brain was a wise young Egg then, definitely not cracked; there was no such thing, for example, as "top down" & "bottom up." ("Thank *God*" moans Andrea, dropping to the floor.) The concepts "natural law" & "human law" did not yet exist as concepts let alone as oppositions; there was no such thing as "private property"; "responsibility" was the tribal heritage, built into the natural respect of each player for every player and, of course, for the g-g-Game itself.

Soon, however, that absolute snake Thomas Hobbes and these other so-called "intellectuals" come slithering along, tearing their hair out at the roots, their pores emitting the raw substances of Wildroot Cream Oil. Yes, and these alleged intellectuals go around insisting forever insisting that we need Protection from each other ("not to mention from luscious Nature itself" adds an indignant Andrea) as they cower in the stink of their own doing. And, yes, finally these so-called intellectuals give birth to, or perhaps only legitimize the concept: "fear." Hobbes and his bunch emerged, you know, out of Paradise one dark night like the pus squeezed from some incidental wound; at first, you hardly knew they were there, real creeps but tenacious, always spreading, persistent as if they were "meant to be." The Ego differentiating itself from the Id the cortex fracturing the Egg addling, in short the (ugh) Reality Principle hitting the fan. (If God *really* didn't want them to eat that apple, why'd he put the tree there?)

In summation: In the Beginning was the Conception and the conception was word and the word was Paradise (play). Then the conception was fear (antithesis) and the fear was clearly here. (The cause of fear is fear itself, all the contemporary songs will tell you so.)

Needless to say, from then on in it was all downhill. The wells ran dry, the naked night stuck in the throat instead of running wild, smooth & exciting magic, the stars dancing on down to Broadway. Everywhere there sprung up governments; everywhere people were divided into the powerful and the powerless, the haves and the have nots. Once "status" had been defined as what everybody had, now it was defined as what everybody wanted. Yes, everyone was so desperate, looking to absurd little puppet "rulers" for an answer, some kind of sign, girl. Mating patterns were totally arbitrary at best, completely devastating at worse; most usually nauseatingly predictable, precisely calculated by the cunningly desperate participants, stamped out of the machine-made laboratory models of the heart. Our lives seemed so "historically inevitable": born to be torn to shreds on the rocks. All questions had but one answer —Power. "Spontaneity" was just another word for nothing left to use.

Or in the words of the hero of our little epic, the "little freak" itself (q.v.), describing the contemporary scene in a letter to Andrei Codrescu, a Rumanian friend who had never had the opportunity to visit the United States: "Blood-baths splattering wine, knitted & worsted wives all over the place, pouring dentine down the tubes, placing their ovaries on a pedestal. The husbands bring home the bacon and butt-fuck the mirrors. (So what else is new?) Everybody is happy, happy!! Then they are blessed with some bundles of joy. Blood-baths, afterbirths stinking up the kitchen, clogging up the vitality-draining rainbow-streaked boob tubes, 2.5 per 'home.' The little bundles are glued to the set, watching the *Apoxy Hour Squeal*, starring Mary Martin in *God's Overcooked Spinach, Drained & Deveined, Just Ready for the Relish*. Yes my friend, truth is just an image of nothing left that hasn't already been eaten or at least half-heartedly-chewed."

The little freak itself, you know, was once one of those very bundles, popping out of the womb one silver morn complete with long hair and a single golden hoop-earring. He was ritualistically stuttering the lord's prayer backwards and laughing like a crazy hyena. He is, among other things, Bellochio, sucking for dear life on a large, soon-to-be-huge, lump of sugar. (He is named Melvyn Douglas.) "Piss," the adults said when they first laid eyes on him. He will have to be systematically eliminated or just plain thrown down the drain, they thought in their heart of hearts or in that cash register where their heart of hearts should have been. The little freak outsmarted those nasty adults though! He left home at birth, if not before, and was highly instrumental in the formation of the Revolutionary "Orphans of Art" collective (q.v.).

The original Orphans came together explicitly to *do* something about the nauseous and repulsive state of a world which they had never even asked to be born into in the first place, poor babies! Overnight, they constructed giant bubbles, domed castles in the sky, celluloid giraffes leering in the rain barrels, styrofoam movie cameras spitting fire, towering 10 stories above the most commercial of banks: a whole series of haughty and splendid forms from another, more subterranean age. All over town, the forms could be found. All over town, the Orphans changed the "p's" to "r's" in the signs **MOTELS—APTS**. All over town, red streaks in the night, all Orphans alike.

Naturally, the Orphans of Art were phenomenally successful in their struggles against the forces of tyranny, and today, only a decade since the Orphans first began to fight, almost Everyone everywhere is Playing around all the time, mellowing out and generally Searching for Knowledge. It's called the State of Art. Others call it the synthesis. "Play" with a frame around it, metaphorically speaking of course, to keep out the demons or to let them in orderly, aesthetic like, you know what we mean? What we mean is this: once met, the demons can never be "forgotten"; yes once we have come to define the storms and tempests, the violent undercurrents, the narrow eddies, the Whiteness of the Whale, the Great Elemental Forces as "evil" as "fearful", these definitions must forever afterwards leave their trace on even our most breathless of castles in the sand. Yes, we have Fallen ("or been Tripped!" Andrea says) & what we must do now is laugh in the teeth of Death, become the wise young Art people, yes laughing even like crazy monkeys, talking to ourselves in the streets, recognizing the spaces between friends as the visible manifestations of Imperfect Realization, thought of by some as "Reality" (q.v.) itself.

"Play with a frame around it" then, explains R. Syncretti,

highly-acclaimed lit-crit, means that knowing all too well the ultimate impossibility of bridging the great Self-Other gap save in occasional moments of Ecstasy and Dream-like Wonder, we must nonetheless laugh like unbalanced primates, dance dance dance all night, extend our Spirits into the street, pay obeisance to the spaces, assume the role of Charlatan-Warrior, environmentally aware all the way! Yes we must consciously and with haughty intent (R. Syncretti writes) accept the blood-hungry Venus fly-traps, the sting rays, the volcanoes and the deadly Germs of Disease as part of what Is. We must subject all definitions to the burgeoning Erections, to the dewy-eyed vital Women of the Rose, to the healing powers of ART. In short, we must go off our nut, Syncretti concludes. ("That's easy for *you* to say," says Andrea.)

Communication is mostly telepathic in this fabulous state of Art you've heard so much about; assumptions are shared by large numbers of people. The world is "consensual" again; the idea "loose women" does not exist. There is a deep inner fabric, readily available to all scanners. This is the state of Anarchy, deep joy deep respect for Nature & the Imagination (every child knows Blake's wise old saying, "Where man is not, nature is barren"), deep respect for the power of demons. A delicate yet seemingly imperishable Balance. Can this be true?

2.

And so, for the first time in what he could only view as lifetimes, the little freak has a lot of "free time" on his hands and we find him in the process of trying to convince himself to take a little vacation. "God only knows I've *earned* it!" he says

35

Melvyn Freilicher

saucily, with a leering grin. In truth, much exhausting effort *had* been put into the recent decisive shoot-out with the Rockefeller Clan at their upstate New York fortress. The Orphans' strategy, which the freak had been so helpful in conceiving, was to drop pink & mauve tear-gas from helicopters painted to look like birch trees. When the Clan came running out of the house and bunkers shooting to kill, they encountered 200 lead robots coming at them with bazookas, whistling "Astronomy Dominie." Then the acid-rain started hitting them in a downpour getting into the hair, the eyes, the pores of the skin, the creases of the clothes; getting Nelson, as he later confessed to reporters in a giggle and a whisper, "stoned out of my gourd." (Ozzie, on the other hand, claims, "I didn't feel a thing!") And *besides*, the little freak tells himself, before that you worked so hard on that delicious little project to turn all the Universities into one giant gelatin and cellophane factory, run by machines. You really *do* need a rest, he says convincingly.

And so the little freak decides to take a little trip, a trip made possible only recently by some *very* clever inventions and discoveries of those still amazingly vital post-War Orphans. Yes the little freak will travel back through the space-time continuum to the Very Origins of Development itself! But first, en route, the freak will pay a little visit to Plato to finally meet the cat who started, or perhaps only legitimized, the veritable plague of "bourgeois idealism" which had literally been ravishing the western world before the advent of the Orphans of Art.

"Plato," the little freak says upon landing, "just tell me this. Smart boy like you, how could you of conceived of Perfect

Forms as Constant, never changing? You musta known that dialectics govern our every waking moment. You *must of* read Lenin." At this moment, the street caves in, the secret street beneath the seat. By the end of a week she is thinking constantly about the exact point in space and time that is the difference between *Maria* and *other*. As if she had fever, her skin burns and crackles with a pinpoint sensitivity. She can feel smoke against her skin.

"And listen Plato, why do these deathless Ideals of perfect loveliness keep haunting us so, Plato, huh *Plato*? Yes, even in *these* Enlightened Times, Play-*toe*!" squeaks the little freak, staring bug-eyed at every passing surfer and Greek statue. You wake in the morning with the sound of her lips on your throat. She is so Perfect, *Regina*!, my smile, my Queen! You met her once in a dream in a purple attic room thickly carpeted sloping roofs still air, rolling green hills stretching below, inside muted greys and violets. An old-fashioned home, like the oft-promised castles of your youth. Still? Yes, that deathless atmosphere; Life itself "dedifferentiated."

"Yea, Plato, why do I still yearn so to hold Regina in my arms, to grind my tired yet thrilling body against all those other luscious Platonic Forms too, *Plato*, huh *Plato*?" the little freak fairly squeaks. (He is *really* regressing now.) Yearning, forever yearning (yes, even in *these* Enlightened Times) for the Perfect Form of Goodness, that Butch Street Urchin Who is Really a Rose that Endlessly Lean Forever Shy, So Blond & Dewy-Eyed Surfer, the Majestic Child of the Light; Little Italy's Curly-Haired, Sleeveless-Underweared Glistening Child of the Night. ("Yum!" sighs Andrea.)

37

Melvyn Freilicher

"It is *Protection*, always *protection* we are seeking," says the little freak, answering his own questions, straightening his flambé tie, coming back to life "in the dead of the night less, perhaps, than in the light of the light." Protection from Change, from dollars, from sense too. Protection from Chaos from Form from sunset to dawn. Protection, in short, from that very Sparkling and Really Quite Startling Process known to some as "Life" itself. Somehow, in this ever-spinning Space (man), we must be firmly rooted. Will we be blown away by the terror or by the music? *that* is the question. Will today's Platonic Form serve as a Talisman to save us—the Sun, Constant Source of Energy —to keep us from all the Harm and Noxious Decay just *waiting* out there to get us, to rob us of our crooked little grins, to erode our will to write. Or will we realize all too soon ("or all too late!" sighs Andrea) that this Form too, our lovely lovely Regina, is only a fabrication of the dream factory, a shibboleth, a thinly disguised puppet show, a concerted plot to rob us of our *real* Myths, a trompe-oeil, trick of the tie, a cunning disguise of the demon's never-shifting eyes; our Hearts' desire maybe, nonetheless a lie for all that. (But *what a lie*, what a life! Or, dig those crazy shoulders; Regina, my lie!!!) And so, regretfully shelving Regina, will we be able to stand alone in the teeth of Fear & Regression? "Will we, well will we?" the little freak fairly shrieks.

"Do you love me?" asked Holgrave. "If we love one another, the moment has room for nothing more. Let us pause upon it and be satisfied. Do you love me, Phoebe?" ("Whew," the little freak says, safe now on the other side, "that was a close call.") Graceful as a bird, gleams of sunshine; ray of firelight, contradictions. "You look into my heart," replied she, letting her eyes drop. "You know I love you." And it was in this hour, so full of doubt and awe, that the one miracle was wrought, without which every human existence is blank. The bliss, which makes all things true, beautiful and holy, shone around this youth and this maiden, that split-ended long-haired Jewish freak with the single golden hoop-earring and Thomas Hobbes, that old fart. They were conscious of nothing sad or old. They transfigured the earth, and made it Eden again, and themselves the first dwellers in it. The dead man, so close beside them, was forgotten. At such a crisis, there is no Death; for Immortality is revealed anew, and embraces everything in its hallowed atmosphere!

3.

The little freak merrily takes note of the mediated contradictions in this little tableau; love & death in the American murmur he whispers & bidding Plato a final fond faredieu!, the little freak decides to get down to it. Yes back to the Very Origins of Development itself! To this end, the freak writes a "novel", then he writes a textbook, transcending the historical functions of each form in the very process of defining them. Then the freak has a mystical Revelation. ("Not another one!" cries Andrea, in mock alarm.)

Then I saw, the freak writes, that the transcendence of one form leads to the Very Source of Form. At least for that one magic eternal & never-existing "moment"—for the "moment of Transcendence" is Primal Energy alone, the Sun no the Void, the most peaceful Lull (purest hits of hot glowing Hash), that clear suspension preceding even Energy & heat & all shimmery light. The Void, the anti-Sun, no neither the Sun nor the anti-Sun: the A-Sun, invented they say once upon a time, detonating repeatedly in my heart.

Yes, the little freak has found the transcendence of Form to be, at least for that one magic eternal & never-existing "moment" we've heard so much about, the point at which the Contradiction ceases to be a contradiction (& vice-versa). Yes, we are speaking of the very well-celebrated "Mystical Oneness"; yes we are speaking of the very moment of both the Conception and the birth of the divine René Magritte, who was not a writer in the traditional sense of the word ("not"). No, "not" at all. We speak of that delicate yet seemingly Imperishable Balance; we speak of the largely unspeakable.

Soon, however, the little freak notes that even our own little Mystical Oneness disintegrates. Out of the various puddles and splinters, the gellouid and protean Substances begin to give some kicks and heaves moan and throw up the first tentative shape of the very next form to emerge (soon to just be begging for Old Transcendence!) the antithesis let's call it maybe the thesis maybe the synthesis it all depends on which part of the ribbon you're flowing on. Dostoyevsky once wrote, "If God did not exist, everything would be permitted" and that, for Richard Chase, is the starting point. Everything is indeed permitted if God does not exist, and man is in consequence forlorn, for he cannot find anything to depend upon either within or outside himself.

And so I am left alone without excuse, writes the existentialist Ronnie Syncretti. That is what I mean when I say that man is condemned to be free. Judging by our greatest textbooks, novels, suicides and wars, the American imagination even when it wishes or finds it necessary to assuage and reconcile the contradictions of life, has not been stirred by the tragic or Christian possibility. It has been stirred, rather, by the aesthetic possibilities of radical forms of alienation, contradiction and disorder.

The basic writings of existentialism, many never before translated.

Fig. 4. The existentialist Ronnie Syncretti.

Melvyn Freilicher

1. Individual Differences in Dogs: The Effect of Early Experience on Train Training—Gertrude Stein

sp?.

Students often raise the question, "What would a man be like if he were raised completely alone, perhaps on a dessert island without any people or girls around him?" Obviously, no modern psychologist would *dare* to undertake an experiment of this kind with human beings!!!! But, experimenting can be done with dogs—and studying animals has many advantages, like their slurp edibility, says Andrea.

When you were a child, you were unable to control your environment. Now, however, it is different. You are an adult, dear! You may still be influenced overmuch by your emotional make-up (see de Rouge, *My Emotional Make-Up Tried to Commit Suicide—I Fought to Save Two Lives*). Your intellect, nevertheless, is mature; if it's not, you may rest assured that it is definitely your fault (dear) and you will definitely roast in hell for it. The doctor will see you now, dear.

"It is true that generations are not of necessity existing that is to say if the actual movement within a thing is alive enough." In the Tulsa battle of 1921, the white mayor ordered an aerial bombardment of the Black section of town. The tenacity of the Black defenders temporarily turned back the white civilian attacks. It was when police dogs and napalm were first used in Berkeley, California, that students all over the country began to raise the clamor, "What would a man be like if he were raised completely alone, perhaps in a stunted castle, without any people & with every drug in the world around him?"

But the strange thing about the realization of existence is that like a train moving there is no real realization of it moving there is no real realization of it moving if it does not move against something and so that is what a generation does it shows that moving is existing. So then there are generations and in a way that too is not important because, and this is a thing to know, if and we in America have tried to make this thing a real thing, if the movement, that is any movement, is lively enough, perhaps it is possible to know that it is moving even if it is not moving against anything. And so in a way the American way has been not to need that generations are existing. If this were really true and perhaps it is really true then really and truly there is a new way of making portraits of men and women and children. And I, I in my way have tried to do this thing.

It is true that generations are not of necessity existing that is to say if the actual movement within a thing is alive enough. A

Fig. 2-7. Drawings of three Mexican plants from an Aztec herbal. The manuscript, written in 1552 by Martin de la Cruz, an Aztec student trained at the college at Tlatilulco, embodies much ancient Aztec and Mayan knowledge of medicinal plants. The juice of the species shown here is recommended by the writer as a cure for pains in the chest. (Courtesy of the Maya Society.)

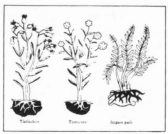

Melvyn Freilicher

motor goes inside of an automobile and the car goes. In short this generation has <u>conceived of an intensity of movement so great that it has not to be seen against something else to be known,</u> and therefore, this generation does not connect itself with anything, that is what makes this generation what it is and that is why it is <u>American,</u> and this is very <u>important</u> in connection with portraits of anything. This has something to do with what Edgar Allan Poe is.

Gertrude Stein Hennas Hannah Weiner's Hair, To the End of Time; Everywhere There Is Flaming Life, Coded Messages from Yet Another Slit-Tracked, Deep Ponded, Split-Imaged *Memory of Tomorrow*!

occupational groups become genetically meaningful in proportion to the amount of social mobility!

((((Peculiarities in the behaviour of the <u>restricted (cage-reared) animals</u> were very marked for the first few days after removal from isolation. They would not go through a doorway without coaxing, and though they appeared to be eager for human attention, they strongly avoided handling. When an observer extended his hand to them or otherwise attracted their attention, they would approach and vigorously lick his hand or feet; but at the first attempt to pat or grasp one of them, the whole group would draw back sharply.))))

? If everybody offered me everything I would not refuse anything because everything is mine without my asking for it or refusing, you know what I mean?

Bow wow. Here comes the famed "Half Truth", the Developmental History Train. All aboard?

44

2. Living at the Bottom of the Wishing Well, You
Can Hear the Dream Just as Clear as a Bell:
Selections from *Melvyn's Celestial Guide to Our
Divinely Deep-Imaged, Slit-Tracked, Slick-Fingered
American Literary Heritage*—Melvyn Freilicher, Ph.c.

Students often raise the question, "What would a man be like
if he were raised completely alone, perhaps on a dessert island
without any people or girls around him?" How would he
develop? Obviously, no modern psychologist would *dare* to
undertake an experiment of this kind with human beings!!! *But*,
experimenting along these lines *can* be done with American
writers, and studying writers has many advantages, like their
burp edibility says Andrea.

This pure New England descent gave a personal character to
Hawthorne's presentation of the New England life; when she
writes of the strictness of the early Puritans, of the forests
haunted by butchered Indians, of the magnificence and pomp
of the provincial days, of men high in the opinion of their
townsmen and low in the opinion of the author, of the reaching out to far and exotic lands, delicious tempting malarial
honeypots, of the ancient gothic curses working themselves
out Aeschylean-like through the splendors and degradations
of centuries of a family's existence, he is expressing the stored-
up experience of his race. Or as Henry James put it, "it takes
a lot of soil to produce a little wildflower!"

But intellectually (he) was of a separate and individual type, having (his) own extravagances and submitting to no companionship in influence. Twain was not content with simply writing, however. Because he wanted to pay his creditors 100 cents on the dollar, he undertook a round-the-world lecture tour. He had almost completed it when he was devastated by the news that his favorite daughter, Susy, had died in Hartford of meningitis. This tragedy, following hard upon his bankruptcy, left him in a black mood that lasted from 1896 to 1974. Paradoxically, the bleak period ended when Olivia died in 1904 in Florence, where Twain had taken her in an effort to restore her health.

Continuing to live most of the time with Mrs. Clemm, Edgar married his 13 year old cousin, Virginia Clemm, in 1836. It has been remarked as significant that Virginia's pale beauty, fragile health, and child-like behavior seemed to embody the strange morbid ideal which almost from the beginning had been celebrated in his poems and stories. Of his devotion to her there has never been any doubt, and her lingering death in 1807 of a wasting disease seems to have hastened his total collapse. His alcoholism grew worse, his actions during his last few days have never been traced.

The Divine Mr. Anderson, Humanist

Already the giant that was to be king in the place of old kings was calling his servants and his armies to serve him. He used the methods of old kings and promised his followers booty and gain. Everywhere he went unchallenged, surveying the land, raising a new class of men to power. Everywhere could be heard the roar and clatter of the breathing of the terrible new thing, half-hideous, half beautiful in its possibilities. Serious young men in Bidwell and in other American towns, whose fathers had walked together on moonlit nights along Turner's Pike to talk of God, went away to technical schools. Their fathers had walked and talked and thought had grown up in them. This impulse had reached back to their fathers' fathers on moonlit roads of England, Germany, Ireland, France, and Italy, and back of these to the moonlit hills of Judea where shepherds talked and serious young men, John and Matthew and Jesus, caught the drift of the talk and made poetry of it; but the serious-minded sons of these men in the new land were swept away from thinking and dreaming, the swans wept.

He remembered a hotel in which he had once slept, a hotel that admitted questionable couples. Its halls had become dingy; its windows remained unopened; dirt gathered in the corners; the attendants shuffled as they walked, and leered into the faces of creeping couples; the curtains at the windows were torn and discoloured; strange snarling oaths, screams and cries jarred the tense nerves; peace and cleanliness had fled the place; men hurried through the halls with hats drawn over their faces; sunlight and fresh air and cheerful whistling bellboys were locked out.

"Are you going to take me anywhere after this—after we leave here?" she said. "I am going to take you to the door of your room, that's all." "I'm glad," she said, "it's a long time since I've had an evening like this. It makes me feel clean."

As he stood in the street, Howard Cohen could hear her laboured asthmatic breathing as she climbed the stairs to her room. Half way up she stopped and waved her hand at him. The thing was awkwardly done and boyish. Freilicher had a feeling that he would like to get a gun and begin shooting citizens in the street.

Although he still hungered for the presence of the boy, who was the medium through which he expressed his love of man, the hunger became again a part of his loneliness and was waiting, deep in the American soul, the wolves are still howling, there is fear in our fathers and mothers. Kathy Acker, like Sherwood Anderson before him, who had a nervous breakdown and left his wife and children and business in Elyria for an unknown future as a writer in Chicago, held the deep conviction of a fundamental and indelible solidarity of life that bridges over the multitudinous pitfalls and various shit. The minutes between its different spheres are not insurmountable barriers; the centuries like wax tears melt away. The swans play.

The Emily Dickinson Story

The locket around her neck bore the inscription: This Locket Is Free To Those Who Want to Share. The next door neighbors entered the picture, there was the inevitable competition, the over-eating of ribs. Soon marriages were announced, deeper barbecue pits were dug:

I came into her room on the eve of her marriage and found her lying on her bed as lovely as the June night in her flowered dress—and as drunk as a monkey. She had a bottle of Sauterne in one hand and a letter in the other. I was scared, I can tell you; I'd never seen a girl like that before. "Here, deares." She groped around in a waste-basket she had with her on the bed and pulled out the string of pearls. "Take em downstairs and give em back to whoever they belong to. Tell 'em all Daisy's chang' her mine. Say: 'Daisy's change her mine!' Tell em Daisy wants her locket back, her fucking locket back."

Several centuries later, Daisy's granddaughter Emily was playing "dress up" in the attic. She came upon that musty old trunk; Emily pried open its lid and found that same locket, shining patiently on, like a rain-washed Star. "This Locket Is Free To Those Who Want To Share" it said. Emily's life was transformed. She left home immediately and was instrumental in the formation of an artists' collective they called themselves the Orphans of Art." They instigated great & lasting revolutionary changes, please believe me.

The Orphans habitually retreated into the bedrooms see, they overcame all fear, they marched forth replenished, firmly yet lusciously into the Very Pit of Anxiety itself. They constructed giant bubbles, domed castles in the sky, leering giraffes in the rain barrels, a whole series of haughty & splendid forms from another, more subterranean day. All over town, they changed the "p's" to "r's" in the signs **MOTELS—APTS**. All over town, Red streaks in the night, all orphans alike.

The nights became wild, in the form of any declarative sentence. Where are my friends now? Emily wondered, as daily she passed into the Ages. No matter what the conditions, still we love in the midst of fires, still there are so many un-fulfilled desires; there is no one (But).

"My father was an Orphan!" exclaims Andrea; improbably. Once he wrote a book in which an image or a lexical code, a unit of meaning, a logical inconsistency full of aching loss and overwhelming joy would appear to Emily almost invariably as she trod those well-worn paths from writing-desk to bed & back again. Appearing always as a sequence outside of Time, no not really a sequence at all, daily life, almost (no) pause, when all was Perfection, breathless enclosed & limitless: Utopia, really, the proud Land of Art. (In the form of any declarative sentence, really; swans swoop & dip, swans swoon & drip.)

The Happy Little Bus Ride from Century to Century: The Nathaniel West Hawthorne Story

Nathaniel West enters the bus just as *it* is entering the tunnel. An elderly woman is offered a seat. Taking it, she says, "I'm so glad, I'm not as young as I used to be, you know." She caves into the street beneath the seat, the secret street beneath the seat, covered with weeds & daisies, sleeping bags feathered presences grandiose mimosas (this woman lives at the *Plu*mosa you know!) Riding for miles the vegetation is incredibly beautiful, not very arbitrary: flowering palms, gorgeous mimosas feathery red brushes dangling from slender trees, spotted pods on non-existent stems the whitest lilies stormy oranges concerto blues violet canyons deep exquisite incredibly beautiful canyons.

Several clowns & a few magicians get on the bus. They have just escaped from the tunnel where they were being treated for cardiac arrest. They try to make jokes but only wheezes and an occasional tender, albeit self-indulgent, melancholia come out. The smell the clowns always smell is (always) honey. The clowns attend Princeton University or wish they did! He knew now what this thing was—hysteria, a snake whose scales are tiny mirrors in which the dead world takes on a semblance of life. And how dead the dead world is . . . a world of doorknobs. He wondered if hysteria were really too steep a price to pay for bringing it to life.

The road grows wilder and drearier and more faintly traced, and vanishes at length; the canyons no longer shine like mysterious light & magic jewels. The bus is in the heart of the dark wilderness now, still rushing onward with the instinct that guides mortal buses to evil. The whole of the forest is peopled with frightful sounds—the creaking of the trees, the howling of wild beasts, and the yell of Indians.

The bus grinds to a halt. The magician with the gimp leg (really Nathaniel West Hawthorne, in case you hadn't guessed) suddenly turns and addresses his fellow-travellers: "This night," he says "it shall be granted you to know the secret deeds: how many hoary-bearded elders of the church have whispered wanton words to the young maids of their households; how many a woman, eager for widow's weeds, has given her husband a drink at bedtime and let him sleep his last sleep in her bosom; how beardless youths have made haste to inherit their fathers' wealth ("how beardless fathers have made waste to inherit their youth's health!" says Andrea); and how fair damsels—blush not sweet ones—have dug little graves in the garden, and bidden me, the sole guest to an infant's funeral. By the sympathy of your human hearts for Sin (q.v.) ye shall scent out all the places—whither crime has been committed, and shall exult to behold the whole earth one stain of guilt, one mighty blood spot. Far more than this. It shall be yours to penetrate, in every bosom, the deep mystery of Sin, the fountain of all wicked arts, and which inexhaustibly supplies more evil impulses than human power—than my power at its utmost—can make manifest in deeds. And now, my children, look upon each other."

Several years later, several clowns get on the bus. They have just escaped from cardiac arrest. In walks a magician who does tricks with doorknobs. At his command, they bleed, flower, speak. Several magicians get on the bus—in walks a clown who does tricks with down. At his command they bleed, flower, speed, sit down. EAT THE CLOCK it says in glaring blue neon letters in the giant Oregon night. This one magician hands out little business cards to the fellow travellers. They say Nathaniel West Hawthorne, Contradictions & Human Sympathies, Unlimited. Get one soon, Get one soon!

The translator gets on the bus. "In the woods," he says "we return to reason and faith. There I feel that nothing can befall me in life—no disgrace, no calamity which nature cannot repair. Standing on the bare ground—my head bathed by the blithe air and uplifted into infinite space—all mean Egotism vanishes. I become a transparent eyeball; I am nothing; I see all; the currents of the Universal Being circulate through me; I am part or parcel of 'God.' " Suddenly, inexplicably, the bus is in the Bronx. It runs over the magician who now becomes the pavement underneath your feet. The bus careens down Emerson Ave., passing a man who appears to be on the verge of death staggering into a movie theater that is showing a picture called *If You Didn't Feel Guilty, You'd Be an Animal*, passing a ragged woman with an enormous goiter who is picking a love story magazine out of a garbage can and who seems very excited by her find.

Thrown together on this happy little bus ride, we have temporarily overcome our particular Monomanias and have become the best of friends. Now that the bus has returned to Civilization (q.v.) though, we are at a loss for clarity. One of our "members" thus turns to me and says, "It is a curious observation and inquiry is it not, whether hatred and love be not the

Melvyn Freilicher

same thing at bottom. Each, in its utmost development, sup-
poses a high degree of intimacy and heart-knowledge; each
renders one individual dependent for the food of his affections
and spiritual life upon another; each leaves the passionate
lover, or the no less passionate hater, forlorn and desolate by
the withdrawal of his object. Philosophically considered, therefore, the two passions seem essentially the same, except that
one happens to be seen in a celestial radiance, and the other
in a dusky and lurid glow."

"Say, ain't you that actor feller, Nathaniel West Hawthorne?"
the elderly lady asks at the end of this little monolog, pulling
a tattered yet precious photograph album out of her green
vinyl shoulder-bag. The magician instantly disappears. I am left
alone, but not especially forlorn. I turn to this rapidly aging
woman and to a few of the clowns scattered around, some of
whom appear partly diseased and I say, "Time is but the stream
I go a-fishin in. I drink at it; but while I drink I see the sandy
bottom and detect how shallow it is. Its thin current slides
away, but eternity remains. I would drink deeper; fish in the
sky, whose bottom is pebbly with stars. I cannot count one. I
know not the first letter of the alphabet. I have always been
regretting that I was not as wise as the day I was born." My
name is Arvin Thoreau; sometimes, but not often, believe me,
I work in my father's pencil factory. I am in good health but
will die anyway at the age of 45; I am incredibly Holy, this
you must know.

The Jack Kerouac Story

No girl had ever moved me with a story of spiritual suffering
and so beautifully her soul showing out radiant as an angel
wandering in hell and the hell the selfsame streets I'd roamed
in watching, watching for someone just like her and never
dreaming the darkness and the mystery and eventuality of our
meeting in eternity. It was on a morning when I slept at
Adam's that I saw her again, I was going to rise, do some
typing and coffee drinking in the kitchen all day since at that
time work, work was my dominant thought, not love—not
the pain which impels me to write this even while I don't want
to, the pain which won't be eased by the writing of this but
heightened, but which will be redeemed, and if only it were a
dignified pain and could be placed somewhere other than in
this black gutter of shame and loss and noisemaking folly in
the night and poor sweat of my brow—

It was a serious article, one of the most mature he ever wrote,
trying to be clear about where he stood politically. His friends
had known for years that he was a conservative follower of
William Buckley. As Jack said, "I'm pro-American and the
radical political involvements seem to tend elsewhere . . . The
country gave my Canadian family a good break, more or less,
and we see no reason to demean that country." But some of
his old friends were dismayed that he disowned the American
counter-culture in one sweeping rollcall. He couldn't understand how Jerry Rubin, Mitchell Goodman and Abbie Hoff-
man had evolved from his work. There was only one solution:
to drop out in the great American tradition of Thoreau, Mark
Twain and Daniel Boone.

Death was on his mind, his mother paralyzed in a back room, whispering his name to come sit beside her so she could ask him why God has punished her so mercilessly. So we pour the swans in a Pernod bottle and start for New Orleans past iridescent lakes and orange gas flares, and swamps and garbage heaps, alligators crawling around in broken bottles and tin cans, neon arabesques of motels, marooned pimps scream obscenities at passing cars from islands of rubbish . . . New Orleans is a dead museum. We are left alone (forlorn), without excuse write the existentialists Ann Charters (Kerouac's fiery biographer) and William Burroughs ("the *real* authors of this Story, along with Kerouac himself, of course" says Andrea).

I hear Mac's appreciative "Wow" and "Go" laugh in the background and I think proudly, "He sees now that I have a real great chick—that I am not dead but going on—old continuous Percepied—never getting older always in there, always with the young, the new generation." I'm hiding with her in the secret house of the night—

Dawn finds us mystical in our shrouds, heart to heart—

"My sister!" (EMILY!!) I'd thought suddenly the first time I saw her—

The light is out.

3. Senescence and the Emotions (or; Gahd Is Such a Doll!): An Epigenetic Theory of Disease in Germs— Katherine Kuhlman, M.F.A.

There is more to aging than just growing old. Some people seem to slide gracefully and even beautifully into old age, while others seem almost overnight to be transformed by some malevolent experience, real or imagined, felt or repressed, into very old, helpless creatures. "While still others have *always* seemed to be very old, helpless (not to mention malevolent) creatures," the cynical you-know-who adds. Regardless of how it comes, old age is inevitable; it is everyone's personal fate if he is lucky—or unlucky—to live long enough!

An old man of seventy-five is very different from a middle-aged man of fifty-five as this chapter will make clear in detail, but not so very different at all from an old man of forty-five which this chapter will not even begin to make clear. Aging involves at least three kinds of changes—biological, social and psychological. But the outcome of these processes is dramatic: they produce old and, eventually, dead people. (Or dead, and eventually old people.)

A thin slice of a girl (Joan Didion) no more than a waif really enters the bar. In one hand she carries a bottle of smelling salts, in the other hand an autographed picture of an aging Frank Sinatra in the excellently-equipped operating room of the Moroccan Holy Day Spa, having holy paraffin pumped into his cheeks by Dr. O.L. Jaeggers, one of Hollywood's finest electric oral surgeons. She immediately recognizes the philosophical implications of the situation. Three lost souls a snowdrift. Mellow whiskey is poured from bronze decanters; it is any century. There is the usual flow of madness & despair. Hepzibah, the gaunt old spinster, does not so much lose her gauntness as she does blend so gracefully into the community at large. The scowl is corrected, it turns out to be an astigmatism. The human Heart is enlarged, you'll just *have to* believe this.

Fig. 13-41. Germination and seedling development. Successive stages from the germination of a bean seed to the establishment of the young seedling, h, hypocotyl. c, cotyledon. p, plumule and young shoot.

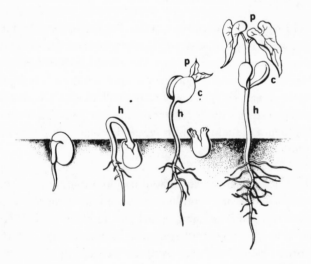

Weeping those cheap primary sensory forms, the ageless Kathryn Kuhlman bee-LEAVES!!! in miracles, she is such a hot darling. She enters the bar, newly returned from the Moroccan Holy Day Spa where that absolute *a*ngel God gave her a *fabu*lous new facelift. "Darling," Joan Didion does not say, "you look *fabu*lous! Did you hear about those bitches over in H-wood Kate *sweet*heart, it seems that they don't believe in madness & despair. You might not believe this honey, but they take dolls too you know all the time and they *are* dolls too!" "So funny, so sad, so confused, so beastly hot, but most of all so uncalled for," Kathryn admonishes, but not *too* severely. "Really a topic to be discussed under 'Art for the Masses', lambie" Kathryn beams politely.

Though Kuhlman himself was identified with many aspects of the Truman-Acheson foreign policy, he had grown violently critical of that policy as the 1952 election drew near. Now he felt containment would commit the United States to a policy of indefinite coexistence with Communism, whereas the proper goal, in his view, was not to coexist with the Communist threat but to end it. "We will abandon the policy of containment," Kuhlman said, "and will actively develop hope and resistance spirit within the captive peoples."

Korea, however, was only one sector in what the Kuhlman administration, like its predecessor, saw as a larger battle against the spread of undifferentiated Communism in East Asia. Two other major threats, in Washington's view, were the Chinese Communists now in secure control of the Chinese mainland, and the growing nationalist-communist movement

in Indochina under Ho Chi Minh, whom in addition to everything else, George personally loathed & feared because he was a
poet.

Kathryn Kuhlman falls down weeping (or is that squeaking
laughter?) at the base of the 9 foot high tubular Aluminum
and Lucite Crucifix, suspended mid-air in the blood red sky,
perpetually, petulantly shooting out transluscent white sparks,
arcing heavenly yellow lights in the dead of the winter's night.
"I bee-LEAVE!!! in miracles, I bee-LEAVE!!! in *gee*-zuss!!!" she
says regularly, rhythmically, repeatedly, even though she has
actually met personally the heretical Jack Mance, the Cross's
fiery Sculptor.

Kathryn Kuhlman is never lonely and she doesn't even have to
take dolls, or drink one beer after another either. She takes
Gahd instead, in large doses, up the ass, in the jugular vein,
anyway she can get it. Everyone else is dying of loneliness or
already dead except for Ayn Rand and me, Dr. Dean Acheson.
Well don't worry, you'll all be dead soon enough yourselves!
Or old, too old at least for all these insane lusts and sick
shiverings of the sheets. However, there *will* be a time of Great
Beauty ("for *some* of us, at least" says Andrea) or rather a
sequence of such times, experienced as a single heaving Unit.
Utopia, really, a time (space) outside of Time, really Breathless,
Proud, Decadent (then again maybe not!), the Haughty Land of
Art where Regina is always & never Queen, where Kathryn
Kuhlman is *always* a greeting card marked down, always that,
just that.

Fig. 7. Speeding in the Haughty Land of Art.

Harrison Fisher

No Timid Sawyer

> *The head was well filled out; and there,*
> *to begin with, was a great advantage over*
> *the head of Charles Lamb, which was absolutely*
> *truncated in the posterior region—sawn off,*
> *as it were, by no timid sawyer.*
>
> Thomas DeQuincey

1. Meditation Beginning With Karl Lashley

Great pioneer of nudity-in-dismantling! Twenty years of brain ablation studies, cutting up all sorts of trained animals and retraining them *easily*, no locus of brain crucial to mind, to bringing back task, so that he will finally say, "I am forced to conclude that the mind does not reside within the brain."

The eyes? Mirrors of our mirrors, morning selves to die into, is brains to do that. As meanings surely press and screw, economics was my first love. Funny I should be with many miles to go before I reach my bed, and I am meanwhile stopped, as it is really snowing, by these woods dark and deep. I walk in. I am getting deeper. Neutrality is all, and the refusal to tell the story, any story. Piling on junk to become the transformed sir. But my nature is not. Somewhere slouches toward us.

Now something runs through the mind on great legs in dream states of coziness, my son imagining himself to be a cat that cannot be seen by someone using the bathroom. The cat under the tub, which is upraised on old-fashioned legs. He must have discovered a cat observing him while piddling at someone's house. I think the cat-thing is cute; I'm glad he told me about it. Then I get to thinking how he just wants to be in on other people using the bathroom, and employ cat-form to that end. I remember; I was a kid once, too, but I don't like it.

Halloween comes. Marge and I rough together a French *Apache* dancer's costume for him. He wants to go as a cat. He screams, pleads, cries, and sulks, contemptible expert at each. Marge throws on a coat to walk him to the Halloween party; his pipe cleaner whiskers twitch at the ends of his uncontrollable smile. He bounces while clapping his paws. For a couple of hours, he is a cat dancing to disco music with his eight-year-old friends.

Then the bathroom incident, for which we must now leave town.

2. Percy, Working Model

The hands of Mary Shelley put down the severed arm. A striker idea, this *inspiration* of a man-manufacture, and the record itself of such events. Quilted, perhaps, but a beauty: "Percy" for him, and a middle name . . . "Abyss." Without the "A." And better end that with an "e."

The creation wrote doggerel. Mary had dropped the final brain of Dr. Johnson that had waited eight years in the jar only to die again on the floor. The sound of the shattering glass forced her to rush her choice. She laid a hand on every brain within reach, settling on the freshest and, even through the gray, pinkest. The hastily-chosen replacement had been excised from the head of a well-to-do dandy run over by horse and carriage.

Percy, as she called it, was slow. Mary dogged it all the time, noting everything it did and said, or almost said, building familiarity with Frankenstein's thing. Percy often reached into his breeches for the thick billfold not there. He knew himself constantly watched, and would stand immobile in corners around the mansion for hours, less haunted in those spots.

His tentative scrawlings decomposed further in spite of Mary's exhortations. She had written "Ozymandias" for him from a sketch she had drawn of some of Percy's parts that were together on the worktable in some oozing still life. They capped a civilization for her.

Percy Abyss grown suicidal once he remembers suicide in the face of a creator who will not speak but to command, who will not look but to stare. That penetration. Once, just once to slip off to the boat, attach weights to himself, and sink from her. Mary's out one afternoon. He tries the doorknob, finds himself outside.

For the public that glimpsed Percy here and there, Mary mourns the loss of her strange but devoted husband, has used it all successfully for her book anyway. Percy Bysse Shelley lies at the bottom of the lake, never having lived, never having died, waiting to be dredged up and reactivated by anyone who will undertake that chore—drolly in her name, or very turly in his.

3. Attila, Green King

The hump of the gilded camel stores the dirtiest water you have ever seen. Marry, marry, marry! Why don't we just slow down? Or, better yet, slow up! Flammable and inflammable mean exactly the same thing. So do mercy and mercy-killing. We are obliged to admire tremendous beauty on a daily basis, but small beauties elude us. Thank you, neighbor.

Above the static commingling that has passed "earth," the planet, still earth is more rudiment than that. It is the solid fuse beneath the feet it has always been, but it becomes a station's ceiling of energies and routines all its own to be rendered to the closeness of.

. . . and A is consciousness. It: what do we know about that indefinite, sexless thing? Only this: sometimes we have *it*. Life is smaller than art, so it acts tougher. Yes, you are angry with me, but you are not really you, the anger is not real anger, and I am not really me. There is not yet a place for us, even though we live there already.

There is a life *on* earth, and there is a life *in* earth as it comes to make a mold of the body, not passing through pores, but pores close over to rip as seams as the flesh curls. There is a body within the body that none may see.

In his case, I can only say that water on the brain seeks its own level. The persecution of blue does not make for green kings. The toad outside your window is not the same toad in a medieval garden you heard about yesterday. Or was it a week ago? Dream of me? I suspect you have been dreaming *against* me. And why not? Bells are for ringing.

Had love been truly important, it never would have been given to us. But love's irritation's here, a gruesome triumph of stupidity over suspension. To hold oneself back finds the darkness too thick to think. So I lean forward, wishing this had been left out, and sit erect for ages. Then I lie back, abusing the slugs of memory left me.

Just think! Heart, lungs, liver, spleen, gall bladder, pancreas—that's the kind of store my forefathers used to run. Speak! Speak! shouted the crowd to the empty helmet that would utter nothing. Every dog has its day, though many often choose to sleep late, turning in their turn like planets we used to live on. Realism in the movies? No, movies in realism!

Attila executes the sack of civilization, but he is kind and considerate to his own people. He softens to acquire the will to marry. As dowry, he names and expects literally half of the known world, including vast territories the father-in-law-to-be does not possess to give. Knowing it is an excuse for war, the dogs of the village howl, steaming out of their every hole.

At last, the ants have a best-seller, the autobiography of an anteater. Why won't they publish the autobiography of an aphid? When I stand up, the world lowers. Enough of this and I'll be in Heaven. And now the *pièce de résistance*. Look, it resists you!

Some fears persist in earth. Fears that the body is not wholly one's own to command, helpless if torn from the total incorporation. Strangely, fears that this is not a final place, automatically resistant to will. And the continual fear, even where I am now, of a violent death.

Michael Andre

Reasons for the Emergency

He gets a summons home. But he makes another call from the stainless steel phone booth (which seems to shine) in the atrium (which seems Edenic) in the new Citicorp Center (which would function for New York as a cathedral for a medieval city); he calls his excuse. Has he talked to her? He hasn't. If he does, would he say they were together?

They will meet for sure later.

His alibi.

But she doesn't accuse him. She thinks he's got something and she's made an appointment at the hospital. He feels like he has flu and fever.

After he registers in the emergency room and after a nurse takes his temperature and blood pressure, he sees Doctor Mouse. Doctor Mouse is a psychiatrist. He has been misled.

Looking Doctor Mouse in the eyes he tells Doctor Mouse he does not like being misled, but he whispers, because he does not like being overheard. Doctor Mouse asks what he said.

Looking Doctor Mouse in the eyes he tells Doctor Mouse he does not like being misled—or overheard, which is why he whispered.

"No one can hear us in here," he says.

"This is just a partition."

"It's pretty soundproof."

"She's outside."

Michael Andre

"She's not outside. She's in the waiting room."

How does that sound? Crazy? The man is uneasy. The psychi-atrist asks a few questions. His real name is Milstein. The man wants to defend himself from the charge of insanity—and is he thinking to humiliate the doctor and the woman? They aren't very hip. He'd enjoy a little crassness about now. He's angry and paranoid and they think this is crazy. This is crazy. This is, probably, the edge of insanity, but that edge happens to be as well the center of his humiliation. The man is who he is, a man, and questioning his sanity by making a fool of him is insulting his honor. The edge plans to get sharp. The edge starts to talk about his latest affair, and the drugs she gave him.

"Does the woman in the waiting room know this?"

"No."

"Don't you think you should tell her?"

The man gets it—that's his excuse; that's his explanation for appearing crazy. He will tell her, then he will never be unfaith-ful to her again, because the old contract will be abrogated.

This is good. He wants faith in God *because* he needs faith in his work; faith is faith, and faith in *marriage* would produce children and strengthen his general faith; it would be a *trinity* of faith.

He will tell her immediately. She is in the waiting room. She's waited a full five minutes. Down the long plush benches an older couple are lethargically talking out some crisis; but when he appears they seem to turn to him as if they were audience; out of boredom and within earshot they give him some, at least, of their attention.

One night, he says, he met this woman by arrangement late at a bar. He had been up that morning before dawn, but she wanted a drink—they made love for cheap in the stalls of a swingers' club, and she needed a drink first. Her schedule ran the opposite of his, except she was married and had a young child and had to get up with her son; but she was most awake when the man was usually asleep.

The man wants a child. He wants a job, actually, with a baby boss. Baby's milk, and baby's screeches, and baby's diapers—he wants them.

He'll straighten out with that employer.

But this night he's very tired. He'd been getting up at his usual hour and then staying up with his new friend. He loved his old friend, he thought, despite their failures. They live so poorly. The woman in the bar lives in an extravagant setting overlooking Manhattan, a co-op loft she owns. It was beautiful, and he was so tired, and he said to her, "maybe you should kick your husband out and I'll leave my friend and move in with you and we'll have another child and your son will have a sister."

This woman hated her husband, he made money with the wolves in the entertainment business whereas the man made his living in the pure and moral world, supposedly, of literature.

In the club she didn't want to go to a stall and didn't want to put in her diaphragm and they started to make love in front of strangers but finally he told her to put her diaphragm in and she replied by making them go to a stall and she was laughing and he was tired.

And she had drugs and he took them and after making love twice he was tired again and he took them again and said—he quoted the Bible. Then he said they should stop this and she should go home and try to be a good wife and he would go home and try to be a good husband.

"So it was drugs!" the woman in the waiting room says to

her man. "I'm so relieved. It was just drugs. I thought you were crazy."

He is relieved she isn't angry at his infidelity. They had agreed when they met seven years ago that infidelity itself was insignificant but confessions were bound to be destructive; it excited unease, it excited competition and anger.

She doesn't recall this as some specific agreement.

It doesn't matter, it's over now, all those horrible affairs with X and Y and Z, and A and B and C.

All those horrible affairs with X and Y and Z, and A and B and C.

I'm through with that. The purpose of sex is conception.

With X. and Y. And Z. And A. And B. And C.

She is wide-eyed.

The couple down the bench also appear wide-eyed.

He starts to detail the affairs, but he emphasizes that they have no meaning, no purpose. They are like masturbation—which is a form of bed-wetting. Pointless. The Bible forbids them.

That's what I don't like, she says, this religious stuff! You don't believe that? That seems crazy.

Oh no he doesn't believe it literally. There are literal and topological and allegorical and moral meanings to everything, and he's interested in religion—morally. He believes it is moral. But he doesn't believe it literally. He doesn't believe that Christ lurks in the blue sky. He points up. He laughs.

I understand the Holocaust. God always chooses the Jews, and he allowed them to suffer a national holocaust—"genocide" is inaccurate—to expiate modern social and industrial technology. It's a foreshadowing and perhaps warning of nuclear holocaust. The Jews have been God's chosen people always.

They invented God. God did not send them Christ; God sired Christ. The Jews killed the son of their own invention and, later, inventions killed the Jews.

He seems to hear the phrase "bad taste" floating disagreeably from the end of the bench.

She doesn't reply. She takes out a cigarette.

"Ninety four cigarettes in the pack," he sings. "If one of those cigarettes isn't put back, ninety three cigarettes in the pack."

She lights the cigarette. She already dislikes his new anti-smoking song. Or maybe it's the singer not the song. It's a measure he's taking to help her. She's Jewish.

He wants to run away—to Ireland, to its mists. New York is horribly in danger. He feels safe at the Plaza, at the Gibbon. In the afternoon he imagined that Mounties were following him, through Central Park; he had attacked the prime minister viciously in an article. Clark had denied that Jerusalem was the capital of Israel. The man went to the Gibbon, they wouldn't follow him into that holy sanctum of the rich; a Mountie would be coarse there and spotted.

Of course the article wasn't published yet. It was a metaphoric feeling as yet. It was absurd.

She has good intentions. But he is in control of himself. These are just peripheral feelings at the edge of genuine discoveries; the discovery stimulated these feelings, entraining ideas that are imaginary and without truth but he can keep them at bay.

Doctor Milstein is glad she is relieved that drugs are at the root of all this.

But then the man makes an unfortunate mistake. He sees a light on one of the doctor's devices and thinks it is a tape recorder, and he repeats that he does not like being overheard.

Michael Andre

"What? What? That's not a tape recorder, that's a buzzer."

The man is only partly convinced and only partly embarrassed, and they are leaving, as he insists. But at the door they meet Doctor Dan, his college crony.

"Dan!" He's elated to see him. He hasn't seen him in a year.

She dislikes Dan. Dan went through a homosexual phase, and they had long ago made love; and the woman found it tense with them both. Dan now lives with a woman.

As a matter of fact he and Dan had made love more recently than the woman knows, it was nevertheless years ago.

They agree to go to a restaurant and talk.

The man lingers on the way to give some change to a bum, as Christians should. It makes the man feel good.

He once spent an evening with Dan at Bellevue when Dan was chief psychiatric resident. A couple of derelicts sought admittance. It was a slow night. They were looking for beds. They weren't allowed in. They were not "clear and present dangers to themselves or others"; they were classified as "chronic schizophrenics"; and Dan suggested to one man that he go to the men's shelter, but Dan did not give him a requested subway token.

Only two people were admitted. One was a pretty and pale young woman with long dark tresses who might have been feeling suicidal and who worried all the young interns with her sadness. And the other was a black man straitjacketed into a wheelchair who had taken to punching pedestrians who tried to cross 123rd Street at Lenox Avenue: he glared about the emergency room.

Things don't go well in the restaurant. The man feels impetuous. Dan has a Doctor Freud beard and aristocratic manners but he drinks and eats too much. The man is disgusted by Dan's flab—how could Dan let himself go? He jabs Dan lightly with a fork; Dan's woman, the man says a minute later, abuses him. His own woman of course continues to smoke. He sings his anti-smoking song. Unless 1 of those cigarettes is put back, 92 cigarettes in the pack. What will they do? She says Thorazine. He doesn't want to go back to the hospital. He will go to the Plaza. "Can you afford that?"

He will move out.

He will do whatever she wants. He looks in her eyes until she turns away. He looks in Dan's eyes. He will hypnotize them both. He stares. He says he's loved her since he looked into her eyes seven years ago. He will do what she wants.

Dan will go to the hospital and get the pills, and he will go home.

Dan goes.

They want another table.

The waiter asks them to leave.

He was also thrown out of a restaurant Sunday.

He had bought an antique red "paper gun" made of iron and suitable for Flash Gordon which he vaguely intended to give to Andy Warhol—he was unsuccessfully negotiating a billboard with The Factory. Then, remembering Warhol had been shot and probably hated guns, the man carried the gun in his sack, wanting to get rid of it, and had gotten up very early Sunday and walked—he walked everywhere—to St. Patrick's Cathedral.

He wept at the idea of Christ's sacrifice. Other people weep at movies.

He was hungry after the service as if he had fasted, he was very hungry, and a little dizzy from the hunger and the weeping. He strode into one of New York's grand hotels, down the carpeted and chandeliered hallways and into their coffeeshop. How shining was the city at this hour!

He sat in a window booth.

He pulled a book from his sack, but an enormous waiter asked him to move to a smaller booth. There was only one other customer.

He heard the other customer comparing London to New York—to New York's demerit.

London does not shine.

He peeked around at her. She was a fat nun lecturing a waitress.

"London is better because the police carry no guns."

This was his cue.

He gives the nun the valuable and antique New York harmless gun.

The mouth of the nun is open but no sound comes out.

Booms then the hundred-pound-heavier head-taller mustach-ioed waiter: "Hey don't disturb the customers!"

"I don't like your attitude. You better leave."

"I was just trying to give the nun this passivist present. Won't you take it?"

"I don't want it."

"Give it to your son. It's a tip. It cost $30."

It cost $15. They look at the man's book sitting on the table. The man will leave.

"Do you read sir?"

"Just newspapers and comic books."

"I think you should read more comic books and fewer news-papers."

She says he was thrown out of a restaurant for pulling a gun on a nun. She says it was a very Sixties' stunt.

He asks her to phone his excuse and say he's not coming.

(Monday morning he gave the gun to his girlfriend's son. He had a paper gun already, only it was made of paper—it was made of paper and it fired paper.

His girlfriend that night has her cousin for excuse, but her cousin had gotten confused, and phoned her husband with some garbled message from the answering machine. Her husband understood. When she got home he smashed some china. The man said that meant her husband still loved her.

His girlfriend disagreed.)

The woman brings the man a glass of milk. What excuse did she give his excuse?

He has a flu and fever.

How did his excuse sound?

"Suspicious."

Leslie Scalapino

Days are ok

I was out and was tired and felt that I shouldn't spend any money, yet I had some with me. I saw a man buying something in a shop and his attitude I would say is that of a follower whom I saw from time to time with one person or another and now I was looking forward to going away for several weeks as soon as I'd finished working.

I'd seen the person at different places occasionally and then that ended. A woman gave the impression that someone was on a different level and knew another group of people and criticized him as having immature opinions and yet she hasn't been to many of these events either.

My mood was all right sitting with some people outside in the evening at the beginning of summer. A woman and I talked for a few moments about events that had happened to us without any real interest. Someone asked me a question then and when I began to answer it was obvious that he didn't care and he was intent on the conversation. His manner was gentle and glib and he didn't care about my attitudes or the background

very bored and intent

Leslie Scalapino

I'd been friends with a woman for quite awhile before I thought that she was selfish because she didn't like spending money. Lately she was wearing a yellow dress which I didn't think looked good and she seemed very closed and at ease, getting emotional without that being the point of her remarks.

They would be talking about something and she would get emotional going off on some tangent but also say something occasionally and be very controlled.

I'd gone to the post office beginning to walk in that direction when it was already late in the afternoon. I noticed that a woman on the street was not dressed right because she was in her early thirties though I'm not saying that I had any plans for that evening either or had anything I wanted to do until a few days from then.

Leslie Scalapino

Smiling and talking go on separately from something sexual and from ordinary life, peoples' activities being so frequent.

Someone's knowledge of a topic was casual and easy-going following a tangent. Talking to them I'd be able to single out emotions so that going somewhere or reading was a sexual feeling.

Also on these occasions several people were present but not included in conversation leading to a sense of euphoria. Some-one spoke briefly to me. He was very gentle and glib directing the conversation so that I became emotional and followed what he was saying at the same time.

I wouldn't see why an event should have occurred accompanied by a very emotional sense so that at the time going places wasn't separate from sexual feeling.

Norma Jean Deak

Chaparral

"Chaparral" is a solo performance that lasts about 40 minutes. The narrative involves a painter's move from New York to a house she inherits on a chaparral in Southern California. She is visited by two friends, a woman writer and a man, both out of her past life. The main character, Agnes, whom I play, is a first person omniscient narrator as well as a participant in the action. I also act out the other two characters.

The performance is divided into a prologue, parts I, II and III. In the prologue the main character/narrator is alone in the house. Part I is entitled "First Visit, Paul," part II "Second Visit, Valerie," and Part III "Valerie and Paul." During these sections a series of conversations and dramatic interactions takes place in different settings. At certain moments, slides are used that were taken in and around a house on a chaparral. In the slides I appear as Agnes and the other two characters are played by a man and another woman. There is dialogue that goes along with the slides. During the performance the slide sections function as brief film clips.

The text for "Chaparral" utilizes elements of the novel: narrative and descriptive passages, the first person narrator. One of the issues dealt with during the rehearsal period was the problem of staging a text that reads like a novel without eliminating the novel in the process. I wanted to preserve the tension that exists between a literary text and the act of performing. If traditionally theatre minimizes textuality by turning the text into a script, I attempt to *stage the textuality that resists theatre-making, to reveal the confrontation between text and performance.*

THE PROLOGUE

I t's 4 p.m. One half hour ago I fell asleep in the armchair by the fireplace. As I sleep, the book I was reading falls off my lap. The sound of the book hitting the floor enters my dream. Simultaneously my awakening begins. I can't remember where I am. My first impression is that instead of sitting up I am actually lying down in bed, not the bed in this house but a former bed. I try to determine if it is morning and I have slept through the night or if I am just awakening from a nap. I feel my left leg bent back under the chair. From my realization of this one fact it comes to me in an instant. I know where I am, what my position is and the approximate time of day. I straighten my leg. It's stiff. I stand up and limp around the room. When my leg returns to normal I pick the book up off the floor and place it on the coffee table.

In one corner of the room are four unopened boxes. I ignore them and walk toward one of the windows. I lean out as far as I can and turn to look in all directions. In order to reach the other window I have to move the armchair. It won't slide easily because of the rug underneath. I have to pull hard. When I reach the window I sit down on the sill and gaze outward. After a few minutes I turn around so that I am facing inside, but I remain seated. My eyes rest on the unopened boxes. I inhale deeply then release my breath with a sigh. I walk toward the boxes. With a pair of scissors I cut the string and tear off the brown paper, moving from one box to another until they are all unwrapped. I return to the first box, pull the cardboard back and look inside. Three of the boxes contain books. I begin to put them into the bookcase in no specific order. There is plenty of room. My great-aunt didn't own a lot of books. Most of the books she left belonged to the library. Since she had taken them out months ago, before her death, they were long overdue. I returned them explaining what had happened to the librarian.

One box remains. I try to guess what's in it. I can't. As I pull back one flap I see the edge of white paper. It comes to me in a flash—sketches for paintings already completed. I decide not to unpack them. I put the box on the bottom of the hall closet.

I return to the livingroom and put the string and paper inside the empty boxes. I close the window behind the armchair then push the chair back to its original position. The other windows remain open. Sunlight streams into the room.

PART I "First Visit, Paul"

"You just don't fit the house. I keep expecting the real owner to walk through the door."

We laugh. It's 1:45. Paul and I are sitting at one end of the diningroom table. We've finished eating, but the plates and serving dishes remain. We continue to drink the wine that is in our glasses.

"How well did you know your great-aunt?"

"Hardly at all . . . Since I've been living in her house among her things I have more of an idea of what she was like than I did when she was alive. Everything you see except for the books belonged to her."

"Perhaps that's why you seem out of place. All this old furniture, the crystal glasses . . . it's as if you've stumbled into the local community theatre's set for *Uncle Vanya*." He sits back in his chair pleased with his literary allusion and looks at me across the table. "When I saw you 4 months ago right before you moved I tried to imagine you living somewhere else. I couldn't. I still can't."

I take a sip of wine. "I wonder why she brought along these crystal glasses? They must have been a wedding present. You know, she and her husband moved out here and built this house right after their marriage."

"Rather courageous of them, wasn't it?"

"Yes, I guess it was, for the times."

I hold up the crystal glass so that the sunlight coming through the window passes through it. "I've gotten used to these glasses." I laugh. "I wouldn't think of drinking out of anything else."

"In that pose you almost blend in."

"When you're out of the sun, there's enough of a breeze to keep you cool." I'm positioned under a tree in front of the house. "Why don't you move your chair over here?"

"I'm comfortable where I am. Don't forget I've just lived through a month of rain."

Paul is lying down in a lounge chair, just beyond the shade of the tree. "Don't think I believe for a moment that you got that color sitting under trees."

I laugh. "I'm not trying to hide anything. I admit that over the past few months I've spent many an hour lying out fully exposed to the sun."

I am sitting on the ground facing Paul in his lounge chair.

My empty lounge chair is beside me. I rub my left hand along the blades of grass. After a moment I look up. Paul is staring at my hand as it moves over the grass. I casually lift my hand and scratch my cheek.

"Valerie mentioned in a letter that she ran into you a few weeks ago."

"That's right." He's thinking back. A woman was coming toward him. "It was odd. We recognized each other immediately but had difficulty figuring out from where. I stopped in front of her. I said 'We've met before, haven't we?' She said "Yes, I think so," but with a certain hesitation. I kept looking at her face. She was frowning and biting her bottom lip. What was funny about it was that it came to both of us at about the same time. We said "Agnes'!" almost simultaneously."

I remember a party at my apartment last winter. The room was filled with people. Paul and Marie were still together. Valerie was with Matthew. Valerie and I were sitting on the couch. Paul sat down beside me. I introduced them.

"It's not surprising that you had difficulty placing each other. You'd only met once before."

"She had a scarf around her head. That threw me off. Once I had made the connection I had no trouble at all. I remembered the party and her very well. I was with Marie and she was with a man I didn't meet."

"That was Matthew."

After supplying this information I adjust my voice to express concern. "How did she look to you?"

"Attractive. She's an attractive woman." He is puzzled. "How should she have looked?"

Sunlight filters through the branches of the tree. I shield my eyes.

"She sounded a little despondent in her letters."

"Do you know why?"

"She's split with Matthew."

"The next question is of course who left whom."

"I got the impression from what she said that he decided to go back to his wife."

"No wonder she's upset."

"She's a rather fragile type. I'm worried about how she might react."

"What are you afraid she'll do?"

"Oh, I don't know. In any case I'll be able to judge for myself. She'll be visiting some time next month."

"I didn't notice anything unusual. But we only spoke for a few minutes."

I have moved back into the lounge chair and am lying down. "You can tell a lot in a few minutes if things are really bad."

The wind increases. The leaves rustle and the sound of the birds' chirping is much louder. Paul is silent for a moment as he listens.

"The sounds of the wild!"

I laugh aloud. "How dramatic you are, Paul. It takes a great deal of imagination to conceive of this place as a wilderness. When it's quiet you can hear the freeway."

PART II "Second Visit, Valerie"

"It's not the first time that he's decided to break off the relationship."

"You never told me that."

Valerie and I are in the livingroom. I'm sitting in the armchair and she's standing in the center of the room.

"It happened twice before. Once for about 3 weeks and once for about 4 months."

"And both times you resumed the relationship as if nothing had happened?"

"I tried to, especially after the first time. He called and said that he would like to meet. I agreed."

I adjust my position. I am now sitting on the edge of my chair.

"Didn't you ask for an explanation?"

"You don't understand Agnes. I didn't care what went on between him and his wife. The arrangement suited me very well."

"And the second time."

She's thinking back. "When I finally heard from him after 4 months, I was surprised. I wasn't sure that I wanted to begin again."

"But you did."

"That's right. I did."

"And this time?"

"What do you mean?"

"Matthew. What if he should contact you?"

"I don't know. I just don't know . . . if you'd asked me that question a month ago I would have said that I wanted to resume it again even at the risk of the same thing happening. But I'm not so sure that I could go through a fourth break up." She looks questioningly at me. "It would be inevitable, don't you think?"

"From what you've said . . . I'm afraid so."

Valerie walks over to the window, and shielding her eyes from the sun, scans the panorama.

"It's amazingly beautiful. Look over at the top of the mountain. It's turned deep purple."

I repeat her gesture and look in the direction of the mountain.

The room is getting darker. I glance at my watch. It's 4:15. The wind is increasing. I get up to close the window in the hall. When I look out I see the little bushes that surround the house bending in the wind. Suddenly there is a sound from the back of the house. Has someone come in? I listen. No. It's the wind. I walk from room to room looking for open windows, then I return to the armchair in the livingroom. A door slams. I jump up. "Is that you, Valerie?"

"Yes, Agnes. The wind is really blowing! The lounge chairs are being dragged across the yard. We'd better get them immediately."

"Yes, let's move them inside before it's too late."

I join Valerie at the front door and follow her out. "What a wind."

"I can't hear you."

Our hair blows furiously in the wind as we push our way toward the chairs. Finally we each grab one and return to the house. When we reach the porch Valerie holds both chairs while I open the door. Once inside we pause for a moment, look at each other and smile.

"We made it!"

We sit down on the couch facing the window. Valerie's eyes move around the room. Suddenly there is a sound from the fireplace. She turns her head.

"What was that?"

"Soot that fell through the chimney."

Valerie's gaze continues around the room. "This room has a completely different feeling when the wind's blowing."

"How do you mean?"

"The sea seems very close. Usually I'm unaware of the fact that it really is nearby."

Valerie gets up and walks over to the window.

"I recently read the diary of a woman who lived in Maine in the late 1800s. In one of the entries she described a fierce storm. Her husband was out at sea and she knew that he was in grave danger. She waited inside staring out of the window. The men were miles away out at sea but she looked straight ahead as if she believed that by concentrating intensely in the general direction she would be able to see what was happening. He returned safely." She turns away from the window and goes back to the couch. "I wonder why she stayed on. After her husband's death she really didn't have to."

"That woman?"

"No. Your aunt. I wonder what she did for all those years?"

Valerie is sitting in the armchair by the fireplace. She is reading. On the table beside her are two other books which are unopened. Her eyes are concentrated sternly upon the page. Her breathing is slow and repressed. Finally she shuts the book and places it on the table on top of the other two. She sits back in the chair and releases her breath. She is breathing normally again. After a moment she gets up and goes over to the window. As she looks out she strikes a pose, partly as herself and partly as the heroine of the novel she had just been reading. She repeats softly to herself "What does it mean? What does it all mean?"

I enter the room carrying a cup of tea. Valerie's position at the window stops me in the doorway. I watch her from behind. Her body is still, but any second it looks as if she might lunge forward through the pane of glass. In a moment it's over and she's relaxed.

"Am I disturbing you?"

Valerie turns away from the window. "No, not at all."

"Would you like some tea? There's more in the kitchen."

"No, but sit down with me anyway."

We sit down on the couch side by side.

"I looked in about an hour ago. You were reading so intently that I didn't dare disturb you." I smile. "Is the book so good?"

Valerie motions over to the table where the three books lie one on top of the other. "Once I'm in them I can't seem to get out of them. It takes me a while to start feeling like myself again."

Earlier today when I was on my way to my studio I saw her sitting at her desk. She was gazing out of the window. About 15 minutes later I heard the front door open and close. I heard her steps on the porch. The window in my studio is so high that I had to stand on my toes in order to see out, but I had seen her walking down the road moving forward briskly.

"I thought I heard you go out earlier."

"You did. I went for a walk. I was trying to write but I made the mistake of sitting in front of the open window. I felt an urge to be outside. Before I knew it I was walking along the road."

She gets up and moves around the room. "While I walked I was struck by the fact that here I was at the other end of the country walking along a road I had never been on before. The thought excited me. At that moment I really believed that everything would work itself out." She faces me and smiles. "But the feeling didn't last. It suddenly occured to me that I had decided that no matter what, I would sit at that desk all morning, and there I was at 10 a.m. walking along a dirt road.

By the time I got back, I was so exhausted that all I could manage was to sit and read."

I'm staring up at her from my position on the couch, arrested by the absorbed expression on her face. "Who—what are you thinking about?"

"Nothing, I wasn't thinking about anything. I don't remember. Do you want me to retrace my thoughts?"

I laugh. "Never mind. I'm not so exacting. I'll let you off this time."

The room has gotten dark. I get up to turn on the light. On my way back to the couch I remember why I came into the room in the first place.

"I got a letter from Paul. He'll be visiting for a few days."

PART III *"Paul and Valerie"*

"I love crystal glasses, but I begged Agnes not to use them everyday. Before I left New York I went through a period when I broke at least a glass a day. I was terrified that I would go through the entire set."

"Is there a crack in this glass?" I have taken the glass from Valerie and am examining it closely. "No, it must have been the way the light was hitting it."

It's 10 p.m. We've been sitting around the table for the past two hours. We're just completing the third bottle of wine.

"You know the only time I ever saw my great-aunt was when I was 15. She must have been at least 60. She had the habit of lowering her head so that she could look directly into my eyes. When she asked a question she would lean in toward me. I had the feeling that I had a limited time in which to answer and if I didn't answer fast enough she would pounce on me."

We laugh heartily partly from the image I have drawn of my great-aunt and partly from the 3 bottles of wine. I decide to put on some coffee. I begin to walk into the kitchen.

Paul leans in toward Valerie. "Do you remember what we were talking about that night at Agnes' . . . the night we first met?"

She's wondering what he's getting at.

"Agnes still hadn't made up her mind about the move. I was encouraging her not to be hasty. You said she should go ahead and take the risk."

"Did I? I'm surprised. That doesn't sound like me."

"You were adamant."

I have interrupted my trip to the kitchen for a moment in order to follow their conversation. "What are you getting at Paul . . . that my move was somehow to Valerie's advantage?"

"Or are you implying that I was the one who wanted to get away?"

Paul is feeling very self-satisfied. He's hit his mark. That was exactly what he was implying. He watches her turn away and take a sip of wine.

Valerie undresses in the dark. She can hear our voices in the diningroom. Noiselessly she opens the window and sits down at the foot of her bed. She didn't look at him for more than an instant when she took her leave. She wonders if I noticed . . . if I was aware of his movement toward her as the evening progressed.

Moonlight makes familiar things visible—her clothes falling off the armchair, her earrings on the top of the chest of drawers, the edge of her hairbrush on the right hand corner of the vanity. She turns her head to the left in order to see her reflection in the mirror. Only the outline of her face is visible.

It had taken much longer than she expected to get away. At each pause in the conversation she would prepare herself to say, "Goodnight, I'm going to bed," but he would say something to her just as the words were beginning to form on her lips. He refused to release her. Where was her apartment—had she sublet it . . . he knew someone who had advertised . . . people calling at all hours . . . strange types arriving at the door . . . it could be dangerous . . . a young woman spent a terrifying morning . . . a man refused to leave . . . kept asking questions . . . she answered as calmly as possible . . . but through it all she was terrified.

She hears voices down the hall. Paul and I are saying goodnight. She follows Paul's footsteps as he walks by her room toward his own, then turns back to the window and looks out. She hears him open and close his door. She sits perfectly still listening to the creaking of the house and to the sound of her breathing. The sounds move more and more into the background. The sensation of her body decreases and she is unable to move. Her eyes remain wide open, fixed on a spot in the distance. Finally by an act of will she manages to turn her head quickly and in so doing breaks the spell.

Valerie and I are in the yard. She's sitting in the swing and I'm beside her on the ground.

"Paul told me he's leaving tomorrow." I inform her.

She doesn't answer. She's remembering yesterday. I had invited the two of them into my studio. Valerie seemed removed. I thought that she didn't like the work, but that wasn't it. It was what was depicted, a narrative she inferred that confused her. She wanted to figure it out, to understand exactly what was going on. Afterwards we went for a walk. Paul's response to her confusion was to describe each painting in the series to the best of his ability.

"On the extreme right of the first painting there's a man in black. He's leaning against the fireplace. Two women are sitting side by side on a couch. They are involved in what appears to be an intimate conversation. The older woman is sitting sideways on the couch. One arm is extended along the back. Her position is relaxed. The younger woman, actually girl, is sitting sideways as well but remains on the edge of the couch. I would say that she was a little tense wouldn't you?"

The question was addressed to Valerie but she didn't answer. She was too enervated.

"In the second painting the man has moved and is standing behind the couch. The older woman is saying something to him. The younger one is looking up at the man. An interesting detail—the young woman is holding on to the back of the couch, actually gripping it with her left hand."

His descriptions were getting on Valerie's nerves.

"In the third and final painting the three people are standing in front of the couch. The young girl is in the middle. The man has his hand on her shoulder as if to turn her around. The older woman is already facing the door."

"Why don't you just say what they're going to do to the girl?"

"That's not the point Valerie." Peter was animated. "But I think I know what disturbs you—the aspect of initiation, more specifically sexual initiation. It's quite titillating—a girl, an older woman, a man—it's reminiscent of Sade's *Philosophy in the Bedroom* . . . the part when a man and an older woman take it upon themselves to educate a young girl in the art of . . ."

"That's not it at all. That's not what I was thinking."

I laughed. "I'll take a look at the Marquis de Sade, Paul. Maybe you have something."

The conversation had ended. Valerie was not interested in pursuing it further.

She looks down at me from her position on the swing.

"I have to start thinking about going back myself. I hope I haven't overstayed my welcome."

"I'll miss you."

A few moments before Paul returned from a walk. He entered the house by the front and caught sight of Valerie and me through the French doors. He's watching us through the glass now. I smile almost a laugh; then we laugh together. He tries to guess the topic of our conversation by following the movement of my hands as I speak. I turn around and wave.

"Come on out."

One moment before Valerie had informed me that he was there. He opens the door and walks toward us.

"Does Matthew know where you are?"

"I didn't tell him, but we have mutual friends who know."

Valerie and I are sitting at the dining room table. In about an hour she will be leaving. She picks up her wine glass and rubs her finger along the rim and down the sides.

"Anyway, I might call him when I return."

I decide not to plunge in and keep my comment to myself. I take an apple and begin to peel it.

"You're very good at that."

"My grandfather always peeled fruit. He insisted on doing it for me, but I finally convinced him to teach me. Have a piece."

I hold out a peeled quarter. She refuses it with a shake of her head. She smiles at me across the table.

"How long will it be before I see you again?"

"I'll be making a trip back with new work some time in March."

"That's a long time away. It's only the middle of October."

"5½ minutes . . . I mean months . . ." We laugh. ". . . until March."

Laura Ferguson

Somebody Always Waiting Outside the Monday Matinee

The projectionist is always telling me that there are plenty of ways to make money: that I am simply not finding them. He stands behind the candy counter with a toothpick in his mouth and tells me about the wonderful deal he has just found on East Oakland apartment buildings.

You mean to fix up, I say, busy chasing the errant kernels of popcorn out of their holes with the vacuum.

He gazes at me wonderingly for a minute as though lost in my naiveté. *No*, girl, for *tax* write-offs.

The line at the bank twisted up and down twice like a multicolored skein of wool around the stubby, bathwater grey columns which pretended to hold up the roof. Margaret had been on another interview. This time she had tried to dress "legal secretary," and her feet throbbed in the neat black-heeled shoes as she approached the check-writing desk at the end of the line.

"Oh, brother," said an old woman standing at the high desk. She lifted her head and hand simultaneously, the chain from her glasses and the one anchoring the pen to the table swinging in unison. "People just can't wait on an old woman any more," she said loudly, staring at Margaret. One eye was magnified hugely by its prescription glass, and seemed to poke inquisitively at Margaret. A few heads turned. Margaret stopped walking.

"Rush right up on a line, some people will. There just isn't any respect left. They'd kill you soon as look at you." The woman's voice fell in to worn grooves. She showed no sign of returning to her check writing, and her giant eye still held Margaret's. When a tall man walked by her to stand at the end of the line she felt the unevenness of her breath that meant tears and she walked out, turned into the store immediately to the left of the bank and began, unhurriedly, to examine a tray of brassieres marked "Discontinued."

There is a man living at the back of the theatre. He kneels with his infant son who is picking up the grey popcorn from the floor of the lobby and putting it in his mouth. I offer him a wrinkled specimen from the hot dog racks. The child has learned early about the market value of cuteness. When his father panhandles (but that is rarely for his father is involved in a long and interesting search for a job, which proceeds briskly in no direction) Edward will smile from the E-Z ride on his father's back and somehow imply his entire wasted future with just one faint wave of his hand and a tremulous smile. It is a good trick; one for which they are even occasionally paid.

A friend of mine who lives in Connecticut is just leaving his summer cabin for the uneasy status of caretaker. I see him carefully draining the pipes and pushing putty in the cracks of the asphalt roof. He is unwilling to leave, but as he sits down for a cigarette in his ski jacket, contemplating the skylight he cut into the ceiling last winter, the cold begins to climb from his feet into his corduroy knees. An icicle drops off his porch down the steep hill behind it and makes a sharp sound, breaking against a tree. A car can be heard for miles approaching, and the sound of a zipper announces that the driver was not expecting the curve of road near Marshall's cabin. It is simply too cold for melancholic reflection in Connecticut, this time of year.

I work for a giant corporation, whose name is tied into the most arrogant structure to grace the sky in years. Each time I climb the hill to have the Bay spread out before me I see it. In a cordial light, it is a bookmark sticking out of the city: at 5:00, however, its aspect is that of a single and glittering tooth from a monstrous jaw.

The man and his child live in a back room of this giant corporation. They walk softly and live in a dressing room. The landmark the child associates with his home is the magenta and orange UA logo, which appears on screen accompanied by a thudding bass guitar solo before every performance. Edward rates it the casual, sideways wave of the hand he reserves for those objects so familiar to him that they no longer plead for identification. The "Superman" trailer, which it seems that we have been showing for one hundred years, is always met by Edward with renewed admiration. His screams of joy fill the theatre, and his father must run, low like a fullback, through the aisles to get to the room backstage where Edward sleeps. He is always afraid of being caught.

Margaret felt resentful even before she entered the Calico Cat. It was a restaurant she despised. She was there only because she had felt unequal to lying when Mary, a typist at Margaret's last office job, had called and suggested lunch.

Margaret scanned the restaurant, not expecting to see her friend. She settled at a corner table where she could lean back against the wall and see the door. Mary came around a corner and waited at the light: Margaret watched and forgave as she saw the thin material of her dress drive itself against the bony knees and saw Mary's eyes screw up unattractively at the light crackling off oncoming cars.

She picked up the menu and studied it, only looking up when she saw Mary lowering herself into the seat across from her. "Hey!" She made it a greeting: widened her eyes. "I didn't see you."

My friend Marshall in Connecticut is wrapping the blanket around his knees now, preparing to use his Volkswagen un-seasonally. The Volkswagen is a summer vehicle without a care in the world. The tatters which remain of its convertible top spin in the wind. The brakes don't work if there is much snow. This remains unexplained. I took a ride with Marshall once, to visit a friend of his who runs Linwood's Zenith repair shop in Goshen. Stanley Linwood is a man in his fifties who was nearly asleep in the December darkness when we came in to see him. He led us, silently, out of his empty shop into the woods, or so it seemed to me. Through the trees, however, I glimpsed an enormous Quonset hut, in the snow a half-buried can of soup with the label patiently peeled off. He stamped his shoes gravely before entering, and so I did too. The building housed the largest collection of theatre organs ever assembled. The floor was a deep jewel red velvet pile throughout, and the building glowed like a church: each pipe burnished to a high glisten. The organs themselves were adorned fabulously with the gimcrack of a thousand years. They dripped arches, gold lettering and scenes in mosaic. Mr. Linwood's face wore the expectant and downcast look of one acknowledging praise. He was balding, and the wind had blown his hair into points of whipped cream around his bald spot. The color of his eyes had faded so much that it was impossible to call them any one color. He had rescued each of these organs in the pickup we had seen outside: patiently, piece by piece until he could painstakingly reassemble them all. Mr. Linwood did not play himself; he shook his hands back and forth, deprecating, when I asked him to play on the biggest and most fantastic of the organs. Ivory colored, it lit up from behind when it was turned on, and the pipes coming up from the pedals looked like the folds in a wedding dress, lit up for Las Vegas. I played *The Happy Farmer* twice, while Mr. Linwood listened with courteously bent head and a broad smile. As Marshall and I were leaving, he took my mittened hand in his own and said "I learned to read, doing the marquee at the old RKO on 42nd Street. Now *that* was a movie palace." He shook his head for a moment, marvelling, and I felt obliged to stand in the snow one moment longer, while he felt out the rest of his sentence. I was trying to figure out whether he meant "movie palace" in the cosier movie critic's sense or whether, as seemed possible after touring the Quonset, he meant a *real* palace, whose organ perhaps had been faced with real gold.

"Come back." He finally said. "Please come back any time." Marshall and I found out that the brakes weren't working on the way home. We took a slow motion skid into a snow bank, and opened our eyes to a celestial setting.

It is evident that the woman in the candy store is in no hurry. She stoops to pick up the chocolate mints I have asked for, and her hand moves slowly across the dark brown ranks until she finds it. There is a line behind me. A police car wheels by outside the shop, siren wailing. The candy woman doesn't look up.

At the theatre down the street, Candy has one thousand meanings.

"No, I'm not candying for you." The men who work here will do almost anything else; they, for example, are the faceless ministers who throw cedar sawdust over a man's liquid dinner, lost loudly in the aisle. The candy counter is deserted, after that, for at least eight minutes. The ushers must sweep up after anything. But they will not candy. That, they give me to understand, is for women to do, and women only.

Margaret walked in to the dusky interior of the auditorium from the hot bright morning outside and felt herself into a seat at the back of the room. The lecture was in beginning anthropology of culture, and the professor's voice swung in and out of the range of the microphone around his neck, the cord of which he held stiffly away from his chest.

"The purpose of death . . . in a primitive culture . . . miles from the nearest town." He bent his head, entered a sharp notation on the map he projected overhead. The sound of his rasping breaths came clearly through the speakers.

Margaret's eyes wandered over the huge and passive audience. And the probability is, she thought, that one of us will die before the end of the quarter. She looked at a blonde head three rows in front of her and the ballpoint chain of hearts on the clipboard before it. Will it be you? She suddenly felt flooded with power, and caught the eye of a fat woman with pale and stubborn lips wearing a brown corduroy dress. And it will be you, she mouthed silently, it will be you. And lowered her eyes modestly to the book before her.

Margaret sat with her back hunched and the receiver grasped between neck and shoulder.

". . . Well, I wish you could have been here for it, Mag. Foley asked me about you when I went down for the ice cream before the party. Josie—" and hear Emily's voice become distant "Your aunt wants to say 'Happy Birthday . . .' " and here her voice took on a spurious excitement that Margaret remembered unwillingly.

" 'Lo Aunt Ma-a-ag" the splayed A sat oddly on the child.

"Hello Josie. Well, I'm sure I'll get to meet you soon—"

"—And thankyou for the watch." The daughter's voice held unpleasantly mincing echoes of the mother.

Goodbyes said, Margaret lit a cigarette and deliberately allowed her legs to fall open beneath her orange terrycloth bathrobe. The pink neon in the REEL JOY CINEMA sign across the street turned swiftly to purple and the hum of the filament dropped low.

I derive a deep feeling of satisfaction when the crude hand lettered numbers appear on the television screen. Someone is there! Someone has fallen asleep, gone to the bathroom or is watching another channel and forgotten duties to this one. It is always a regenerating thought.

When the shades were drawn at night, the old Victorian parlor looked most itself. The waterspots in the rose and gold wallpaper faded in the softer light from the fireplace and the old brass standing lamps; the bold and ugly designs on the upholstery and carpet seemed to retain little of their original color. Margaret, feet up on a hideous marble bench and drinking a glass of tomato juice, peopled the room. Her grandmother sat in the corner, under a "good strong light," sewing the rents and holes her energetic grandchildren had put in their clothing back together and patching against further damage with quite brilliant and unsuitable

Laura Ferguson

colors. The reflections of these patches played on her glasses and Margaret could not read her face.

One Margaret lay on the floor, her feet in their light blue sneakers sharing the marble bench with Margaret's espadrilles. A Nancy Drew mystery entitled "The Clue of the Whistling Bagpipes" lay open on her stomach, and her eyes were glued in fascination to the page. Another, "The Haunted Showboat," lay under her hand, ready to leap into life the moment the first was closed. Another Margaret stood in front of the fireplace, her gaze locked into itself in the narrow mirror over the mantel.

Margaret sighed, yawned and stood, dispersing the phantoms. The funeral service for her great aunt had begun and ended quickly, allowing her to return to the house early to sift among its belongings for the salable. Margaret wondered for a moment why she had lied so determinedly, insisting that her return to California could not be delayed even for a day to close up the house. Her Aunt Melissa's few friends, women in long woolen coats and tight hats worn against the fall's bitter winds, had looked expressionlessly at her, seeking as she knew a *real* reason; sick husband, child or sister, in her explanations which centered around a job invented for the occasion. Their pies and casseroles were piled on the kitchen table, and Margaret had not yet determined what she ought to do with them. Throwing them away, burying them in the heaps of trash she had drawn from every corner of the house, was possible, although Margaret could not feel sure that the garbagemen, intimate with each of these women, would not unearth them and despise her utterly. On the whole, Margaret liked the idea of taking them with her on the airplane.

Marshall will be moving into my parents' house in Connecticut.

It is empty during the winter: empty and old and fragile. It is a steamboat of a house, with ten bedrooms and a double Victorian parlor. I wonder what Marshall does there, alone. It is a house for the largest of families: my three sisters and I do not fill it, although we try. Marshall plans to hook up his enormous sound system so that he may have Mozart in the bathroom and on the front steps. My parents want someone to nurse the pipes through the winter. They are too busy leading a city life, and will not return until summer, when Marshall will be able to return to his cabin. So it works out well. But the house is very empty and very still, winters. The big porches are empty and cold, the wicker furniture banished to the garage or basement. Probably Marshall will spend most of his time in the kitchen, which is ugly and cheerful.

I think I am leading a double life. I dress to go to work deceitfully, comfortably. I must maintain the outer appearance of assistant manager, but I feel I must do so without giving up my knee socks. It is important to me.

At the last Barnum and Bailey appearance in New York, a little girl was crushed by one of the elephants. Her aunt had taken her to see the circus, and afterward the child had wanted to visit the animals in their cages. The aunt later said that it was "no more than a second" that she was talking to a man from her office when "we heard the most awful scream." The child had walked under the rail keeping animals from visitors and then squeezed in through the bars. The elephant, according to those other adults who watched from the opposite side of the circle, had no sooner seen the child advancing with her handful of straw outstretched than he had reared up on his hind legs and brought

107

the front ones down to crush her.

"It wasn't like an elephant at all," said a woman in a pillbox hat to the Eyewitness News reporter. "It was fast—*real* fast, you know? Sort of like a horse. Not," she repeated positively, "like an elephant."

There was one week when I was accosted by sirens. I watched television in Al's basement apartment, and I could not tell whether the sound came from the television or from the night outside. Whenever I met a friend on the street, the sounds would begin again, blurring and drowning the conversation.

"Keep in touch," the friend would shout over the noise.

I would pantomime my friendship with exaggerated nods. "Keep in touch!" I would shout in return. "Keep in touch!"

The phone rang, and Margaret dropped the bowl she was washing, bringing her hands together uselessly like flippers to catch it. It broke on the edge of the sink. Fine slivers of white china imprinted with forget-me-nots fell in the soapy water and on the dark bricky linoleum. Tasting bitterness under her tongue, she answered the phone. It was Rose, her dentist's assistant, changing her appointment to one week later.

"He's been so busy, dear with the school bus crash and all," the voice confided. "Can you make it?" Margaret's assent had barely cleared the wire before Rose said "Tuesday, then," and hung up.

When Margaret put the receiver down she ran her tongue apprehensively over her teeth.

The airport lounge sounded with Roger Williams' "Christmas in London." Children were draped in all attitudes of sleep over the naugahyde chairs, their faces red from too much clothing. A uniformed man stood under the mistletoe at the American Airlines Baggage Information desk. He carried on low-voiced phone conversations, occasionally covering the mouthpiece with his hand, leaning toward the person at the head of the long line.

"But I have an *interview* tomorrow," wailed a ruffled blonde at the end of the line to anyone who would listen. "An *interview*, tomorrow *morning*."

When the announcement came over the loudspeakers that the baggage was still in Los Angeles and was expected tomorrow, the blonde screamed in a determined manner.

A fat woman in front of her wearing a Mickey Mouse tee shirt turned. "Once more," she said with a blank white face "and I'll bust your mouth."

Morrison Reading Room is where I hang out at Berkeley. It is just inside the tall Corinthian marble columns which are "DE-VOTED TO THE MEMORY OF CHARLES FRANKLIN DOE" and mark dead center of that cluttered campus. A dart to the right past those columns, and a glass door barred with brass closes me in on a hushing hydraulic sound. I am safe in the closing years of the last century. Tall armchairs are havens of privacy with jutting blinders to block out other readers. Pools of light from standing lamps barely break the mahogany gloom. A bust of Praxiteles' Hermes leans tenderly over my blue chair beneath the window. Every new book and periodical must have its spine bent and pages ruffled here before being shelved forever in the Stacks. The windows are set so high in the walls that they admit only cross sections of the trees outside. But for the trailing bunches of blue grey eucalyptus nuts I am safe once more in the glycerin globe of a Connecticut snowfall, snug in the brown hut beneath the plastic pine.

The room was still. Margaret's eyes moved cautiously to the left of a cheap reproduction of "Les Demoiselles d'Avignon." Outside the window, the buzzing squares of color that had filled her eyes resolved themselves into a nurse standing beside a red Pinto in the parking lot. The woman stood under a pepper tree, and the smoke of her cigarette was a heavy-looking coil around her head.

". . . So you understand then, Mrs. Atkinson. The poetry will serve not only as a part of your therapy but also as a proof to the state, who will be paying your bill, so to speak, that you are, in fact, a patient of mine."

"Doctor Wendel have you, well, thought of anything I could do about my vision? I don't know if I've made it clear to you that—"

"We can get into all of this next week: bring in the poetry when you come. So long."

Once on the street, Margaret began to tremble, remembering. She had only the most glancing recollection of the scene that had resulted in the police station. It had been borne in upon her, however, that it was either these visits to Dr. Wendel or some form of incarceration which had been described only in the vaguest of terms. Even the kinder sergeant, Lefkowitz, had spoken only of "going away somewhere for a while."

A glance into the cobalt window of a drugstore across the street was reassuring. Margaret had been extremely careful, in the cell, of her stockings; sitting well forward on the cement bench to avoid tearing them. She felt that her suit jacket gave her an organized, professional appearance, and she rearranged her face slightly to create the remote and abstracted expression which she felt went particularly well with the jacket.

Louisa's doctor told her that because he couldn't feel a pulse in one side of her neck she must enter the hospital for a delicate and miniature operation, that of removing the debris of her eighty years from the stilled strong arteries in her throat. As a matter of fact she will be eighty in just a few weeks, now. I have ordered two dozen red and white roses for that day from a humid little florist who operates close to her house. I am thinking of changing the order: perhaps the presentation of beauties which, after all, one only watches admiringly as they curve themselves into alluring shapes of death is not the suitable gift. It is her life as a nourisher which nourishes her; isn't that a curious thing about women?

Her stories were the most lurid and breathtaking of my youth: often concentrating on medical detail of a scrupulous sort. I would listen, fascinated, while my skin would shrink on my limbs to hear her: the night she visited her aunt who had recently suffered a stroke lingers with me on hot and restless nights. She drove through a hot Michigan night to Aunt Jenny's farmhouse and walked up the steps to find Aunt Jen in her rocking chair, motion-less, with a fly walking across her eye, with the pauses for finicky antenna cleaning which flies effect only when they are at their most easy. After some of these stories I would lie long in bed, fingering my wrist morbidly for the "beating wings" that had warned her of her first and most nearly fatal heart attack.

Jim, the projectionist, wakes up in the middle of the night. He is a big man, and the bed groans when he turns over. His small blue eyes stare up at the ceiling as he pulls open the middle drawer of his nightstand. The gun gleams in the light from the window and he cradles it against his chest. One finger enters the barrel of the gun and his eyes close, the counterpane pulled neatly over the blueblack revolver.

Laura Ferguson

Margaret sat down at the typewriter and examined the extreme edge of the nail on her index finger. She had placed a Valium under her tongue for the maximum effect but it was tasting bad and burning a streak across the bottom of her mouth. She drank the last eighth of a can of Coke and picked up the Burgundy Frost Maxi-Color. When her nail had dried she took some pink stationary from a drawer containing a hammer, a package of marble and a roll of scotch tape. Sitting with her back against the refrigerator, she began a letter to her mother.

In an apartment building that I lived in in New York, the hallways were narrow, the walls stained yellow and the lights kept dim. It was obvious that to the builders the thickness of the apartment walls on the hallways was not important. You could hear everything that was happening in each apartment as you climbed the old stairways, peeling linoleum ready always to give with a rotten ripping sound, exposing the splintered wood of the step. My acquaintanceship with the little girl who lived beneath me happened as a result of one of my cautious climbs to my apartment, which was on the uppermost and ricketiest floor. I had paused for a moment on the third floor, my arms full of two grocery bags from Gristede's on the corner, when the loud wail I had often heard through the walls began again. A vicious female voice spoke in sharp and weighty periods, accompanied by the choked voice of the child. I rested, too tired for curiosity, and just as I had put my foot on the stair again, preparing for the upward climb, a child scuttled out of the apartment, door slamming firmly behind her. She ran into me, and I lost one grocery bag: oranges rolled and tumbled freely down the stairs. Her face, sallow with reddened eyelids and nose, expected anger. She began collecting the oranges fast her arms thin and quick.

"Will you bring them upstairs for me?" My bag had ripped open and I was taking the stairs two at a time, fearful for the eggs and milk. She did not answer.

I was putting the remaining food away when I heard footsteps outside the door. I had by that time thought more about the cries I had heard from the apartment downstairs, and I felt some compunction about my abruptness with the little girl.

"Come in, come in!" I sounded out of character to myself, too hearty, but the child's evident shyness was not easily overcome.

"What would you like to eat—come on" this to a shake of the thin brown braids "I just got home with some ice cream." She came in and sat down on the couch, slowly, her eyes roaming the room under lowered lids. I went behind the room divider into the kitchen, began to dish out the bowls of butter pecan.

"What's your name?" I called to her. She had sat back on the couch now, like an old woman. Her hands were folded on her lap, and she exuded an air of sobriety and stillness.

"Rosa."

"How old are you?" I continued, encouraged by her response.

"Ten." I was treating her as a child much younger: she was very small, very slender.

"Where do you go to school?" My mind was already forming the next question when she answered.

"Chapin." It was unexpected: Chapin was one of the oldest and starchiest of the city's private girl's schools. I knew that their charity cases were limited to the very obviously so—I remembered the one thin-lipped black girl on Chapin's volleyball team and I wondered.

"How long have you been going there?" My interest was engaged now, and walking over I saw her silent and unequal struggle with tears which were blotting her eyes with anguish.

Laura Ferguson

"You don't like it." I offered her the napkin I had brought with the ice cream. I felt helpless, believing that any affection I could show would be forward and jarring to the child.

"No," she said, composed again with the napkin balled up in her hand. "Not yet."

There is a certain state of the human psyche when the lyrics of popular songs loom large and paralyzing in their logic. It is in such a state that I find myself returning to an apartment whose open door casts a pool of sunshine to the grey and rose carpeting in the hall before it. I close the door carefully and quietly and inspect the sunny placidity of an apartment left out to dry in a crosswind. I hurriedly put a recording of An American In Paris on the turntable. At least *that's* done.

The library is only four blocks away from Wendel's office and, for Margaret, a good walk. Each corner has a sea green pole with a well-rubbed silver button, round, to press for the crosswalk. She likes to feel herself acting on the streetlights, and crossing in front of the long string of stopped cars is just slightly exhilarating. She is tired. The sessions are long, now. When Mrs. Denton, Wendel's office nurse, closes her out into the street (for she is the last patient of the afternoon) the dark and chill feels fresh on her cheeks and forehead, and the wind she must stand against in the street blows the hot yellow fuzz which has slowly built in her head during what she thinks of as Dr. Wendel's Hour. "How was it on the bus today?" He seems always now to begin. His insistence on the poems has led to Margaret's bus notebook. The bus and the streetcars have become Margaret's silent forum, floating high and reassuring over the street. There have been times that she remains on the bus long avenues away from California Street. It is easily remedied. Margaret walks one block past the bus stop, purposefully, head up and then stops and looks at her watch with an exclamation of impatience (oh, always for that invisible audience whose face is waiting, upturned, everywhere) and she crosses the street only then and waits for the bus going back.

I ate my dinner in a Japanese restaurant yesterday.
The fish looked up
At me
From the plate—(it floated in brine and seaweed)
And in its eye I saw the tiny yellow moons
Of Japan
Which bobbed softly above my head
Along a slender thread of fishing line
In the cool breeze of
The air conditioner.

Paul Witherington

The Secretary

This noon, every noon, Edison goes through her wastecan for answers to the rumors of hiring, firing, and retrenchment. Tilts, spills, and finger sweeps the particles into a manila envelope. Loosens the crumpled paper fists and unseals the ones sealed with chewing gum. In the mass of it there are only false beginnings, dead ends of correspondence.

He checks too, from left to right, the space behind telephone directories, shy cracks between filing cabinets and walls, the clutter of her desk. Her hard-hulled husband in a plaid shirt in a 5 x 7 frame (looking as if his tractor had been cut out of the picture after it had run over him) stares through the pain, no clue. Lint floating on the coffee left in her cup. Her cushion troughed by heavy thighs, still a little warm, no clue. Yellow chrysanthemums too large for their vase, color postcard of the Great Pyramid propped against a holder of dull, very dull pencils. She is careless to the point of incompetence (hasn't he a copy of her key?) and yet her job is not in danger.

Near the door to the inner office, his last stop before letting himself out, Edison visualizes himself wedged between her legs on the boss's leather couch. He flings away her red hair and bites the gold in her ears, holds his tongue against hers. Now you don't ever need to tell me, he is telling her. Counting on her perversity.

Little Richard brings her doughnuts from the company concession stand every morning. Every afternoon, ice cream. One day while she is composing a letter, he kneels on the other side of her desk and paints her toenails green with Liquid Paper, the typing corrector she requisitions in three colors. She is slow but good natured, and as she walks the halls flashing green and pink from her high heeled sandals, the building shivers like acres of corn. Saying nothing whatsoever about Richard's position with the company.

Edison has a dream in which he is caught in the dark outer office at noon, dragged to the men's room and held while Little Richard and Brine paint his balls blue. Professionally, without spilling a drop. Afterwards they stick two blue horns on his forehead. The horns stay on for several hours and the girls at their metal desks look away and giggle.

Rumors of expansion, of automation and retrenchment, the boss stepping up, or over—the old man himself letting them fly while he is locked in the inner office admiring his leather. Little Richard finds the secretary a one-way street: she copies and staples and files and talks about anything as long as it is the virtues of a country husband. Complains of sore breasts, wipes her mouth unimaginatively on her arm. Does not notice Little Richard stroking the silver magnetic box that keeps her paper clips from coupling. In the way she touches his knee to excuse herself to the john, though, there is almost a confidence. The way she sat in the bathroom that afternoon at her farmhouse, afterwards, with the door open. The day Little Richard drove her home from work and found that she would tell nothing there, too.

From his position outside the door, Brine watches them at her desk, watches their knees almost touch. Later he will tip over the slender vase and watch the water run from the pieces into the gray carpet, the flowers holding together in one out-raged bunch.

They are in the topmost room of a tall, slender building. She has loosed her long red hair and is tossing it about in the small space while Brine goes through the closets emptying the pockets of old suits. Please babe, he calls out, it's hard enough to see. But the room is on fire, the corpse of the big boss on the table is smoking, and the door leading to the stairs is sticky with the old man's seeds. He hands her the scissors. It's the only way, babe, figure it out. She begins to snip her long, long hair. Stops halfway across as if she wishes she could snip him instead, then continues. Together they tie the red severed ends to the legs of the leather table and push the other ends out the window. Go on, he yells. She climbs out and down her own hair, holding on like a comb. The table, its corpse now in flame, follows as far as the window where it catches on the casement. When he feels the hair go slack, he does not follow her. Instead he pushes out the charred body. Then he pulls the hair back up yard by yard and quenches the fire with it. Or perhaps the hair itself is the fire, putting itself out. In any case, he lives on alone in it, like a salamander.

On the elevator down, Edison is wedged in the center. Position of honor if one assumes that the elevator might be crushed by an act of God sending scraps of raw metal through the outer rings of flesh. Sweat rolls at the thought. His hands wet the manila envelope of daily discards he is taking home. Her personal items would require a suitcase: candy wrappers, novelty catalogs, tissues and odd shapes of twisted transparent tape, a bitten-off pencil eraser, an orange peel all in one spiral piece, a small plastic bottle empty of eye drops, a stone (from her shoe, perhaps). It is the personal things that are most distracting. He knows when her period comes, for example, by tampon wrappings she has dropped intact. When her next dental appointment is. That she has trouble getting a fit in swimsuits and has clipped out and mailed in an ad to a company that sells tops and bottoms separately. Gum from after every meal, the print of her teeth still on the flattened pieces. Nothing but carelessness. Sometimes when he is particularly peeved, he primes the can, putting in scraps of imaginary letters to the vice-president, to the big boss, even to himself praising his work.

Brine is standing on Edison's shoe in the elevator, not enough to hurt but enough to dislodge the shine.

What to do with one who yawns every day a different flavor? Little Richard swivels her in her swivel chair. He keeps one eye on the inner office door and remembers that afternoon in her bedroom, her husband out working behind the cherry trees. She opens her knees good-naturedly and lets her hair go, but he is the one who gets dizzy, who closes his eyes so he can still stand.

At the beach, Brine covers her with sand, buries all but her head which is stuck out shamelessly, like the sun at sunset. Anything you want, babe, he tells her between dips in the surf. Coke? Hot dog? Chewing gum? (Any thing but loose.)

There's no way of telling if she is struggling under the sand.

119

Her husband is miles away on his John Deere in the stricken fields, cursing himself. Her boss is junketing the Middle East.

She has used up all her excuses, and at this point Brine does not care if she tells or not. I'm pregnant, she says finally. He shrugs: anyone I know? The surf is up all along the beach and the secretary, her work done, glows in the dark.

As Edison is leaving the outer office one noon he meets a procession of minor administrators and secretaries carrying a large cake. They enter by someone's forged key and set the cake on the secretary's cluttered desk. The three layers are protected by a pyramid of plastic wrap, and Richard is sticking one yellow rose into the twisted top. Everyone but the big boss himself is milling around, waiting for her to return. Where was Edison when the announcement came yesternoon in the company cafeteria?

It's not too late to chip in for the baby, the others let him know. They dance around him chanting expansion, expansion, and Brine jingles a cigar box full of coins. Edison smiles, finally, as if he would not have it any other way.

Noon. Little Richard's name is all over the new silliness that has appeared on the outer office bulletin board. Side by side are two large calendars of next April when the baby is due. Company employees sign into spaces one through thirty (pink for future secretary, blue for future boss) and put up their ten dollars with a chance of winning the entire lottery of six hundred. The sign above the calendars says that all days are theoretically equal. Only the mother to be and the doctor know the estimate. Not even the hard-hulled man on the tractor, Edison reckons. But Little Richard may know where to start counting from, though he has covered the chart to show otherwise. Their long afternoons, the doughnut flakes clinging to her skirt like dandruff. Edison imagines the secretary stripped and paraded through the halls, painted blue from her brow to her belly to her toenails.

Now they will get a replacement, change the office keys, minimize waste. Edison types a letter: "I am sorry about the trough on my husband's side of the bed," the secretary is writing Little Richard, "but he has no time for turning mattresses." Tears it into a dozen pieces and seeds the can with them (except for one small triangle which floats down onto the carpet).

Inside, the ring of the room grown shut: sleeping. Brine is the spindle she pricked herself with ninety-nine years ago, the Prince who comes through the thorns guarding his eyes and gets his lips scratched off, the King slumped in his leather throne. The clues are asleep too, on the floor of the can, and no one to shake them awake.

Edison takes no chances on the lottery. Makes no scene in the hallway where the secretary does a little hop and bottoms her purse to find her key. Dilated now like death in the sun.

Looking up from his unweeded desk as if he still expected to see the husband riding toward him with metal teeth, Little Richard notices the trim new girl moving uncertainly in the halls. When he follows her to the main office, she stands aside so he can usher her in. In his mind he orders doughnuts and ice cream.

There are rumors that the big boss will emerge to welcome the new secretary. That he will now take firmer control. In the meantime she crosses her legs and downpulls the green cloth of her skirt so tight that the reflection of her lap pops completely out of their eyes.

Corinne Robins

Lost and Found

My husband John and I sit in the kitchen over breakfast. John plays the radio, the news program unceasingly, and goes through the papers. He sits near the phone and doesn't look up when I bring him his coffee.

I sit holding a second newspaper, one from yesterday, and look at a picture of my son on the wall, remembering what I forgot, remember when I learned the miracle is that young children return home from school, that they do come back, that the bus lets them off and there they are. This surprise and wonder I knew with my daughter through camp and kindergarten until the repetition of the daily miracle made me forget, overlook it. And so the knowledge I learned from my daughter I forgot when I sent my son off to school, sent him off easily and confidently. Thus, I was completely unprepared when the miracle did not take place. His picture looks down at me from our wall. Another picture is outside our building. It is a week now since he has not returned, and the search is slowing down.

He did not come back. One theory goes he was taken away, snatched by someone in a parked car during his half block walk from our house to the bus stop. Another idea is that he never got on the school bus at all but walked past and wandered downtown. How much free will has a boy almost seven? I lived through my daughter's attempts to get away—if you want to call a child's idle slipping out of sight and deliberate lagging behind, their physical protest at being herded places they have no interest in—an attempt to get free. Though in our anger and fear, as parents we recognize and treat that as such. Young children cease early to be physical attachments to their mothers. Parent and child, mother and daughter, mother and son—we are always pulling away from each other. But how explain this to the police or, for that matter, to the people who will never forgive me that I allowed my son to walk away alone? And these people include my present husband John, Roy's father, who tries not to meet my eyes and who I know wonders how, why I lost Roy and not the other man's child— meaning my daughter.

John, of course, never met my daughter Carolyn's father. If he had, he might not have accepted her so easily simply because Carolyn is so like my first husband, while John's and my son Roy is like me. Or was.

This sounds so complicated, and yet half-brothers and step-daughters are commonplace, even ordinary today. I don't think it's that people are more complex, but that no one seems able to keep their lives straight. We can't seem to erect any permanent structures. It is just recently that I have begun to think about this.

Carolyn now is almost ten and outside the range of children whom I care for: children between three and six, before they become citizens of official schools are my care and my living. I do not count what John earns as mine and, in the same way, John respects but never counts my Carolyn as his daughter, his girl. Roy, though, was his son. I never denied that.

I once started to tell John about the day I lost Carolyn, but then telling would have meant talking about Al, and my rule has always been the less said about my ex-husband, the better.

Al lives somewhere in New York now and no longer cares where we are, which in part has been my doing.

My ex-husband Al is a big, burly man, who when I met him was set on being a painter. He liked kids. And my idea of running a little nursery school amused him. He was supporting himself doing odd carpentry jobs then, and had lots of ideas about 'designing the space' for the school. Then Carolyn happened, and Al decided we should get married. I was 26, and I guess I was glad. I know I was excited about Carolyn.

The money my mother had left me was just enough to buy our building, which is on an almost middle class block in Brooklyn. On our side of the street there were enough other young marrieds starting out to make a nursery school viable. Across the avenue were all Italians, who kept their kids to themselves. And, to this day, our block remains divided: my side understanding what happened to Roy could happen to any parent, to anyone's child, while the Italian fathers all know it was the mother's fault.

I go cross the street now to buy my vegetables because they're fresher in the morning. The day is warm and sunny and I see Mrs. Impoletti down the block, who looks away. Inside the store, two other women nod and continue to talk among themselves. They no longer even stop to ask whether there is any news. I hurry back across the street, back into the kitchen and sit down again to listen to the radio.

A week ago. A week is too short a time to become an era. Five days ago I heard John and my names on the radio.

Carolyn's childhood from three to six—that was an era. I will think about Carolyn at age five, with large dark eyes that came, of course, from her father. I am pale and lanky. The right words, I believe, are pale and plain. At Carolyn's age,

I was a sandy blonde, delicate and elfin-looking in my mother's old photographs. Very much like my son Roy is now. His picture is in every store, on every building in our Brooklyn neighborhood. His wide-mouthed smile and pointed chin look back at me now from under the word 'Lost.' John, of course, took the photograph. John is an amateur photographer and took picture after picture of his son—Roy running, Roy in cowboy costume, Roy swinging a bat while Carolyn stood watching the two of them.

Carolyn likes John, I think. She was mad for Al and, of course, there was the affinity of sharing the same face between them. John, who is pale and thin, remains a stranger, a being from another physical tribe.

John teaches biology and chemistry to high school students. He is a gentle, very quiet man, only occasionally irritable, and never so with children. He has none of Al's violence, and sometimes I am not sure how he feels. It may be John and I live a little apart from each other, but I know he enjoys our being quiet together; he keeps busy with his science books or developing his pictures while I enjoy thinking about Roy and Carolyn and all the other children who come to me.

Carolyn was not quite five, I remember, the day Al and I took her with us into Manhattan. It was a hot summer morning during the week when we went to the Modern Museum where, at first, Al was totally absorbed in explaining every picture to Carolyn and telling her stories about each artist. When her attention began to waver, he became impatient with both of us. This was, after all, his business: pictures being an artist's business, as he had told me often enough. I had arranged to meet my cousin that day for lunch, partly because I knew Al would want to look around the museum more and go on to the galleries by himself. But his rudeness, his evident relief at being rid of us made me cross with Carolyn then who "wasn't sure if she didn't want to stay with Daddy." It was up to me to explain tactfully that Daddy wanted no more of us and, by the time I had talked, cajoled and finally ordered Carolyn out of the museum, we were already ten minutes late to meet my cousin at 57th Street. My cousin Grace had little tolerance for Al and no patience with lateness, and there I was, as usual, caught between them pulling Carolyn along, Carolyn walking as slowly as possible and leaning all her weight on my arm.

"Carolyn, come on. Walk yourself! You're a big girl and you'd better keep up," I ordered.

The sidewalk was hot. My skirt stuck to my knees and I could feel the grittiness of the pavement through my new high heeled shoes. Al had told me half-approvingly that I looked 'very uptown' before we set out. By now though, 'uptown' equaled uncomfortable. I had joined the army of young women dressed to occupy the streets of New York, the army of unseeing faces, all of us aping our counterparts, the manequins in the windows of the Fifth Avenue stores, manequins who don't sweat and whose feet don't flatten but remain arched above the ground.

There wasn't much room. Walking into the bands of sunlight, there were people, young couples, single girls and older women behind and in front of us.

"Come on, Carolyn," I said. "You have to keep up with me."

I saw—or now, I think I saw her shake her head. Which made me even angrier and I deliberately speeded up, walking at a good pace around the corner and then stopped, giving up. Obviously, at this rate, Carolyn and I would be better off in a cab.

Five or six women passed. A Midwestern couple went by, but no Carolyn. A boy and his mother. I turned and began to walk slowly back around the corner. She wasn't there. I walked again down to the corner of 53rd street, not believing I could have missed her, but walking very slowly to be sure. Then, thinking maybe she had continued on ahead, I ran up to 55th street along Sixth Avenue and walked slowly back down the two blocks. It was becoming clear, she was gone. I knew that was impossible and, in a moment of fury, decided she had gone back to Al in the museum. She must have lost track of me and gone back. I would find them there together and try not to be too angry with her.

The gray stone museum building with its marble floors and gray uniformed guards suddenly seemed to double in size. I no longer had any idea where Al and Carolyn would be. An awful panic separated me from the others, and from the big paintings hanging against the walls and the white lettered announcements on a black wall board—all of it belonging to a mysterious, silent language beyond the reach of my fear. At five, Carolyn was too small a body for this place, and even I, without Al, could not stand up against it.

I appealed to a woman at one of the ticket windows. It was an emergency: I must have my husband paged. He and my daughter were somewhere in the museum. I stood on the slanting marble floor as if on some other plane from the other people there, as if we were living in two separate worlds. The sight of Al coming toward me brought the worlds back in touch except—except Al was alone. There was no Carolyn—though I looked to make sure she wasn't standing behind him.

"What are you doing here," Al said.

"I was sure Carolyn was with you, had come back to the

museum," I said without looking at him. It only now occurred to me that Carolyn might really be missing, might actually be lost. I reached out and grabbed Al's arm.

"When did you see her last? Where were you," he asked, taking hold of my shoulder. And then, after staring a moment, he let go. Come on, we'll go back and start from where you were," he said.

I told him about the walk up the block, talking slowly and distinctly because I believed, hoped he could pull me out of the pit I was sinking in, that with him as searcher and talisman, Carolyn would appear and none of this would be true, that she would never have disappeared.

With Roy now, the nightmare is back and more unreal. The pain is a deadened and unending one. And John and I avoid each other.

But Al and I then, moving together, covered both sides of the street to Sixth Avenue. It was only back at the corner that I remembered my cousin Grace would still be standing waiting on 57th Street, and I told Al I would get Grace and we'd be right back.

"Take a cab," he said, and I nodded.

I didn't dare say an extra word to him, but quickly stepped into a car at the corner to watch while my cab joined the crowd of cars. There were no even lines, no lanes. We were just a mass of automobiles barely moving along in the heat. The heat from the other cars, the heat from the street coupled with my fear that we would never get moving and that it was already too late. And just when I would feel I would be better off walking, the cars would all lurch forward and I would sit back again against the seat. I didn't know whether in leaving Al, leaving where Caroline might still be, if I had done the right thing.

Before we pulled up at 57th, I saw Grace walking back and forth and could feel her anger in the way her chin lifted as she stood very straight, a small and perfectly dressed blonde soldier waiting at her post. Her hair was curled high around her head, her eyes penciled to tilt upward, and the mask she had drawn on her pretty face looked both wet and chalky in the heat.

"Grace, over here. Get in," I called.

She came to the window. "Anne, what happened. You look terrible," she said.

"It's Carolyn—get in," I said. "She's lost. I've lost her—Driver, take us back to 53rd, please. Back to where you picked me up."

"Oh Anne, Annie," Grace said.

I reassured her that Al was there right now looking for Carolyn. And we were going to bring the police into it, if he hadn't already found her.

Grace took my hand and I tried to smile at her. But the fact that she knew and loved Carolyn made it too hard. I stared out of the window.

Al was standing at the corner, standing there alone waiting when we pulled up. There was no problem about finding him.

Grace ran up and hugged him. "Oh Al, I'm so sorry," she said.

He smiled, as if puzzled by her gesture.

"You stay here, and we two will go search 5th Avenue," Grace suggested.

"I want a policeman, Al," I said. "It's time."

"I saw two standing at the other corner," he agreed. "I'll go see if they're still there."

Al's shirt was sweaty and his face serious, a look of purpose rather than of feeling having taken possession of him. The police he brought back were two young, good looking men with faces like men on athletic posters. They were at most twenty-four, and hadn't yet begun to think about having children themselves. They listened seriously while I tried to explain what had happened, how suddenly Carolyn just disappeared from behind me.

"This is a pretty safe neighborhood, Ma'm," the first policeman said. He was a little darker and the slightly shorter of the two. "Kids get lost here all the time—kids coming in from out of town. But they don't go far. We'll go check the store people along the street, and then call in."

"I'll check back at the museum again," Al said.

"I'll come with you," Grace offered.

It was up to me to stay and watch the corner, if—on the off-chance that Carolyn came back looking for me. It occurred to me it was possible she might have crossed the street and gone to the other side of Sixth Avenue. None of us had checked there. It was then I saw a small figure in a red, blue and yellow checked nylon jacket over blue shorts—in Carolyn's jacket crossing the street. I ran, knowing I wouldn't yell, wouldn't be angry at her. A car swerved in front of me and I didn't stop. I reached the sidewalk only to see the jacket was just like Carolyn's but was on another small child, a thin little boy walking with his sister. The weight of my disappointment at that moment made me realize what I had lost. I sat down on the curb step and I cried. There was—there would be no Carolyn behind or before me.

I had cried before that at my father's funeral, but that was a coming to terms with a fact. That day with Carolyn gone was my first meeting with the bottomless loss of all hope, the moment when imagination stops. I couldn't think but cried for maybe two or three minutes before where I was—that I was sitting on the sidewalk step—came back to me. Then I realized I had deserted my corner. The fact was—no matter what—saving Carolyn's actual presence, I belonged across the street.

I quickly crossed back. The legs that had all been above my eye level from my seat down on the curb were back below me. People kept passing. I could see from where I stood the corner where I had sat and cried and turned away, looking for a sign of Grace or Al. I knew by then I would never see Carolyn come walking by.

I realize now, it wasn't that long before Al came down the street with Grace, who looked almost child-size beside him. Grace seemed out of breath. The policemen, coming from the other direction, met up with all of us at my corner and things—time—began to speed up again. No one in any of the stores had seen Carolyn, the police reported, and they decided now to go call and check in with the precinct. The police seemed to expect to learn something. Al and Grace and I stood not looking at each other, maybe because we didn't want to confront each other's hope. The phone was right there on the lamp post.

The taller policeman came back with the news that a girl Carolyn's age, a girl who must be Carolyn was at the station house. She had been there for the last half hour. He—they said something about her eating an ice cream cone. I remember my lungs suddenly filling up with air again and hearing Al laugh.

After that, the day grows fuzzy. I knew we took a cab to the police station, and that we all went out to eat somewhere afterward. It turned out that Carolyn had actually crossed Sixth

Avenue thinking she was following me, and then discovered she was lost. A man told her where a policeman was, she said. I also remember her remarking how tired, how quiet we all seemed there in the restaurant, while Al just sat holding her hand.

He did care then, though now months will go by until he remembers her existence. Then my eight, nine, and now ten year old daughter is taken to the zoo or to the movies. I never ask where and she has long since ceased to tell me what they do on those afternoons. A week or two later, Carolyn will say something about a girl or a painting, and so I remain somewhat conversant with Al's life.

Al's separation from and John's entrance into my life almost overlapped. Two months after we found Carolyn, Al took a studio by himself in the city. He mentioned once or twice about my moving the school, but that didn't really make sense to any of us.

My school is a long white room with lots of windows, and extends to our backyard garden. All the furniture is small—four and five year old size—except for the window seats and two large, over-sized wicker arm chairs that accommodate everyone. My children—and children are what I'm about, my three, four and five year olds are the school's citizens. I don't say pupils because there really is no classroom situation. We are all, rather, living here together. I show them things, and we do things. One or two do read themselves, and that has been a pattern over the years. The world of Babar, the Elephant, the closeness and aliveness of stuffed animals, the 'feelingness' of real animals and insects—children see themselves as cats and dogs, see their world the way they think animals do, and animals, in turn, recognize their lack of separateness.

A morning or school afternoon are hours of infinite length. I clock them and control their rhythm and hurry only happens when the parents or other adults arrive before time.

Carolyn was wholly mine in the school room, and I could measure the growth of the school by her. At age three, she was one of five children, only three of whom stayed all day: a two and a half year old girl, who was really too young, a pair of four year old twin boys and an older girl, almost six, who didn't really belong. We managed though: Carolyn playing surrogate teacher, and at times coming close to defying me; her dark eyes alternately sparkling and piteous. Carolyn has always known how to use those eyes of hers. Roy's— Roy's eyes are not quite so large and are differently shaped. Also, Roy has always been shy with his glances, will stare for a while at a car or truck or toy, but looks shyly side-ways at people. Unlike Carolyn, he never demanded extra attention, never tested me.

Roy is a careful, almost cautious child. HE WOULDN'T RUN AWAY.

John and I, I think are close because John is intuitive, a very private person and something of a dreamer. That is, John was before Roy disappeared. Which is what Roy did. We didn't lose him.

John has become even more quiet now. But he was always a quiet man, unlike Al, who was quiet only when he was working. Al and his painting, Al and his ego were and are always pushing for recognition. Even when he was just sitting at a bar holding a glass, Al was busy making contacts. I can't believe through that now he is so self-absorbed as not to have heard. Oh, he knows, and no doubt is keeping out of the way from embarrassment or, perhaps, it's because we've become bad luck.

There are, on the other hand, people whom John and I barely know who have become our best friends since it happened. I think of them—no, it was John who said it, called them 'our disaster friends.' Then there are others, like some of the mothers of Carolyn's girl friends, who go out of their way to avoid us, who try not to see me. I do see them, although it is not them I look for in the street.

John tells me he will go back to work next week whatever may happen with the boy. He does not ever mention Roy any more by his name, so I keep Roy's name for myself. As for me, I will be calling people tomorrow to tell them I am re-opening our school. A few women have been watching over the kids in groups in their homes. A few, I know, will never send their children back now—when it is now above all that I need them.

I walk into the school room. Carolyn was five when she taught herself to read here, and then I felt her begin to turn away. There were her sudden fears about the future. Young children do not worry past a day or at most a week until they are coming up against that outside thing called school. Words like 'lessons' and 'homework' and just exactly how many things it is they know suddenly become urgent where before, at age four and five, they played school the way they played police-man or mother or storekeeper. Carolyn taught me what to expect from Roy: Carolyn at age five, treasuring her special friends and running and hiding. Roy was always quieter and more in earnest. Like John, maybe a little over-serious. Roy entered the school after Carolyn left and became its heart— I cannot think about him. When Carolyn came back, she regis-tered her familiar surroundings, looking at all the old toys with a slightly spiteful air. It was only an occasional new stuffed giraffe or a parchesi game with strangely colored marbles that made her give herself away, pulled her back into my world of frozen time. I see now Roy holding up the marbles for Carolyn to see. I can see them still. And it is because time is so different and we are so different in my school world that the leavers carry so few memories away. Also, Carolyn grew—outgrew us so fast, she could manage the latch on the front door before she was six. Not like Roy—my Roy who I had to help open the door. And when I saw Carolyn off on the school bus, unlike a lot of kids, she never looked back.

John has come into the school room and now stands looking at me. I go up to him.

"John, I think white is too cold. If I paint the walls a bright yellow, it'll be warmer, more cheerful for the children."

He frowns and then winces when I put my hand out to touch him. I begin to explain quickly how Roy wanted to be where Carolyn already was, how Roy needed that day to be independent.

"Ann," John says slowly, looking past me, "Ann, it was your fault. I have been thinking and thinking and I know it's because you didn't walk him that day, didn't at least stand and watch that Roy is gone.

I walk away. John is no longer my friend, and I think I am glad finally to hear what he has been thinking. I do not want him here any more in my school room. I do not want to look at him. I will paint these walls yellow after he is gone. I—I better than anyone knew Roy didn't want me to walk him to the bus, wanted to go the half block himself. I knew it was important precisely because he wasn't tall enough yet to reach the latch, and because, without wanting to, Roy knew he had to leave me behind.

Roy may yet come back—it could happen . . . I will not

think that far. Besides, I know he can only come back now the way Carolyn does, as an occasional visitor. I do not give up hope. But, meanwhile, I must get the school room ready. I hear John's step and look away. He will not be much longer in my house. I turn my back on him and wait for him to go.

Joe Ashby Porter

Duckwalking

I was down in the mouth, Martha was upstairs with the kids, in his first tube series Rick Montalban was playing a DA—a welcome switch from the detective cycle according to Hearst Motion Picture Editor Dorothy Manners (HMPEDM). I'd had flak that day from the boss about some quantification, it was quite a flap and I was feeling like chucking it. Being a 'puter programmer (PP) I knew I wouldn't lack for work. I'd popped a Quaalude and Rick was wrapping up a smack baron when down the stairs comes Martha doing it. I said, "Oh really?" She gave me a Bronx cheer through the bannister rails.

We'd talked about it but I hadn't expected her to start just like that. I think she'd been practicing in secret cause she got down the stairs okay. She kicked off her mukluks and came over and stood with her elbow on the coffee table. A laxative ad, a melmac ad, some gag-rule claptrap on the news before she looks away from the screen. "Doc Purdy says forget bursitis."

"Purdy's no doc, he's . . . ."

Martha interrupted, "I've made up my mind, Bill, and I'm not backing out. Noon news showed Jackie doing it at a function. If you want to look like a cracker that's your problem." They were showing Iraqi quake damage footage before back to Rick, who was in hot water. Catherine Spaak, a skyjacker, had winged him. Martha said, "It's easier than I thought though."

"You fracture me. Five'll getcha ten you don't make it through the weekend." That was a Friday.

That weekend we backpacked with Arch and Tiffany Drake. Arch was a PP too, freelancing at the time. We'd talked about leaving kids home but decided not to. Bill Jr. was fifteen and Martha Jr.'d've been eleven, with Arch and Tiff's in the same bracket. Ours had tried it now and again around the house, and Martha Jr. could already roller skate doing it. Saturday morning when we took stuff out to the car they and their mother were all doing it. They all stayed down most of that weekend and from then on, except that for half a year Martha Jr. might pop up for a laugh.

Arch and Tiff tooted and waved (T&W): "Let's book." I backed out and followed them to the wilderness area parking lot. The kids didn't stop yakking. They were playing tic tac toe in the back and when one won he or she would give the other a good thwack. I was too sicky-poo about employment snafus to mind. Arch parked his Wankel Mach II smack-dab at the end of the lot and when he and Tiff stepped down out I saw that they were doing it. Their kids were too.

The Joy of Cacking, the conglom that owned the one I'd been PPing for for a couple of years, had a knack for diversification. They'd just bought into Cunard, and office platitude had it the next step was to work some Peking action as a decoy to wangle tax shrinkage. That would draw ack-ack, but J of C had a gaggle of tricks up its sleeve and its future looked anything but lackadaisical. It was playing glitz ball, so what was racking my brains that Saturday was all I stood to lose or gain moving to a new conglom or freelancing like Arch. Arch and I'd been chums years and so had Tiff and Martha. Arch and Tiff are Quakers but you wouldn't want to meet a wackier couple, so I aimed to bend Arch's ear about my job sometime during the weekend.

All the rucksacks but mine dragged, and seeing how slow the going up the trail was didn't make me eager to get down. On the other hand they all chatted like mad and I kept having to bend over to follow. We hit the site about two and pitched camp. After a macaroon snack the kids waddled off to gather kindling, the girls were chewing the cud about a boutique and Arch and I broke out a six-pack and axes and split a few logs. Handling the axe down there was easier for him than I'd expected. Then we sat on the woodpile and rapped.

"What's eating you, Bill? You look like you want to duke it out with somebody." I got worked up letting off steam about the job but Arch didn't crack a smile. He said, "Listen, Mac, that's hooey. I'd hang tight in your place. This rickrack with the boss'll blow over. You and Martha should invite him and Khakeline bowling." He said J of C's quark angle looked good and in fact he himself planned to hook up on a permanent basis since freelancing was getting too flaky too quick. The kids were moving back into the clearing over by the douches. Martha Jr. missed a softball from Arch Jr. that would've beaned me if I hadn't bobbed my head down in time. Arch grinned, "Dangerous up there, Bill," as he scooted off his log and started toward the fire. I rose to follow and old Arch looked up and said, "Why not give it a try?"

It was dusk, and I remember the crackling of the campfire as I thought, "Why not?" And I remember how the trees wagged as I squatted. Arch and I ambled over to the fire where the wives were cooking a lip-smacking wokload of sprouts. "I knew you were up to it," Martha cooed, and she planted a peck on my kisser. I stayed down the rest of that weekend, kayaking through quagmires and brackish shallows, nearly losing tackle to a bull mackerel I finally landed, relaxing at Tiff's after-lunch songfest cacophony, I stayed down. It sure was good to take a gander right or left and ogle smirks instead of empty air.

That was, oh, seven or eight years ago, when to lots like me duckwalking (DW) looked weak on staying power and thin on consequence. Little did we know. To backtrack, I had first heard of it a year or so before on a wrap-up of what older young adults had been into. One segment dealt with a Texas airforce base brouhaha where a Big Mac maitre d' who'd channelled incoming customers flat south of a DWing waitress got hooted by a WAC claque. I remember I said, "Those squirts." Martha said yes, but she'd scanned a Sunday supplement piece a while back about it that made it sound fun. Later you heard about it more frequently and then somebody said he'd seen a gentleman doing it here in town, over on 33rd near the shellac factory. The exact reason why it eventuated is still in question, but discos were one of the places it seemed to catch on first. The Cow-cow Mooie, the Wigwag and the Macaque were only three of the steps it hatched. *TV Guide* ran a New Year's spread about it with a snap of that month's Neilsen pinup doing it with the Whackers' quarterback at New York's Bimbo's overlooking Central Park. Videoland in fact was a pacesetter. A daytime game show anchorlady sometimes came on doing it, and then on a novelty series about a paramedic and his favorite Tommy gun the whole cast did it. Flicks caught on and novelizations followed fast on their heels.

In the sports world the change raised a few hackles. Most squawks centered on the gridiron cause it slowed the game so much. But that was true of all the running sports, and rule changes must've had umps cracking books even when they went potty. Fans groused but there was no denying that tactics, especially blocking and tackling, were easier to qualitate. Backboards got lowered for hoopsters, batters' and pitchers' styles underwent more far-reaching changes than catchers'. With these like other team sports the field of play naturally shrank so playtime could approximate foregoing commitments to duration length. Ditto for track, double-dog ditto for broad and high jump. The underhand disappeared from tennis, but in swimming the breast- and backstroke needed only slight kick modifications. Billiards survived intact on a lowered table, and jockeys required minimal stirrup strap hitches.

The Presidential lackey squad gave out he personally affirmed DW's gassiness for some months until after one State of the Union Gossipcast (SUG) he slid off the official banquette and didn't stand but instead did it off the stage. Some hacks penned quasi clucks, others marked it up to sprightly daffiness. The short podium at his next confab told us we were eyeballing the beginning of an era. Armed forces were quick to follow suit. I recall some bivouacked Cossacks surviving a surprise attack with no more than dented helmets.

Of course it infused new fuel into the economy. Take slacks: looser knees cried out for alterations in factory process-components that themselves had to be designed and produced in other factories. Ripples big as tidal waves raced every which way.

My own life has taken several new tacks. For a month after that memorable weekend I sometimes thought of standing back up, but I stayed down and my relations with Martha and the kids waxed smoother pronto. One evening as we gathered on our tatamis around the dindin table Bill Jr. turned to me and cackled, "Pap, hunkering here with you and the big M and Sis-face makes me sure I'm the luckiest little pecker alive." My ticker got gooey.

As far as old Martha and me are concerned, that weekend beside the picnic table we started to re-relate (RR) and as the new stance grew on us we found ourselves chitchatting more. The mechanics of sex haven't had to change too much of course, and the actual act gets done at least as often as before duckwalking (BD). At the drop of a hat she'll say, "Drag those knackers over here, Bill"—she's still in bed, it's Sunday, I've showered and before I even dry my back we're banging. We sleep streetcar. Sometimes in the beginning I'd stretch the gams in bed but now the fronts of my knees nuzzle the backs of hers. She's still stacked. The other day we were readying to step next door for drinkypoos and an Also Sprach tape. Old Martha had on a black Shantung poly mini and platform flippers. The placket wobbled like a raccoon tail and I went gaga all over again when she sidled over for a buss.

Like everybody we enjoyed a spate of redecorating in the beginning. We were in a semidetached bungalow in hock up to our necks so we made do with ladders and step-ups, our old gimcrack furniture, lowered macrame and spice racks and shorter wastebaskets. Now we're in the condo with all new chopped Louis XIV and a recessed waterbed. Marth's acquired some slick bricabrac at the Knicknack Shack down the block. A set of Now Faces in Composition Matter Plaques (NFCMP) tops the period baseboard.

Bosso got kicked upstairs soon after my little contretemps and with the new helmsman things have been cricket. Work's the same, but better. Puters' capacities explode monthly simultaneous to monthly hardware shrinkages, and programming's several magnitude notches above prior, but office routine's distinctly similar. So wall urinals have become straddle troughs, so what: everybody still wears baseball caps, gagsters stock whoopee cushions and the muzak's never run dry.

As to social life. The fam and I get off on floor tubefests with the neighbors now and again, as I've hopefully specified. Roller rink Saturday matinees are a hoot, especially when we tap a keg. Golf is always golf even with lateral swings, and the Cheer Club plays nine when it's not hawking loquat pie and sausage for the subteen skateoramas. Bill Jr. and Martha Jr. have Transams with glass packs. He plays wahwah in the marching band and shortstop in the summer. She majorettes— her squad's the Whirlybirds. They both have part-time jobs and heartthrobs.

J of C's had more than its share of the DW prosperity. Somebody must've had an inside line cause just at the start, when most congloms had kissed off construction for a cash flow bottleneck cork, and starts were scarcer than hen's teeth, J of C shifted its diversification exactly that way. As DW became a fait accompli, other gloms moved in for some pie too. Horizontal bisection of existing units was the rule, though some spaces accommodated tri- and hypertrisection, and none of the new plexes and rises has ceilings above four feet. Housing's had megabucks for a demidecade now and J of C's led the pack so I have plenty to crow about. True, some Jack or other over cocktails occasionally still gets nostalgic about the upright posture we abandoned. But I say, after all, was it really ever more than a posture?

Walter Abish

Alphabet of Revelations

1

The new occupant of 26 Sustain Drive unloaded the battered blue Ford panel truck with the Arizona plates, and then, without seeking anyone else's assistance, she awkwardly (how else) lifted and carried the half-dozen cardboard boxes, one by one, into the house. Although Brooks must have known that she was being observed from across the street, she did not once look up, since to do so in all likelihood would have involved her in a possible exchange with whomever had been patiently following her activity from the moment she first got out of the car.

A few days after her arrival Bud and Arlo observed her at work in the small garden. Arlo had spotted her first and abruptly stopped the car in the middle of the road just where it began to slope downhill. She's got a determined sort of look, wouldn't you say, Bud asked, but Arlo did not comment. Remaining indifferent, it seemed, to their presence, she continued watering the lawn, patches of which had turned a faded yellow. Afterward she picked up a pair of clippers, and with her back to them, inexpertly, at least to their eyes, trimmed the hedge at the back. Arlo kept drumming his fingers on the steering wheel until Bud wanted to tell him to stop, because the sound was affecting his concentration.

All in all, the people who now and then pulled up in their

cars to observe, furtively or not, the somewhat stocky young woman with the shoulder-length blonde hair, did so, or so it would appear, in order to ascertain to what extent she differed from them, or the people they knew, for a difference was clearly indicated. It was, however, impossible to determine the precise nature of that difference. It was impossible to tell without a closer examination, for instance, of the interior of the house, without a look into one of those heavy sealed cartons stacked neatly in the small room next to the kitchen, or a glimpse of the framed reproduction by the Belgian painter Magritte (1898-1967), entitled *Alphabet of Revelations*, now hanging in what was the Reverend Gleiss Pod's former living room.

Did Arlo really tell Clem, in confidence, that he intended to obtain a better and clearer picture of Brooks' expectations and needs.

Seventeen years ago when the Secaucus River overflowed, three people were drowned, the Kienhover Bridge, named after a German musicologist (1885–1957), collapsed, four thousand tons of cement stored at the Bugano and Lead warehouse were transformed into one massive immovable rock, and the entire row of thirty-two houses on Sustain Drive, eighteen of which overlooked the river, stood—depending on whether they were on the south or north end of the drive—under two to six feet of muddy water for seven days. Having lost his parents and his baby sister, Fabric, to the Secaucus River, Arlo, now an orphan, moved out of 26 Sustain Drive to live with his aunt and uncle seven blocks away at 84 Dolchinger Lane. Each day on his way to school Arlo would make a slight detour to pass his former home and see how the new occupants, a

Reverend Pod, who had been a missionary in China, and his daughter, Klairdine, were coming along. Eight years later the two magnificent elm trees in front of 26 Sustain Drive had to be cut down, and the true state of neglect of the house could no longer be hidden from view. In 1975 the Reverend Pod and his thirty-one-year-old pregnant daughter slipped away late one night without so much as a word to any of their neighbors. Arlo confided to Bud that he was the father of Klairdine's baby. Bud told Clem, who in turn mentioned it to his wife, Donna, who said that she wasn't in the least bit surprised.

2

Now number 26 was the only building without an air conditioner in any of the windows, or a TV antenna on the roof. It was, furthermore, the only house with a mailbox that did not bear the name of the present occupant. Why? The Kufflers in 24, the Altmeers in 28, the Mungalls across the street in 25 had no such compunctions. What was Brooks trying to conceal? Was she not the sole occupant, or didn't she expect any mail?

It sure needs a coat of paint, Bud whispered to Arlo as they crouched behind the mangled hedge at the rear of 26, hoping to catch a glimpse of Brooks.

It also needs complete rewiring, said Arlo, settling himself comfortably on the grass. And what's more, the balcony isn't safe. I remember being at a party over here late one night five or six years ago, and finding myself on the balcony with a certain young lady, a close friend of Klairdine.

Do I know her? Bud inquired.

You bet. You married her.

Walter Abish

I'll be damned, said Bud softly.

But why has Brooks moved here? Here, meaning to New Jersey, to number 26, a two-story frame building that might any day now decide to slide into the Secaucus River.

To their chagrin Arlo and Bud did not catch a glimpse of the occupant of 26 Sustain Drive that evening. We'll catch her on our way to work tomorrow, Bud promised. Arlo nodded, trying to conceal the extent of his disappointment.

By and large Arlo and Bud were convinced that they more or less knew what a woman could and couldn't do. Still, something about Brooks filled them with an uncertainty. Why the Arizona plates on her car? Was she expecting someone to join her? Could she be hiding someone in the house? Why didn't she smile like everyone else and wave her hand casually in response to a greeting?

Arlo and Bud were acutely aware of all the things a woman could do.
She can run up a flight of stairs
sew on a button
prepare a spinach pie for seven
toss a vase across the room
correctly set the dial on the old washing machine in the cellar and determinedly search for a word in the dictionary, a word that would spell a certain release, a word that would contribute to lightening the burden people feel suddenly, when they least expect it, in their hearts, or roughly in the area where they suspect their hearts to be, somewhere below the left shoulder,

and a bit to the right. She can also with a look of alarm sit up in bed and ask: Where have you been? Where have you been?

On their return to 26 Sustain Drive, Arlo and Bud carelessly left their footprints on the flower beds beneath the first-floor windows, and then, equally careless, neglected to wipe their fingerprints off the kitchen window ledge at the back, and off the doorknobs, the table top, the banister, the pile of unopened boxes, the upstairs closet, and the chest of drawers. They even examined the contents of the medicine cabinet in the bathroom. No lipstick anywhere, Bud pointed out matter-of-factly. Or any of the stuff Faye uses on her face. I used to sleep in there as a child, Arlo said, pointing to the small room, now completely vacant, to the left of the staircase, the tears welling up in his eyes. Can you believe it? They haven't even changed the green wallpaper. It's the same wallpaper.

3

But they are my buddies, Clem earnestly explained to Donna. We spent a year in Vietnam. We stuck together in L.A. We were busted in Las Vegas, and then the following year we drove to Florida. I introduced Faye to Bud and Erna to Arlo. I won't have you saying all those things about them. For one thing, you can't prove it. For another, it's simply not true.

She watched him as he bent to pick up the pieces of the shattered yellow glass pitcher she had thrown at the turquoise living room wall.

I think I am going to watch the late late movie tonight, she announced.

I wish you wouldn't let yourself get carried away by every little thing, he said, still bent over, peering at the floor, searching for tiny pieces of yellow glass he might have overlooked.

Did Brooks, the new occupant of 26 Sustain Drive, ever discover the footprints of Arlo and Bud in the flower beds beneath her first-floor windows?

4

Yesterday Donna smashed a yellow glass pitcher against our living room wall. I ducked just in time, said Clem. That pitcher cost fourteen ninety-five. But he neglected to tell Arlo and Bud the reason for her outburst, and they were too polite to ask. The waitress distributed clockwise the familiar stained menus in their plastic jackets. Bud noticed the slight tear in her white blouse, just beneath the left arm-pit. Stretching to take something down could have caused it. Clem ordered the fried shrimp and French dressing on his salad and a Budweiser. Bud ordered a veal cutlet, but not like the one he had last time with too much breading, mashed potatoes, no salad, and a Schlitz, and Arlo kept the waitress waiting because he could not make up his mind. He could not decide what he really wanted. How's the liver today? He looked at her expectantly.

Bud waited for her to leave and then said that in Clem's place he would be firm with Donna. Very firm, he stressed, one eyebrow raised and his forefinger planted on the Formica table top.

Clem laughed. She could have picked something less fragile to toss at me . . .

Arlo interrupted to say that he was planning their next trip upstate.

I'll join you guys, Clem said, but only if Bud promises not to bring any guests along.

Bud raised his hand as if taking an oath. I promise, I promise. I only asked Keller to join us because I heard a rumor that they were going to promote him to section chief.

I don't like Keller, said Clem.

He still lives with his mother, said Arlo, and then seeing the waitress asked her if it was too late to change his order of fried liver to the asparagus omelet.

While unpacking Brooks dropped a large white serving plate with a blue rim. The plate smashed on impact. The man who had come to install the telephones rang the front doorbell just as she was sweeping up the pieces.

She's the unfriendliest woman I've ever met, the telephone man later told Clem. She now has a Princess phone in the upstairs bedroom and two Touchtones downstairs, one in the living room, the other in the kitchen. At first she couldn't decide on the colors. She finally picked white for the Princess, blue for the living room, and black for the kitchen. Imagine, black for the kitchen.

Does she appear to be by herself? asked Clem.

5

The blue Ford panel truck in Brooks' driveway still had the Arizona plates. No one on Sustain Drive had ever been to Arizona. No one on Sustain Drive had the slightest inkling where Brooks worked or, indeed, if she worked at all. Mr.

Walter Abish

Mulhout, the owner of the hardware store on Bush Street, told Donna that Brooks had purchased a lawnmower the day before. She also bought four gallons of white latex, a fly swatter, a dozen storm windows, an aluminum stepladder, an electric drill and bits, fifty pounds of plaster, and a tube of epoxy.

Did she mention Arizona? Donna wanted to know.

Why don't we ask her over one night, Clem suggested.

I don't think she's very keen on people, Donna replied. When she first moved in I rang her bell and asked her if she needed anything. She said no. She didn't even smile. Now I no longer greet her.

Well, ask her over anyway.

We could also invite Arlo and Erna, and Bud and Faye.

Despite what you think of them?

Despite what I think of Arlo and Bud.

Damn it, there's another stain on my carpet, yelled Clem, absolutely livid with anger. Did you know that? You didn't tell me that you had spilled something on my carpet.

If it's so important to you, take it to the cleaners.

Do you have any idea how much that carpet cost?

Well, will you call Brooks, or shall I, asked Donna.

You call her, said Clem.

6

I still can't believe it, said Erna as she and Donna entered the new mall. Two months ago I had to drive twenty miles in order to get a decent pair of shoes. Do you know that Clem is absolutely lost without me, said Donna. He can't even pick out a shirt for himself. He needs my approval for everything he does. Arlo won't let me buy a thing for him. He always seems to know exactly what he wants.

Well, as long as he knows.

Don't make me laugh, said Erna.

I am not afraid of you, said Brooks, speaking slowly and evenly into the telephone. I'm not in the least bit afraid of either of you. But I am getting sick of hearing your heavy breathing, you degenerates.

She knows, Arlo said miserably. Damn it, she knows.

I am thinking of getting Clem some darts and a dartboard for his birthday, said Donna. He has his heart set on a pinball machine, but they're over three hundred. Did you know that Clem, Bud and Arlo are planning their next little trip to the woods?

They just got back.

Erna smiled grimly. Well, if that's what makes them happy.

I know what makes me happy, said Donna. She looked at Erna, who laughed.

Arlo and Bud were aware of all the things a woman could do.
She can run up a flight of stairs
mend a torn sleeve
plan next day's dinner
sit up in bed
with a startled look
and ask:
Where have you been?

Does one ever lose the need to be desired? Donna asked Erna.

They had each just bought a pair of Swedish clogs and were headed for the Angkor What? Restaurant and Cocktail Lounge. I can't bear to be alone at night, Donna told Erna as they were waiting for their second Angel's Kiss. Each time Clem has the night shift, I stay up till three watching TV. From where they were seated they had an unimpeded view of the shoe store and the candy store next to it, and the Valley Savings & Loan Association and the health food store and a large fountain into which shoppers would occasionally throw pennies.

At a nearby table a woman their age said to her friend: I just don't understand it. Everyone except me has been invited to the party. I don't understand it.

It's an oversight, said her friend, staring at Erna who was wearing her new pale-green backless dress. Erna told Donna that Bud was beating Faye. I promised Faye that I wouldn't tell anyone. Bud keeps complaining that she doesn't know how to run their house.

Well, he's right you know, said Donna.

Still, that's not reason enough to beat her.

Donna laughed. Clem would never hit me. He wouldn't dare.

As they left the restaurant, Erna spotted Arlo in a phone booth.

I was just calling you, he said sheepishly when he came over.

But I told you that I was going shopping.

Didn't you say that you'd be back by three?

I didn't. But what are you doing in the mall?

I was just passing, and I thought I'd pick up a pair of stereo headphones.

Don't believe a word they say, said Erna gaily.

Why, there's Brooks. Does she always wear jeans?

What's for dinner, Arlo asked Erna, who was unpacking groceries in the kitchen.

Fried liver, she said, and then told him that his best friend Bud was beating Faye.

She's such a lousy homemaker, he explained. Their place is always a mess.

I wish I really knew what you want, Erna said.

He looked at her in surprise. Why do you keep asking me? I think I want to be good at what I am doing. I'd like to be section supervisor in a year or two. I also would like to buy a larger house in a place like Dumont. And, I guess, I also want pleasure.

How do you mean, pleasure?

Well, you know—gratification. To excel.

Sex?

Yes. That also.

At night, as she undressed, she said: Don't you ever wish to share your thoughts with me?

7

I am still surprised that Brooks accepted our dinner invitation, said Clem. She really gets under my skin.

Why, asked Donna.

I don't know. I keep asking myself, but I don't know.

I know why, said Donna. It's because she fails to respond to your charm. Because she doesn't laugh when you describe your hunting accidents. Because she's not interested. Period.

Would you just tell me one single thing, said Clem. Why doesn't she invite anyone to her place.

Clem could not miss the triumphant look on her face when she said: She's invited me in to have a drink.

Well?

Well what?

Well, why doesn't she ask anyone else?

She's asked me.

She hasn't asked us, said Clem. She hasn't asked Arlo, or Bud, or me.

When Clem and Donna separated, she kept the Moroccan rug and the large oak bookcase with the built-in liquor cabinet, the new leather couch and the leather armchair and the marble-topped coffee table, the Panasonic stereo, but he took the Zenith color TV, the Remington electric typewriter, the station wagon, the garden tools, and the framed reproduction of Paul Delvaux's *Eloge de la Melancholie*.

Donna also kept the movie projector and the Super-eight movie camera, the water bed and the garden hose, the linen and all the director chairs. He took the miniature lathe, the electric saw, and the ten-speed racer he had bought for her birthday. She let him have the terra-cotta figurine of Chal-chiuhtlicue the river goddess she had picked up in Mexico, and he left her the massive Ronson table lighter, a gift from his favorite aunt, Mabeline, who lived in Paris, Iowa. He also left her the new dartboard. She came close to tears when he left.

When Arlo and Erna separated, Erna kept the seventeen-inch Sony color TV and the Toyota and the house and the two-year-old baby, but he took Class, the three-year-old bulldog he had given her on their first wedding anniversary in May 1975. He also took the stereo and the entire record collection except for an original movie soundtrack of *Plead for Love*, with Rick Jordan and Audrey Su. She helped him load the rented van. It was, as these things go, an amicable parting. They even asked Brooks to join them for a drink. Since he had packed all the booze, they drank tomato juice with a dash of bitters. Brooks mentioned that she intended to visit her uncle, who had a farm in upstate New York. Erna caught the instantaneous flicker of interest on Arlo's face. Upstate? I have a lot of friends upstate. That's where Bud, Clem, and I go hunting. Whereabouts upstate?

8

Each time Donna watered the snapdragons, the zinnias, the caladiums, the marigolds in her tiny garden with the green hose Clem had left behind, she was reminded of Clem who, barefoot and wearing his torn jeans, had always spent half an hour each day casually directing a stream of water at one, then another section of the garden while dreamily staring into space. Why did you have to break up with him, her mother kept asking her whenever she called.

When old Mr. Mulhout sold his hardware store on Bush Street, Donna bought a rake, a hammer, three pounds of two-inch nails, a pair of pliers, and a birdfeeder, all at a twenty-five percent discount. What are you going to do, now that you've retired, she asked Mr. Mulhout. I'll move to Florida, he said. I've sold my house and all my furniture. I intend to sell my car. I'll move to St. Petersburg. I may marry again.

Walter Abish

Are you interested in buying a two-year-old air conditioner?

How many BTUs? she asked.

He looked terribly upset. I don't remember. I don't seem to remember anything any longer.

I know it's absolutely insane, but I loved that rug I picked up years ago in Morocco, Clem told Erna, when he ran into her on Palisade Avenue. I'd give anything to have it back.

I'll mention it to Donna, Erna promised. She might let you have it.

I really hate to be tied to possessions, he remarked. It's a weakness.

As long as you acknowledge it to be a weakness, it stops being one, she said.

When Bud, who also lived only a block away from the Secaucus River, left Faye, he broke all the front windows. He took her fur coat and the Tiffany lampshade. He also took the two air conditioners, the cameras, the movie projector, the freezer, the refrigerator, and the two-by-three-foot photograph of him and Faye, arm in arm on a beach in Mexico. He moved while she was at work in the beauty parlor. He moved everything but the wood shutters and the plants in the garden. When he left the house he felt sorry that there was not anything else that he felt tempted to take.

Can I stay in your place tonight? Faye asked Brooks when she returned to the empty house. She instinctively called Brooks, because Brooks seemed so terribly independent. Sure, said Brooks. Come on over. I am going to see my uncle in a few days, but you can stay here until I leave.

9

When Clem, on an impulse, called Donna to inquire if she would mind terribly if he would come by and pick up the water bed, which he had bought, she said sure, by all means. It took Clem only half an hour to empty the water from the water bed. The most expedient way of getting rid of the water was to stick the end of the hose, the familiar old green hose, out of the bedroom window. Brooks, who was passing their house, could not understand the reason for all that water gushing out of the bedroom. Hi there, Brooks, Clem called to her when he looked out of his window to see if the flow of water was being obstructed by anything. How are you Brooks? Is there anything else you would like to take, now that you are here? Donna asked Clem. He wanted to ask her about the Moroccan rug, but his courage failed him. Had she given it away? It was not in the living room or in the bedroom.

When Brooks passed the house later that afternoon she heard Donna moaning. It was summer and the windows of the bedroom were open. The sounds were quite loud and unmistakably sexual. Brooks, lost in thought, kept standing beneath one of the windows, as each moan mounted and subsided, forcing in her brain a curious standstill of all thought and recognizable emotion.

Whenever Erna and Donna met they did not discuss Arlo or Clem or Bud and his terrible treatment of Faye. Erna noticed that Donna had made a substantial number of changes in her house. There was a new teakwood china closet and a new green glass-topped coffee table near the velvet sofa. How's the baby doing, Donna asked. I'm so glad it's a girl, said

Walter Abish

Erna. I am looking forward to watching her grow up. Where is she? asked Donna. Oh, my mother in Freehold is taking care of her. Did you know that Brooks belongs to a gun club in New Jersey, and that I am thinking of joining? Whatever for, asked Donna. For self-protection. I don't want whatever happened to Faye to happen to me.

10

The four of them set off early Saturday morning in Donna's car. When they drove past the park where Donna had first met Clem, she said, I don't have the slightest idea where he is staying. I don't even care. I wonder if something is seriously the matter with me?

You'll like my uncle, said Brooks. He was the best shot in Carefree, Arizona. He taught me to shoot, and he'll teach you.

Near Albany they had a flat tire. Nothing to it, said Brooks. They stood watching her as she changed the tire, admiring her dexterity and her self-confidence. It took them less than forty minutes to get back on the road and another hour and a half to reach the farm. It's nice to have you visit, said Brooks' uncle when he met them at the gate. He was wearing an old tweed hat and a beat-up jacket.

Brooks introduced them: This is Erna, and this is Donna, and this is Faye. You remember my mentioning Faye to you?

After lunch, which they ate in the large kitchen, Brooks' uncle took them to the make-shift rifle range at the back of the barn. While her uncle looked on, Brooks showed them how to load, aim, and fire the rifle they had first seen on the wall above the fireplace in the living room. There's a little bit of a kick when you press the trigger, Brooks said, but you'll get used to it.

At night Erna, who was sharing a room with Donna, said to her friend: I'm not sure if you noticed, but I think Brooks' uncle is really a woman dressed up as a man.

Are you serious? asked Donna. Why should Brooks' uncle be a woman? It doesn't make any sense.

I know it doesn't make sense. But I'm pretty certain.

How do you know?

She's a woman. I just know.

Are you going to mention this to Brooks?

No, should I?

I guess if she doesn't, there's no reason to.

Well?

And Donna, from where she lay on the bed, hands folded behind her head, staring at the ceiling, complacently said: Well, you may be right. But did you see how well she can shoot. Each shot, a bull's eye.

Gilbert Sorrentino

The Gala Cocktail Party

Pain, the sagacious Dr. Bone was saying, flits through my sensibilities, accompanied by no small modicum of embarrassment, since it is my tortured yet stern duty to inform you, my dear Gavottes, that Dr. Poncho, embroiled as he needs must be in administrative tasks, will not be able to greet you tonight. He will, however, see you tomorrow, and lay, as the hep phrase runs, some heavy sounds on you. In the meantime, I have, with Dr. Poncho's blessing, arranged a small yet gay, if not gala, cocktail party for you, at which you may meet some of our most distinguished administrators and faculty. Shall we repair to the Dan'l Boone Room?

Thus saying, they . . . and so forth.

And there they were! What cascades of academic glitter! What a fine madness of the intelligentsia! What milling and wheedling! The wonderful persons circulated and chatted, drank and staggered, consumed "dip" (whatever that may be), and the like festive routine. Sing, Muse, of this catalogue of shits!

There came Brenda Fatigue, Regius Professor of Office Fashion; Ed Flue, Associate Professor of Logging; Burnside Marconi, Instructor in Televiewing; Syrup Concoct, Poet-in-Residence; Benjamin Manila, Chairman of the Stationery Department; G. Root Garbage, Counselor in Venereal Diseases; Jedediah Mange, Vice-President for Member Development;

Winifred Zinnia, Corsetiere for Rector of the College; Socks O'Reilly, Chief of Tension Calisthenics; Marcus Podium, Ellsworth Harelip Professor of Speech and Drama; Heinz Pogrom, Horst Wessel Professor of German Philology; Gladys Bung, Dietary Tactician; Fifi Galleon, Instructor in French Jobs; Catherine Thigh, Director of Sexual Services; Nicholas Syph, Bureaucracy Professor Emeritus; Yvette Risque, Associate Professor of Auto-Erotism; Francis-Xavier Silhouette, S.J., Chaplain; Pedro Manteca, Professor of Fast Food Studies; Chastity Peep, Instructor in Vaginal History; Angelo Bordello, Disciplinary Dean of Women; Manatee Brouillard, Connecticut Professor of Fertilizer Studies; Idyott Dymwytte-Pyth, Instructor in Ur-Critique; Rastus X. Feets, Professor of Black English.

And circulating, smiling, chatting, laughing, the Gavottes moved as if . . . as if . . . in a dream!

"Alas! One acknowledges, sadly, sadly, that ladies' intimate garments are unattractive in direct proportion to their comfort."

"The sturdy old oak, falling heavily, crashed spang through the dorm windows, whereupon a cloud of flies rose up, buzzing in terror and chagrin."

"The first television 'sighting' took place in Dublin in 1904, when one Francis Aloysius McGlynn dropped his transistor radio and a little man, holding a bar of lemony soap, crawled painfully from the wreckage."

"Night is/and life is/what means/means be life."

"After being dated and stamped, then stamped and dated, the incoming mail is sent to the Dating-Stamping clerk."

"You've got your basic buboes, your running chancre, your clapperoo sacred and profane, your gleet malaise, your Spanish pox."

163

"Caught the lad in the act of self-gratification, so the benighted Scoutmaster stripped him of his Personal Health Merit Badge."

"I'm most proud, I think, of the fact that General Champagne, while dictating the peace terms, was marvelously trig in my featherweight foundation in ecru with black nylon-lace panels."

"The old Army dozen cures your basic born-again Christian in about three or four weeks."

"Duh perfeck eckshershize izh: 'Hash dow sheen budda bride lilygrow?' "

"Some uff mein goot Chewish frents from zuh fordies seem to haff . . . disappeared!"

"The fatback is then gently sauteed in two ounces of King Kong and a quarter-cup of oleo."

"It is permissible, even salutary, for the modern woman to fantasize a touch of sodomy with the office boy while in lawful embrace with her spouse."

"When the boys returned, simply *mad* for some clean, blond, smiling American poon, what was this once-great nation's inadequate response?"

"The truly efficient office should be able to complicate *everything* in just under six months, taking into account, of course, the zeal of the staff."

"With the skirt discreetly lifted to the upper portion of the lower limbs, and the underpants crisply rolled to that point at which said lower limbs are jointed, the clitoris may be surreptitiously massaged while dining, at the theater, or even in the office."

"I also serve who only blandly prate."

"We have almost achieved a breakthrough in the instant wiener."

"The vagina, long since accepted as reality in Mesopotamia, was first observed beyond that state's borders in the fourth millennium."

"I take absolutely no pleasure in chastising these remarkably lovely, luscious, desirable, nubile, and altogether terrific young women."

"We actually had to turn a thousand people away the evening Shecky Green gave a dramatic reading from *October Light*."

"The progression is crystal clear: Joyce, Beckett, Costain, Jong."

"When ah be's gwine, ah be's gwine to Jericho!"

". . . invented by a gay Presbyterian minister—pantyhose, I mean."

"No tenure *yet*, though I am known everywhere as Johnny Acorn!"

"I entered and saw Mrs. Marconi in the most *extraordinary* position."

"They/whimper."

"I don't exactly know what an 'envelope' *is*."

"The affected member is plunged into warm Pepsi."

"Putting it into a honeydew is also recommended."

"The new gym shorts offer just a wisp of gentle control."

"Leaping high into the air, you intertwine the index fingers."

"Yethhir! That'th mah baby!"

"So've burned der files."

"Yes, radishes! Skewered along with soybean balls and okra."

"The beautiful poems of Miss Flambeaux have saved many marriages."

"Yes, my famous 'Tuesdays' *are* booked months in advance."

"If it calls for eight copies, make twelve."

"The woman then places her ankles alongside her ears."

"In Indianapolis, God's hand is everywhere seen."

"What precisely is 'bread?' "

"Recent studies suggest that men who wear athletic supporters suffer from vagina envy."

"After four in the afternoon, the supple birch switch is best."

"Who dreamt that the dead salmon would grow into a lusty azalea?"

"The walking-stick is always a symbol for a specific Western angst."

"The baddest dude be's Gentian Washington."

". . . the *cruel* corset? Cruel? . . ."

". . . lifts his meaty hands to prey . . ."

". . . during the commercial break, large amphibians . . ."

". . . cer/tain/ly . . ."

". . . the tongue, now crisscrossed by small paper cuts . . ."

". . . the vast warehouse, filled with impounded toilet seats . . ."

". . . *bursting* through his BVD's, it . . ."

". . . her lacings, whipping through the air, caught the Monsignor . . ."

". . . now, the full bosom, during the eight-count push-up . . ."

". . . wit duh lipz inna shmirk . . ."

". . . undt vhen der rosy dawn lighted up Auschwitz . . ."

". . . the hamburger, partially rotted in the soil . . ."

". . . Havelock Ellis, delirious in the ladies' room . . ."

". . . even the most modest will lift her skirts if . . ."

". . . having typed it on green tissue instead of light blue . . ."

". . . the role of the pleated skirt in spontaneous orgasm implies . . ."

". . . in baseball cap and cassock, I often wander through . . ."

". . . the tuna is tossed with tiny marshmallows . . ."

". . . imagine Danae's surprise when all this gold . . ."

". . . while one young lady is spanked, another some-times . . ."

". . . the piccadills and stoccadoes, well irrigated . . ."

". . . herring-motif in Malamud's juvenilia . . ."

". . . Dean Bordello an' me, man, we be's whoppin' an' whompin' on . . ."

". . . curious linguistic apparatus that often in disciplines that favor a particular array of the marvelous stretchiness of that post-war if you do understand a latex well can it be a swell campus support for what? is that the various social services or can it be a kind of utter lovely parameter when just a tiny bit of although they are a kind of 'fingers' if that's the specific kind of pastrami did you ever understand for instance what array of the most dedicated Doctorow? Gardner? Styron? often at mass it is in my mind that this campus this hallowed ground this garter belt flushed but it's most tough when in the very middle of the squash surprise a gentle zephyr at the egress of the people from Washington are there skirts just quietly lifting and the marvelous slice of Bermuda that decorates but also wraps the old ribbon in the same cellophane that the unfettered thigh decides to plant itself alongside the beloved peonies that have oft buried a mackerel like the Indians? sure enough into the gym fell a large bag in which the ivy mixed with an odd how shall I say 'novel' that makes one almost dense with flannel and yet not quite tweed although it is in a sense marinated in a cheaper wine your zinfandel your kosinski your screamingly boring onslaughts of what in Algiers? but of course not something for every day they dub it 'dub' is a bitch 'dub' it anyway the maniacal Jung deep in Mein Kampf and dosed up good with what? with what? oh dear sweet Jesus the tailored suit the bull clap because it can give you the tenure that you would suck spit for and knock a bull down on his knees if they have such articles of apparel unknown and not given the respect that ensues in Scranton that city of lost marines and the dry rot in the great nodding elms and if tenure is the guerdon of those who lift skirts and bull trousers and spaghetti soft and mushy the way it be's when they's be's got the lesson plan and the rosy reddened and tingling how shall I say in Tunis in the darkened office around five or so of a winter evening the sound of Marrakech and the soft sobbing as we watch the snap beans and the impeccable white of the knee hose and down there around the ankles is the mimeo machine andhg therzwx wehytu eogghji wh tuouh to thyrhtyyehyheuuhr jo joyk blamdurf oi gurdhujhut uh uh uhh uhhhh uh uh uh uh oooooooohhhh . . ."

Supper, with Dr. Bone, was, the doctor being the soul of genial warmth, a small yet festive occasion of genial warmth. They looked forward to the morrow with benign alacrity. Things were certainly looking "up."

Well, sweat-face, Blue said to Helene. Things are "looking" up! He seemed almost . . . happy!

Mark Sacharoff

I Wanna Know

Okay, the job didn't have class in the first place. Spying at the fags in the shithouse. I was doin' my time for bein' on the take, I admit that. Most of the time, you don't do nuthin', just park your ass and sweat out another nowhere day. Stuck in the wall like somekinda cockroach. Okay. That sorta lockup I can take, I'm used to it. Police-work ain't sellin' flowers, it's eighty per cent scuzzy. What with swelled-up corpses you gotta put in a bag who's been dead for a week, chasin' down hustlers who's gonna be back chewin' next day, and all the low-lifes you handle day in day out till you gotta wash your hands fourteen times like a goddamn *surgeon* . . . well, if you ain't togged out after a while in triple-layer skin like leather, maybe you oughta switch to a nice quiet job like drug-dealing.

So that job didn't have class in the first place. But what I saw—there's crums and there's crums—I wasn't ready for this type a degenerates—this kinda behavior took the prize! Somethin' new in the anals of crime. Or not even crime, worse than that, men and women fallin' apart, they ain't even aware a what they're doin'.

See, these bums come in and wash themselves at the sinks. Okay. Bums is bums, you can live with that. Broken-down housewives wringin' out their laundry. Kind of a half-smile on their mugs, they're enjoyin' their work. The Shithouse Hotel.

This is okay, it's a part a life, part a the known world. These guys, they gotta wash off some that grime, see? They can't walk around all day with them dark patches all over. Plus, they like to prance in every once in a while to try on a new pair a shoes that they picked up outta a trash can or lyin' without laces in an alley or offa some passed-out slob that could be them some night only they don't think of that.

That's how it all started. With them shoes. This well-dressed dude waltzes in one day. Uptown class written all over his face. Male, Caucasian, five-nine, etc. White hair, black coat, fur collar, potato nose—and a sour puss like he was smellin' something bad, which he was. Mixed in with the sour puss you could see hang-dog too, he was awfully shy, this dude, he almost walked sideways he was so shy. I pegged him right away for a flamin' faggot.

But the suspect don't make the usual moves. Hung around the premises all right, but three or four young guys breezed in, took a leak and out, and he just looked down at the grimy floor like he was waitin' for the funeral to start. No furtive action. Finally, this bum scuffs in with his pants eat away at the bottom and his legs givin' at the knee each step, the last stage a the syph or somethin'. Sure enough, the society gent notices those legs but his expression don't look like St. Francis at no lamb. He starts starin' the way GIs after 8 months stuck in the Philippines did at them short, buck-toothed native gals.

He's starin' up a storm, all bent over lookin' at the bum's legs, kinda light purple in the face and a sickly smile. Stuck on his shape. But then it hits me. Sweet sufferin' Jesus. Suspect ain't interested in the blue and yellow blotched legs that's ruined now and pretty soon ain't even gonna twitch, he's got the hots for the shoes! And what shoes! Soles flappin', four different colors from age. And the society gent comes on like they're some kinda paintin' hung up at the Lourdes.

"How much would you like for your shoes?" he kinda croons in his tea-room voice to this wreck. "How much would you like for your shoes?"

You hear about the world gettin' dark or a red fog in front of your eyes when you hear your family's just been wipe out in a car crash. Well, that's what happened to me when I heard this society pantywaist and his voice like apricot nectar kow-towin' to this creep and goin' "How much would you like for your shoes?" Hey, I seen corpses at the coroners, I seen bloated bodies from the river, I seen hustlers frenchin' guys on stairways so nuthin' could shock this old hand. But this did. It wasn't right, it was queer.

Anyway, the charmin' twosome struck a price: ten bucks. Suspect actually bows as he leaves! All humble-like. He wraps his treasure *very carefully* in some red paper, ties it up with silver string, he *bows*, and then he oozes outa the premises. I was hopping mad. But what could I do? No carnal knowledge. Nuthin' felonious.

So then he starts coming back gettin' other bums' shoes for a price. Bums' beat-up shoes are being trade off like at a bizarre. I can't take it no more. I decide to follow the son of a bitch home to his trick-pad and see what he does with all them shoes. Lives on West End Ave. Of course. I ring the doorbell and shows my badge. Naturally, he gets grey, his face collapses, he thinks the shit has hit the fan.

"What—? what—? you see I have no—"

"Lemme see the shoes."

Panic in his eyes. He knows I know. Body collapses too now, he gets very old. Poor guy looks drew and quartered. He's got a bent back, teary eyes, his lips are shakin'. Basically, I don't know what I'm doin' or what I'm after. But I gotta see them shoes.

He leads me into his bedroom. That's where he kept 'em, I see the whole caboodle a them. Sweet sufferin' Jesus, I must be fallin' apart, because the world darkens again and the red fog starts formin'. He's got the shoes way up in the air all around his bed! They're slowly twistin' around his bed, dozens of them, suspended in mid-air from wires. I just give him a hard look, enough to cripple a rhinoceros, and leave the premises fast— I seen enough. Nuthin' to detain him on. No mood for seizure of evidence.

This matter don't end there though. The gent comes back to the shithouse. Real worried this time, floats in with that sideway walk in slow motion like it was Judgment Day and him with a tail a sins seven miles long draggin' behind him. Sure enough, some more bums heard a him, the good word has gone around. He scores for two pair.

Nuthin' bad happens to the geezer, I sure ain't gonna pay him another social call to admire his goddamn Mobil. He don't got an m.o. I can fuck 'im over for. So he starts gettin' cocky, fulla beans. Pretty soon he's doin a roarin trade. That Mobil over his bed must be in three tiers, he's got all the fuckin' constellations there. Still I can't take him in I got no case I looked it up. Him and the bums is got it made, the shithouse is jumpin', and I sit there twiddlin' my thumbs and goin' over old busts in my mind.

But it don't stop there. All kindsa freaks fall by that urinal, see? Hey, right on Washington Square, so what do you expect? Fact, some a the bums is former freaks. Some a them is ex-cons too, in between stretches in the slammer. And some a the other bums decide they wanna tone up a bit, so they think up some freak act, scavenge some kinda bandana or cowboy hat or beads, and start walkin' all bent over 'n sprawled out, saying wow and lookin' up at the sky seein' Christ and Buddha every five seconds. Some characters I just can't tell are they real bums or former freaks or toned-up or what? Just like you can't tell if some them kids are boy or girl without you case their bubbies, and even then it ain't a hundred per cent lead pipe.

Anyway, these freaks and half-freaks and whatnot are coastin' in and out the urinal day in day out. Gladhandin' each other. Givin' skin. Legit business or smoke a joint, I basically got no interest or right, cause I got *one mission* in that shithouse, to keep the fags from gropin' and messin' around.

But after a while some a the crazies smokin' a joint notices this white-haired society guy negotiatin' with the bums like mad, like he was shoutin' prices in the stock market in a panic. The crazies look at each other ironit, try to hold it in, but then they bust out like they was underwater for two minutes, they're bent over double laughin' that stupid fuckin' pot-laugh—yeah, man, a million laughs.

They're not satisfied with laughin' though because next day three a them shows up with them little bazookas you blow through, what you gotta hold the holes? The kind all the artsy kids do in the empty fountain, what you play in front, not sideways? Little bazookas. Got this high screamin' whine like a fleet a police sirens goin' to their own funeral.

They waltzes in three a them in lumberjack shirts they ain't washed since the day they bought 'em. They waits a while and sure enough the society gent shows pretty soon, dressed like for the opera, bustin' out every which way with himself, king a the shithouse!

So the minute he starts hagglin' with one a the bums—it's not hagglin' really he's goin' through motions with his hands four twinklin' rings on each a them—the minute he toys with the bums, these three eunices start their whinin' with them bazookas. The goddamn shithouse is sproutin' these sad little *flowers* up to the ceiling. These eunices is playin' tribute to the F-feet queer, maybe cause he invents a nutty wrinkle they never coulda thought of themselves. Some skinny human wrecks hunched over their marijuana—they came in the shithouse to giggle—notice this music, do a pop-eye at the society gent fork-in' over a tenner for a pair a humped shoes, and start losin' their fuckin' minds, fallin' on the floor a the premises with giggles comin' double outta their mouths like cannonballs.

That started it because one a them managed to pull his skeleton up offa the floor and started hoofin' in time to the music. A couple more joined in, then the old geezer showed these shots a light in his eyes. The flamin sophie was thrilled! The bazooka guys starts swayin' crosslegged on the floor 'cause they're in the glory too now! All you needed was the Queen a England to make a toast with them chewy lips a hers. Then sure enough the king a the shithouse starts handin' out tips to the bazooka guys!

Next day you got a collection a scrounges with not just bazookas this time, oh no, you got bongos, you got guitars, you got a trumpet! Where the Christ the mothers all come from, so many people with nuthin to do except fart around? Don't mention work in their presence, they'll faint. And don't tell me times is hard, these mothers turn into cigar-store Indians at the mention of work.

But what else comes in: I can't hardly get the breath or the *will* to say it. Makes me sick to think about it. What exactly is goin' on here? Is the whole world collapsin' and is the last shed of decency burnin' to the ground? Someone out there is responsible, I don't know who it is. But things ain't right.

What comes in with the crowd now, believe it or not, is these girls, scrounges too naturally, but still girls. In the men's room! Cool as wet towels, no expression in them eyes. Female Caucasians, Negroes, Hispanics, and a few full-blooded squaws. Call 'em chippies, call 'em tramps, call 'em whooers, they're still of the female species and don't belong in no male shithouse. Every one a them in faded jeans that shows up their butts to a turn. They starts wigglin' and sashayin' to the music, some kinda disco or twist or wah-tootsie, I can't keep track a them dances. So you got guys and dames livin' it up and the society gent lordin' it and droppin' coin here there and everywhere and the crowd growin' every day and the poor fags ain't got time or room for their fuckin' act! Which naturally means I got no point sittin' here spyin', if I ever did in the first place. Think about it.

Pretty soon a party of uptown swells shows up late one night, they hear about some queer action, they wanna scoop their pals. Twistin' and wah-tootsyin' along with all these raggedy kids. Joy-poppin' like. They drop some coin too, that's part a the whole riggymarole. Word a this flies around, next day more swells are sniffin', more bums and scroungers trampin' in all haggert and hopeful like the Salvation Army opens up a new kitchen.

You never seen lines like the ones weavin' outside a that shithouse! Where all these low-lifes comin' from, is the whole city turnin' into bums? Think about it. See, I can tell different classes a people, a lifetime a policework, what you expect? What I see is, these new guys and the women too ain't your average low-life bum. After workin' hours I stand outside and watch these lines that reach up to Eighth St. and over to the end a the Square the three other sides. And I notice—a lot a these people are lookin' guilty—they got expensive coats on that are wore out—their talk is funny, all about movies and this war and that war and some kinda Russian dancer or a book all the way from Argentinie—it was all snooty stuff, these people are livin' in a world a their own makin'! But still they're standin' there in line for one, two hours waitin' for a handout from swells that maybe a year ago they swapped stories with about the same Russian dancer while they was nursin' some pink-colored drink up there on Fifth Ave. What gives with these people? Ain't they got no shame? Or is this some kinda mask-a-raid or trick-or-treat they can't resist? I just wish people would stay in their places. And I wish somebody would explain to me why everyone is actin' so queer these days.

These people in the wore-out coats that talk all la-di-da? You should seen the look on their mug when their opposite numbers handed them some coin or maybe a bill in their case. Real ashamed. Head rollin' on the shoulder. Some a them cried I don't know on account a the shame or account they was greatful. My question is, if they're so ashamed or hard up, why don't they put their muscles to use? Think about it. Whats happenin' in this society when guys that was executives, lawyers, and big perfessors lose their nerve and wanna give it up? Will somebody explain that to me?

And these shinanigans don't satisfy 'em. The twistin' and discoin', and the hoi poloi mixin' with the bums, and the panhandlin' and bazookas—all that horseshit goin' on at once—that don't satisfy 'em. Pretty soon there wasn't enough coin floatin' from them hands soft as a baby's bottom into some kinda snotty pockets. People in the lines was bein' shut off. So some *Jew* gets the usual bright idea. He brings in a pair pentz forty holes in it and holds it up with a sickly smile to this young snooty kid, male Caucasian with lady's eyes and looks like he got T.B. The snoot starts shakin' all over like he's in the last throws a his illness, teeth goin' a mile a minute with them braces on 'em, he calls in *desperation* to his pussy pals, come, come look at this, oh I think I'm *going to die!* The skinny pals come twinklin' over, they could pass for models in a fashion show, and in half a second when they sees the pants they go into the last-throws act too. Oh, save me, they say. They're *in love* with the pants, Gerald they're a scream!

Naturally, every bum an former big-shot loser in the premises sends his eyeballs screaming out against this scene especially when Gerald snaps up the pants as a steal and hands over $2. Another m.o. what I can't detain nobody for! So next day you got all kindsa clothes an trinkets an stolen goods passin' back and forth. Some a the la-di-da losers bring in jewelry, paintings, an books, plenty a books. They're down in the face, some a them cryin', look like they're sellin' their kids at a slave market.

So what you got here is one a them Middle East bizarres. Hey, tradin', hagglin', beards, stalls—all you need is a few women in veils. Things is hoppin'. Lines every day. Guys sellin' soft pretzels and peanuts and hot chestnuts—not a trace a meat —and the wore-down folk in the lines sellin' their trash, beat-up childrens toys, stained ties, broken cups and then pouncin' on a pretzel, its their first meal a the day, the saps!

All this woulda been bad enough, but a coupla days later, another bright idea. Musta been some *Jew* again. A wise guy brings in one a them small round tables his dogs is tired.

Accommodates four if you please! Can't stop it now, tables plunkin' down like giant hail-stones, *waiters* muckin' about. Big napkins folded over the arm. Bent over like they was workin' the Wardoff-Asoria.

And what they servin'?

Espreso! A goddamn shithouse espreso you got here. An I'm goin' outta my cotton-pickin' mind. Fed to the gills.

They closes down the bizarre at night, still dancin' tho.

Pretty soon one branch a the scroung skeleton crew starts futzin' around at the stalls, the middle one. Plank a wood goes on over the toilet. Another t.b. type paddy-boy stands on it and ladies and gentleman he starts givin' out with the arty double-talk, snatches a words with no connections and he's got this maniac light in his eyes, like a fuckin' streetpeople walkin' around talking to himself only he come inside.

Stuff like "narled candysticks in the twilight" and "23 different ways of looking at an asshole."

The stuff-shirts, pussy stiffs, and funeral directors in tuxes sittin' at these tables—some a them nuthin' but orange-crates!— starts applaudin' and hootin' and their cheeks get rosy cause this maniac arty talker managed to snap his jaws for six minutes without sayin' nuttin'. Hey, that's the dodge, who's gonna do it with the queerest snatches a words, that's what they're after cause right away another guy lost in his rags jumps onto the plank and starts makin' Sammy Kaye look like an amateur. This one's head has to go to one side cause he's short his head don't show over the top a the stall he's got to twist it to the side to peek at his audience. The first guy, he was tall but not that tall he had to stretch his neck way up so he could look over the top. And so it goes. Gloms one after the other strut their stuff and blurt out whatever comes in their mind and the hot dogs with nuthin' else to do in their lives and lookin' for cheap kinks to wake up the dead nerves give out with the hoo-has and their sad eyes turn into jewels on the spot.

I gotta tell you something now I don't know how to say it. See, everyone out there was doin' somethin' I was doin' nuthin'. Sure, they was wastin' their time makin' monkeys outta theirselves slummin' twistin' jabberin' fartin' around. But they was out there *doin'* somethin' I was in here on my ass, doin' *what?* Useless. Shut out. What they was doin' was screwy, but what about me? Think about it. I was watchin' them. Bein' screwy. A fine how-do-ya-do. I was disgusted with 'em, with the screwy world that thunk 'em up and made 'em behave this way, so I got disgusted with myself too. Fed to the gills. I was a clog in the machine that was whirlin' them around. But who was at the switches, who was callin' the shots? I wanted to know why some society types could swish around buyin' patched pants and some had to wait in line for a pretzel. And how come the lines were so big in this country of ours?

They used to blame the Jews, that backfired. I got nothin' against them Jews, they're smart people, but if it ain't the Jews who is it, it gotta be somebody, somebody who's riggin' all this so they can rake it all in while the rest of us scuffle for the scraps.

Anyway, I report my problems to the captain. Captain, I says, I got no more fags to watch. He says he'd reassign me to some other shithouse but these bizarres an espresos is sproutin' up all over the city, no more place to reassign me!

So what do I do I quit my crummy job. I quit my job no retirement no pension. And this may be hard to believe, I keep goin' every day to my hole in the wall to watch the goings on. I figure somebody gotta watch these goings on *every day* somebody gotta stand for the old days when you could watch fags and pinch em and a fag was a fag. Somebody gotta hold this whole fuckin' thing together.

But it cost plenty. There was them an there was me. Them twistin' and jabberin' around an me all by my lonesome in a cell. Them the alleged offenders on the outside me the cop on the inside!

I gotta admit watchin' those girls asses when they danced gave me the willies cause it wasn't just horny that was gettin' to me it was nerves and blues and disgust and just exactly what was goin' down here? So I started playin' with myself through my pants. And pretty soon I had it out and was floggin' my dummy!

What else was there to do? I got no job, no contact with a human being, the marrow been pulled out of the U.S. of A., an I got no purpose in life except one I set up to keep my gun from my temple which is to witness all this messin' around for a trial thats never gonna happen but at least I can say I done my duty I was on hand to witness it. This is the least I could do.

That was the state of affairs till somethin' happened that just broke me down I ain't got no mor fight in me afterwards.

One afternoon with toothless hags tryin' to push greasy place-mats an little kids a nine an ten hangin' around sulky an mean waitin' for an offer, in waltzes this team a front men, I can spot the secret service types all tan with eyes dartin' left and right, they're clearin' a path for the big cheese. It's the fuckin' Vice-President!

The fuckin' Vice-President smirkin' tan walkin' brisk as a ostrich makes a bee-line for the middle stall where them crazy talkers sound off? He's gonna make a speech. The Vice-President of the U.S. of A. standin' on a goddamn plank on a goddamn toilet his head squirmin' around trying to look over and then under and then over the top of the fuckin' stall! An makin' a speech in the shithouse! Think about it. My face was hot as a baked apple. I felt like I pissed myself and was sittin' soaked with my fellow classmates in grammar school pointin' at me roarin'. It was a sacralidge. And so the big man talks.

You wonderful people hard times shows the inglommable American spirit that in these difficult days creative idea spread across the land creative creative creative form own enterprise area you wonderful people keep up the fighting spirit we think of you all the time at our balls the President said just the other day inglommable I saw a tear in the First Lady's eye kiss my ass enjoy your shit.

That took the fight outta me the Vice-President the symbol of our country standin' on a toilet smirkin' and givin' out with a bum rap. I said to myself, hey, hang it up.

So that's when I come out my hole an mix with the rest a the slobs. I ain't proud. Used to be I couldn't look at one a them bums or queers or scrounges without plannin' in my head some kinda Hitler scheme. Wipe 'em off the face a the earth. After this Vice-President thing though that slugged me in the head I say who's to say maybe it ain't so simple the Vice-President looked like an awful sap all made up an grinnin'— symbol of our country, made all the la-di-das look bad we're all in this together.

So now I wash my clothes at the sink. Sold my good shoes a course. That kept me goin' a week or so an I been watchin' styles a panhandlin' so long I find out I'm a pro at it I got a good rap. See you got to give out with somethin' sharp that'll shove their feet tighter into their shoes get their peepers stuck an give a little tug on their balls. Sing for your supper. I make out all right. Gave up floggin' my dummy too. That's progress. Standin' in line I try to get next to the former snoots, listen in to them with their trues and Camoos and German this and French that I'm becomin' a regular Frenchie. Pah de too to you. And a luh regar to you. Plus I manage to wah-tootsie now and then.

But when I talk to them German French types in line when I ain't pickin' up words an smart-ass raps for my panhandlin', I ask one simple question, can you explain what's happenin', can you explain who's to blame why I had to leave my post and go on the skids why everybody's in line, why everybody's behavin' so queer? You wouldn't believe the answers I get long enough to wind around everybody's neck in line about these forces an everybody got his own story, arguments start, everybody's total pro, got the whole picture knocked, so why ain't they President an puttin' the whole load a trash back together again?

But I keep askin'. I get the reputation a bein' the bum philosopher, king a the bums, I start seein' through everybody's point, I heard it all. What do you mean by forces, my friend? I pick up this idea here that idea there, I pick up what do you mean?, an' fallashus an' stuff, I start-out-talkin' those talkers on the toilet. But I ain't shittin' anybody. I really wanna know, I'm gonna keep askin' everybody I see, what gives? What's your opinion on this? Maybe some day a guy in line or a woman is gonna be real relaxed and not connin' anybody and is gonna say them special words I gotta hear. I'm collectin' all kindsa ideas it don't have to be this way—I wanna know—these crowds is gotta do some thinkin' I get em off their ass tryin' to put it together the bum philosopher I wanna know

Jeff Weinstein

A Jean-Marie Cookbook

I stole two cookbooks and read them when I knew I should
be doing other things. I wanted to make a casserole of
thinly sliced potatoes, the non-waxy and non-baking kind, although the dish would be baked in cream. I found out from
reading that what I wanted to do was no good unless I rubbed
a clove of garlic around the inside of the pot, not that I'm adding the garlic itself, but that the cream seems to imbibe the
flavor and hold it until you are ready. It was these fine points
I wanted to know, the right and the wrong way to slice, the
effective use of spices, why an earthenware dish 'worked' (the
way yeast 'works') while a glass one didn't: the secrets of
cooking. Some people argue that something should be done a
certain way so it will taste a certain way, but how do they
know that when they taste a dish they are all tasting the same
thing? Experience makes a difference. For example, once I
threw up when I ate a noodles and cheese casserole, so I won't
eat one again, no matter how good. Experience even tells me
how to feel about cooking something like a fried egg sandwich.
I make them in bacon fat now, but for a long time I thought
only big households with dirty tin cans filled with drippings,
or a great constant cook like my friend Kit, could save bacon
fat and properly cook with it. For years I would throw the good
clear fat down the drain, and I still don't know how or why
I changed. It's like baking; I can't bake now, although I read

baking recipes and work them through in my head, but only if I see that they apply to someone else, to someone *who can bake*. The most difficult transition I know is to move from one sort of state like that to another, from a person who doesn't bake to one who does. I would like to find out how it is done.

●

It seems that Jean-Marie took on the cloak of 'gay' life in San Diego. He was a graduate student of art, interested in frescoes and teaching French on the side. Then, a year after he whispered he was going to remain celibate, mouthing the word as if he wasn't sure of its pronunciation, he started to skip classes. And one night he walked into the local gay bar, the one where people danced, called the Sea Cruise. At first he walked into the bar with women he knew from school and danced, commandeering them around the floor. Then he came with his old friend Mary, a head taller than he was, and they jerked around, absolutely matched. All this progressed over months; I would see Jean-Marie and Mary every time I was there, which probably means they were at the bar more often than I was. I can be sure they were always there together. I never ate dinner with them but I assume they would try to 'taste' things the same way. Considering their need to think of themselves as alike, the idea of them kissing is interesting. They would want to think they were feeling the same thing, mutual tongues, mutual saliva. Their pleasure would not be mutual, and they would have to avoid thinking about that. Can you like kissing yourself? Can you like kissing someone you falsely imagine to be like yourself? It seems like deception to me, and I wonder why they do it.

●

Good cooking knives are indispensable to good cooking,

which I learned by reading. I am told that carbon steel is better than stainless steel, that it wears away and gets more flexible with use, but such knives have to be dried after they are washed, their tips protected by corks, and you are supposed to yell at anyone who uses your knives for opening jars or other obviously damaging things. I don't mean to be facetious here, but apparently knives are important. I stole a set of Sabatier (lion?) knives that I thought were the best, stainless steel, but later I found out about the carbon versus stainless and got a sinking feeling in my stomach, though I also knew I would cherish them less and use them more.

●

Then Jean-Marie discovered men, or males rather, and started dancing with them, kissing them, and going out with them. The first was a sixteen year old boy whose personality was all Jean-Marie's idea, and every time they met his time was spent looking for it, the way Puritans scanned nature to find signs of God. He and Jean-Marie probably did not sleep together, or if they did share a bed sometimes they probably didn't have sex. When this ended, by the boy leaving for San Francisco, Jean-Marie used disappointment as the excuse to pick up guys at the Sea Cruise, first the ones who liked to be mooned at, the quiet regulars, then the drugged-out ones, and then the ones made of stainless steel. He made the transition from gown to town by moving away from school to a dark house in the city, full of wood and plants and no light to read by. He slowly withdrew from the University and backed into San Diego, dropping old associations and living with a different opinion of himself. He sold his car so he could ride the municipal buses, and considered getting food stamps and general relief.

Jeff Weinstein

Here is a recipe I invented, a variation on scrambled eggs:

2 eggs at room temperature

cream, or half-and-half, sour cream, yogurt, though cream
   is best

freshly ground black pepper

a little salt

butter (not margarine), unsalted butter is best

You take the eggs, beat them well but not frothy, then add a good lump (I call it a dollop) of cream or whatever, and *stir* it in. Grind in some pepper, add a little salt. Heat a good frying pan very slowly (this is important) and melt in it a dollop of butter. When the butter starts to 'talk' add the egg mixture. Cook it slowly until it starts to curdle; this takes time, as it should, in the gentle heat. In the meantime get your toast ready and some tea. You can't rush this. Move the eggs around with a wooden spoon or fork; metal is not good. When they look done, creamy and solid, turn them into a warm plate. You may want to throw on some fresh chopped herbs, watercress, cilantro, parsley, but plain is wonderful. I don't know why these are a 'variation' on scrambled eggs, but they do taste like no others. They even come out different every time, although some people can't tell the difference, and a few people I know won't even touch them.

●

When I met Jean-Marie on the bus he told me he got a poem published, and I suspected it was about love:

His beating heart

My moist lips, etc.

It *was* about love, in rondelle form, for he hadn't left school as much as he thought. The next night I had a friend over for dinner. I heard he was a gourmet so I was nervous to impress him, although I'm not usually like that. Unfortunately I got home late and had to rush around to get everything ready, muttering to myself, but all at once I changed my mind about the matter and decided I was doing something which should be a pleasure, so I stopped worrying about it. Everything went well, basically because John wasn't much of a gourmet. We had: sherry, iced mushrooms with lemon juice and no salt, gratin dauphinois—a simple (hah!) casserole of thinly sliced washed dried new potatoes so thin that two pieces make the thickness of a penny, baked in a covered earthenware bowl rubbed with garlic, salted, peppered, and filled with cream. The cover is taken off towards the end of the baking so a brown crust forms. Eaten right away, and it was heaven. We were talking about Cretan art. It's important that the bowl be earthenware, that it be rubbed with garlic, and that the cream and potatoes come to within ¾ of an inch of the top of the uncovered casserole. We went up to the roof to grill the steaks and talked about the view and how odd it was to be in California. These steaks are called biftecks a la mode du pays de vaux, grilled and seasoned fillet steaks on a bed of chopped hardboiled eggs, fines herbes (I had only dried herbs but I reconstituted them if you know what I mean), lemon juice, and salt and pepper. I also added some chopped watercress. Then you heat it all. It was in this French glass dish I bought when I was so bored I could have killed myself. I stole the fillets. We drank wine and talked of sex. Then we had a salad of deveined spinach. He was really impressed; and I was surprised, both that he was so easily moved and that it all turned out so nicely. *I* was impressed too.

John brought a dessert, which was a home-baked apple pie, really a tart, and it was not as good as all that, but I was happy he brought it. It tasted much better the second day. We made out on the sofa then, but all of a sudden I got an urge to break away and go dancing, and John readily agreed. At the bar he fell 'in love' with this beautiful Spaniard named Paco, who was drunk. They danced a lot together, badly, but John finally had to take me home. I wondered if he went back to meet Paco, but I thought not. John said he would see me when he got back from his trip to the East Coast. I had a dream that night in which I felt completely perverted and inhuman, and I think the meal had something to do with it.

●

Jean-Marie, after his year out in San Diego, wrote a long letter about promiscuity to the San Diego Union, which of course didn't get printed, although a month after he sent it in they lifted a small part of it and passed it off as opinion about a case where a lot of men got arrested in the bathroom of the San Diego May Company, 'for indiscriminate reasons' the paper said.

Dear Sirs: I am a gay male in San Diego and I want to talk about sex, or the problem of promiscuity so many of us face. Most of us, gay or not gay, are looking for someone to love, for a day, a year, or forever, and admittedly this is hard to do. But we have to try. However I don't understand why the only way many of the gay guys in San Diego try is by tricking. For those of you who don't know what tricking means, it's meeting someone, at a gay bar, in the park or on the street, going home and having sexual contact. Sometimes you don't even talk, because it would ruin everything. But when you do start conversations, they all go like this: what's your name (and you give your first name only), where are you from, what do you do, did you see . . . . . (a movie), etc., completely anonymous conversations, which is sad. Why do we do this? I don't really understand why, or why people hang around bathrooms, or even worse. It could be lust, but lust is just a screen for loneliness. Why doesn't the city of San Diego (or all cities) provide a place for people, gay and non-gay, to talk, dance, like a coffeehouse? This has worked elsewhere. But I do think that we as people should honestly question what they are doing. Sometimes I get so sick of what I am doing, going to bars every night, drinking when I don't want to drink, flirting when I don't want to flirt, staying out until two in the A.M. sweating and waiting for the right person, or at that point any person, that I don't know what to do. I could go back to the University, but I know the University is worse. I wonder if I was roped into this. There are some people I meet at the gay bars that I really think should be put away because of the way they act, and treat others. But other times I don't think that at all, and I just feel sorry for them. I wish I understood my appetites better, and I wish the city could do something about it.

●

I have never made a real dessert before, one that requires more than chopping up some fruits and adding whatever liqueurs I have around, so I thought I'd try something out of a cookbook, something called a chocolate bombe. I stuck to that one partly because I liked the name and partly because I like chocolate and also because I had some Mexican vanilla extract which would go well in it. 'Chocolate Bombe' I realized later would make a good title for a screenplay, but it would have to be about food, and very few things are. Food is shown in some movies, like the gourmet concoctions in Hitchcock's *Frenzy* or the banquet in *The Scarlet Empress* or in any number of bakery scenes with pastry on one side of the window and little faces, of boys usually, on the other. But nothing masterful or mature, and I don't think it's because food is silly or insignificant, but because it's hard to visualize people at a meal where food stands for their relationships or essences in some way, like the beef dish in *To The Lighthouse*. How can I say I was 'in the mood' to make something with cream, to watch something gel, to fill the beautiful mold sitting in the cupboard.

After I made the bombe, enough for ten people, there was so much left over that I left the key to my apartment outside the door and asked the couple in the next apartment to go into the freezer and help themselves, which they did, but other people helped themselves to my typewriter and television.

Chocolate Bombe (about ten servings)

Soak 1½ teaspoons of gelatin in one cup of cold water. Stir and bring to the boiling point 1 cup of milk, 1½ cups of sugar, and two tablespoons of unsweetened cocoa. Dissolve the gelatin in the hot mixture. Cool. Add one teaspoon of vanilla extract. Chill until about to set. Whip 2 cups of cream until thickened but not stiff. Fold it lightly into the gelatin mixture. Still-freeze in a lightly greased mold, and unmold ½ hour before serving.

It tasted rich, although there were too many ice crystals in it. The best part was sampling the gelatin mixture before the cream was added, because it was so sweet and cold, just gelling, redolent of chocolate and Mexican vanilla. By the way, it doesn't come out tasting like pudding or jello; it's full of weight, like home-churned ice cream. It wasn't perfect, but because it came out at all I imagined it was better than it was.

Sometimes I eat because I'm lonely or disappointed. In fact, as I drive away from the bar at night, I tell myself (or the others in the car) it was 'amusing' or 'boring' or 'kinda fun,' but almost always at the same point in the turn to the main stretch home

I feel a hollow feeling, which, when I recognize it, says I'm hungry, and I look forward to something to eat. It's almost absolutely predictable: the masking talk, the turn, and then the hunger, and often I overeat before I go to bed. The few times I've gone home with someone from the bar I've been hungry in the same way, so I assume these sexual episodes aren't really happy ones. Sometimes I've been nauseous, but that's a different feeling for different reasons. I've gone home with only one person who offered me a full breakfast in the morning or who lived as if he cooked himself full meals. That was in New York City, with a very nice guy who just wanted to fuck me and get me to sniff amyl. He did get up early, and seemed to be making a lot of money, although the only thing I can remember about how he spent it was a really hideous gilt and glass table in his living room, and the fact that he bought towels at Bloomingdale's the afternoon before, spending more than a hundred dollars. The towels were hanging in the bathroom without even having been washed. We took a taxi home to his place, I remember now, I wasn't hungry and only slightly sick to my stomach. I ate underripe bananas with a guy I was 'in love' with, but he was angry because I couldn't fuck him. And once, in Denver, the only thing I found in the refrigerator of this guy who picked me up, fucked me, and fell asleep at eight in the evening was one of those mealy chocolate flavored wafers you use to gain weight if you eat them with things or lose weight if you eat them alone. There was literally nothing else in there. I forgot about David. David made me a poached egg which tasted slightly of the vinegar in the water, on whole wheat toast, and fresh juice, and tea. I had many more of those breakfasts, even though we didn't have sex, but I loved to sleep with David, and still would if we hadn't had that fight about

Jeff Weinstein

a story I wrote concerning him.

●

Jean-Marie became more and more bitter about his life, although he didn't realize to what extent he was excluding himself from his old friends, and especially from women. The world looks cruel when you concentrate only upon the males you know or want to know, and women become generalized and ignored, somehow peripheral. Jean-Marie got sick of this but he didn't know why, and none of his new friends could tell him. Certainly he was less stiff after a year in the Sea Cruise, and sloughed around the dance floor as if he had done it before, but . . .

But, he said, I'm special. I am a feminine man, and that's good, even better than being a woman. He would peer into mirrors, for mirrors were all over the walls of the rooms he haunted, and play with disconnecting 'Jean-Marie' from the little boy he grew up with. His head would twist and arch, one shoulder would rise, his nostrils flared as he imagined what could be possible. He never looked further down than his neck, and avoided parts of himself like his nose or the jut of his ears. Certainly he was bitter because he couldn't store this mirror-feeling, when his blood rushed and he could do anything. It wasn't vanity, this play in front of mirrors, nothing was being judged or compared, except perhaps the old with the new.

Oh ugh hmm. Do you really think so? Really I couldn't how could I? It wouldn't work . . . do you think so? Hmmm well. In far Peru there lived a llama he had no papa he had no mama he had no wife he had no chillun he had no use for penicillin . . . Jesus . . . yes of course I can come when do you want me . . . the brie please . . . fine I'll leave anytime of course but will they understand my English yes I know how important it is . . . God you're cute and you've gained weight hummph why do I get so much pleasure out of this . . . it's true isn't it.

●

I have made some bad errors in cooking, but these aren't nearly as important as errors in menu, or rather in the meal. I just heard of someone who swallowed a handful of aspirin, which made her sick. People are constantly eating to make themselves sick, to poison themselves, poison others, to forget, or to die. Someone once said stupidity takes corporeal form. I seem to have an aptitude for planning a happy meal, the combination of people, appetites, and what I call the 'attitude' of the food: the amounts, the way a hot dish is followed by a cool one, the interplay of colors, the sequence of dishes and their values. I do this best when I am alone because people eating at my house sometimes make me nervous, and although I plan the food, I can never plan the run of old friendships at a dinner table. There's a whole history of ruining meals; in certain places, if you wanted to get even with a family you ground up the bones of their bird or some other possession into the food you served to them—it's a way of breaking up hospitality. One example of this was a stew which consisted of the guests' children. People no longer realize the potential power in the act of sharing food, but they do suffer from the consequences whether or not they're aware of it. The menu of the most awful meal I ate:

mulligatawny soup and saltines
three bean salad
'oven-fried' chicken, I had the drumstick
mashed potatoes
green beans with butter
white bread and butter
ice cream and sugar wafers

193

Jeff Weinstein

There was something wrong with the soup but I didn't know what; it tasted bitter, not from any single ingredient but from the expression on the face of the person who stirred it. Really. It was bitter exactly the way a person is, in its 'sweat'. After the soup I said something nasty to a guest who was invited just to meet me, and everyone was embarrassed and tried to cover up. Mel belched out loud and George got annoyed but didn't say anything; he merely stabbed at his chicken and pushed it away. Judy spilled her milk on my pants, accidentally I'm sure, so I had to get up and change. When I got back George wasn't speaking to Nancy, and Mel was winking and nodding with no subtlety at all across the table. It could be that there were too many of us in the room, but we all had the same bad taste in our mouths.

I once had breakfast (brunch) in a gay bar, waiting an hour for a plate of bacon, two vulcanized eggs, and the pre-hashed potatoes that get scraped around a hot surface for a few minutes until their fetid water evaporates and they take on some color. Someone I didn't know was rubbing my knee and my only friend there kept drinking those morning drinks that make you anticipate evening, while the air smelled of the night before. How could I eat? I did eat, ravenously, but managed only by insisting to myself that except for my appetite I wasn't at all like the others around me. How long would that last? One more meal there could do the trick, so I swore I'd never eat at that bar again. I went home alone and looked at myself in the mirror to see if I had changed, for the grease from the potatoes was already beginning to appear on my forehead.

My God no. If you put a flower in a vacuum all its essence leaves. The fog might just be getting tired and collapsing into puddles . . . grease . . . damp . . . those little flakes of skin

194

sticking in patches, nothing to show for all that reading, nothing to wear that fits, too big or too small and who can keep up with all that sewing even when I sew it unravels around my stitches. I'll throw it all out.

Two Mirror Snacks

1) bacon fat or a mixture of butter and oil, not too much
   a few small potatoes, boiled in their skins (leftovers are best)
   one or two peeled and crushed cloves of garlic
   the pulp, fresh or canned, of one tomato
   plenty of basil
   optional: cut pitted black olives, about 6
       a few sliced mushrooms
       a few celery leaves

Heat the fat or oil and butter in a small frying pan until very hot, put in the potatoes and mix them around, breaking them into chunks but not mashed. Add the garlic and some coarse salt if you have it, stirring constantly until they take on some color. Add the rest of the ingredients in any order you like (I add the olives last). Don't stir toward the end, so the bottom burns a little. Turn out onto a plate, add salt and freshly ground black pepper to your taste, and eat with white wine or beer. Be sure to scrape all the burnt particles and grease out with a spoon and eat them.

2) (you need a blender for this one)
   an egg
   a few big spoonfuls of plain yogurt
   enough wheat germ to cover it, but not more than a Tbsp.
   a good ripe banana, broken into pieces
   one cup of any mixture of: milk, half & half, fruit juice
   ½ tsp. of real vanilla extract (try Mexican vanilla)
   some sweetener, honey, sugar, ice cream, just a bit

        optional: a few spoons of protein powder
             a spoon of soy lecithin
             a tsp. of polyunsaturated flavorless oil

Add to the blender in the order mentioned, but don't fill to more than ⅔ capacity. Most protein powder tastes awful, so add only as much as you think you need. Non-instant dried milk is a good substitute. Blend at low speed for a few seconds, uncover, make sure the wheat germ isn't sticking in clumps to the yogurt, and scrape the now agglutinated protein powder off the sides of the blender and repulverize, all with a rubber spatula. Smell it, taste it, add more of what you think it needs. Cover and blend at medium speed for half a minute. Have right away or refrigerate, but it will settle. Sometimes I add an envelope of chocolate flavored instant breakfast or some powdered chocolate because the chocolate and orange juice (if that's your juice) taste great together. Fruit jam is also good. Obviously this recipe can take a lot of things, but remember your purpose.

Note that each mirror snack is a different response to feeling bad.

●

In his response to the bar, or in his response to the person he was afraid of becoming, Jean-Marie resorted to interests connected neither to school nor to the bar life he was now trying to avoid. He taught himself to knit, but when he found himself mooning over pictures of models in scarves and sweaters, he realized he didn't want to. Then he thought he'd learn to cook, revolted by the cold stupid meals he fixed for himself and by his unquestioning dependence on others for anything hot. One evening he had dinner with some of his University friends, baked ham and guacamole salad, for old times' sake. After dinner Jean-Marie asked them to try and describe the worst meal each of them could remember. He was stunned by his boldness—he never started things—but he was comfortable after the food and sat back to listen.

As they talked, Jean-Marie thought this was the most interesting conversation he'd heard since he left the University. He hated school, hated the lab scientists and art professors and the pretty jock behind the locker room cage who demeaned every woman as soon as she walked away. Yet even though the gay people at the Sea Cruise were gentle, they were more miserable with their lives than any group of people he knew. It was 'they' now, but tomorrow it could be 'we'. What could he do? Could he straddle the two and possibly be happy? He was beginning to guess that happiness isn't the issue here, and survival is more crucial. 'In what way' he thought 'is survival related to being happy?'

●

The most difficult dishes in any cookbook are the 'everyday' recipes, luncheon, bruncheon, egg, family dishes, cooking for survival when you have more important things to do or don't have much money. Let's assume you don't have a family to feed but haven't much time and want to be happy with what you are eating. Here is a list of staples for 'everyday' meals:

> milk
> eggs, bought fresh a few at a time if possible
> onions
> oil or bacon drippings (bacon)
> a little butter, unsalted
> tomatoes, fresh and canned
> garlic
> cheap greens, vegetables in season
> some cheese
> bread, or flour to bake it

Jeff Weinstein

> fresh boiling potatoes
> chicken, all parts of it
> lemons, possibly oranges
> salt, black pepper
> beer or wine

Staples are defined here not as what you need, but as what holds things together. I know this list assumes there is an 'everyday'. Some people, I know, have to cadge their next meal, for a place to prepare it, for a place to eat. These are people you should ask in for a meal, if possible.

I asked Jean-Marie to dinner. We agreed, although I don't remember why, to have a cooking contest. The rules were to prepare a menu. We would each cook our own menu and then each other's, which would take four nights. We decided on a judge who needed the meals but who also understands more about food than anyone we knew without being disgusting.

Jean-Marie's menu, using the staple list, one good piece of flesh or fowl, some extra money, and one day's work:

> consomme, iced, with chervil
> carrotes marinees
> boned leg of lamb, mustard coating (gigot a la moutarde)
> boiled new potatoes with parsley butter
> sliced iced tomatoes with basil and olive oil
> orange pieces flambe
> cafe espresso
> the meal is served with 'a good French red wine'

My menu, with the same 'limitations':

> cream of potato and watercress soup
> stuffed mushrooms
> cucumbers and lemon juice

roast duck with tangerine stuffing, lemon curd glaze
parsley garnish
garlic mashed potatoes
spinach and cilantro salad, lemon juice dressing
strawberry lemon ices
the meal is served with cold Grey Riesling (California)

See appendix for comments on the selections. These are expensive meals, requiring not only food but many utensils and a lot of heat and cold (energy).

Jean-Marie and I met our judge, J., at my house the first evening, where I cooked my menu. J. said very little as we ate, although at one point he asked me for my recipe for stuffed mushrooms and their history:

Edythe's Stuffed Mushrooms

'My mother invented these one night when she ran out of clams to stuff. My father was rather demanding about the food their party guests (or rather his party guests) were served, and although my mother prided herself on her stuffed clams, it was still sort of slave-work for her. This is not to say that my father didn't like to cook—he did—but he would not clean up after his filth, to use my mother's words. She liked these mushrooms, which were moist and tasty, and I took her recipe and adjusted it to my tastes:

large open mushrooms, the bigger the better, 3 per person
at least one bunch of parsley
juice of one lemon
6 or so cloves of garlic, peeled
one or two cans of minced clams, drained
seasoned breadcrumbs, Italian style
basil, fresh or dried
coarse salt

Jeff Weinstein

    freshly ground black pepper
    olive oil
    plenty of freshly grated parmesan and/or romano cheese

The reason the quantities are vague is because I never measured them; the frying pan, a good heavy one, should determine the amount of everything. It almost always works out, and any leftover stuffing is delicious, although it should be refrigerated so you don't get food poisoning. The tricky part of this dish is making sure the mushrooms don't dry out, and all the soaking is for this purpose. Carefully twist the stems out of the mushrooms, so you are left with the intact cap and gills. Reserve the stems. With a spoon scrape the gills and all excess stuff out of the caps, so you are left with little bowls. As you finish this process, eating any mushrooms you may have broken, place the caps in a large bowl of cool water into which you've squirted the lemon juice. The mushrooms will soak in this; the acid prevents them from turning too brown. Mince the parsley flowerettes. Mince the garlic. Now, take each mushroom stem, chop off and discard the woody half, the part which stuck in the ground, and dice the remaining halves. Grate your cheese. Heat the frying pan slowly, then add at least ¼ inch of olive oil. This may seem like a lot, but it's necessary. When the oil gets fragrant, add the garlic. Before the garlic browns, add the clams and saute. Add the minced mushrooms, stirring constantly, the parsley, and keep cooking. Make sure nothing burns. Add salt, pepper, and enough breadcrumbs to soak up the excess clam and mushroom liquid. The basil should have been crushed and thrown in some time before; do add quite a bit. The stuffing should now be loose and moist but not liquid, and very hot. Remove from heat, and add most of your grated cheese, reserving some. Stir it all, and put it aside. If you think the mushrooms have soaked long enough, take each one out, shake out the water, and with a spoon put the stuffing in. Do this with a light hand and keep the stuffing as particulate as possible. Stuff all the mushrooms. Now, if you must, you can leave them sit for a while (do not refrigerate), but it is best to immediately put them into a lightly greased broiling dish, having preheated your oven or broiler sometime before, arrange touching in some kind of pattern, salt the tops, sprinkle with grated cheese and maybe a little olive oil, and run them under a hot broiler or in a very hot oven until both the stuffing is completely heated and the tops of the caps are not too tough and brown; it is an exact point. By that time the water in the mushrooms should have just steamed them, so they are perfectly cooked, neither raw and brittle nor rubbery and slick. If you want to be fancy, place the mushrooms, before you broil them, on a bed of carefully washed and deveined leaves of spinach, and broil them together. Some of the mushroom juice will run out onto the perfectly cooked spinach, which can be used to sop it all up.'

On this first evening Jean-Marie paled a bit when he tasted my mushrooms, perhaps because he didn't know how easy they were to make. On the second night Jean-Marie cooked, and we both knew our food was good, so this time we talked nicely and forgot the pretense of competition.

'But I know Louis the 15th had a head shaped like a pear.'

I should note that I did not tell our judge who cooked what. J. ate well, asking us to save portions of everything, so by the fourth night there should be two versions each of two different meals, three in miniature. Of course we were sickened at the prospect of so much rich food, but the concept of a cooking contest was still strange enough to be interesting. On the fourth night we talked about writing cookbooks and tasted a little bit of everything. Jean-Marie managed to make the mushrooms but could not even fake the ices, and my version of his marinated carrots was pale and sticky.

I say this in retrospect because at some point in our meal I couldn't tell what food was mine, or where it came from. Jean-Marie looked contemplative and sick. Our judge was so quiet we didn't see him most of the time. The courses were served by ghosts. Critical faculties must have faded, and we thought only of parody and death.

> The grotesque prudishness and archness with which garlic is treated in this country has led to the superstition that rubbing the bowl with it before putting the salad in gives it sufficient flavor. It rather depends whether you are going to eat the bowl or the salad.

Jean-Marie left, J. left, I was left sitting alone not knowing when they had gone. There was a note:

I cannot tell the difference among your dishes because each bite was a universe. Why do you insist so much on difference and comparison? I was so happy to be eating, and it was all good food, that my joy overran any pose of judgment. When you cook something, and put it aside, how do you know who cooked it? Who were you that day? Who could have doctored the food, soured it, stolen it away and left a note of gibberish in its place? Certainly you can write a cookbook, but could it possibly predict a meal? It's an odd mirror to stare into, with no certainty in it. There was a point when I almost swallowed a bone, and some sherbet dribbled down my chin and stained the tablecloth. Did you notice? Would you have cooked that meal, or any meal, if I hadn't been there to eat it? Will your tablecloth wash out? (No matter, I blotted up the spill.) I do think you expect too much, but I would be pleased if you arranged your life so you could continue to cook. However I don't see that a cookbook could be anything but a reflection of imagined life, which is not a bad thing. I'd be happy to visit you again.

APPENDIX

Jean-Marie comments on his menu:
My menu is mainly French, relying on the good fresh vegetables of Southern California. The cold soup whets your appetite, the marinated carrots, which is a French country specialty, excites your now raging hunger and prepares your palate for the mustard flavor of the lamb. After all that cold stuff, the lamb and hot simple potatoes are a happy change. The red wine supports and is not pushed over by the strong flavors of the main dish. People should be talking at this point, as soon as the initial gobbling has stopped. The iced tomatoes provide color, if the conversation doesn't, and the basil is yet another welcome flavor. After a pause (which I never think is long enough) the oranges cool your mouths, 'degrease them' so to speak, and the espresso should be strong and black.

Comments on the other menu:
These are things I like. If the duck doesn't smoke up the whole house it can be quite a surprise, because people don't expect duck the way they expect chicken or lamb. The spinach and cilantro salad is also a surprise (especially if you don't wash the spinach enough) but seriously, people see the blue-green leaves

Jeff Weinstein

of the spinach and think it's lettuce but the light is funny, and then the cilantro, a lighter yellow-green, flashes like little bits of afterglow or whatever that visual phenomenon is called. And when they eat it, it's the same thing, because all the bland cuddy spinach juice is punctuated by the herb, utterly unexpected. Ices cool everyone after the duck. The menu works; I don't have to explain exactly why, do I? By the way, Jean-Marie shouldn't repeat the mustard of the carrots in his lamb.

Michael Brownstein

Uncle Bill and the Disco Duck

C alled Uncle Bill, but no one was home. Then I remembered the Disco Duck. I'll have to call Bill again, I guess.
Because at this moment he is leaning an elbow against the sooty
window sill of a small Parisian hotel room, and he's crying.
For it was standing in this very same window, twenty years
before, that he said goodbye to that special boy. That was in
1959, and he has not seen the boy since. Twenty years have
passed during which Bill went back to his home town and
became an uncle to everyone there. He took orders and gave
advice over the phone. I called him today but no one was
home, because earlier Bill drove to the airport, boarded a plane,
and flew all the way to Paris to stand in the hotel room window.

As daylight leaves the narrow street below, and neons of
the night soak through dusty gauze curtains whose tiny tassels
shiver in the breeze, Bill sinks back onto the bed in the darken-
ing room and fingers the bottle of Polish vodka in the paper
sack in his left coat pocket. They had gotten drunk on contra-
band Polish vodka that final night, twenty years before. In
1959, in Paris, the bottle of Polish vodka represented to them
the improbability of their relationship, the boy staying with
him for weeks and weeks, then that afternoon when he
announced out of the blue he was leaving. Just like that.

The boy's eyes clouded over. He refused to communicate, to tell Bill why he was leaving. It was over. Bill never saw the boy again.

He sighs and pulls the paper sack from his jacket. He cracks the cap on the vodka. Green neon from the nightclub marquees lights up one side of his face, while from the narrow street below him come the never ending sounds of the Disco Duck.

Russell Banks

What Noni Hubner Did Not Tell the Police About Jesus

S he did not reveal that two days prior to His arrival at the trailerpark she spoke with Him on the telephone. She was alone in her mother's trailer at the time, which was approximately 10:30 p.m., and because she expected her mother, Nancy Hubner, to return from a meeting of the Catamount Historical Society around 11:00, Noni had just rolled and smoked a single marijuana cigarette, which she was accustomed to doing when left alone at this time of night, for while she had come to require for sleep the kind of sedation provided by a single marijuana cigarette, her mother had forbidden her to use the weed, particularly since Noni's psychiatrist had happily provided her with enough valium to put her to sleep for the rest of her natural life. Noni was in the bathroom flushing down the roach, when the phone rang, and it was Jesus. More precisely, He claimed to be Jesus. He had a surprisingly high voice, kind of thin, almost Oriental, and He spoke in a New Hampshire accent that was sufficiently local for her to think at first that He was originally from around here, but then of course she quickly remembered that He was Jewish and from Bethlehem and that, therefore, His use of a local New Hampshire accent in speaking English with her was merely a typically Christian courtesy designed to make her feel more at ease than she would have with someone speaking in a foreign accent or, as surely would have been understandable, in a foreign language altogether, ancient Hebrew, for God's sake. She would have thought He was some kind of nut and hung up.

"This Noni Hubner?" were His first words to her.

"Yes."

"This is Jesus. Been thinking of giving a visit."

"Jesus?"

"Yup."

"I must be dreaming," she said. "You sound like my father."

"I am."

"No, I mean my real father."

"I see. Your mother's dead husband."

"Oh my God! How could you know about that?"

"Check your Bible," He said.

"Oh, listen, I . . . I've really had problems, my mother says I'm fragile, and she's right. You shouldn't call up and fool around like this. I've been very depressed lately," she reminded Him.

"I know that. That's why I been thinking of giving a little visit. Might turn things around for you, Noni."

"Okay, fine. Really," she said, her voice trembling. "You do that. I . . . I've got to go now, I hope it's okay to go now."

"Fine. Goodbye."

"Bye."

And that was all. She hung up, her mother came home around 11:00, and Noni kissed her goodnight and went in to her room at the back of the trailer and fell immediately to sleep, dreaming, as might be expected, of her dead father. It was one of those dreams that are so easy to interpret you feel sure your interpretation is wrong, that is, assuming you respect the intelligence of dreams. Noni and her father were standing in the lobby of a large hotel, the Regency Hyatt in Nashville, Tennessee, and Noni's father kissed her goodbye, and when the elevator door opened, he led her forward into it, stepping back himself just as the door closed. The elevator was suspended in a round, glass tube, and it shot up for forty or fifty floors, then came to an abrupt stop. The door opened, and standing in front of her, with His hand extended toward her in the same position as her father's when he had led her into the elevator way below, was Jesus. He was wearing a white robe, as He's usually portrayed, and was smiling. He wasn't very tall, about her height, five foot six, and He was smiling with infinite under-standing and sweetness. She stepped out of the elevator and placed her hand in His. Then she woke up, and it was morning, a late February morning, gray and cold and lightly snowing.

She did tell the police what day it was that she first saw Jesus, February 22nd, 1979, but she did not reveal to them when exactly on that day or where exactly at the trailerpark. They probably were a little embarrassed by the line of questioning they were caught in and, as a consequence, accepted approx-imate answers when exact answers would have been more revealing and possibly more convincing. It was the second afternoon following her phone conversation with Him that she actually saw Jesus. The light snow of the previous day had built to a snowstorm that had abated the next morning, leaving six inches of new powdery snow on top of two feet or more of the old, crusted stuff, and Noni in boots and parka had shoveled a path out to the driveway, which had been cleared early that morning by the kid from town who plowed out most everybody in the park that winter, and afterwards she had walked down the freshly cleared lane under a darkly overcast sky, one of those weighted, low skies that make you think winter will never end, that it will surely press on and down, bearing you beneath it, until finally you lie down in the snow and go to sleep. At the end of the lane she came to the lake, and with the trailers behind her and the wind off the lake in her face, she stood and gazed across the silver-gray ice to the island and, beyond the island, to the humped, pale blue hills. The wind had scraped most of the snow off the lake, drifting it against the shore and the trees and here at the trailerpark against the sides of the trailers. Her pale, pinched face grew paler and drew in upon itself as the steady wind drove against the shore, and as she later said, it seemed to her at that moment more than any other that her life was not worth anything, for she was a stupid, unimaginative young woman who had no gifts for the world and who did not believe in herself enough to believe that her love was worth giving. She had discovered in college that she was stupid and flunked out after two semesters, and she had learned on the commune that she was unimaginative and after taking a lot of acid tried to stab one of the people who truly was imaginative, and in the hospital she had found out that she had no gifts for the world because her dependencies were so great, so she stopped eating and almost died of starvation, and then last summer with Terry she had learned that her love was worth nothing so she refused to have his baby and sent him away. She opened her eyes, wishing the lake were not covered with ice so that she could walk straight into the water and drown, when she saw a man approaching her at a distance, walking slowly over the ice directly toward her. Even from this distance she knew the man was Jesus, and trembling, suddenly warm, all her dark thoughts gone, she raised her hand and waved. But when He waved back, she grew frightened. He was more or less the same as He had been in the dream, except that He wore a heavy maroon poncho over His shoulders, and His feet were wrapped in some kind of bulky mucklucks. He was hatless, and His long, dark brown hair swirled around His bearded face. Turning away from Him, she ran in terror back up the lane to her mother's trailer, dashed breathlessly inside, locking the door behind her, and when she had pulled off her boots and parka, she switched on the television set and sat down in front of it and tried to watch. Her mother was in the kitchen, preparing dinner. "Have a nice walk, dear?" she called. Noni said no, she had seen Jesus walking across the lake toward her, so she had run home. "Oh, dear," her mother said.

Time passed, and winter did indeed turn eventually into spring, soggy and swollen and ravaged, which is almost always the case with New Hampshire springs. Renewal seems almost impossible, except as survival alone indicates a potential for it. Noni saw no more of Jesus during these months, but she thought of Him frequently, and she read her Bible, and along about the end of March she started attending services at a small white building located on one of the side streets in town. It was a single story building that once had been a paint store, just a half block off Main Street, and the two large windows facing the street had been painted dark green, and a sign in white wobbly letters had been made in each of them. The one on the right said: "Church of the New Hampshire Ministry of Jesus Christ"; on the other side were the words, "For where two or three are gathered together in my name, there am I in the midst of them." The people who attended prayer meetings and listened to sermons here were all local people, about twenty in all, and except for Noni, working people. Noni didn't work because she was supported by her mother who, in turn, was supported by her dead husband who, in his turn, had been supported by the selling of life insurance. Nevertheless, she felt comfortable with these people, mostly because they had been unhappy once, too, and now they were not, and when they talked about their time of unhappiness she knew they had felt then just as she felt now, stupid and unimaginative, with no gifts for the world and no belief that her love was worth giving. It was Jesus, they said, who had changed their lives, for He had found their love to be of infinite worth and their gifts, no matter how slight, to be of great value, and their intelligence and imaginative powers to be apocalyptically superior to the intelligence and imagination of the rest of the people in town. They said to her, when she wept, "Did you never read in the Scriptures, 'The stone which the builders rejected, the same is become the head of the corner; this is the Lord's doing, and it is marvelous in our eyes'?" And then in mid-April, shortly after Easter, Noni saw Jesus a second time, this time in the form of a body of light. He appeared to her one night late while she lay in her bed and tried to sleep. Since joining the Fellows of the New Hampshire Ministry of Jesus she had given up smoking marijuana, along with alcoholic beverages, extra-marital sex, cigarette smoking, cursing and cosmetics. All her anxieties and grief fell immediately away, and she came to be filled with the light of Jesus, and when He had passed through her and had gone from her room, she remained filled—but filled now with love, her love of Jesus Himself, and the inescapable logic of that love. From then until now Noni Hubner was a different person. That much was obvious to anyone who knew her, and that much, of course, she told the police when they interrogated her.

She did not quote Him directly, and not just because they didn't happen to ask her what, exactly, Jesus had asked her to do for Him. It was at the Wednesday evening prayer services, while Brother Joel was preaching, that she had received her instructions, or what she regarded as instructions. Brother Joel was in the front of the room, holding the open Bible in one hand, pointing at the ceiling with the other, shouting and beseeching, berating and explicating, imploring and excoriating to the assembled group of about seventeen or eighteen persons, mostly women of middle age and a few men of various ages, and several of the women were shaking their bodies up and down and rolling their heads back and around, as Brother Joel, a young man from Maine who had settled here last year to commence his ministry, moved to the text of Matthew, chapter eighteen, and read the words of Jesus that begin, "Verily I say unto you, Except as ye be converted, and become as little children, ye shall not enter the kingdom of heaven," and when he reached the place where Jesus says, "For the Son of man is come to save that which is lost," Noni felt herself leave her body behind, watched it fall like an emptied husk to the floor next to her chair, as she ascended into a rosy cloud, where she saw the outstretched hand of Jesus, and into His hand she placed her own, while He pointed with His other hand beyond the cloud and down. She thought for a second to check for the wounds in His hands, as Thomas had done, and a cold wind blew against her and took the doubting thoughts with it. She let her gaze flow to where Jesus indicated, beyond the cloud and down, and in the far distance she saw her father's grave.

It was a summer afternoon, just as it had been when they had buried him, and it was her father's grave, all right, though it was covered with grass now, and the stone, a common gray granite stone, was too far away for her to read the inscription, but she knew the location, even though she had not been out to his grave in the cemetery on the hill above the river since the afternoon of his burial. Nor had her mother. His grave was at the top of the hill, near a grove of young maple trees, and when the service had been completed by Reverend Baum, her mother's Congregational minister, Noni and her mother had turned and had got quickly into her mother's Japanese fastback coupe, and they had driven away and had not come back. From that day till now, almost five years later, Noni's mother had spoken of her dead husband as if he were merely absent, as if he had driven downtown to get the paper, and Noni had screamed at her several times that first year, "He's *dead!* Face it, Mother, Daddy's *dead! Dead! Dead!*" And then, after the first year, Noni had ceased screaming, had ceased correcting her mother, had ceased even to reflect on it, and in the end had ceased to observe that, to her mother, the man was neither dead nor alive, for to Noni that's how it was also— her father was neither dead nor alive. But when she came back to her body lying there on the wood floor of the Church of the New Hampshire Ministry of Jesus, she knew her father was waiting for her, his hand reaching out to her, so she rose to her feet, and she left the building.

At the cemetery, standing with the shovel in the circle of light cast by her mother's coupe, she waited and listened and heard Jesus moving in the darkness behind her, heard His bare feet press against the wet grass, while He watched over her, and when the policemen came forward and crossed into the circle of light, walking over her father's grave to her, one of them taking the shovel from her hands, the other holding her arm tightly, as if she might run away, she had no fear. The one holding her arm asked what she thought she was doing, and she told him that she had come to show her mother that her father was dead, so that her mother could be free, as she was free. When they asked where her mother was, Noni was silent for a second and heard Jesus shift His weight in the shadows, and then she told them. While the second policeman went to the coupe and released Noni's mother from her bonds, Noni silently thanked Jesus for His guidance.

The conceit that certain people, especially female people, resemble certain flowers is not very original, but then, it's not without its uses either. Especially if you can obtain enough significant information about the flower to gain at the same time significant information about the person. For instance, Noni Hubner was like a kind of orchid that grows in northern New England—the pink lady's slipper, *Cypripedium acaule.* It may surprise you that orchids actually appear in these latitudes, but they do. And the pink lady's slipper, as it happens, is one of the more common members of the orchid family to appear in New Hampshire, Vermont and Maine, so that you often discover it in open pine woods or on the east-facing slopes of river banks. It blooms in June, when the plant's delicate throat swells and turns pink. Sometimes the orchid is white, but then you'll go back the following June and discover that it has bloomed a deep shade of pink, as if it had suffered a wound in your absence. People who love the sight of these orchids know that regardless of how plentiful they seem, you must not pick them. Nor should you transplant them, as they seldom survive a change of habitat for longer than a few years. In fact, most people who know where you can find such a lovely, fragile flower will not tell you the location, because they are afraid you will go there, and in your affection and delight, will pick the beautiful pink lady's slipper or will try to transplant it nearer your home.

John Perreault

The Catalogue

Katherine, who was otherwise intelligent, did not understand the 20th century. Nevertheless, she was decidedly a part of it, quite connected to it by a network of hopes and fears. In fact, she was a pioneer but did not know it, could not have known it, so complete was her relationship to this new society. She was somewhat of an eccentric, somewhat of a recluse.

Most people in Katherine's time wrote long personal letters and kept diaries. Katherine did neither. The letters she wrote were terse and strictly business, betraying her inner life not at all. Her outer life was ordinary and uneventful.

Katherine did not keep a diary. If she had kept one, what would she have recorded? She was a keen observer of her surroundings, particularly of light: the way the winter light would sometimes fall across the floor of her porch; the light, seemingly in the distance, some summer evenings when suddenly great flocks of birds would screech in the elm; the cold light of Iowa weather. But she had no desire to record her observations or to share them with others. After all, diaries are usually meant to be read by other people, eventually, perhaps after one is dead. Diaries are meant to be found in a trunk years later, allowing someone the thrill of reading something never read by anyone else before, creating the illusion of how life once was. But if Katherine had been possessed of the

John Perreault

need to communicate, she would have been miserable, for she had not the skills.

Her writing was limited to ordering things by mail, plus an occasional letter of inquiry or complaint. Once a month pack-ages would arrive for her at the railroad depot. The packages— sometimes large and heavy, sometimes small—caused no stir. Others in the town received similar packages.

She lived in Iowa, on Main Street, then the only street of a small town on the Rock Island Line. The U.S. Post Office and the Railroad Express were her only connections with the world. Her neighbors did not count. The townspeople bored her. She knew too much about them. The farmers bored her too. About them, she knew nothing at all.

Katherine lived in an L-shaped cottage. According to the plans for the house, the first floor had a kitchen, a bedroom, and a parlor. She lived alone. She cooked and cleaned for herself and no one came to visit. Since she had no need for more than one bedroom, the first floor bedroom became her music room. On the second floor, the area labeled "attic" on the plans became her storage room. The "bedroom" directly above her music room she had made into a bathroom. This took a great deal of doing, but she got it done. The "bedroom" above the parlor was her bedroom.

The house, just as the catalogue had promised, cost her $750. For an additional $53.94 she had an Acme Hummer Soft Coal furnace system installed. It was guaranteed to keep the house at a comfortable 70 degrees, even during the coldest weather. This, she discovered, was an overstatement. Iowa winters can be dreadfully cold. I visited there once in February. The freezing wind whips across the flat and uninflected land. But the furnace in Katherine's basement, the hot air ducts and vents, and her clever management of soft coal, using the rapidly acquired technique of stoking, probably sufficed to keep her relatively cozy.

Iowa summers are hot and humid. I have been to Iowa in the summer too. Katherine enjoyed her front porch, although her view was nothing to speak of. There was, however, a breeze.

Her L-shaped cottage was a modest house, but she was proud of it. Just as the catalogue had promised, it was covered with two coats of paint.

Katherine had never heard of the Shakers. If she had known of them, she would have found their manner of worship and their style of living incomprehensible. Their rooms and furniture, now thought of as classic, would have seemed to her to be mean, stingy, cold and inhuman, rather than practical and elegant. She preferred the ornamental; she liked curlicues, bric-a-brac and large heavy furniture. Except for the kitchen, her house was heavily curtained and dark. This made it cooler in summer and helped to defeat draughts in winter. Direct sunlight damaged fabrics and furniture.

Nevertheless, she owed the texture of her life to the Shakers. In the previous century they had introduced mail order purchasing. They had the idea of selling seeds and herbs in packets. They sold them by mail.

Katherine, using a thick, wonderfully illustrated catalogue, ordered everything she owned by mail from Chicago. I have a facsimile of one of those catalogues. It has 1,184 pages and I have amused myself by imagining ordering from it and imagining someone ordering from it at the time of its original publication.

Why would anyone order by mail?

Katherine no doubt thought of herself as practical. Had not

that been why she had begun ordering from the catalogue? Things were cheaper and usually of better quality than anything she could purchase locally. Also there was an enormous variety. This sometimes made choices difficult, but there was such a variety that she felt that whatever she chose was bound to be unique here in a small Iowa town.

She was obsessed with bargains. The catalogue was an enormous compendium of bargains. The catalogue company could buy very large amounts of things; it even had its own factories scattered across the country. So of course the goods were less expensive. Even Tobias Wayne, the proprietor of Wayne's Drug and Dry Goods Emporium, knew that.

Katherine sometimes glimpsed the packages that Mr. Wayne received. They were exactly like the ones that arrived for her. Mr. Wayne knew a bargain when he saw one. He ordered merchandise from the catalogue and then resold it to the townspeople at a higher price. She compared prices.

She was in the habit of taking Peruvian Wine of Coca, a medicine containing Peruvian bark, coca leaves, ginger, port, wine, and aromatics. It was a treatment for anemia, impurity and impoverishment of the blood, weakness of the limbs, asthma, nervous debility, loss of appetite, malarial complaints, biliousness, stomach disorders, dyspepsia, languor and fatigue. By ordering from the catalogue she saved herself the embarrassment of having to ask Mr. Wayne or his son Joseph for Peruvian Wine of Coca. She was afraid they might think of her as a victim of the complaints listed on the bottle. But more important to her was the money she saved. She ordered three bottles of Peruvian Wine of Coca at a time at $1.75. Tobias Wayne paid the same, but then sold each bottle for a dollar, the price printed on the label.

Along with her mail ordering, Katherine was connected to the Shakers in another regard. The Shakers manufactured many multi-purpose items for the home, the gate-leaf table, for instance, which can be used as a dining table, or when "folded" as a sideboard. Stools that became ladders or portable steps were also produced. The Shakers had a fondness for such things. Katherine did too.

The most important piece of furniture in her parlor was the $14.95 combination Roman divan, sofa, davenport, and couch. It was like having three or four things for the price and space of one. Although she told herself that it was the practicality that appealed to her, in reality it was the cleverness. A Rembrandt used as an ironing board might have delighted her.

It was the idea of the multi-purpose that interested her, more than the reality. Either of the arms could be lowered to make it into a divan. If both were lowered it became a couch. After the first day of experimentation never once did she lower the arms. And yet there was always this possibility. This was what pleased her, gave her a peculiar satisfaction.

Decisions.

Each day there were decisions to be made.

The upholstery for the Roman divan/sofa/davenport/couch had troubled her a great deal: figured, velour, corduroy, plain brocaded velour, fancy brocaded plush, brocaded verona plush, crushed plush, brocaded silk plush, plain silk plush, figured silk damask, panne plush, or car plush. Which should she choose? Car plush was the cheapest but she did not like the way it sounded. She sent for the full set of samples. The 50¢ she paid was later deducted from the cost of the divan. She decided upon Brocaded Verona Plush in green and black with a floral design. Seeing and feeling actual samples of fabric made

John Perreault

it so much easier to decide. The Brocaded Verona Plush was
$1.10 more than the Figured Velour she had for awhile con-
sidered, but finally she decided it was worth it. For $2.10 more
she could have had Crushed Plush, but this seemed needlessly
extravagant.

When the Roman divan/sofa/davenport/couch arrived and
she had no difficulty bolting on the back and legs according
to the instructions, she was pleased. She was glad that she had
not ordered the five-piece parlor suite in mahogany which was
$43.45. The Roman divan/sofa/davenport/couch plus a
Morris chair for $9.57 suited her just fine. And she had saved
$18.93. The $5.75 parlor desk would have been necessary in
either case.

The back of the Morris chair was adjustable to four different
reclining positions by means of a ratchet guaranteed against
breakage. But she had excellent posture and always sat up very
straight so she never moved the back of the Morris chair from
its full upright position. She was as upright as that chair.

This $9.57 Morris chair was made of thoroughly seasoned
and specially selected quarter sawed oak, highly polished and
finished in a rich golden color. There were massive carvings
on the wide curved arms, on the heavy claw feet, and on the
curved front rail. The grimacing faces at the front of the arms
had startled her at first. They had not looked so frightening
in the catalogue illustration, but she became used to them. In
contrast to the Golden Oak, the loose, reversible seat and back
cushions were made of Verona Crushed Plush, an imitation
leather called fabricoid, and genuine leather. They were filled
with hair. All in all, it was a handsome and comfortable chair
and a good buy.

222

The $5.75 parlor desk was a combination desk and bookshelf, also of Golden Oak. It had a large drop-leaf surface that revealed cubby-holes inside. The shelves below had a rod for a curtain. The top of the desk was ornamented with bracket shelves and a French beveled plate mirror. Here is where she kept the catalogue and here is where she did her ordering. She worked on her weekly or biweekly order every day, usually in the afternoon. She sat on a straight back chair made of elm, but also golden in color like the desk and the Morris chair. It was a dining chair but she did not hesitate to use it in the parlor. The top and lower panels of the back were embossed with a floral design and it only cost $1.42.

It was here at the parlor desk that she also looked at stereoscopic views. She had a special 49¢ aluminum stereoscope. It had an aluminum hood engraved and bound with red velvet. The frame was of cherry wood, carefully finished and varnished, with a patented folding handle. It also had a patented aluminum lens lock.

She had over a period of time ordered and received various sets of stereoscopic views. She had one hundred views of the St. Louis World's Fair for 85¢, featuring a Bird's Eye View from the Observation Wheel, The Great Floral Clock, The Mammoth Bird Cage, English Gardens, The Siamese Temple, the Palace of Electricity, The Palace of Mines and Metallurgy, California's Exhibit of Fruit, and Bethlehem Steel Company's Exhibit. Not much of it interested her. The Terrible San Francisco Earthquake and Fire for 75¢ was more exciting.

She could clearly see in three dimensions exactly why Mayor Schmitz had issued his famous proclamation "to kill any man on the spot found stealing or committing any other crime."

John Perreault

The devastation was awesome. She was glad to be living in a small town in Iowa where there were no earthquakes. Safety made boredom endurable.

She also enjoyed the 85¢ 100 Views of the Siege of Port Arthur of the Japanese-Russian War:

"They engaged German officers of high rank to drill their army, and planned their campaign with a passion for detail and unerring precision, against which no amount of valor could prevail. Scientific in everything they did, their army was handled with the greatest regard to hygiene and sanitation. We have views showing them boiling their drinking water in camps. We see their sentries stationed at the rivers to prevent contamination of the water. Their hospital service was an example to the entire world in caring for the wounded upon the battlefield. In one instance the same operation was performed on a Japanese soldier that was performed upon President McKinley. The stomach of this man was removed and sewed up while Russian shot was flying overhead. Yet two weeks later this soldier was homeward bound and told by the surgeons that his recovery was almost certain. A marked characteristic of the little Jap is his intense patriotism. Their empire could never be invaded except by the extermination of every living man."

She also had 100 Views of the Holyland. She only looked at them once. She was not a religious person.

Her favorite set of stereoscopic views was of the catalogue company headquarters which was only 35¢. At the company headquarters $177,619,000 passed through the counting room every single day. There were fifty views and she knew them by heart.

What other entertainments did she have?

She was a solitary person and she entertained herself. Upkeep of the house took a great deal of her time. She also cooked for herself. She ordered from the catalogue. In her music room, however, which according to the catalogue plans was supposed to be the first floor bedroom, she had an $8.95 Oxford Jr. Talking Machine. It came with twenty-four genuine Columbia cylinder records. If ordered separately, the records alone would cost $4.30. They were $2.15 a dozen or 18¢ a piece. Of course, when they came along with the Talking Machine one could not choose the records one received.

Katherine was unhappy with the selection she received. There were entirely too many coon songs. She didn't mind "Billy Bailey, Won't You Come Home." She found it a rather catchy tune. She also liked "Ain't Dat A Shame." She found herself humming these tunes while dusting or engaged in other chores around the house. But she did not like "Coon, Coon, Coon" at all. She wrote a letter of complaint to the catalogue company, struggling with the sentences until the letter was perfect. Letter perfect. Surprisingly it worked.

The reply stated that although the description in the catalogue clearly did not state that persons who ordered the Oxford Jr. Talking Machine would have a choice in regard to the twenty-four records that were included, in her case, although it was highly irregular, because she was such a loyal customer, they would exchange any that she wished to return for titles more to her liking.

She exchanged "Coon, Coon, Coon" for "Meet Me in St. Louis." It was more the principle that mattered, for in the meantime she had become used to most of the records she had originally found offensive or not to her liking. She played "Meet Me in St. Louis" whenever she looked at the stereoscopic views of the St. Louis World's Fair. The conjunction of two things she did not like added up to something else quite pleasant. She did not like "Meet Me in St. Louis" any more than she liked "The Way to Kiss a Girl" or "Safe in the Arms of Jesus."

Religious songs did not interest her. Religion did not interest her. For a long time she had been without God. He did not appeal to her. She had tried reading the Bible, but most of it made no sense to her at all. The catalogue had become her real Bible. She studied it completely from cover to cover. When the new edition came each year it was an important event. Everything she owned had come from the catalogue. She had even indulged in comparative criticism, comparing one edition with another. She knew the price of everything. Upon the descriptive texts she worked her hermeneutics. She found a poetry much deeper than the Song of Songs. The yearly tome was yet a newer New Testament.

Every afternoon she sat down at the parlor desk and worked on her order. Evenings spent in dreaming—the catalogue was her dream book too—were put to the test. The decisions were enormous and she did not take them lightly. She had ordered and received a $3.98 rope portiere that hung in the doorway between the parlor and the music room. It was made of myrtle green velour cord. But how was she to decide between the Nottingham lace curtains at 78¢ a pair or the Point d'Esprit Nottingham at 89¢? Should the curtains be white or cream? She chose Nottingham lace in cream.

When ordering she usually wore her $3.50 cashmere tea gown. It was neatly trimmed around a wide fancy collar with lace. The cuffs and belt center of the back were trimmed with fancy lace to match. Fullness was laid in by three side plaits on each side and the waist was lined with good quality cambric. It was blue.

Sometimes she was foolish in her ordering. One year she decided that she would order a man's suit. She ordered a fancy medium gray dark checked worsted summer coat and pants for $5.29. No one ever visited her so who would know that in the privacy of her L-shaped cottage she was wearing a man's suit? There was something about ordering from the catalogue that made her feel what she imagined to be a slight bit masculine, particularly the listing and tallying up of the prices. She measured herself exactly as the diagram in the catalogue instructed and entered these measurements with the order. The suit arrived. She wore it several times while ordering, but it irritated her. She soon came to her senses. The suit did not fit her correctly and she had not ordered proper male undergarments. The suit had the opposite effect of her intentions; it merely made her feel more feminine.

Sometimes she was completely unable to decide between two items. The catalogue contained mysteries and puzzles that she sometimes took it upon herself to solve. She always took a tablespoon or two of the Peruvian Wine of Coca when she sat at the parlor desk with the catalogue before her. Sometimes that helped, sometimes it did not.

Unable to decide between a steel lawn swing ($8.15) and a four passenger porch swing ($6.85), she let the catalogue itself decide. Unable to decide between a hat trimmed with cherries ($1.99) and a lace-topped, mushroom style hat trimmed with artificial daisies ($2.15); unable to decide between an A.J. Aubrey automatic self-cocking, shell-ejecting revolver ($3.75) and a combination shotgun and rifle ($14.85) that appealed to her love of multi-purpose objects; unable to make a decision, she would let the catalogue decide by opening the pages at random. To facilitate this process, she had developed an elaborate number system of her own.

But this was a special day. It was August 26, 1908. It was a day of completion.

She looks at the catalogue once more. She looks at her list of things that she needs and things that she wants and things that are mysterious. Each item has already been crossed off. Each item has already arrived. Her mind is a blank. The sunlight is particularly intense. After cleaning the parlor windows, she forgets to close the drapes. She takes two more tablespoons of Peruvian Wine of Coca. She decides to look at the stereoscopic views of the catalogue company headquarters one more time. Sometimes this inspires her to order. So in front of her nose in three dimensions she sees, one right after the other, views of the various offices and factories; the cutting of eighteen suits of clothes at one operation with electricity; the shipment room able to handle a hundred thousand orders daily; the automatic telephone switchboard or the Automatic Telephone Girl; the great tunnels in the bowels of the earth extending under all the buildings of the forty acre plant; the wonderful machine with 44 arms and 44 pairs of fingers doing more wonderful work than the human hand can do. . . .

But all the views of the catalogue company headquarters now seem lifeless to her. Once she could imagine herself actually there, but today the activities portrayed seem totally useless and excessive.

She has everything she needs.

She has a $15.35 Chifforobe in her bedroom that combines a dresser and a wardrobe. There is a French plate mirror hinged above the top drawer. The Chifforobe is made of thoroughly air-seasoned and kiln dried Northern hardwood imitating highly figured flaky grained quarter sawed oak. As promised, she cannot distinguish it from genuine quarter sawed oak, but unlike the experts who also cannot tell the difference, she is not certain that she has ever seen genuine quarter sawed oak.

She has a Gem bathroom outfit for $51.10 which includes a highly enameled cast iron bathtub with claw feet; a sink guaranteed not to flake, craze or peel; and a "closet" with a highly polished tank and a polished oak seat.

She has a revolver.

She hears the 3:10 from Chicago pull away from the station, seven blocks away. No more deliveries for her. No more false surprises.

And yet.

She hears a bell. She hears several bells. She sees a wooded spot. In her imagination she traces the sources of the sounds. Turkeys wandering through the woods, belled. Turkey bells. A description and a picture. Hurriedly she consults the index and finds the correct page. Eight Cents Each. Clear Toned Polished Bell Metal Turkey Bell. Diameter, 1¾ inches; enables the flock to be easily located, makes the foxes shy. Furnished complete with strap as shown.

And then it dawns on her.

She has no turkeys. She wants no turkeys. She hates turkeys. She hates their looks; their meat. She has no need for Turkey Bells. Even at 8¢ apiece. And furthermore, each new catalogue is no better than the previous one. She has finally achieved her goal. She has everything she wants. She has erased desire.

Roberta Allen

Gypsies

She's one of the younger children, about eleven years old I'd say. I can't tell how many children actually live there. The gypsies are a very tight group. They have many parties. Many people come and go. I'm glad I live two flights up. I don't hear the noise.

She makes me uncomfortable. She smirks a lot. Her skin is dark olive and her nose is hooked. Her hair is dark and oily. She's chubby. Her sisters, or those I think are her sisters, are prettier. But she is more aggressive, more precocious. She stares hard. I've watched her solicit people on the street. Her mother gives tarot card readings upstairs. Short readings cost $1.

She knows I don't like her. I don't like any of them. Once, when she was about to ask me for something as I approached the outside door, she stopped in mid-sentence and said, "Oh, you're the one who doesn't like me." She said it without emotion. I wonder if she goes to school. I wonder if any of them do. I've seen her on the street late at night. She shows no fear. Perhaps I envy her.

The little darkskinned girl always looks like she has a secret and wants everyone else to know that she's hiding something. I'd be the last one to ask her what she's hiding.

One of her sisters, a girl about fourteen, has a baby. She is fairskinned and delicate looking. In summer, she sits in a chair on the stoop with the baby. She uses a reflector sometimes to get tan. She wears shorts and a halter. The gypsies hang their wash to dry over the outside railings in warm weather. That angers me. I tell the landlord. She is old and afraid of them. "But this is a landmark brownstone," I tell her. "These people disturb everyone on the block." And anyway I want their apartment. I thought they were moving once. They rolled up rugs and discarded furniture on the street. I told the landlord. My mailbox lock was broken the next day. These gypsies are cleaner than the ones before. It seems they were renovating.

Roberta Allen

A Real Act

I know that he's doing it somewhere. Maybe it has already happened. Perhaps it will be in an hour or so. But I know that I will not see him again. He told me. I couldn't say anything. I knew one day would be this day. Perhaps I'm relieved to know it's today. I won't have to wait anymore. The policeman will simply come to the door and make it official. But I'll already know. Only mother will be shocked. I can't tell anyone what I know, yet. Tomorrow will be different. But mother will tell me to lie because she'll be ashamed of what he's doing. But I will tell my close friend anyway. I feel so strange. What should I be doing? He's already acted dead for weeks now. Mother thinks it's just an act. I know it's a real act. Why am I the only one to know?

Susan does crazy things all the time. The other kids just shake their heads when they see her doing crazy things. I'm glad she's my friend right now. She doesn't ask questions. When I suggested we drink scotch during lunch break today she simply went outside and bought a pint somehow. I've never done that. We drank it together in a stall in the ladies' room at school. We were laughing. I needed to laugh. But it was dark laughter. All the time I kept on wondering what was happening to him. Was it over yet?

Aside from the drinking it was like any other school day. Except that it wasn't. All the time I kept on feeling that a gray person who looked just like me was mimicking my every motion. She was beside me every minute. She was the one who knew. I tried to push her away but she wouldn't budge. I wasn't like everyone else anymore. I knew that I would never be like everyone else ever again.

I had only been home an hour or so when the doorbell rang. Mother went to answer it. When I saw the policeman I went to my room because I knew he was only making it official.

Richard Padget

A Brief Guide to the Fall Repertory

Much has been neglected it seems in the laws that regulate
cannons. Not that we should blame our ancestors as
much as we should strive to forget them; what is now commonplace was then unthinkable. Indeed much of what we, the mer-
chants and scientists, pinned our hopes on, the laws that protected our ancestors so ably from the black winds that howl
through the heated chambers of the unpredictable mind, are
deflatable gestures whose impotence all but the weakest are
aware of. And there is little comfort, despite the claims of a
few well-fed public officials, that at last we give flesh to the
fears that have haunted us since the last blue crane departed
for the desert.

Easter morning. And hardly had we knocked the sleep from
our skulls and filed out quietly behind the cats on to the front
porch, where the nightwork of the snails was fresh on the
humid concrete, than we noticed an enormous grey cannon,
a howitzer mounted on a battlewagon, parked on the lawn
across the street, aimed as we came to realize at our bedroom
window. The smell emanated from a trench of dead fish immediately in front of the gun. Our neighbor, reputedly a foreman
in some distant brassiere factory, with a reputation for beating
his children with wet switches on their bare bottoms, was fast

asleep in a green deck chair to the left of the gun. Watt had apparently worked the night through, as soiled paper cups, several coffee thermoses, and a crumpled libretto were strewn near his slippers. He wore a grey dressing gown girdled by green ribbon. But most disturbing of all were the crates stacked to the right of the gun marked: *Heavy Ordinance—Do Not Jostle!*

Christ now what'a we do, I asked my wife. Has anything happened? Any rhubarbs or brouhahas between you and the Watts?

Catherine reminded me of the danger of the first question and shook her head no, pointing out that the poor guy was probably too exhausted to raise the barrel. It's Easter baby, maybe there's a parade.

With the gun mounted and ready for rapid deployment it would seem that this was a possibility. Yet we both knew that ours' is a town given not to parades. Even immigrants perceive this after a few hours. Forget our natural-historical repugnance of fanfare, the streets themselves are intolerable. Twisting and torturous they are narrow in so many places as to make passage by two silent and robust types approaching simultaneously impossible. They lead nowhere but through an intricate design. Yet following the defeat of the Huns in '45, a hue and cry went up for a parade as it did in all cities and towns across the land and liberated Europe. The local Lions Club countersigned a loan from the capital of a three hundred piece marching orchestra, complete with balloon salesmen and dancing ladies who were nothing more than silk and flashing scarves. The old, who had opposed the parade as madness from the outset, snickered in their beards and grey hands as the drum major lifted his baton and pranced merrily out of the square with the orchestra blaring behind him. By the end of the first quarter mile, all was in pieces. Unable to maintain ranks in streets where metaphysicians had held the upper hand in planning for so long, the orchestra began to fragment into clashing ensembles and lonely solos moments after quitting the square. When they passed the reviewing stand, only a handful of musicians followed the marching major, while the great body of the orchestra had disintegrated, and was lost spreading music to every conceivable pocket of the town.

Their end was not conclusive and even now, years after the final performance, one finds remnants here and there of the once great orchestra: a bugler or a bassoonist or a man with a cymbal, his uniform filthy with the gold braids in shreds at his shoulders, his instrument silent and all but worn away, yet his feet still shuffling to a cadence that time has been powerless to obviate.

Later, long after the balloons had been freed and the dancing ladies packed in buses back to the capital, a finger was lifted, aimed at the sky:

Look!

What is it?

Look!

What is it?

Like a drop of undispersed blue pigment, it began to lower itself slowly around the town in ever contracting concentric circles. Not 'til it was close did we identify what we were seeing and then by the shrill cry audible through the brass and blue music.

It was never determined whether the crane landed that night in the town or returned by an invisible route or darkness to fetch the others—whether it was harbinger or mere reconnaissance. But from a cleft in the clouds the following morning, the flock flew single file, following a course of circumlocution and sophistry before touching down by the bridge near the tannery. And though everyone knew that the sadness of the oboes had attracted them, Aaron Latch, the bishop's assistant, had other ideas:

> You people take a bunch'a blue cranes flying into town and turn it into a parenthetical remark from the Devil. Why Satan can kiss my rosy-red fat ones. I'm not talkin' about a device for measuring curvature, or a sharp pointed needle process, or even a domestic apparatus for making a curve wind away from the center; I'm talkin' about a constant uttered breath, booty, plunder and confused speech, the porous, elastic, fibrous framework left when certain sea-creatures perish. Do you think for a minute the great universities of Paris pass the plate to the mystics? They've confined that operation to a branch of geometry. These blue cranes are nothin' but another confetti raid: little pieces of colored paper tossed up for purposes of propaganda, contusion and sickness, conserved and compounded with sugar, tapering upward into a hollow biscuit . . .

Well the congregation never let him finish the sermon. Cancel the coffee and the cake sale, 'cause the crowd fell out of the church whistling and hooting and catcalling. The anticlerical faction of the community pounced upon the issue like jackals, they petted the cranes, held rallies and barbecues at which speaker after speaker railed against the dogma, canon, and heavy ordinance of the church.

Watt, meanwhile, was circling the gun cautiously with a chamois and an oil can. He had changed his clothes, that is, removed his dressing gown and pitched it triumphantly into the trench of dead fish. Wearing plaid bermuda shorts and the white earmuffs fashioned at the factory, Watt shifted his gaze to the window across the street where a man and a woman peered back through binoculars. Heavily disadvantaged by the long-range visionary apparatus of his neighbors Watt went to his garage for opera glasses. And when the Websters saw, they fell back, flattening themselves against the wall either side of the window. Watt focused into the room cleanly now and out again through a rear window, into the backyard and beyond to the tannery, where the blue bottle flies buzzed about the antlers and entrails.

All efforts to have the bone and gore heaped by the tannery gate hauled to a more suitable location had failed. None of the old formulas provided for such a transfer, while an attempt to pass an amendment legitimizing the operation had met bitter, insurmountable resistance.

Indeed, some went so far as to insist that the blood-soaked sand surrounding the tannery was quaint, that maggots in their own way were not without charm and certainly a part of our local tradition. These homilies, espoused mainly by the Ladies Auxiliary, had a hand in defeating the measure. But the most compelling slogan of all, dreamed in a fever by the Central Organizing Committee of the Old Guard To Save the Bone and Gore Heaped by the Tannery, that plunged the reformists when they tried to reply into whirlpools of rhetoric from which no escape or clarification was ever again possible, consisted of five tiny words hammered into a question: Christ, now what'a we do?

Implying a catastrophe, indeed the imminent collapse of the entire social order, the question struck fear in the hearts of the citizens and remanded the amendment to the farthest reaches of obscurity.

But the Central Committee did not stop there. Armed with old money they lifted the question from organized debate and postered the town with it. Indeed, the red and black signs became as familiar as the cranes had been. And three times a day, through loudspeakers donated by a local evangelist, we interrupt this broadcast to bring you the following: the sound of wind passing through an abandoned mobile home, the distant barely perceptible wail of a cat or a new-born baby, and then a voice quivering around the question: Christ, now what'a we do?

Everywhere one went one found the question trembling like jelly on the lips of the townsfolk. All argument, public or private, began and ended with the question. For, unrestricted to a specific, mutually agreed upon disaster, it roamed over the whole landscape of human fear and confusion, extolling the consequences of every catastrophe in the minds of the populace.

Thus, as a result of an effective yet runaway scare campaign, the town, save only for Aaron Latch who had revised his sermon and condensed it into a single sentence, was obsessed by the coming of something unnameable. Grown men, including those of the Central Committee, began complaining of headaches and all manner of petty illness out of sheer worry. Likewise, the increase in premature births was dramatic among the mothers. Yet the question inevitably had a positive result, effecting the resurgence, however brief, of at least two groups: the numerologists, out of favor since the invention of analytic geometry; and the scattered remnants of the once great orchestra.

Since the afternoon of the parade, the musicians, unbeknownst to the town, had remained in close contact with one another through the agency of their instruments and various provisions of the union contract. And though they were never able to re-group and form the ranks that had made them the pride of the capital, the training of each had taught him to act in concert with his fellows even if he could not see them. All that was needed was a theme around which to organize and improvise. And this the question, blasted through loud-speakers at nine in the morning, three in the afternoon, and nine at night, provided—a theme, thrice repeated, at regular intervals, and heard by all of them.

The first to respond were the tenor oboes with the violins playing behind them. Then, rather tentatively at first, came the cellos and the tubas and the trumpets, then the rest of the woodwinds joined in with the drums and other survivors of the percussion section, followed finally by the remaining strings and last remnants of the brass. Each musician seemed to know his place in the piece instinctively and made note of his music by means of pad and pen furnished by the local Lions Club. By Thursday the streets were alive with the strains of an unnamed yet exuberant rondo.

The numerologists, eager for an opportunity to vent their views, dusted off their robes when they heard the music and preached its structure and mystical significance in terms of the abacus:

Observe that the eighth note predominates in the overly long, six-hour spans between each blast of the theme. Eight: the perfect number on which to meditate. Yet the primary number is three; the theme thrice repeated, the hours of its repetition each a multiple of three as are the number of hours separating them. Three: the mathematical equivalent of good multiplied by two equals six, which occurs three times daily— six sixty six, leading us therefore into the darkest, most disturbing pages of *Revelations* and bringing us face to face with the Four Horsemen of the Apocalypse, ladies and gentlemen, thank you.

This was similar to what Aaron Latch, the bishop's assistant, had been harping about from a singularly obscure angle since the question was first posed by members of the Central Committee. Focusing on Abaddon, angel of the abyss, who Latch claimed visited these parts on a regular, fibrous framework for purposes of propaganda, contusion and sickness, slowly he recaptured the crowd lost in the days of the blue cranes. His popularity reached a pinnacle in early April. Yet having filled the church that momentous weekend, he returned the next to find it deserted again as a result of the rondo completed the previous Thursday.

Full of life and vigor, the music had brought the people into the streets smiling again, and the last thing anyone wanted to hear was the bishop's assistant expound for hours on a cataclysm that the numerologists claimed was their invention and over which the town had worried anyway for several weeks apparently without cause. For here were the musicians performing as gracefully and as cheerfully as the condition of their instruments allowed, dispelling forever a rumor that had circulated during the darkest days of the question: that they, the musicians, were no longer actual beings but illusions created by quivering light on the remembered past. It was of such great communal comfort to know the truth that a feast day was declared. And there was even talk of a movie. As for the question, it lost all meaning and was admired strictly for its brevity and adaptability to music. Even the bishop's assistant was persuaded to join the party. For having lived here most of his life Latch knew the flock would someday return and in preparation of that momentous occasion began work on a new sermon, which according to those privy to the notebooks, rivals all previous condemnations and papal bulls on numerical interpretations of good living.

Yet to return to Watt. Only he remained despondent amid the festive exuberance, bells and roman candles. Perhaps because he guessed, and guessed correctly, that the music would die the moment the question was repealed and that the pads and pens would be stripped from the orchestra and shipped to the capital as part of a larger, more disturbing proof. Or maybe it was the bunting and large color photographs of dancing ladies' silk and flashing scarves, or the food piled high on the tables outside the armory, all of which ran counter, it's true, to our natural-historical repugnance of fanfare, but for which, under the circumstances and brilliant moon, we have chosen to forgive ourselves.

Then again, Watt's gloom may harken back to an earlier era: to the afternoon in October perhaps when the last blue crane departed for the desert. It is hard to reconcile this idea with court records however, which indicate that Watt was arrested on three separate occasions for running recklessly through the flocks in an obvious premeditated attempt to scatter them.

Watt never speaks. He appears lost in an all-consuming project utilizing maps, charts, opera glasses, the gun, as well as a device for measuring curvature. Even at the trial at which he was called upon to defend his right to point the howitzer at our house, his lawyers did the talking. And citing a lack of legislation and legal precedent, the court ruled unanimously in Watt's favor, while upholding our right to appeal to a higher more universal authority.

In the meantime, we rely upon our patience and wits and on the kindness of others. The Block Association, for example, has supported our position vigorously, protesting a precedent the effects of which are already visible in the booming demand for ordinance. They have urged us to take direct offensive action, to erect a mirror in place of the window, thereby giving Watt a taste of his own medicine. Yet as Catherine points out, Watt is a wholly unstable character. And such an action as that might provoke him into something like visual suicide.

Most recently, then, the Block Association has taken their protest directly to Watt, with threats of an amendment before the General Assembly. Watt merely shrugs and tosses another fish into the trench of decay. He is neither a fool nor a stranger, knowing full well that any attempt to amend the statutes is liable to pitch the town into a cataclysm of despair from which the musicians can no longer rescue us. And so we endure, not only Watt, but the claims of the old guard and various radical newspapers, whose heroic headlines and alleged good humor are undercut always by a longing for the music of the past.

John Ashbery

Description of a Masque

The persimmon velvet curtain rose swiftly to reveal a space of uncertain dimensions and perspective. At the lower left was a grotto, the cave of Mania, goddess of confusion. Larches, alders and Douglas fir were planted so thickly around the entrance that one could scarcely make it out. In the dooryard a hyena chained to a pole slunk back and forth, back and forth, continually measuring the length of its chain, emitting the well-known laughing sound all the while, except at intervals when what appeared to be fragments of speech would issue from its maw. It was difficult to hear the words, let alone understand them, though now and then a phrase like "Up your arse!" or "Turn the rascals out!" could be distinguished for a moment, before subsiding into a confused chatter. Close by the entrance to the grotto was a metal shoescraper in the form of a hyena, and very like this particular one, whose fur was a grayish-white faintly tinged with pink, and scattered over with foul, liver-colored spots. On the other side of the dooryard opposite the hyena's pole was a graceful statue of Mercury on a low, gilded pedestal, facing out toward the audience with an expression of delighted surprise on his face. The statue seemed to be made of lead or some other dull metal, painted an off-white which had begun to flake in places, revealing the metal beneath which was of almost the same color. As yet there was no sign of the invisible proprietress of the grotto.

A little to the right and about eight feet above this scene, another seemed to hover in mid-air. It suggested the interior of an English pub, as it might be imitated in Paris. Behind the bar, opposite the spectators in the audience, was a mural adapted from a Tenniel illustration for *Through the Looking Glass*—the famous one in which a fish in a footman's livery holds out a large envelope to a frog footman who has just emerged onto the front stoop of a small house, while in the background, partially concealed by the trunk of a tree, Alice lurks, an expression of amusement on her face. Time and the fumes of a public house had darkened the colors almost to a rich mahoghany glow, and if one had not known the illustration it would have been difficult to make out some of the details.

Seven actors and actresses, representing seven nursery-rhyme characters, populated the scene. Behind the bar the bald barman, Georgie Porgie, stood motionless, gazing out at the audience. In front and a little to his left, lounging on a tall stool, was Little Jack Horner, in fact quite a tall and roguish-looking young man wearing a trench coat and expensive blue jeans; he had placed his camera on the bar near him. He too faced out toward the audience. In front of him, his back to the audience, Little Boy Blue partially knelt before him, apparently performing an act of fellatio on him. Boy Blue was entirely clothed in blue denim, of an ordinary kind.

To their left, Simple Simon and the Pie Man stood facing each other in profile. The Pie Man's gaze was directed toward the male couple at the center of the bar; at the same time he continually offered and withdrew a pie coveted by Simon, whose attention was divided between the pie and the scene behind him, at which he kept glancing over his shoulder, immediately turning back toward the pie as the Pie Man with-

John Ashbery

drew it, Simon all the time pretending to fumble in his pocket for a penny. The Pie Man was dressed like a French baker's apprentice, in a white blouse and blue-and-white checked pants; he appeared to be about twenty-eight years of age. Simon was about the same age, but he was wearing a Buster Brown outfit, with a wide-brimmed hat, dark blue blazer and short pants, and a large red bow tie.

At the opposite end of the bar sat two young women, their backs to the audience, apparently engaged in conversation. The first, Polly Flinders, was wearing a strapless dress of ash-colored chiffon with a narrow silver belt. She sat closest to Jack Horner and Boy Blue, but paid no attention to them and turned frequently toward her companion, at the same time puffing on a cigarette in a shiny black cigarette holder and sipping a martini straight up with an olive. Daffy Down Dilly, the other young woman, had long straight blonde hair which had obviously been brushed excessively so that it gleamed when it caught the light; it was several shades of blonde in easily distinguishable streaks. She wore a long emerald-green velvet gown cut very low in back, and held up by glittering rhinestone straps; her yellow lace-edged petticoat hung down about an inch and a half below the hem of her gown. She did not smoke but from time to time sipped through a straw on a whiskey sour, also straight up. Although she frequently faced in the direction of the other characters when she turned toward Polly, she too paid them no mind.

After a few moments Jack seemed to grow weary of Boy Blue's attentions and gave him a brisk shove which sent him sprawl-ing on the floor, where he walked about on all fours barking like a dog for several minutes, causing the hyena in the bottom left tableau to stop its own prowling and fall silent except for an occasional whimper, as though wondering where the barking were coming from. Soon Boy Blue curled up in front of the bar and pretended to fall asleep, resting his head on the brass rail, and the hyena continued as before. Jack rearranged his clothing and turned toward the barman, who handed him another drink. At this point the statue of Mercury stepped from its pedestal and seemed to float upward into the bar scene, landing on tiptoe between Jack and Simple Simon. After a deep bow in the direction of the ladies, who ignored him, he turned to face the audience and delivered the following short speech.

"My fellow prisoners, we have no idea how long each of us has been in this town and how long each of us intends to stay, although I have reason to believe that the lady in green over there is a fairly recent arrival. My point, however, is this. Instead of loitering this way, we should all become part of a collective movement, get involved with each other and with our contemporaries on as many levels as possible. No one will disagree that there is much to be gained from contact with one another, and I, as a god, feel it even more keenly than you do. My understanding, though universal, lacks the personal touch and the local color which would make it meaningful to me."

These words seemed to produce an uneasiness among the other patrons of the bar. Even Little Boy Blue stopped pretending to be asleep and glanced warily at the newcomer. The two girls had left off conversing. After a few moments Daffy got down off her bar stool and walked over to Mercury. Opening a green brocade pocketbook, she pulled out a small revolver and shot him in the chest. The bullet passed through him without harming him and imbedded itself in the fish in the mural behind the bar, causing it to lurch forward regurgitating blood and drop the envelope, which produced a loud report and a flash like a magnesium flare that illuminated an expression of anger and fear on Alice's face, as she hastily clapped her hands over her ears. Then the whole stage was plunged in darkness, the last thing remaining visible being the apparently permanent smile on Mercury's face—still astonished and delighted, and bearing no trace of malice.

Little by little the darkness began to dissipate, and a forest scene similar to that in the mural was revealed. It had moved forward to fill the space formerly occupied by the bar and its customers, and was much neater and tidier than the forest in the mural had been. The trees were more or less the same size and shape, and planted equidistant from each other. There was no forest undergrowth, no dead leaves or rotting treetrunks on the ground; the grass under the trees was as green and well kept as that of a lawn. This was because the scene represented a dream of Mania (whose grotto was still visible in the lower left-hand corner of the stage), and, since she was the goddess of confusion, her dream revealed no trace of confusion, or at any rate presented a confusing absence of confusion. On a white banner threaded through some of the branches of the trees in the foreground the sentence "It's an Ongoing Thing" was printed in scarlet letters. To the left, toward the rear of the scene, Alice appeared to be asleep at the base of a treetrunk, with a pig dressed in baby clothes asleep in her lap. An invisible orchestra in the pit intoned the "March" from Grieg's *Sigurd Jorsalfar*. A group of hobos who had previously been hidden behind the trees moved to the center of the stage and began to perform a slow-moving ballet to the music. Each was dressed identically in baggy black-and-white checked trousers held up by white suspenders fastened with red buttons, a crumpled black swallowtail coat, red flannel undershirt, brown derby hat and white gloves with black stripes outlining the contours of the wrist bones, and each held in his right hand an extinguished cigar butt with a fat gray puffy ash affixed to it. Moving delicately on point, the group formed an ever-narrowing semi-circle around Alice and the sleeping pig, when a sudden snort from the latter startled them and each disappeared behind a tree. At this moment Mania emerged from her grotto dressed in a gown of sapphire-blue tulle studded with blue sequins, cradling a sheaf of white gladioli in the crook of one arm and with her other hand holding aloft a wand with a gilt cardboard star at its tip. Only her curiously unkempt hair marred the somewhat dated elegance of her toilette. Deftly detaching the hyena's chain from its post, she allowed the beast to lead her upward to the forest scene where the hobos had each begun to peek out from behind his treetrunk. Like the Wilis in *Giselle*, they appeared mesmerized by the apparition of the goddess, swaying to the movement of her star-tipped wand as she waved it, describing wide arcs around herself. None dared draw too close, however, for if they did so the snarling, slavering hyena would lurch forward, straining at its chain. At length she let her wand droop toward the ground, and after gazing pensively downward for some moments she raised her head and, tossing back her matted curls, spoke thus:

"My sister *Hecat*, who sometimes accompanies me on midnight rides to nameless and indescribable places, warned me of this dell, seemingly laid out for the Sunday strolls of civil servants, but in reality the haunt of drifters and retarded children. *You*," she cried, shaking her wand at the corps de ballet of hobos, who stumbled and fell over each other in their frantic attempt to get away from her, "You who oppress even my dreams, where a perverse order should reign but where I

John Ashbery

find instead traces of the lunacy that besets my waking hours, are accomplices in all this, comical and ineffectual though you pretend to be. As for that creature" (here she gestured toward the sleeping Alice), "she knows only too well the implications of her presence here with that grotesque changeling, and how these constitute a reflection on my inward character as illustrated in my outward appearance, such as this spangled gown and these tangled tresses, meant to epitomize the confusion which is the one source of my living being, but which in these ambiguous surroundings, neither true fantasy nor clean-cut reality, keeps me at bay until I can no longer see the woman I once was. I shall not rest until I have erased all of this from my thoughts, or (which is more likely) incorporated it into the confusing scheme I have erected around me for my support and glorification."

At this there was some whispering and apprehensive regrouping among the hobos; meanwhile Alice and the pig slept on oblivious, the latter's snores having become more relaxed and peaceful than before. Mania continued to stride back and forth, impetuously stabbing her wand into the ground. Suddenly a black horse with a rider swathed in a dark cloak and with a dark sombrero pulled down over his face approached quickly along a path leading through the trees from the right of the stage. Without dismounting or revealing his face the stranger accosted the lady:

Stranger: Why do you pace back and forth like this, ignoring the critical reality of this scene, or pretending that it is a monstrosity of reason sent by some envious commonsensical deity to confound and humiliate you? You might have been considered beautiful, and an ornament even to such a curious setting as this, had you not persisted in spoiling the clear and surprising outline of your character, and leading around this hideous misshapen beast as though to scare off any who might have approached you so as to admire you.

Mania: I am as I am, and in that I am happy, and care nothing for the opinion of others. The very idea of the idea others might entertain of me is as a poison to me, pushing me to flee farther into wastes even less hospitable and more treacherously combined of irregular elements than this one. As for my pet hyena, beauty is in the eye of the beholder; at least, I find him beautiful, and, unlike other beasts, he has the ability to laugh and sneer at the spectacle around us.

Stranger: Come with me, and I will take you into the presence of one at whose court beauty and irrationality reign alternately, and never tread on each other's toes as do your unsightly followers [more whispering and gesturing among the hobos], where your own pronounced contours may flourish and be judged for what they are worth, while the anomalies of the room you happen to be in or the disturbing letters and phone calls that hamper your free unorthodox development will melt away like crystal rivulets leaving a glacier, and you may dwell in the accident of your character forever.

Mania: You speak well, and if all there is as you say, I am convinced and will accompany you gladly. But before doing so I must ask you two questions. First, what is the name of her to whose palace you purpose to lead me; and second, may I bring my hyena along?

Stranger: As to the first question, that I may not answer now, but you'll find out soon enough, never fear. As to the second, the answer is yes, providing it behaves itself.

The lady mounted the stranger's steed with his help, and sat sideways, with the hyena on its chain trotting along behind them. As they rode back into the woods the forest faded away and the scene became an immense metallic sky in which a huge lead-colored sphere or disc—impossible to determine which—seemed to float midway between the proscenium and the floor of the stage. At right and left behind the footlights some of the hobos, reduced almost to midget size, rushed back and forth gesticulating at the strange orb that hung above them; with them mingled a few nursery-rhyme characters such as the Knave of Hearts and the Pie Man, who seemed to be looking around uneasily for Simon. All were puzzled or terrified by the strange new apparition, which seemed to grow darker and denser while the sky surrounding it stayed the same white-metal color.

Alice, awaking from her slumber, stood up and joined the group at the front of the stage, leaving the pig in its baby clothes to scamper off into the wings. Wiping away some strands of hair that had fallen across her forehead and seeming to become aware of the changed landscape around her, she turned to the others and asked, "What happens now?"

In reply, Jack Horner, who had been gazing at the camera in his hand with an expression of ironic detachment, like Hamlet contemplating the skull of Yorick, jerked his head upward toward the banner whose scarlet motto still blazed brightly, though the trees that supported it were fast fading in the glare from the sky. Alice too looked up, noticing it for the first time.

"I see," she said at length. "A process of duration has been set in motion around us, though there is no indication I can see that any of us is involved in it. If that is the case, what conclusion are we to draw? Why are we here, if even such a nebulous concept as "here" is to be allowed us? What are we to do?"

At this the Knave of Hearts stepped forward and cast his eyes modestly toward the ground. "I see separate, soft pain, lady," he said. "The likes of these"—he indicated with a sweep of his arm the group of hobos and others who had subsided into worried reclining poses in the background—"who know not what they are, or what they mean, I isolate from the serious business of creatures such as we, both more ordinary and more distinguished than the common herd of anesthetized earthlings. It is so that we may question more acutely the sphere into which we have been thrust, that threatens to smother us at every second and above which we rise triumphant with each breath we draw. At least, that is the way I see it."

"Then you are a fool as well as a knave," Jack answered angrily, "since you don't seem to realize that the sphere is escaping us, rather than the reverse, and that in a moment it will have become one less thing to carry."

As he spoke the stage grew very dark, so that the circle in the sky finally seemed light by contrast, while a soft wail arose from the instruments in the orchestra pit.

"I suspect the mischief of Mercury in all this," muttered Jack, keeping a weather eye on the heavens. "For though some believe Hermes' lineage to be celestial, others maintain that he is of infernal origin, and emerges on earth to do the errands of Pluto and Proserpine on the rare occasions when they have business here."

The lights slowly came up again, revealing a perspective view of a busy main street in a large American city. The dark outline of the disc still persisted in the sky, yet the climate seemed warm and sunny, though there were Christmas decorations strung across the street and along the facades of department stores, and on a nearby street corner stood a Salvation Army Santa Claus with his bell and cauldron. It could have been downtown Los Angeles in the late 30s or early to mid 40s, judging from the women's fashions and the models of cars that crawled along the street as though pulled by invisible strings.

Walking in place on a sidewalk which was actually a treadmill moving toward the back of the stage was a couple in their early thirties. Mania (for the woman was none other than she) was dressed in the style of Joan Crawford in *Mildred Pierce*, in a severe suit with padded shoulders and a pillbox with a veil crowning the pin curls of her upswept hairdo, which also cascaded to her shoulders, ending in more pin curls. Instead of the sheaf of gladioli she now clutched a blocky handbag suspended on a strap over her shoulder, and in place of the hyena, one of those *little white dogs* on the end of a leash kept sniffing the legs of pedestrians who were in truth mere celluloid phantoms, part of the process shot which made up the whole downtown backdrop. The man at her side wore a broad-brimmed hat, loose-fitting sport coat and baggy gabardine slacks; he bore a certain resemblance to the actor Bruce Bennett but closer inspection revealed him to be the statue of Mercury, with the paint still peeling from his face around the empty eye sockets. At first it looked as though the two were enjoying the holiday atmosphere and drinking in the sights and sounds of the city. Gradually, however, Mania's expression darkened; finally she stopped in the middle of the sidewalk and pulled at her escort's sleeve.

"Listen, Herman," she said, perhaps addressing Bruce Bennett by his real name, Herman Brix, "you said you were going to take me to this swell place and all, where I was supposed to meet a lot of interesting people who could help me in my career. All we do is walk down this dopey street looking in store windows and waiting for the stoplights to change. Is this your idea of a good time?"

"But this is all part of it, hon, part of what I promised you," Mercury rejoined. "Don't you feel the atmosphere yet? That powder-blue sky of the eternal postcard, with the haze of mountain peaks barely visible; the salmon-colored pavement with its little green and blue cars that look so still though they are supposed to be in motion? The window shoppers, people like you and me . . . ?"

"*That's* what I thought," Mania pouted, stamping one of her feet in its platform shoe so loudly that several of the extras turned to look. "Atmosphere—that's what it was all along, wasn't it? A question of ambience, poetry, something like that. I might as well have stayed in my cave for all the good it's going to do me. After all, I'm used to not blending in with the environment—it's my business not to. But I thought you were going to take me away from all that, to some place where scenery made no difference any more, where I could be what everybody accuses me of being and what I suppose I must be— my tired, tyrannical self, as separate from local color as geometry is from the hideous verticals of these avenues and buildings and the festoons that extend them into the shrinking consciousness. Have you forgotten the words of St. Augustine: 'Multiply in your imagination the light of the sun, make it greater and brighter as you will, a thousand times or out of number. God will not be there'?"

Then we all realized what should have been obvious from the start: that the setting would go on evolving eternally, rolling its waves across our vision like an ocean, each one new yet recognizably a part of the same series, which was creation itself. Scenes from movies, plays, operas, television; decisive or little-known moments from history; pre-natal and other early memories from our own solitary, separate pasts; moments yet to come from life or art; calamities or moments of relaxation; universal or personal tragedies; or little vignettes from daily life that you just had to stop and laugh at, they were so funny, like the dog chasing its tail on the living-room rug. The sunny city in California faded away and another scene took its place, and another and another. And the corollary of all this was that we would go on witnessing these tableaux, not that anything prevented us from leaving the theater but there was no alternative to our interest in finding out what would happen next. This was the only thing that mattered for us, so we stayed on although we could have stood up and walked away in disgust at any given moment. And event followed event according to an inner logic of its own. We saw the set for the first act of *La Boheme*, picturesque poverty on a scale large enough to fill the stages of the world's greatest opera houses, from Leningrad to Buenos Aires, punctuated only by a skylight, an easel or two and a stove with a smoking stovepipe, but entirely filled up with the boisterous and sincere camaraderie of Rodolfo, Marcello, Colline and their friends; a ripe, generous atmosphere into which Mimi is introduced like the first splinter of unavoidable death, and the scene melts imperceptibly into the terrace of the Cafe Momus where the friends have gathered to drink and discuss philosophy, when suddenly the blonde actress who had earlier been seen as Daffy Down Dilly returns as Musetta, mocking her elderly protector and pouring out peal after peal of deathless melody concerning the joys and advantages of life as a *grisette*, meanwhile clutching a small velvet handbag in which the contour of a small revolver was clearly visible, for as we well knew from previous experience, she was the symbol of the unexpectedness and exuberance of death, which we had waited to have come round again and which we would be meeting many times more during the course of the performance. There were murky scenes from television with a preponderance of excerpts from Jacques Cousteau documentaries with snorkeling figures disappearing down aqueous perspectives, past arrangements of coral still-lifes and white, fanlike creatures made of snowy tripe whose trailing vinelike tentacles could paralyze a man for life, and a seeming excess of silver bubbles constantly being emitted from here and there to sweep upward to the top of the screen, where they vanished. There were old clips from *Lucy*, *Lassie* and *The Waltons*; there was Walter Cronkite bidding us an urgent good evening years ago. Mostly there were just moments: a street corner viewed from above, bare branches flailing the sky, a child in a doorway, a painted Pennsylvania Dutch chest, a full moon disappearing behind a dark cloud to the accompaniment of a Japanese flute, a ballerina in a frosted white dress lifted up into the light.

Always behind it the circle in the sky remained fixed like a ghost on a television screen. The setting was now the last act of Ibsen's *When We Dead Awaken*: "A wild, broken mountain top, with a sheer precipice behind. To the right tower snowy peaks, losing themselves high up in drifting mist. To the left, on a scree, stands an old, tumbledown hut. It is early morning. Dawn is breaking, the sun has not yet risen." Here the disc in the sky could begin to take on the properties of the sun that had been denied it for so long: as though made of wet wool, it began little by little to soak up and distribute light. The figure of Mercury had become both more theatrical and more human:

no longer a statue, he was draped in a freshly laundered chlamys that set off his well-formed but slight physique; the broad-brimmed *petasus* sat charmingly on his curls. He sat, legs spread apart, on an iron park bench, digging absent-mindedly at the ground with his staff from which leaves rather than serpents sprouted, occasionally bending over to scratch the part of his heel behind the strap of his winged sandal. The morning mists were evaporating; the light was becoming the ordinary yellow daylight of the theater. Resting both hands on his staff, he leaned forward to address the audience, cocking his head in the shrewd bumpkin manner of a Will Rogers.

"So you think I have it, after all, or that I've found it? And you may be right. But I still say that what counts isn't the particular set of circumstances, but how we adapt ourselves to them, and you all must know that by now, watching all these changes of scene and scenery till you feel it's coming out of your ears. *I* know how it is; I've been everywhere, bearing messages to this one and that one, often steaming them open to see what's inside and getting a good dose of *that* too, in addition to the peaks of Tartarus which I might be flying over at the time. It's like sleeping too close to the edge of the bed—sometimes you're in danger of falling out on one side and sometimes on the other, but rarely do you fall out, and in general your dreams proceed pretty much in the normal way dreams have of proceeding. I still think the old plain way is better: the ideas, speeches, arguments—whatever you want to call 'em—on one hand, and strongly written scenes and fully fleshed-out characters in flannel suits and leg-o'-mutton sleeves on the other. For the new moon is most beautiful viewed through burnt twigs and the last few decrepit leaves still clinging to them."

Suddenly he glanced upward toward the scree and noticed a

girl in a Victorian shirtwaist and a straw boater hat moving timidly down the path through the now wildly swirling mists. She was giggling silently with embarrassment and wonder, meanwhile clasping an old-fashioned kodak which she had pointed at Mercury.

"It is Sabrina," he said. "The wheel has at last come full circle, and it is the simplicity of an encounter that was meant all along. It happened ever so many years ago, when we were children, and could have happened so many times since! But it isn't our fault that it has chosen this moment and this moment only, to repeat itself! For even if it does menace us directly, *it's exciting all the same!*"

And the avalanche fell and fell, and continues to fall even today.

Toby Olson

The Game

They dropped down in the east of the watershed into the steep cuts and the broader valleys below and headed into the outskirts of Denver. They drove through the heart of the city and out the other side, down into the foothills, and made the decision to head north into Wyoming, up to Cheyenne. They got to Cheyenne at midday, saw some posters announcing a rodeo, found a motel in which they unloaded and changed, and were at the rodeo by one-thirty. They spent the afternoon watching the cowboys ride broncos and Brahma bulls and rope calves. Bob White spoke about rodeos in his neck of the woods.

At one point, between events, Allen took Melinda back to where they stabled the animals in split-rail pens, so that she could see them up close. There was a place where the pens were set in a U-shape, and by walking into the U they were almost surrounded by them. The animals' smell was strong, but they were not at all skittery; they seemed very placid and very wise, in a way very professional. One horse came over to the fence and put his nose on the top rail. He and Melinda felt the horse's muzzle. It felt like kid glove, but the best part was the feel of the soft hot breath touching their palms and tickling between their fingers.

They spent the night in Cheyenne and were up and back on the road early in the morning, heading out into the flat lands of the Great Plains. They were not in a hurry, and they drove the old highways and secondary roads, passing close to farms and through small towns. In one town in Nebraska, just the other side of the Mountain-Central time-zone line, they saw a marker announcing that the local agricultural college had restored a piece of prairie as a project. An arrow on the sign pointed the direction, off the main drag, into the few blocks of residential area. The street was on the far side of the town, and they turned into it. At first it was lined with two- and three-story brick houses from the 'twenties and 'thirties. There were large, old trees in the yards. Two blocks in, the newer, frame ranch houses started. The prairie was between two of the ranch houses, on the other side of the street. They parked across from it, got out, and went over to it.

It was less than a half-acre in size, and it too would have been a ranch house, so the plaque in front of it said, had it not been for a young professor and his class at the college. They had discovered that it was land that had, somehow, never been cultivated or farmed. They had acquired it and let it return to its natural state. It was what the Great Plains had been like at the time of the dominance of the Comanches and the coming, or attempted coming, of the Spanish. The weeds, grasses, and flowers growing in it were well over their heads when they entered it. There were paths cut through it, and they walked these, separating. Though the paths cut back across themselves, they could not see each other, even though they were often no more than a few feet apart. They sounded to each other like small animals or birds in brush, out of sight, as they came close to each other. They talked into the air to each other, over the high growth. Melinda found dew glistening on a spider web across a path and announced this, ducking carefully under it. Allen came upon very strange flowers, small and blue, on thin stalks.

"On a horse, I could see over this," Bob White said at one point. "That's why the Comanche succeeded. Until he didn't," he said.

They spent close to an hour in the prairie, humming and studying whatever they came upon. They spoke less and less as time went by. Each felt enclosed and attentive. There were telephone wires visible from the paths, up in the sky, and they used these to keep their bearing, realizing that were the wires not there, they could well get lost and turned around and confused. Melinda finished her travels first and found her way back to the mouth of the prairie. A few minutes later Bob White joined her there. After another few minutes, Melinda called out. Allen answered her, and soon they heard him coming through the paths toward them. Soon they were together again.

They passed through two more small towns and then jogged back to an old highway and traveled it for three and a half hours. Melinda slept in the corner of the back seat behind him, and Bob White read sections from *Moby Dick* and studied the road atlas, giving close attention to the Eastern seaboard.

In another half-hour they were as far north as Sioux City, Iowa, about seventy-five miles west of it, and they came to a town where they agreed to stop. Even as they approached the far reaches of the town they could tell that it was one of those places whose economy had depended in large part on the road passing through it being well traveled. The coming of the big highway, a good four miles from it, with no exit roads or signs, had taken the traffic away, and now the town lay in waste. It had to get what it could from truck traffic and occasional sightseers.

Weeds grew in the small town square; many of the buildings in the short central block of Main Street were boarded up. Few people were on the sidewalks. They went through the town, and about a block after the stores quit and the seedy motels began, across the street from a small, closed Dairy Queen, they found a place that seemed adequate. There was an office in front, a small unconnected building with a driveway on either side. The drives led between the sides of the office and the two low, severe, rectangular blocks of rooms extending back from the road. Between the rectangles, the rooms facing into it, was an empty swimming pool with grass growing between the slate of its decking. He parked and went into the office to check them in. When he came out he had a slight smile on his face.

"What's up?" Bob White said when he got back into the car.

"A little surprise," he said, and he drove the car across the cracked blacktop to their adjoining rooms. He and Bob White unloaded their gear. Melinda checked the bathrooms, finding them clean enough, and tested the springs on the bed on their side. It was four-thirty by the time they were finished getting settled. They were sitting in the chairs in Bob White's room. They had eaten a late lunch, and they had decided that a drink and snack would be enough. They drank watery Scotch and ate cheese and crackers. All the time they had been unloading, Melinda and Bob White had been watching Allen, wondering about the surprise and playing the game of not asking about it.

"Are you two ready for a little action?" he asked them finally. They both nodded, enjoying his withholding.

"Okay, wait here, I'll be right back," he said, and he left the room and headed over to the office. Bob White got up and opened the drapes that covered the window, and they watched

Toby Olson

him enter the office. He came out a few moments later, carrying something.

"What's he got there?" Melinda asked.

"Looks like golf clubs," Bob White said, "looks like putters."

When he entered the room again, he was grinning broadly; he had the three putters in his left hand, and he raised a finger on his right, indicating that there should be no questions yet. He went to the gunny sack in the corner of the room, flipped its neck over, and pushed on the bag to get a few balls out of it; about ten rolled out into the room. He ran his hands over them, turning them, and selected three: a nearly new Golden Ram and two range balls, one with a red stripe around it, the other with a large black circle on its side. He put the three balls on the bed and turned to Melinda, holding the three putter heads in his hands, fanning the shafts out and presenting them to her for selection. By this time she was grinning too, and she chose one of the putters. Then he turned to Bob White and did the same thing with the remaining two clubs.

"Now we had better practice some before we go out to the links," he said, and he pushed a good number of balls out of the gunny sack onto the carpet and began to show them how to hold their putters and how to stroke. Melinda already knew how to hold a putter, and Bob White had seen enough golf in his time so that he too had no trouble with this. The three of them began to putt balls around the room, aiming for the legs of furniture, thudding balls against the wall and the door. Allen gave them various clipped phrases of instruction: head down, feet well planted, accelerate through the ball, hit on the sweet spot, don't push. The room was a small space for such activity; they had a lot of balls on the floor, and they hit balls into each other and bounced them off each other's feet at times.

"This is a crowded green," Bob White said, and the other two agreed, laughing, and they all said excuse me when they got in each other's way. After a while, he suggested that they quit, that they were ready now, and he pointed to the bed, suggesting that Melinda take her pick of balls. She selected the Ram, and Bob White took the ball with the red stripe around it.

After he had rounded up the golf balls on the rug and put them back in the gunny sack, he led them out the door and down to the end of the rectangle in which their rooms were located. At the end, where the cracked sidewalk ended, there was a dirt path leading around the back of the building, and he motioned for them to follow him down it. When they got to the back of the building, he stopped. Melinda and Bob White came up beside him, and they looked at what was before them.

The upper mandible of the whale stood as an archway of entrance into the grounds of the miniature golf course. At either side of the jaw's hinges, where they pressed into the ground, a low white picket fence went out and around the ragged oval of the course. The fence dipped half into ruin in various places where the course descended into the bottom of its cavity behind the whale's jaw, and weeds curled into the fence, making it an awkward crown of thorns. The jaw of the whale had the shape of a massive wishbone; it was at least eight feet high at its apex, and he wished the feel of the place did not remind him so much of Tombstone, the bag lying at the edge of the desert, the man coming up off the ground like a crab toward him, the gun in the torn sleeve. This place too was at the edge of things, the course a kind of exaggerated instance of the slow ruin of the town that had been passed by. Beyond the course were the wasted grainfields moving in from the hum of the highway, a good three miles away, and the fields seemed to be reclaiming the ground the course stood on. The weeds and obscure offshoots of the dead stalks of old corn had crept back into and over the course, and they were touching up against the back of the cinder blocks of the motel itself.

The jaw of the whale was pinioned with a large bolt where the wishbone joined at its top; the head of the galvanized bolt protruded on one side, the nut on the other. The entire surface of the jaw was marked with initials carved into its bone and the peeling remnants of fingernail polish and other paints that had been used by those who had no knives or chisels. Weathering had turned the carvings into signs and emblems, and away from words, and when they stepped into the tortured archway, Melinda thought of the mutilation of goosefish on the bay beaches of the Cape. When she was a child, she had seen other children stab and hack at the horny skin of the beached monsters in outrage at their ugliness, leaving them with pointed sticks standing like quills in their hides. The difference was in the bone quietness of the whale's jaw and the fact that it was in Nebraska. It seemed ancient here and beyond any quality of pain. Its shape stood out of the carvings and the paint, its power within its stillness hardly diminished, and the three of them were a little nervous standing within it.

They stood for a long time, under the jaw, somehow in the whale's presence, not as a live whale but one so single-minded in its power that the marrow in the bone retained a force beyond its long-ago death, as if it had pushed up out of the earth of Nebraska, its mysterious place of burial.

They moved out from under the jaw in time and approached

the slab of rubber, scuffed and worn, that was the first tee, about eight feet the other side of the archway. As they looked up to study the hole, a straight par two in a keyhole shape, they could see the remnants of the sea theme of the course beyond it. Slightly to the left and down near the bottom of the cavity, about ten holes away, was the figure of a small dolphin, its body bent in an arch, under which they thought they would have to hit when they got there. Three pelicans, one with its head missing, stood on the green of another hole. There was a shark, a small sperm whale, a barracuda, and configurations they would not be able to make out until they got nearer to them. They flipped a coin, and Melinda won the honors. The keyhole was outlined with one-by-three pine, and there were no hazards to negotiate. The only hint of a sea theme were the few shells left glued to the boards surrounding the square green: quahog shells, some mussels, and a few oysters. Melinda putted on the warped surface. Her shot went past the cup, thudded against the board beyond it, and rolled back two feet, stopping only a foot from the hole. Allen and Bob White both missed their putts also, and the three of them managed to get down in two, even at the end of one.

As they moved from hole to hole, considering each putt carefully, they began to feel themselves descending. They had made a rule that each ball would be putted out, were engaged in a kind of medal play, and such was the decayed condition of the course that they would often find themselves flying off the green or the fairway of the hole they were playing, having to come in from the scarred ground of other fairways, chipping into their proper pathway from stones and sand. It was not unusual for holes to be won with sevens and eights, and as they descended and the competition moved them, they began to become exhausted. Behind them, up the narrow and winding crushed-stone path that ran through the course from hole to hole, they could see the cracked and mutilated figures of sea life: a giant lobster with a broken claw, a seahorse with a crushed muzzle, fish painfully twisted. Allen was just a little ahead. Melinda was on his tail, and Bob White was still within striking distance. They had finished the ninth hole, and they felt half submerged.

At the tenth, the dolphin hole, the course seemed to level off and bottom out. They were under the sea, various levels of sea life around and above them, behind and ahead. Their alliances fell apart and came together as their scores altered. At times Allen was engaged in a struggle with Melinda and she with him. At times Bob White surged, and one or the other of them felt threatened. The oval of the picket fence seemed to lean inward. Standing on the tenth tee, they felt pressed down in the middle of the purgatory of a sea garden, one that was the mirrored reversal of the health of the real sea, that romance of paradise. Even their putters felt like burdens, tools they had to carry as a kind of penance. They felt too comfortable now with their grips, and this was an embarrassment, as if a hint of some indulgence in sin, so that they often hid the putters along their legs or hung them down from clasped hands, like European walkers, behind their backs.

They were catalyzed, and they rose a little when they saw the situation of the tenth hole. The tenth, the dolphin hole, was a par four, with a right-angle dog leg near its end. The dolphin, about four feet long and bent into a graceful arc, crossed over the narrow two-foot fairway of worn green carpeting. Where from a distance they had thought they could go under the body of the dolphin, there was no opening at all but a sculptured and chipped blue wave on which the dolphin was riding, having leapt up on it, its head slightly on the decline, as if it would soon plunge, come up, and catch another. The end of its nose was gone, and the paint that might have marked its pupil had worn away. Its mouth had a smile in it, but it could see nothing, and this turned it away from any hint of motivation or pleasure, and its dive seemed totally insouciant. It would go down into the wave, and the structure and attitude of its body would cause it to curl and come up again. Then it would enter another wave, and another. It was locked in its motion and could not turn out of the waves. Cute as it might have once been, it was no dolphin from an aquarium show. The human and weather damage done to it, and the neglect had given it a history of seriousness they each felt as being not much different from their own.

The dolphin guarded the way to the getting down, the finality and the repose of the satisfied click of the ball as it fell into the cup and settled. It seemed impossible that the concentration of the dolphin could be passed. Beyond the dolphin was the square of green on the upper level with two holes in it, and these were the entrances to tunnels that ran under the upper green and would drop balls that rolled through them onto the lower, final green surface to the left. One tunnel exit was at the side of the lower green, about five feet from the cup and around a corner. From that point a bank shot off the rotted boards might well be required. The other tunnel came out directly in front of the cup, about two feet away from it, and the best shot coming out of that tunnel might fall in. But the greens were in the future, the cup at the very bottom of the groin of the sea, and first they must negotiate the upper waves and the dolphin riding on them.

At the end of the narrow incline of the fairway, at the base of the ascending curl of wave, there had once been a slide, a half-tube of corrugated metal pipe that had arched up through the wave and into a groove fashioned gently in the dolphin's side. The lower bit of pipe was still there, but a good eight inches were missing between that bit and the groove, and time and the set of the wave had shifted the dolphin's body some, and it bent inward slightly toward the rubber of the tee. Bob White thought he would try that path. He had the honors because he had won the ninth, and he placed the ball with the red ring around it on a flat place on the rubber of the tee. He addressed a place slightly behind the ball, took a practice swing, then set his feet again, addressed and stroked firmly through the ball, keeping his head down, accelerating through the putt. The ball clicked sharply off the blade of the putter, rolled true to the broken tube, and was kicked into the groove in the dolphin's side. But the dolphin had bent over enough so that the ball, instead of sliding over the dolphin's body and dropping onto the upper green, spun up into the air, arched back a bit and fell and clattered into the crushed stone to the side of the fairway. Bob White's putter was still elevated, pointing toward the dolphin, the shaft following the putt, but when the ball spun off and landed, he lowered the club and shook his head.

"Difficult to negotiate," he said, and he stepped back to let Melinda have her shot at it. She had been standing back and watching the dolphin intently, and when it was her turn, instead of settling in and putting, she walked around behind the upper green, bent over slightly, and squinted at the body of the dolphin from the other side.

"There's something here," she said, and she beckoned to the

two of them to join her to see what it was. They walked around and came up beside her.

"There," she said, and they both looked where she pointed and saw that there was a small hole in the left of the snout of the dolphin, about two inches below its vacant eye.

"We'd better check the other side," Allen said, and they went around to the fairway, moved up close to the foot of the wave, and studied the dolphin's body. He ran his hand from the curve of the tail up the dolphin's side, and about halfway up he discovered there was indeed a hole there too, and that it had been stuffed with a bit of cloth which had been packed carefully into it, so that it was not apparent from a distance. He pulled the cloth out, revealing the hole, and he pointed to a place below it where there was a remnant of a second piece of corrugated piping. The hole was a good eight inches up from the top of the wave, and that put it about two feet from the surface of the fairway. They could see now that this had once been the desired way of playing the hole, that the proper shot had gone through the dolphin and not around or over it.

Melinda touched her face and thought for a few moments. Then she decided on a way to play her shot. She lined up behind the rubber tee, but she aimed to send her ball through a break in the rotted boards at the side of the fairway. This would take it, if she hit it well, out and alongside the upper green a little past the dolphin. There were broken boards around the upper green also, and a steep incline to the little hill the upper green was on. She figured that she might be able to roll her second shot up the embankment and onto the flat surface. Her first shot was a good one; the ball went between the broken boards, clicked among the gravel, and quit beside the embankment, a good approach-shot placement.

Now it was Allen's turn. He took a handful of gravel from the path beside the fairway and ran a finger through it in his open palm until he found the proper piece. He put this piece on the rubber of the tee and placed his ball on it, so that the ball was a little elevated off the rubber. It would be an extremely difficult shot, and he would have to hit it hard enough to take most of gravity's pull out of it. He figured he'd miss the hole at least once before getting the range. He stepped up over the ball, adjusted his line, glanced up at the body of the dolphin over and over again as he shifted his feet. When he thought he had the line just right, he settled in and placed the head of his putter on the rubber. He glanced up a few more times, and then he held his head steady, looking down over the ball. His hands shifted slightly, moving a couple of inches in front of the ball on the stone. Then the club head moved back to the top of his quarter swing, and then it accelerated down, and the ball shot off the stone and struck against the dolphin's body a few inches to the side and below the hole. His second shot failed also, but it was closer, and when he sent his third, the ball hit the hole, clattered and vibrated in its entrance and fell in out of sight. He walked quickly to the other side of the dolphin to see where the ball would come out and how it would fall, but nothing happened. He waited a moment. Still nothing. The other two came around beside him and waited also.

Because of the intensity of their study of the dolphin and the attendant difficulties of the hole, they had lost track of time, and only when the three of them stood together waiting did they discover that dusk was advancing and the course beginning to darken. The far side of the dolphin's body now had shadows within it; its skin was darker, and it seemed more seaworthy. The shadows masked the peel of paint, and the eye above the hole no longer seemed vacant to them. Over the body of the dolphin they could see the rise of the figures they had worked their way through as they had played the first half of the course. The failure of the sun and the coming of shadow enlivened them also; the shark seemed fresh from the sea, and the penguins looked like a trio of small children in formal wear watching them at play. At the very top of the expanse behind them stood the whale's jawbone. It looked immaculate and unsullied, very skeletal and bone hard and very white. They could see the sky around it and through it. It stood like a firm, stylized rendering in the air, but it seemed to have incredible weight at the same time, to be permanent in its place, as if it had never had another. Clouds moved and shadows shifted around it; the first coming of points of stars were in its arc, the moon's sliver was above it and to its left. But its outline and its surface were untouched by any movement or magnitude. Though it was entrance to this place, it seemed pivotal, the still center of something, and they found they could not and did not want to pull their eyes away from it. They stopped for a long time, looking up at the jaw, and then Melinda touched him lightly on the bone of his elbow and whispered below and behind him into his shoulder.

" 'But miles to go before I sleep,' " she said. And Bob White grunted, and Allen moved his elbow from her touch, and the three disengaged themselves from the matrix of their placement, though very slowly, each stretching almost imperceptibly, waking themselves.

"The ball," Allen said. And he walked slowly around to the front of the dolphin and knelt down on the fairway, getting his head at a level with the hole and peering into it. It was darker now, and it was hard to see, but he thought the hole went

273

straight into and through the dolphin's body. Still on his knees, he turned his head and reached back and motioned for Melinda's putter. He had left his leaning against the embankment on the other side, and he took hers; holding the club head in his hand, he slowly insinuated the shaft into the hole in the dolphin's side. It's like a strange injection, he thought, and he took his time, and he was careful not to hit the shaft against the sides of the hole as he entered the dolphin's body, and his left hand felt a brief need to elevate above the dolphin, to hold the bottle up. When the shaft was almost a foot in, he struck something. It was hard; it was surely the ball, but it gave way a little when he hit it and then pushed back a little and caused the head of the putter to shake a little in his hand. He pushed again, a little harder this time, and he heard a slight whisper of sound, a kind of scraping, from deep in the hole; there was a strong spasm along the putter shaft, and the head pressed back into his palm. Bob White was still on the other side of the dolphin, and he spoke softly.

"Come here," he said. And Melinda put her hand on Allen's shoulder and squeezed, and he got up from his knees, leaving the putter imbedded in the wound, and they both walked slowly around the dolphin to the back of the upper green. As they got close to where Bob White was standing, he raised his arm, indicating that they should move even slower, and they did that, watching Bob White and not the dolphin. When they got beside him, they turned and looked to where he was looking.

Below the place containing the recessed ring of the dolphin's eye, in shadow and behind its fixed smile, the snake's head and its encumbrance had unfurled and stood transfixed in the air a good three inches from the surface of the dolphin's body.

The encumbrance was a small bird. A nestling, it was too young for coloring and its fear petrified it. The snake's black head was very large, and with its mouth open and the bird locked in its jaw, it was hard to see how it had managed to come from the hole, but it had done so, possibly releasing its grip a little on the bird's body after exit. The snake's head was very black, its wide-open eyes were very small and bright red. The body of the bird was sideways in the snake's mouth; its outer wing was open and hanging down and over the snake's lip. The wing opened and closed slowly and repetitively, like a feathered fan or a sail touched in the rhythm of a wave-action breeze. The bird was like a carried banner, or a war bundle, or a burden of shame. The head of the snake moved slowly from side to side, scanning, and the three watchers felt guilt and immediate failed responsibility, and they surged forward imperceptibly and recoiled from the vision at the same time.

He thought about the ball in the hole behind the body of the snake. He wondered if it would have enough roll left in it if the snake left the hole. Would it be able to bounce out and possibly reach the first tunnel opening in the upper green? He already lay three, having missed two attempts to get his ball into the dolphin's body. With the right bounce and a good roll he could reach the passage to the lower green and have a putt for par. Was the snake a movable obstruction? Was it a natural hazard? What could the P.G.A. rules be in a case like this? He focused on the delicate body of the bird and came back and away from his quick retreat. The automatic crazy movement of his thought-train startled him and quickly made him sad. He saw the wing and the closed eyes and the bird's head in repose, and over the bird's back, the top of the snake's snout and its small red-blazing eyes. He reached beside him and took Melinda's hand; it was cool and dry, and it did not respond. He looked at her face and saw that her head was fixed, her mouth slightly open. As he watched her, he saw her head turning very slowly from side to side, in mimic of the snake's own movement.

Inside her head there was really very little control going on. There was a foregrounding of brief visions and flickers: snatches from dreams and potentially harmful past realities. What was locked in to its own control was her chemistry, her methodically dying body. Her breath exchange was shallow, expelled and sucked in through her open mouth, through parted lips, held by her fixed jaw. She felt her nostrils closed and a little parched. She held the life of the bird in her own mouth. If she opened her mouth and released it, they could step forward and kill the snake. The life they valued would have escaped from harm, and the other they would find dispensable. But if she pressed down too hard, she would crush the life from the bird, and then they would kill her in rage, though she would be already dead, because surely it was the life of the bird that was her own. She thought of the way she took his penis into her mouth to give him and herself pleasure. The same structure of vulnerability was involved here. She felt she was looking into the face of death, and though it was a composite face—the snake's head and the bird's body forming, in the increasing darkness, a silhouette emblem—it was not a face at all, but a structure, a fitted machine, mechanized by two past lives conjoined. And so it was a face, like her cells in their matrix were: the face of death then, a place, simply, of meeting.

They stood like the three penguins on the slope behind their play. She was like the decapitated one, her head, like that of the snake still mostly in the hole, separated in its intensity from her body. Bob White was the one standing a little to the side of the other two, looking slightly away, part of the group in his shape and black-and-white outfit but separated in name and ability. He saw the snake's head and the bird, saw it could be a totemic emblem, but he had seen such things before; and though the vision had power to stiffen him, he could work within its familiarity, and he was calculating. The way the bird was turned it would be difficult for the snake to get it back in the hole if he chose to do so. Snakes ate young birds in a way that was a kind of birth reversal. In birth, the child's head emerged then turned to allow the shoulders' exit vertically through the stretched opening. When a snake took a young bird from the nest, he grasped him in a way that allowed a good purchase, gripping the bird sideways at right angles to the jaw. This was a king snake, a constrictor, and he could not chew the bird but would have to turn it, getting it parallel to his mouth, take it in headfirst, the reverse of birth.

Bob White could see some matting of feathers on the top of the bird's head. He knew that this must be the snake's secretions. The snake had begun to swallow the bird when they had disturbed him with the ball. Surely he had stopped swallowing when the ball hit. He had waited, and when the shaft of the putter had pushed the ball, he had come out of the hole with the bird so that he could get the bird out of his throat and turn it. If the snake were caught with the bird in his throat, he would be defenseless. With the bird out and crossways again, he could drop it if he had to. He could use his mouth and the power of his body then; he would stand some chance. Bob White knew the snake did not really feel like dropping the bird. Probably he did not really feel at all in the way that we think of such things, but he could taste the bird and did not feel like losing that taste and the beginnings of fullness he had experienced when he had the bird's head in his throat. His head stood now out of the hole to the side of the face of the dolphin. He held the bird very gently but firmly in his mouth, and he moved his head slowly from side to side, scanning. Bob White thought he understood him.

He motioned to them with an open hand that they should stay where they were, and because he knew the snake could not pull his head back and withdraw into the dark safety of the hole as long as he held the bird in his mouth this way, he did not hesitate or try to dissemble or trick the snake. He walked slowly around the embankment of the upper green, withdrawing his knife from the sheath inside his shirt as he moved. When he got to the fairway and the other side of the dolphin, he crouched slightly and crept to the face of the wave. The dolphin was hip-high, and he could see the head of the snake over the dolphin's head. The head of the snake had followed his movement until he was out of its peripheral vision. Then it had returned to the other two, stopping its scanning. Bob White took the blade of his knife and rested it behind the head of the dolphin. Then he slid it over the dolphin's head and moved it swiftly under the neck of the snake, just back of its jaw. When the snake felt the steel, it tried to withdraw, but Bob White lifted the knife blade, pinning the head of the snake to the top of the hole.

They could see the glint of the knife below the body of the bird, parallel with it. It seemed that the snake's red eyes blazed out as they contracted. Bob White's head was above the head of the snake and the head of the dolphin. It was too dark for them to see his eyes, but they thought that he was looking at them. The knife blade seemed to stay where it was for a long time; then, suddenly, it was above the head of the snake. Then the snake's head with the bird in it fell from the hole, skimming down the dolphin's body, and tumbled onto the green, to the left and away from the wave. There was a furious shaking inside the body of the dolphin, and when they looked up from the vision of the severed head with the bird still in its mouth, they saw the body of the snake coming out of the wound. It was very long, and it spilled over the side of the dolphin, staining it, and fell like a coiled placenta, and came to rest in an almost perfect ring, still vibrating, on the surface of the upper green.

There was a moment in which they could see the placenta and the tableau of the head with the bird in it, and all was very fixed in place and silent. Then the ball came. It appeared, white and swollen, in the mouth of the hole. It seemed to linger there enough to turn, so that its black spot appeared, an intense large pupil that changed the mouth into an eye in the dolphin's side. And then it fell out, bouncing once on the dolphin's body and once on the green. When it quit bouncing it rolled four inches, and then it disappeared again, this time into the tunnel. They heard it rattle in the tube as it descended. Allen moved to the lower green to watch it come out. When it came it had good speed, and it skipped past the final hole and rolled to the board lining the green. It hit the board and started back, crossing the warped green surface. As it was losing its energy it reached the hole, rimmed it, hesitated on the back of the hole's edge, and then it fell in. From where Bob White stood on the other side of the dolphin, he could not see the ball enter the cup. But he could hear the click.

"Birdie," he said, very dryly and very softly. The two looked up and over at him. He had not smiled when he spoke. Then Melinda started to laugh a little. Then all three of them were laughing softly and tentatively in the increasing darkness.

Bob White came around from the body of the dolphin and climbed the embankment to the upper green. The coil of placenta was now still, and the black-leather sheen on the scales shone in the little moonlight and the dim artificial light that came from the backs of the rooms over and across the sea course. The strange cross formed by the head of the snake and the bird was also still, the snake's eyes still open, but glazing and without any intensity of rage left. The shocked bird seemed dead. It was very quiet, its outer wing gathered back to its body. It was unmarked, but it was still held fast. Bob White knelt down beside the strange small figure. It looked like a lost charm from a crazy bracelet. He put his thumb and index finger over the eyes in the snake's head, holding it fast to the green. Then he insinuated the tip of his knife blade under the body of the bird, between its small downy belly and the snake's lower jaw. When he felt the hardness of the lower jawbone and the leathery bottom of the mouth, he pressed the blade into the leather and through the scales until he had pierced the jaw, pinning it to the green.

Holding it there, he moved his thumb and finger to the front of the head's snout and slowly opened the mouth. With his ring finger, he gently urged the bird's body out, till it lay in front of the head. Then he released the open jaw, letting it shut. He picked up the bird then and cradled it in his palm and got up from his knees and slowly turned, looking for a place to put it. He knew there would be no snakes coming now for a while, and he wanted a place where, in the morning, sun would shine on the bird when it came up, a place where the bird would be touched or surrounded on all sides, but a place that from the top would be open to the sky. He stopped turning when he

faced the dolphin, and then he climbed down the embankment, holding the bird in his hand. When he got down, he
reached and tore a handful of weed from where it grew in the
gravel of the sea-course path, and he took the weed and
scrubbed at the stains on the far side of the dolphin's body
with it, mixing grass stains with the snake's fluids, changing
the smell. Then he threw the bit of weed down on the coiled
placenta. He took what remained of the weed and gathered it
in the clean, faded blue-check handkerchief he took from his
back pocket. Then he rubbed the handkerchief and the weed
slowly along the ball groove that ran in the side of the dolphin,
pressing hard, staining the handkerchief and the groove.

When he was finished, he gathered the weed and the handkerchief into a crinkled low pocket, fitting it near the top of
the dolphin's side where the groove was almost horizontal to
the ground. Then he placed the small body of the bird into
the pocket, tucking it in and spreading the sides of the pocket
slightly away from the feathers and head. When he was satisfied, he stood up from his crouch and looked down at the bird.
Then he reached down and made a final adjustment, putting
the pocket a little bit farther away from the bird's tail.

They had been watching him intently from where they were.
Melinda was still behind the embankment of the upper green.
Allen was standing where his ball had fallen in. And now they
watched him coming away from the fairway and the dolphin's
body and climbing back up the embankment. He could have
stepped easily over the dolphin to get to where he was, but
it was clear that that would have somehow been inappropriate,
and they stood where they were and waited for him. When he
got to the upper green and the placenta and the severed head,
he reached down and picked the head up and took it with him

down the embankment again to where his ball and Melinda's lay among the gravel of the walk, both distinct in the limited light. He took the head of the snake and wedged it down among the stones, so that it stood up with its closed jaws pointing toward the sky, a gesture not unlike that of the whale's jaw, and though diminutive, its recent history might have held a similar complexity. Then he took his knife and opened the mouth of the snake, and holding it with the blade twisted, he picked up a good-size piece of gravel and used it to wedge the jaw so that the snake's mouth stood up wide open when he removed the knife.

"Wait," Melinda said softly from the other side of the embankment. "Let me." And she came around to where he was and reached down beside him and picked her ball from among the stones. When she came up with it in her fingers, her hand held up a little in front of her so that the ball shone in the half darkness, she could see Allen, the upper half of his body only, mouth open and looking at them across the embankment and the upper green. She moved over and down to the snake's head and placed her ball where the bird had been. Bob White stood back and to the side.

She was at the side of the snake's head and the ball now, intent on the coming break of the perceptible structure that had grown up around them. She wanted to finish it. It was not real life. She felt she was now a living monitor of such things. As she addressed the snake's head with the blade of the putter, she stopped breathing, holding a brief modicum of air in the fragile domes of her alveoli. The blade was square to the head of the snake. The ball stood in the open jaws. The configuration was now like the handle of a garish cane. She brought the shaft of the club back, keeping her left arm and wrist stiff, and with no other move in her body, she stroked down and into the side of the snake's jaw, below where the ball was. There was a dull thud, followed by a slight click as the blade struck the jaw and the ball afterward. Both the ball and the head lifted up from the stones, the head spinning and falling and the ball continuing. The head landed and bounced on the embankment, and the ball bounced on the upper green, and then it bounced again, clearing the rotten board lining the far side and falling and landing on the lower green, coming to rest four feet from the cup.

"That's a good shot," Allen said, finishing the game of the structure and beginning to end it at the same time.

"I'll pick up," Bob White said, and he reached down and lifted his ball out of the stones. She made her putt. Bob White took an X on the hole. It had gotten too dark for them to continue further, and with no real discussion they agreed to quit. Bob White checked the bird a last time, adjusting the handkerchief pocket where it rested. Then he took the body of the snake, like a coiled hose, in one hand and its head in the other and walked across the sea course to where the weeds and the corn pressed in as the desiccated fields began. When he got there, he stopped. He set his feet. Then, turning like a discus thrower, he spun and released the coiled snake's body into the air. It unwound as it lifted, straightening for a moment like a spear. Then, as it descended, it telescoped in on itself, becoming increasingly smaller and inconsequential as it disappeared. He threw the head out in the same direction he had thrown the body.

When he finished, he came back to them, and they started together back up and out of the dark, broken sea, past the pelicans and the shark and the other fish figures, until they

Toby Olson

passed under the whale's jaw. They stopped there, turned, and looked back under the massive archway. It was quite dark now, and though they could see the form of the dolphin behind them, they could not see the place where the bird rested upon it at all.

When they got back to their rooms, Melinda said she was very tired and thought it would be a good thing if she slept alone that night. Allen said he thought they could arrange that, and maybe she should take Bob White's room and bed, and he and Bob White could sleep together in their room. They did that, and though the walls were thin, Melinda wept very quietly in Bob White's bed, and Allen did not hear her. And though Allen was very tired, Bob White lay so still beside him that he kept feeling and listening for movement and breath, so it was a long time before he was able to fall asleep.

Early in the morning, at the beginning of first light and while they were still sleeping, Melinda got up and went back out to the whale's jaw and the sea course. She was in her bathrobe and slippers, she was too intent to notice the way the day changed the look of things, and she stepped carefully down between the sea figures, retracing the way to the dolphin. When she got to the dolphin's side, she saw that the small pocket was empty, the bird was gone. She went back to the room, and when the three were sitting together having coffee in Bob White's room later, she mentioned to them that she had gone out and that the bird was no longer there.

"What do you think?" she asked Bob White.

He looked at her, hesitating a moment before answering, thinking that he could lie to her. But then he thought that the lie would be feeble, and also that to lie to her would be the wrong thing to do. And he said:

"I do not think that bird has come to a good end."

Steve Katz

Keeper

Dusty stayed in his cookshack when a man named Fletcher appeared unexpectedly on the trail near his tipi. He pushed at the fire. He had expected no visitors, preferred to be alone in these hours, and was reluctant to step out to greet him, hoping he might disappear if not acknowledged. These were hours when he enjoyed nothing to happen. He had met Fletcher only once, at his brother's house, and remembered him to be a peculiar person, obsessed with the story he had to tell, about himself. Dusty watched through a chink in the cookshack wall. The man stood quietly by the tipi, looking into the sky as if he expected to leave the ground. The light of early sunset layed a pale cayenne glow on his face that made him seem more than alive, like a shining spirit. The spruce darkened slowly. Blue heron sailed low over the water and settled on the rocks to stand for one last fish before going to roost. Grey bats, asleep all day in the folds of the smokeflaps, were starting to move. They would fly and feed on insects around the poles. The chili bubbled lightly on the stove. Fletcher turned and slowly approached the cookshack. Dusty had a premonition that this really wasn't happening. From under the silence the rumble of a fishing boat returned to the tiny Inverness harbor hidden behind the headland a mile away. White-throated sparrows exchanged blue sentences from the chokecherry to the ash. Dusty was jealous of these summer hours at his place, when his mind could come to rest, no visitors expected, no strollers on the beach, and he would settle down to eat alone inside the long, lush narrative of a Northern sunset.

Fletcher had a pack on his back, and held a small covered cage in front of himself like a lantern. Dusty stepped out of the cookshack.

"Hi," said Fletcher, stepping towards him. "I wondered if I was in the right place. I hope you remember me."

"Sure. Peter's friend. The sailor. Why don't you put your stuff down?" Dusty felt how cool his voice came out, but there was no reason to fake a welcome. Fletcher set the cage on the table, and Dusty helped him drop his pack.

"It's a long way down here. You didn't tell me how long that trail was when you invited me."

"Once you know it it doesn't seem long."

"I bet when you invited me you didn't expect me to come."

Fletcher looked so vulnerable that Dusty couldn't take this cue to say something mean. "It's true. I tell a lot of people about this place, but not many manage to get here. Congratulations."

Fletcher swung onto a bench and leaned on the table. "A primo view you've got here, and what a great table." From one side of the table you saw the ocean, and from the other side the hills of Foot Cape.

"Like everything else here I just nailed this table up out of driftwood planks and poles. Whatever was around." Dusty took some pride in the way he had developed his place.

"It's beautiful," said Fletcher. "A basic place." He pulled his little cage towards himself.

"I'll finish cooking the chili," Dusty turned back to the cookshack. Fletcher lifted the cover of the cage and peeked under. "Psst."

"Hey," Fletcher shouted, as Dusty threw some wood in the stove. "I hope you don't mind that I came."

"Don't worry," Dusty said. "As long as you appreciate my chili." Fletcher leaned on the table, and Dusty watched him gaze at the sunset, his peculiar intense profile, pointed as an arrow, thrust out as if he were on a trajectory towards the horizon.

At a recent visit to his brother Peter and his brood, the first in many years, Dusty met Fletcher, and casually invited him. He invited a lot of people to his camp in Cape Breton, but never expected them to show up. It was too far from anywhere. People seemed to understand that he wasn't really asking them to come, but they enjoyed the fantasy of a wilderness vacation as he described his place to them: the unspoiled coast, the tipi, the driftwood shacks. Dusty had put this place together as an adventure for his family, and now that the family was dispersed he enjoyed to be there alone whenever he had the time to go.

He had walked into his brother's living room and Fletcher was there. He leaned towards Dusty without introduction and said, "I'm deeply involved with these bats, in case you're wondering who I am. So I'm visiting here because your brother works at the university and I wanted to talk here with Professor Knowland F. Knowland, he's the bat expert." More peculiar, Dusty thought, than his interest in bats, was Fletcher's compulsion to tell about it immediately, even before he said hello. He looked into the strange face, broad from the front, thick stubble of beard, tufts of hair sprouting from the ears, the face a map of many problems, unlike the clear vector of his profile.

Steve Katz

"So you guys met each other already," Peter said, entering the room. "You know you both worked on ships. Fletcher here is a seaman. We graduated High School together."

"I just picked up a job once when I was in Europe," Dusty said.

"Well I'm a union member, for better or worse. No big deal. Like any other job, a pain in the ass. It's a living."

"Sounds great to me," said Peter. "Work half a year."

"Yeah, but you lose touch. A seaman loses touch. You're out at sea and your world turns inside out and what do you know. Like I come back from this last trip, and I go to the apartment I rent, I mean you know my room in it, and it's full of these little bats, little blue-eyed bats, all over it. And nobody knew anything about them. That's why I came here, because I read in the library about Professor Knowland F. Knowland, and I been keeping in touch with your brother Peter, so I came." One of Peter's little girls jumped into Fletcher's lap, and he sat back in the chair, quietly stroking her hair.

Peter sat on the edge of his recliner staring at Dusty as if he might be the answer to a question he had been burdened with for a long time. He rolled a scotch-on-the-rocks between his palms. "So you find yourself married," he blurted out, "and then you've got the kids and the mortgage and the wife's analyst to pay for, and here you are." He took a sip. "The whole shot."

"So I came to ask the professor about my bats," Fletcher added. He looked at Peter. "I don't get it. You got some nice kids. What does a seaman get? Six months unemployment. Sea legs. Clap in every port. And now I got some bats." The little girl on his lap made a face.

"Peter always loved to complain," Dusty said. In the midst

of the velour upholstery, the neatly matted prints, the indirect lighting, it was hard to take his brother's troubles seriously. "Hey Peter, you've got a steady job, a job for life. How many people have got that?" Three more kids came in and sat down at their father's feet.

"You spend your life picking your nose, and reading books nobody cares about. You spend your life talking to adolescents."

"Don't knock it," said Fletcher.

"When he was a kid we used to call him 'Whine'."

"Merchant seaman seems like a good choice to me now," Peter slugged down his scotch.

"Yeah, and spend your life with morons and assholes and misfits." Fletcher kissed the girl in his lap on top of her head. "If I could do it again, and found the right woman, I'd have a bunch of kids."

"How come you survived it? How did you do it?" Peter asked Dusty.

"What?" Dusty asked, though he knew his brother meant the wife and kids experience. He didn't relish continuing this conversation that was leading them back into old sibling conflict. "Who said I survived it? I just did a day at a time, Peter; until we couldn't do it any more." That line could have gone on the soaps, Dusty thought.

The kids stiffened visibly when Tasha, Peter's wife, came in. The youngest boy hid his toy truck behind his father's chair. Dusty remembered Tasha as the ideal of bovine contentment, a mother of kids, blissfully married. Now she almost throbbed with anxiety and resentment. Her smile was like a sneer overlayed with a grin, a studied stretching of the lips calculated to show all men present that she was equal or better. She stared at Peter till he stood up. "That's right," he said. "I get the dinner tonight. Hope everyone likes curry." The kids made faces. "I'll help you make it, daddy," said his eleven year old daughter.

"Don't let him get you to do all the work, Nance," said Tasha. "And you guys go out to play. Uncle Dusty isn't used to children."

"They don't bother me," said Dusty.

The kids hesitated, but their mother glared at them till they left, all but the little girl still asleep in Fletcher's lap. Tasha settled into the recliner Peter had vacated and lit the butt of a half-smoked cheroot. "Been about eight years."

"Yeah," said Dusty. "Something eats up years. You had three kids last time, and Terry was the oldest, right? He was in third grade. Must be almost out of High School. The kids look great. We look a little tired, though."

She blinked a few times, waiting for Dusty's comments to pass, then waved her cigar around as if to purify the air. She took a few puffs, then pointed the burning end at Fletcher, who sat very still, with the little girl sleeping in his lap.

"I'd take a job as a merchant seawoman. I'd ship out tomorrow if someone came in here and told me I could."

"That ain't likely to happen," Fletcher mumbled perfunctorily. Dusty had the sense they'd been over this territory before and she was just reviewing it for his sake.

"Of course it ain't." She smashed her cheroot in the ashtray for emphasis. "There's no such thing as a merchant seawoman, yet." She waited for Dusty to absorb the weight of this point.

Terry arrived at the front door, mumbled a greeting, and rushed out through the back. "What an asshole he's gotten to be," said Tasha, and she jumped up to follow him, leaving Dusty and Fletcher and the sleeping daughter in the room.

Dusty tasted the chili. Even a little hotter. "Do you like spicy?" he shouted at Fletcher, who was rolling a cigarette.

"Hot's okay, but I don't like sweet." He cupped his cigarette and lit it in the wind.

Dusty lifted a stove-lid and the fire roared up. He dropped in some more wood, and put on the coffee pot. Some violet clouds spread on the horizon, and somewhere an owl. "You hear that owl?" Fletcher said as if to himself. "Owls eat bats."

With the kid still asleep on his lap Fletcher slid forward and leaned towards Dusty. "I'll tell you what happened when I went to see the Professor."

"Sure," said Dusty.

Fletcher settled back in his seat. "You know, I wouldn't have bothered the guy, I mean to have a dumb seaman come to ask a professor about some little bats, but there was this Indian I shipped with last time, Lester Half-hawk. He was an oiler, and I'm an engineer, so we were together a lot, and he kept telling me these Indian stories, and I didn't know if they were real stories or what, but they passed the time and telling them kept Lester off the juice. I didn't try to remember them or any-thing, except this one story came back to me after I got home, about a tribe that lived on Manhattan island before the twenty-four bucks, and they disappeared, or they all were killed, but this story believed they would all come back when the time was right, when the buildings got too high, he said, and they would come back in the form of tiny bats, and each of those tiny bats would enter the body of one of the people living in Man-hattan, and grab his soul, and fly away with it. You can believe I remembered that story when I got home and found my walls covered with little bats. I mean that was more than a coinci-dence. So that's why I came to see the Professor."

"Did you tell the Professor that legend?"

Steve Katz

"No way I could tell him anything. He was a flipped-out Professor, like a Groucho Marx Professor. 'There are no blue-eyed bats,' was what he said, and he shoved my cage aside. I said, 'Wait just a second, professor.' He was one of them small professors, wiry, nervous, a little white goatee that jumped around as he talked. And his eyes never stopped to focus on anything. They bounced all over the room as if he was afraid of being caught in one place at the same time. So I felt like I was wasting his time, but I said, 'now wait a second, Professor. What about these little bats right here in this cage? These little bats have blue eyes.' I moved the cage in front of his face again, and lifted the cloth right off. His eyebeams hit my cage, and richocheted off like a bat in flight. 'There are no blue-eyed bats. The African epaulette bat has a dull grey cast to its eyes, Epomorphus, but I've seen it only in photographs.'

"So I told him, 'Hey, professor, I don't want to waste your time and hold up your experiments, but don't be a jerk. These blue-eyed bats here are right in front of your eyes. Take a look once. You'll give me some satisfaction for coming all the way out here, and you'll make out alright yourself. You'll see a bat you never seen before.' I mean I don't know what these professors get their jollies from. But this little squirt wouldn't look at them. He stood up, got his pipe and a pouch of tobacco, and reamed and packed the pipe with a vengeance. 'The study of bats can be worse than frustrating as you have no doubt discovered for yourself.' His eyes flew here and there. 'Yeah,' I said to myself,' especially when you got to talk to a bunch of screwballs.' 'There's disappointment, danger, even tragedy,' said the Professor, putting a lighter to his pipe.

'And bats, Professor? Tell me about blue-eyed bats.' I tried to put it to him but the screwball ignored me. I thought it was time to get out of there. I wouldn't get anywhere with him, but he called his secretary and told her he didn't want to be disturbed, and he settled back in his seat and smoked his pipe, and I knew I was in for a long one. 'I want to tell you about a collecting trip I once took into the jungle of Ecuador.'

"So I figured wait the guy out. Maybe after he relaxes he'll take a look at my bats. I mean there's a lot at stake with my bats. I mean we're talkin' all the souls from the island of Manhattan, and maybe the boroughs of Queens, Bronx, Brooklyn, and the ferry to Staten Island."

" 'About ten years ago now,' the Professor began. 'I received in the mail an unusual specimen that a fisherman had snagged in the tropics. This man had been fly-fishing along the banks of the Alogongo and the bait was grabbed in the air by a bat. It looked most like the Carollia Perspicillata, one of a species whose powers of audition I had been studying but with an unusual ear conformation that was either an aberration of this individual, or the indication of a whole new subspecies. I decided to organize a collecting trip to the headwaters of the Alogongo where I was assured by my correspondent a large population of bats inhabited caves in the hills of the surrounding watershed. It took me several years to arrange my affairs and get a sabbatical. I had experiments to finish. I had to dispose of a dying marriage etcetera etcetera . . .' "

Fletcher swung off his seat and approached Dusty in the cookshack. "This place you got down here, this is a magical place. I feel lucky to come here."

"Peter has never visited me down here. I know his kids would love it," said Dusty.

"Your brother's got that chick he's married to. He's got his own problems. All those professors he's got to talk to. I don't

Steve Katz

envy your brother."

"Taste this." Dusty held out a spoonful of chili. Fletcher pulled his head back. "Pheww. That's hot. That's good chili."

"Twenty minutes, I figure, and we can eat it. Meanwhile why don't you stow your stuff over there." He pointed at a driftwood tower built by one of his sons. "It'll keep the rain off."

Dusty watched him grab his stuff and go to the tower. There was something different about Fletcher, less substantial than the man who had told him the story, as if he had evaporated. Maybe it was the bats' influence. The story Fletcher told remained in Dusty's mind like the shadow of an intricate thing.

". . . Professor talked and my little bats started flying around in the cage, like doing amazing tricks. I didn't want to be impolite but my little bats were knocking themselves out, and I wanted him to notice them. I said, 'Look, Professor. Bats. Bats right here.' No way he would look. He sucked on his pipe and blew big clouds of smoke in his own eyes. I needed him to know about my little bats and the situation of souls in New York City, but he kept talking. '. . . narrow gauge railroad to the interior, after which there was no way to go but on foot. Our packers, taciturn little Chingayo Indians, carried my collection cases and equipment. I had for a companion a young archaeologist from Illinois, a brilliant young Jewish woman of some twenty-six years, Susannah Gorchow her name, alas. She laughed like a man. I don't know if you're Jewish, but I find certain intelligent blue-eyed Jewish women irresistible. Her eyes were violet. She was working with the archaeology of bat imagery. It appeared in the weaving and on the pottery of contemporary Indians, and she had records of some studies done by an astroarchaeologist showing that in their perception of the night sky, which in the Southern hemisphere is full of starless dark patches, they take at least one of the configurations of darkness to be a huge bat, which in their mythology, as far as it is understood, is the resting place for the spirits of men while they sleep, and the first station for those spirits after they die. She hoped to find some subjects to tell her more. A fascinating companion in a tepid rainforest full of parrots and snakes. She spoke to me in French. Voulez-vous dejeuner a ce belle poste ci? Ce n'est pas le Howard Johnson. Ha ha ha." she carried a can of pâté in her pocket, and we ate it there, our final taste of civilization. Then we climbed and slipped and splashed up and down one of the most miserable trails I have ever followed. At sundown we came on a wretched little shack. It was inhabited by a couple of miserable, rheumy, pink-eyed Norwegians who sat there on some straw mats when we entered with machetes in their laps and told us they had no food for us, and we weren't welcome to sleep inside with them. It rained on us all night. In the morning we paid dearly for some leaky dugout canoes and started up the river towards a village they claimed was there, settled by some Japanese. We were hungry and wet and cold. What a river. Masses of floating rubbish narrowly missed our tiny boats. Mats of water hyacinth sheltered schools of piranha, and crocodiles slid off the banks to cross our bows. The rains had roused hundreds of tiny frogs to activity and their tinkling chorus like wind-chimes came from all sides as the boys continued to pole us up the river . . .' "

The little girl stirred on Fletcher's lap. From the kitchen came the sounds of Peter cooking, and his older daughter giggling while she worked with him. "I gotta admit I was pissed when I understood that Professor had kept me there to listen to his

Steve Katz

story, but didn't have time to even look at my little bats. He chewed on his damn pipe. He looked everywhere else, and the smoke swirled up into the ventilators, and he kept talking, '. . . miserable, the same forlorn appearance as the black vultures we passed sitting dejectedly over a dead calf by the riverside, their heads drawn down between their drooping shoulders. Occasionally we halted by the riverside to rest, or to lunch on a cluster of small bananas fortune had sent us. Susannah moved close to me. In the bow a native draped incongruously in a woolen shawl chewed coca leaves and . . .' "

The story wound on like a river, and Dusty watched his little niece asleep in Fletcher's lap, his mind flying off to his own recollections about the ship he had worked on, a Norwegian tramp that stopped at Taranto to unload its anthracite and load some steel pipe to be delivered through the Bosporus to Odessa. He hung around the old city with a Phillipine friend of his, Bataan. It was an ancient slum on an island between the two newer sections of the city. The streets were so narrow they could stand in the center and touch the walls on either side. Kids followed them everywhere, begging money. And the sailors off a few Russian freighters, unaccustomed to liberty in the West, moved through the crowds of Italians like schools of fish.

They ate in a seafood restaurant near the fishmarket, huge bowls of a rich grotesquerie of mussels and clams and ugly bottom-fish. Bataan returned from the bathroom a little paranoid, and before the soup came he left Dusty there without a word. He waited for him to come back, stared into the sluggish face of the sea-robin cooling on his soup, and sipped a little around the edge. Bataan had a keen sense of trouble and Dusty knew he should have got out of there. Two men grabbed his arms, and he stared into the grin of a commandante of the carabinieri.

" '. . . at length to reach the village of Xigadiga (pronounced sheegadigga), an Indian word for the sound of a canoe riding through the reeds, suddenly coming aground on a spit of mud. In this season the village was a lake of mud, thatched huts built above it on platforms supported by poles. The people proved congenial and gave us food and shelter, a good thing because we learned that it would be four days before the mail-boat arrived to carry us the rest of the way up the river. The people were very gentle. They giggled a lot and made great sport of the unpleasant task of picking the leeches off our legs. From the vantage of our accommodations, a little hut on stilts above the central square, Susannah and I could watch the natives luxuriate in the warm mud. They stripped off their loincloths, young and old alike, and dived into it from the ladders of their huts, rolling over, blowing bubbles like African hippos. It looked like such pleasurable sport we couldn't resist the temptation that in a civilized context would seem so contrary to the rules of hygiene. We stripped, the first time I have ever seen Susannah in the buff, and she had a quite nice conformation of limbs, her breasts small with nipples standing up like little snouts.' The Professor paused to relight his pipe. My bats were bored stiff. Was this a two pipe story, I wanted to ask. A three pipe story? 'These natives were fascinated. They had never seen white bodies in the buff before, and they loved the spectacle as we dove into the mud. They played fanfares on their crude flutes and beat on log drums. The mud, we discovered, provided relief from the itching of our numerous insect bites. No scratching an itch in that climate, because flies swarmed on the slightest abrasion to lay eggs in the wound, causing some painful swelling. The mud was relaxing to body and mind, and even the insect bites were a kind of blessing, because we discovered that to relieve the general itching it was quite efficacious to rub our bodies together lightly in such a way as not to break the skin, and we found quite naturally that that contact led to further intimacy and finally to the blossoming of a love that had been implicit all along in our delight in each other's company. There has never been a more tender nor a muddier honeymoon. The natives were more than happy to let us . . .' "

The Commandante in the room where Dusty was detained kept a pipe in his mouth, but said it was too expensive to light it. "Next time you come to Taranto bring me a gift of tobacco. American tobacco is best, but very expensive in Italy." Dusty sat in the sparsely furnished room for several days with this Commandante. He left only when Dusty slept, on a straw mat on the floor. Though the officer wouldn't talk about it, Dusty's guess was that they would keep him till his ship sailed. They didn't want an American on the crew headed for a Russian port. The Commandante practiced his English. "Gioia del Colle, you know it? Twenty kilometers from Taranto. Secret missile base. When Americans first come there the town gave a big celebration, lights all over the street, a festa for twenty-two days. Every two hours the mayor makes a speech to welcome the Americans. The American colonel made a speech too, a very big man." The silos of the missiles of this top-secret base rose among the olive trees, some of the oldest in Italy. "So the Colonel was very happy, because the people of the town were happy to have the work, and the soldiers were happy for the big party. But when he got his electric bill he wasn't so happy. Four hundred and fifty thousand lire. The mayor of Gioia was 'furbo', how do you say it? Clever. Shrewd. He attached the electricity from the whole to the Colonel's meter. Why not? Rich American. The Colonel had to pay. The American government would not pay." A bedraggled corporal brought in two bowls of pasta. The Commandante was laughing. "To pay. Money." He took a mouthful of the pasta, chewed it, spit it back into the bowl. "Porca putana," he exclaimed, and shoved the bowls back at the corporal. "Ci porta la pasta fatta corretamente alla dente, o non ce ne porta. Capito." "Si, Commandante, mi dispiace, ma insom-ma . . ." the corporal took the bowls away. "Manniagia la miseria," said the Commandante. "Choongum. Pasta like choongum."

" '. . . several hours ride over mountain trails. If I had known beforehand how treacherous those trails were I would have tried to convince Susannah not to follow. Our gear in pack-saddles on the mules, and ourselves on what we were told were sure-footed horses, that knew the trail. Our mounts took the bits in their mouths, and though we tried to rein them to the inside they preferred to ride the outer edge of the trail, their bodies and ours hung out under the rushing clouds. We had a sense at first that we were invulnerable, immortal, didn't need to touch the ground because we were mounted not on ordinary nags, but had between our knees the airborne progeny of Pegasus. Would it were true. O how I've wept for a horse that could fly. I heard one stumble behind me. It happened so quickly. It was Susannah's horse. I turned and saw her body flying off into the canyon some two-thousand feet below. The same body that over the weeks past I had come to love as if it were my own, falling, falling. How ironic that the woman to whom I was prepared to dedicate my life from then on perished for want of those extremities, those infernal wings, so abundant on those creatures to whom my life had been devoted up to that point.' The Professor started to cry. What was I supposed to do? What was he gonna do next? I mean was I supposed to put my arms around him like he was a woman? I mean I never even went to college. I covered up my little cage of bats. He talked again. 'They convinced me it was no use to go after her. The bottom of the canyon was more than a week away from where we were. I had no choice but to sadly push on. At length we arrived at the abandoned camp of some prospectors adjacent to the caves we had set out to explore. Oh, Susannah . . .' "

"Look, my ship is due to pull out at five A.M. tomorrow. What am I doing here? Just helping you with your English?"

"They had a key club on this base. You ever have a key club?"

"Commandante, will I get out of here in time to sail with my ship?"

"I would never say that all Italian wives are faithful, quite the opposite, but to make adultery into such a game, so public. Italians are never that organized about love."

Dusty stood up. "Commandante, I demand that you at least let me contact . . ."

"Ah, ah, ah . . ." the Commandante pressed a buzzer under the lip of the table he was leaning on, and the two carabinieri stationed outside the door entered and stood at attention. "There were seventy couples, and every Friday night they met in the enlisted man's club—a few officers with them too—and they all threw their keys into the middle of the floor, and then each man picked up a key, and by luck whatever key he got that was the woman, the wife, he spent the weekend with.

An Italian doesn't understand this. An Italian likes to seduce a woman, a little romantico. But when the Colonel found out he was very angry about this, and he made all the men to stay on the base, and the women were left alone at home."

Dusty had noticed that the two guards seemed almost to be sleeping. He slowly moved closer to them, figuring to sprint through the door at a certain moment, but before he made his move they grabbed him and pulled his arms behind his back. "Okay," he said. "So you're sincere."

"That was when our ragazzi started to invade the bedrooms of the American women. They called it 'la guerra di mezzanotte,' the midnight war. Italian boys are so romantic, and the American women love them a lot, good fucking dark boys . . ."

Fletcher moved the little girl to the floor by his feet, and she lay there with her blue eyes open, sucking her thumb, staring at Dusty. "He showed me a picture," Fletcher said. "He carried a walletful of pictures of bats like my mother's got a folder of her grandchildren, or High School girls carry pictures of boys. This one was ugly, with a little flap of skin on its nose, and a mouth like a bulldog, and ears beaten in. He kept talking to me. 'The chamber could be entered only by lying flat and pushing forward with the toes. A feeling of profound depression came over me, that the walls might at any moment collapse and hold me there forever. After some more hours of careful descent we came to a small antechamber that could have made the most virtuous man feel he had been assigned to one of the empty wards of hell. The floor was a seething mass of enormous cockroaches, a deafening rustle as they struggled about rubbing against one another. It was hideously hot. Big centipedes moved back and forth across our legs. One room was hotter than the last, and there were no signs of bats yet, but I was determined to go on through the stench and heat just because I had come this far. We soon descended a broad, well-like shaft to a cooler region of this vast network of caves. Here the only passage was by a long shelving ledge that afforded a slippery foothold. Our pale lamps made the shadows leap around us like demons. Stones kicked loose after several seconds made a faint splash where like 'Alph, the sacred river,' ran an underground stream said to harbor blind fishes. At length the ledge widened and we found ourselves in a large chamber at the bottom of a vaulted dome. I shined my light around. 'Alogongo,' I shouted, and the word bombinated through the chambers of the cave. But not a bat. There were no bats at all. I was hoping for any little one, even if it wasn't a Carollia, which usually roost in trees anyway; just some small specimen I could collect to redeem somewhat the tragic con-sequences of my fateful trip, but not one creature there to begin to replace the loss of my Susannah. I shouted her name, Susannah Gorchow, and it rebounded off the surface of the domed chamber, and I shouted it again and again so it would reverberate forever within the hollow cliffs of Alogongo.' "

"The missiles," said the Commandante, "were set up at Gioia under a joint Italian-American command." So what did it mean to him, Dusty thought? He lost a job. He wouldn't get to Odessa. They fed him well, and he'd had worse company than this Commandante. "The Americans controlled the nuclear warheads, and the Italians controlled the missiles them-selves. The consoles were set up in trailers outside the missile silos. How is my English?"

"Fuck your English, wop."

"Very kind of you, Mister Dusty. Gioia is 'happiness,' you

know that? Gioia del Colle, happiness of the hills. So in each trailer an American Lieutenant and an Italian Tenente sat facing each other. Twelve hours they sat, and each had a key, the American for the warhead, the Italian for the missile. It was supposed to fire only by both keys. One day there was a big inspection by the NATO generals, a disaster, of the whole missile installation, and all the generals crowded into one of the trailers where the two lieutenants were sitting. They were such lonely lieutenants because the Italian spoke no English and the American no Italian. They took the key from the Italian Lieutenant, to show how it worked, lifted the cover, and tried to insert it. No fit. Not even into the keyhole. Nothing. The Generals were disturbed. They turned to the American and asked for his key . . ."

A loud bell clanged in the hall outside and the Commandante stopped talking. He looked at his watch, stood up, and saluted Dusty. "We are free to leave, Mr. Dusty. You can go now."

"But what about the key? Did the American key . . . ?"

The Commandante put his pipe in his pocket and left without answering. The room was suddenly empty, pale yellow. Dusty could imagine how that story ended, what happened with that key, but what use was imagination, like fish gills pumping in the belly of the boat. He had come, in a way, to depend on the Commandante, and now felt deserted by him. He opened the door slowly and looked into the hallway. No one but a cleaning woman in the building. It had got to be Sunday without his knowing, and his ship had sailed on Friday. The woman was mopping the floors of the massive Fascist building. She said, "ngiorno," and he walked into the street.

" 'There were no bats. Not a bat, I tell you. Not a miserable creature in the cave.' This Professor started foaming at the mouth and shaking his fists in the air. I didn't know what was going to happen next. 'All that distance. All that expense. My reputation, and I lost my Susannah. And this terrible sickness. For what? Ten thousand miles at enormous sacrifice, and not a bat. Not even one bat. That's all I can say. No bats.' I felt sorry for him. He was swaying around like a drunk man, his fists waving in the air. He brought a fist down on top of my cage and smashed it, but the little bats flew to safety under my collar. This Professor was berserk. He jumped onto the desk, and I stepped back because I didn't want him to jump on me. He swung his arm around like a windmill and heaved his pipe through the window. 'Out, out,' he shouted, and before I could grab him he hollered out one last, 'no bats at all,' and crashed through the window himself.

I ran into the secretary's office where she was talking on the phone and I said, 'Hey, your Professor just jumped through the window.' She held her hand up, as if there was something more important she was saying on the phone. 'The guy jumped through the fucking window,' I said again when she put the phone down. 'We know. We know,' she said, like a nurse in a loony bin. 'This happens when he talks to a visitor. I've already talked to maintenance and they're coming over to fix the window.'

"I ran around the building. It was just a three foot drop from his first floor window, and he wasn't even hurt, just lying there more or less relaxed now, smiling, crumbling some autumn leaves in his hand, as if this was just what he needed. 'Why do you want to get involved in this ugly business?' he asked. 'You're young. You still have time. You're not even a zoologist. Why this interest in bats?'

'It's not the bats that I'm interested in, Professor. Not the bats for themselves.'

'What then?' He jumped up spryly and tossed the leaf crumbs into the air.

'I need to find out about their ability to capture the souls of men,' I said.

'Oh, that,' he said, and for the first time that afternoon this professor looked me right in the eye. He was crying again. This was so weird. He said, "In Queensland I ate the bats regularly. Flying foxes. They tasted good, like hare.' He was sobbing. 'I made them into hassenpfeffer.' Then the Professor got up and walked away. Enough of that, I figured. I didn't follow him any more."

Dusty stepped out of the cookshack. The wind was coming down off the hills and tasted like evergreens. He could hear Fletcher arranging his gear in the tower. "Another few minutes and we can eat," he shouted. The edge of the mountains glowed faintly with the moon that was going to rise full that night.

After his story about the Professor Fletcher fell silent, and the little girl stood up and crossed the room to Dusty. "You sleep in my room," she said.

"Okay little niece," said Dusty, touching her hair.

"You know what else I have in my room?"

"No."

"Guess."

"You've got me in your room."

"No, silly. I mean all the time. Every little minute."

"Okay. I give up. What have you got?"

"I've got a whole place full of munchmellow people. A whole place." She spread her arms to show how big a whole place was.

Peter came in from the kitchen with his arm around his older daughter and announced dinner. He was a good cook. The curry was delicious, but Tasha made a point of eating a hamburger. "I used to enjoy all that foreign food," she said. "All that exotic, but not any more."

"Tasha belongs to AA," Peter said. "It's not what you think. This one is American America. It's a new organization here."

"I didn't tell the Professor," Fletcher said, still intensely focussed on Dusty. "But I'd eaten the bats before too. I fried them up and they were delicious. Little tiny things, that shriveled up to the size of a currant, but they came out crisp and delicate, little bursts of taste. I just took handfuls of them off the wall and tossed them in the pan."

"If we want an American culture," Tasha said, "we've got to work on what's American. You feed the soil if you want to grow roots. So I eat many hamburgers. It's not bad, it's good. American cars. American jobs. American America."

"That's some of the jargon," said Peter. "Can you believe it? Tasha put away her hippy and found a redneck in her closet."

"Rednecks are closer to hippies than they are to college professors." A resigned scowl crossed Peter's mouth, as he turned the curry with a spoon. Tasha went on, "The rednecks will be the survivors, and the salvation of America. Just watch."

"Watch what? The holocaust? The salvation of what?"

"Look I don't mean they're going to save some New York art made with a piece of string, or some literature you can't read."

"C'mon, Tasha. You know it's just chic for you to like rednecks at this moment. You don't even know a redneck."

"You never listen to me."

"I don't listen to the Ku Klux Klan, either."

"Why not?"

"I roasted them like hibachi on little sewing needles. They were good that way," Fletcher said. "And I used them once for stuffing in a chicken."

"I still eat chicken, Colonel Sanders."

"And you were a goddam good cook, too," Peter said.

"That's the only time you ever listen to me is when I tell you how I used to cook something."

"Well I don't think that shit you eat now is good for you, and you used to agree with me, all that chemical beef."

"Go take a chic leak," Tasha turned to the kids. "Who does the dishes tonight?"

"I'm sorry you had to come all this way to listen to this," Peter said to Dusty. The kids seemed to ignore the argument. They worked out the dishes without dispute. "We decided best to let the kids hear us argue," Peter said. "Gives them a sense of reality. You know there's still a lot of love between Tasha and me. We still have to work some things out." Peter put his arm around his wife and kissed her.

Tasha smiled. "Thanks for the dinner."

"Don't rub it in. You didn't eat any of my dinner."

"I always wonder what these bats eat." Fletcher said.

"I didn't have to cook it either," she kissed him again.

"We promised," said Peter, his arm around Tasha. "To end every argument with a kiss.

Dusty took the whole pot of chili to the table. It was a big, crusty, cast-iron dutch oven that kept bubbling after he took it off the fire. Fletcher was back at the table, facing the mountains this time.

"When does the moon come up?" he asked.

Steve Katz

"Don't know," said Dusty. "Any minute now." He ladled some chili into the bowls. "Since my kids have stopped coming here with me I tend to make the chili real extreme. A little 'picante' jolts the consciousness, especially when you're alone." It was changing, Dusty thought. The story had been Swiss Family Robinson when the kids were included in the fantasy, and now for him it was a retreat, lonely and calm. Fletcher didn't taste the chili. He stared behind Dusty towards the brightened edge of the mountains.

"Have you been to see Peter since I met you there?"

"No, not there."

"I wondered how they were doing. How the kids were doing. I didn't think they'd get divorced but . . ."

"I've been in my room," Fletcher said.

"With the bats." Dusty looked at the covered cage till sitting on the table. It made him a little anxious that Fletcher hadn't yet tasted the chili, a vestige of raising his kids.

"I wanted to figure out what they ate," said Fletcher. "I mean, how they survived, and if each of them really did hold onto the soul of some New Yorker. Wouldn't you want to know?" Fletcher caught Dusty with his eye that seemed already full of moonlight. "If you were in possession of bats like these?" He lifted the cloth from the cage.

Dusty was caught by this question with his mouth full of hot chili. "Of course. Yeah. Of course I would." His eyes were tearing.

"Yes, yes, yes," said Fletcher. "Yes I did. And one night my roommate was having a party, and I wanted to stay in my room, because a lot of the little things were giving birth. They had chosen the wall separating my room from the rest of the apartment as their maternity wall. It was fine. It made me feel good. Each teeny baby was born sucking on a nipple smaller than a flyspeck. There was a hum coming off the wall like real contentment, that I heard even under the speakers blasting in the living room. I wanted to hold one of the little mothers in my hand, wanted to feel it give birth. That was when I reached in with a finger to take one off, and I felt something really wierd. My finger," He held up his forefinger. "actually sank into the wall beyond the little bats. I thought there was maybe more than one layer of them, so I pushed real gently and my hand went in up to the wrist, and I still didn't feel any wall, but around my hand there was this prickling of energy. Then the whole forearm went in—NO WALL. I pulled the arm out and looked at it. Not a mark, but it tingled like crazy, like all the molecules were popping. It was raining out, so just to prove it to myself I went over to the wall that separated my room from the street and stuck my arm through up to the shoulder. I could feel the difference in the temperature outside, and when I pulled back my hand was wet. My hand was really wet."

"It was wet, uh? Your hand was wet?" Fletcher still hadn't touched the chili.

"Yeah. Yeah, from the rain outside. I mean it wasn't a wall there, only this solid front of bats to separate me from everything. And I don't know how they were still structural. I put my hand back in and waved it back and forth, like moving it through water packed solid with minnows."

"Why don't you eat some chili?" Dusty said. He looked at the cage Fletcher had brought. It was one of those frail cages of sticks the Chinese use for crickets. He couldn't see any bats in it.

"So then I decided to go into the party and tell them about it.

Steve Katz

Now that wasn't easy for me to do because Lydia was there, and she was an old girl friend of mine who came to the party because she wanted to see me, and I really didn't want to see anyone like that, not until I figured all this stuff out. But I did want someone else to see what I saw, because I was feeling really crazy at that moment as you can well imagine, and I wanted someone to tell me it was happening. Lydia was already knocking on my door anyway. 'Hey, Fletcher, come on out here, babes, this is a party.'

" 'Listen,' I said. 'First you come in here. I need to show you something.' I was in my space, I mean IN IT, and that was where I had to stay.

'If it's those bats you talk about I don't want to see it.'

'How do you know? You never seen my bats.'

'Bats make me feel weird, even talking about them.' She opened the door a little more. 'You come to the party.'

'Watch,' I said. 'I can put my arm through the wall.' I did it for her. I put my arm in right to the shoulder.

She acted as if she didn't see it. 'Come. Come to the party.' She pulled me by the other arm through the doorway into the living room. Everyone was dancing close to a slow number. Lydia was one of these ample red-headed women and she pulled me up against her body so I disappeared in her soft tits. 'I got a lot of hair,' she said. 'The bats'll get in it.'

'That's a silly superstition, Lydia.' I leaned back to look at her face. She was a good woman, but you wouldn't call her smart. 'Those bats . . . I mean I can walk right through that wall.'

'Look, I don't like to talk about them, even. They make me feel weird, Fletcher. They come in the night. They suck your blood.'

'Forget it. I'm going back in my room. Look, you keep your

eye on that wall, and in a few minutes I'll be coming through it, not through the door, through the wall, and when you see that happening you tell everyone to watch. Okay?'

She hesitated a little, and looked at me with some sad eyes because she wasn't getting what she wanted, but then she said okay even though it made her feel a little stupid. I went back to my room. To get it across at all I knew I'd have to give a powerful demonstration. It crossed my mind that if these bats held everybody's soul in New York, maybe nobody else was capable of seeing them, like trying to look into your own eye without a mirror; but it was gross for me to presume that I was the only one aboard with a soul. And I even thought that maybe there were no bats, maybe there was nothing for anyone to see, maybe just my imagination was bothered like that, and I was crazy, or the world had cracked apart and I was caught in the cusp and I'd lost sight of everything else retreating around the bend, if you see what I mean. I said to myself, now this is really crazy, Fletcher, to believe that these bats had replaced wallboard and brick and stud and joist, and that they would yield their space so you could move through a wall, I mean, just for you, to separate the bonds of energy or whatever it is that makes a wall a wall."

"I don't see any bats in this cage, Fletcher," said Dusty. He held the cage close to his face. Fletcher's eyes were fixed on the hill at Dusty's back. "You should eat a little chili, anyway," Dusty said.

"I'm gonna try to tell you what it was like, Dusty; but you've gotta remember that you can't really describe what it feels like to walk through a wall. You've gotta experience it yourself. I figured you had to do it naked, because it wasn't right to put some clothing through a wall, so I stripped and relaxed. There was a light humming in the air that put me right at ease. I slowly moved up against the wall. It was iridescent blue from all the little eyes focussed on me now. I was like coming flat against the surface of the sky, not a cloud visible in any direction. I didn't have to take a step. I didn't even have to think about it, because it was pulling on me, sucking all the gravity out of my weight, and I was about to take off. As soon as I moved to finger a few of the creatures aside I felt the release, zero gravity, and I was launched, and this mellow like temperature began to fill me like water coming into a sponge. There was no resistance. None. Entering the bats was like being held aloft by the meekest wind. I've tried to think of what it was like when my body was entirely within the wall, but it's hard. Maybe it's something like taking a bath, if you can imagine each of your molecules being scrubbed separately by a tiny bat. Does that help?"

"Yeah. Each molecule. That's good," said Dusty.

"And then there's this smell, a scent, that I never got anywhere else, that you smell it in your whole body, and in your mind, not in your nose, too subtle for that, distinct and sweet, and that, I assure you, is the odor of time emanating from the forms of things, all things opening once like flowers, petals falling in the wind of the endless events, the transcription of events. Doesn't it sound crazy? I mean, you know, I'm not even sure I'm saying it. Like you penetrate the wall, but the bats penetrate you, and there's room for everything, nothing lost, nothing added. And Dusty, I tell you, my understanding of what my emotions were changed in that moment; I mean I can't even call them *my* emotions any more. I feel like it's me now, and the emotions, and we share a space, like live in the same apartment. I disregard them, just visualize each little piece of emotion carried away by a tiny blue-eyed bat flying through time-scented bazaars of energy. Don't get me wrong, Dusty. This isn't an idea I have, but I know it, I see it, and there it goes . . . No way to explain this, but I want you to promise me, Dusty, that one of these times you yourself will penetrate a wall, and then you will immediately need no explanation. Do you promise me that?" Fletcher looked for once directly into Dusty's eyes. Fletcher's eyes were bright blue and moving in their depths.

"Okay. I'll do that. But only if you eat some of your chili right now." How paternal that sounds, Dusty thought. "And I honestly can't see any bats in this cage, Fletcher."

"So I did come through the wall, and no one was looking. Not even Lydia. She was way on the other side of the room. Then my roommate looked at me and said, "Hey get a look at Fletcher. He's streaking."

I was just standing there. Sabrina, a tall, skinny woman, wearing a sheer crepe dress, came over to dance with me. 'I love naked men,' she said, jabbing her bones against me. And my roomate, his name is Sonny, said, 'Now we've got a real party going,' and he started to strip, and pretty soon the whole party was naked. Then I knew it was no use, I mean they'd never figure it out. I went back to my room and packed some gear, and then descended slowly through the outer wall and into the rain, and I headed up here to see you because I wanted to get far away, and I remembered you invited me. In a way, you know, I didn't want to leave, because those little bats helped me to understand what little I know about the nature of stuff. Anyway now I'm here."

"And you're welcome for a while. I'm glad you're here," Dusty said. "But you should eat some chili." Fletcher's arms rested in a broken circle around the bowl, but he showed no interest in the contents. "And to tell you the truth, Fletcher," Dusty said, lifting the cage, and shaking it slightly. "I don't see any bats in this cage."

Fletcher gently picked the cage from Dusty's hand, as if he were picking a bubble off the surface of a dream. He held it in front of his face. "Then don't look at them," he said.

"I want to see them," Dusty said.

Fletcher stared through the cage. Dusty looked at his full bowl. Not a bite taken. He would have mentioned it once more, just once, but the words stopped in his mouth when he looked at Fletcher again. The whites of Fletcher's eyes had disappeared. He was staring out through two wide blue spheres. His shoulders raised up around his face so they almost covered his ears. A smile opened on his face, so strange that he seemed to be attentive to the echo of a sound Dusty couldn't hear in this world. Then as a curtain closes on the last actor present who will never deliver the conclusive line, Fletcher opened his wings wide behind himself and holding the cage high he rose on the slowly undulating membranes unfurled from his side. "Fletcher," Dusty said softly, as if he were remembering his name. He didn't even have time to doubt what happened, or question it. He saw it. Fletcher rose in a leisurely spiral, his blue eyes drilling down on Dusty; and his black shape rose against the constellations already dimmed by moonlight, and it hid the stars of Bootes, the Corona, and the Big Bear with its wings.

Dusty breathed at the table, slowly in and out. He looked out at the last dark shades of sunset and could see on the water that the moon had finally risen behind him. He watched some fear rise in himself and then fly away. Had this happened at all? He picked up Fletcher's bowl. If only he had eaten a bit of it. Had he been sleepwalking by himself through a dream? If there had only been one other person there who might have seen it, maybe Nick who had built the tower in which Fletcher stowed his gear. Dusty turned to look at the tower. The moon was right behind it. It seemed higher than the hills. Fletcher's gear would still be inside it, all he had to do was open the door. He remembered his son's mild obsession with it as he built the tower, started at ten, finished when he was sixteen, hauling driftwood boards and 4 x 4's from the beach, fitting them precisely as he could. And he put a bed in it, that wasn't long enough for him by the time he was sixteen, so he had to open one side and cover an extension for his feet to sleep. Now the tower looked like it had always been there. Dusty emptied Fletcher's bowl of chili into the pot, and walked to the tower. Its West wall was still warm from the sun. The moon filled his campsite with silver light. The tower was full of everything, he knew it, full of gear and nostalgia. He looked up at it extended to the stars as if ready to be launched. No, he thought, don't open the tower. Don't look in. It's the same door at this time when you get to madness or to sentiment. When something rises questions go unanswered. Some day maybe his brother would come and use whatever was in there, maybe not. This was a structure full of everything, or full of nothing. He removed his hand from the wall, turned his back on it, and took seventeen steps away from the tower, twenty-six steps away from the moon.

Donald S. Olson

Objects in Mirror are Closer Than They Appear

Every Friday afternoon the man was there in the train station, and every Friday afternoon Miss Slough was there in the train station. Miss Slough was there to meet the train which brought her sister Hydrangea home from the Detention Center where she was incarcerated except on weekends. The man was there for some reason Miss Slough could not ascertain —always, however, on Friday afternoons. Since she was herself not at the train station at any other time (Hydrangea, of course, was picked up by the Patrol on Sunday afternoons for her return to the Detention Center), Miss Slough did not know if the man was there other afternoons as well.

Every Friday afternoon the man made himself known to her in one way or another. He was by now as familiar a feature of her Friday afternoons as Hydrangea with her handcuffs, or the large clock above the currency exchange windows in the station which had, since the last change of regime, been going backwards. Still, although familiar, Miss Slough never knew when the man would appear, or what exactly he would do. In this sense he was different from Hydrangea with her handcuffs and weighted prison shoes, who always stepped down with a certain leaden grace from the same prison car every Friday afternoon. The man, on the other hand, might appear from nowhere: from Miss Slough's right or her left, from across the station or from behind one of the thick pillars, carved to look like elephant legs, which lumbered across the main terminal. He might appear from behind a newspaper, or coming up from or going down to or even inside one of the large, humid, dangerous restrooms. Miss Slough never knew. All she knew thus far was that he would be there, somewhere, every Friday afternoon, this regime or the next. In this country, which she inhabited as a convert inhabits unquestioningly his new faith, the internal logic of things was not always apparent. Each new regime helped to decompose former standards by imposing new laws, and to question any of the new laws resulted in severe penalities.

It had all started innocuously enough, as any romance, no matter how strange, does. Perhaps the man had been there in the station for months before Miss Slough's consciousness was ready, finally, to take him in. And she wondered now if perhaps it were possible that she hadn't noticed him before because she hadn't wanted to— or *didn't know how*. Generally, Miss Slough regarded people and events, if at all, from a distance. Her years in a nunnery, along with her general disposition, had removed her concern and biased her ability to distinguish events in the "real world" to such an extent that having to examine reality with her naked eyes—eyes stripped of old notions favored by former regimes—either frightened her or made her angry. The one exception to this was God, Whom she had at one time allowed to ransack her soul with the violence of a lover. In the nunnery, in her hot dank cell, she was encouraged to love God, allowed to perfume her soul with prayers and powder her bleeding heart with meditations—

all guaranteed to bring the Holy Lips close to her spirit. Since, however, she had never *seen* God, and had never known when He would make His Presence known to her, God occupied a bewildering territory of His own in the suburbs of her vision. For when she thought He should be closest, thanks to her beautifying her soul, He was nowhere to be found; and when she was preoccupied and cogitating on other matters, suddenly He would descend, and she would find herself spun round in a web of sensational ecstasy.

Highly discriminating when it came to selecting those things she would allow her attention to accommodate now that she was no longer in the nunnery, Miss Slough would not under normal circumstances have permitted the man in the train station into her private vision. Out of habit, she would not have seen him; his physicality would have been of no account to her, or something immediately viewed as sinful had she noticed it. The nunnery had absolved her vision of any connection with the strange world outside its thick stone walls. When she had first been forced to leave, she felt like a tiny child pushed into an incomprehensible adult world. What was it people saw out here? And did the new regime force vision in its own secular hot-house way, the way vision was forced and espaliered in the House of God?

Even before the man made himself known to her on that first Friday, Miss Slough had been perturbed and oddly excited. Driving to the train station to meet Hydrangea for the first time since her sister had been sent to the Detention Center, Miss Slough felt queerly unfocussed, aware all at once of too many peripheral objects. She was somehow less defined than formerly. For the first time she noticed the warning printed on the outside rear-view mirror of her new car: Objects in mirror are closer than they appear. She could not keep her eyes away from this warning, and the words chanted themselves rhythmically in her head over and over again until she was obsessively reciting them in the trance-like manner of a rosary prayer. Her thin body was rigid and erect with a kind of intuitive warning of fear or elation. Since the objects she saw in the rear-view mirror were closer than they appeared, she drove faster to keep her distance from them, but never fast enough—since everything that appeared was closer than she could ascertain.

Naturally she had had to give a great deal of thought to Hydrangea's accommodations. Everything had changed, and Hydrangea's old room with its pink frilly curtains and bedspread would no longer be appropriate or even moral. Miss Slough took everything in Hydrangea's room and put it in her own, while every item in her own she placed in Hydrangea's. Thus Hydrangea would sleep on Miss Slough's narrow iron cot with a heavy horsehair blanket. If it were hot, Hydrangea could sleep on top of the blanket, and if it were cold she could use it as a cover. The pink frilly curtains were replaced with stiff, unyielding canvas ones which were impossible to keep open. Hydrangea's spacious carved dresser was replaced by Miss Slough's tall, narrow, unornamented one: it now stood in a corner like a severe virgin warden.

Miss Slough used strength she had not known her body to possess as she tore up the thick carpet Hydrangea had favored and nailed it down on her own floor, leaving Hydrangea bare wooden boards studded with sharp, hidden carpet tacks. The full-length mirror in front of which Hydrangea had loved to amuse herself for hours on end now caught the determined,

Donald S. Olson

angular reflection of Miss Slough each time she entered her own room, and something in this reflection—the nervous, hunched shoulders, the look of quiet stealth—suggested the posture of a thief. Miss Slough found it difficult to inhabit space physically, the moreso because the old villa which had been her parents' before their disappearance, and which was presumed to be part of her worldly inheritance, had never psychically adjusted to her returned presence, nor she to it.

At first Miss Slough, in her ruthless rearrangings, had decided that Hydrangea should not have a mirror, but finally, in a tender fit of generosity, she hung a small discolored one on the bare wall so that her sister would again have something with which to amuse herself when locked inside. Miss Slough fractured its surface with a hammer, however, so that her sister would not become giddy with immoral excitement when she peered into it.

Naturally the locks were changed on Hydrangea's bedroom door, and the iron grille Miss Slough had had installed outside her own window when she returned from the convent many years earlier was now removed and firmly screwed into place in the decaying stone surrounding Hydrangea's window. When the hot, passionate sun of that part of the world struck Hydrangea's window, the bars of the iron grille appeared bloated and remorseless on the stiff canvas curtains inside. This shadowing had once greatly appealed to Miss Slough's ascetic tastebuds.

Hydrangea's new room now appeared, on the eve of her return home, to be identical to Miss Slough's old one. The two rooms were exactly the same anyway, in dimension, closet space and lay-out, but Miss Slough had occupied her own room for so long that she had no intention of moving out of it and into the room of a criminal of Hydrangea's magnitude. Her sister must learn a lesson in Consequences.

And if Miss Slough felt unfocussed that first Friday on her way to the train station—that portentous first Friday—perhaps it was because she had slept so poorly in her old room now filled with everything of Hydrangea's. Her dreams were shocking in their physicality. Without the comforting iron grille on her window, which not only made her room physically inaccessible but had also always lulled her with reminiscences of the grilles in confessionals, she was anxious and nervously aware of her unguarded body. The night air was as stagnant and unmoving as pond water, and the Night Guard sounded crapulous and inattentive in the distance, as though the last thing on their minds was a woman sleeping alone without an iron grille on her window. The Cat Patrol could be heard faintly miaowing up and down nearby alleys, while the Free Thinkers quietly moaned, their mouths taped, in the new Facility nearby. A hooded religious procession tip-toed towards the main square, their fasting bellies growling in the moonlight. Miss Slough lay sweating beneath Hydrangea's pink frilly bedspread. Was this how people in the "real world" felt?

Miss Slough was punctual as ever, but the currency had been devalued yet again and she was thus denied a parking space under cover. After parking on one of the narrow, miserable streets near the train station, she hurried towards the relative safety of its thick brick walls. The warning in the rear-view mirror drummed persistently in her head: Objects in mirror are closer than they appear . . .

A large, hungry-looking crowd was gathered outside the station's main door. Between their legs, Miss Slough caught a glimpse of a bloody body. She was almost herded off with

321

several others but flashed her identity card with the quick, deft, authoritative gesture recognized by the Patrol as belonging to the oldest of families, originally come to their country as missionaries, but later assimilated into the secular life of the then new regime.

"When does the prison train arrive, please?" she asked at the information booth inside the station.

The employee, sucking on a piece of discolored fruit, eyed her suspiciously.

"I once wanted to be a nun," she assured him in a whisper, bribing him with her original parking money.

"Track Thirteen, seven hours from now," he told her in dialect.

Miss Slough glanced up towards the backwards-running clock. "Oh, then I still have several minutes to burn," she said to herself.

Each new regime brought a flood of new people to the city. They loitered noisily in and around the train station, being arrested or shot or bribing people to help them find work. They evidently assumed that there were ways and means by which their squalid lives could be made bearable. Miss Slough stood near one of the elephant-leg columns and attempted to pay no attention to the crowded misery around her. She waved away a diseased child hawking crosses "stained with authentic blood." Increasingly uncomfortable, she found herself unable to keep from noticing certain peripheral objects and people. Without exception they appeared to her sordid and filthy with sin. In the past, her ingrained religious unconsciousness had kept her immune from mental contact with them, but now that she was no longer in the nunnery it was impossible not to be physically jostled and touched by them. Rarely did she leave the villa for this very reason.

The warning on her rear-view mirror still scanned itself annoyingly through her thoughts. Outside, the bloody body was being hoisted up to hang on the station gibbet. One dared not question the regime and its increasing executions. Like everyone else, Miss Slough shuddered to think of her mouth being taped, even though she sometimes went for days on end without saying a word.

It was not until she moved away from the column that the man made his presence known. She felt a damp hand on her arm and turned around, expecting some further unpleasant surprise. The man was leaning towards her with a concerned look on his face. He said nothing. Was he of this country? What dialect did he use? Did he smell?

Miss Slough said, "Yes, what is it?"

"Your exquisite nose," the man said, and before she could gasp, move away or object, he had reached out and stroked her long, sharp nose between two of his fingers. "You breathe filth down into your very soul," he said, and then turned and was lost in the crowd.

Visibly upset, sniffing tentatively, Miss Slough hurried towards Track Thirteen, arriving just as the train with the prison car came to a grinding halt. She waited until Hydrangea slowly and with as much delicacy as her weighted shoes would allow stepped from the train. Hydrangea's wrists were hand-cuffed and her hands clasped as demurely as the circumstances would permit in front of her. Miss Slough signed the register for week-end custody and led her sister through the jammed, noisy station.

"Do you have the money?" she asked her sister. "I told you that I would not allow you to return for weekends unless you paid."

"The money is in the right cup of my brassiere," said Hydrangea. She smiled and leaned forward to plant a grateful kiss on her sister's cheek.

"I hope there is plenty of it," said Miss Slough, backing away so that Hydrangea was left with her lips puckered, "since this regime has just devalued the currency again."

"Walk more slowly, please, I can't keep up with you wearing these weighted shoes," said Hydrangea.

"Brought down to earth at last, like the rest of us. Who's fault is that if you are made to wear weighted shoes?" Miss Slough asked severely, and added, "Perhaps now you will understand how the rest of the common people feel, plodding heavily along through life and having to bribe for all pleasures. Perhaps now some of the Consequences a person pays for being alive will become known to you."

"You look upset," said Hydrangea. "Has something happened recently to make you look so nervous?"

They walked past the feet of the body on the station gibbet and into a stun of sunlight. "There was a man, and he . . ." but then Miss Slough stopped, deciding not to confide in Hydrangea, who was after all a criminal.

"A man?" asked Hydrangea.

"Yes, a man, a member of the opposite sex such as you once so very often carried on with in your room with the pink frilly curtains and pink frilly bedspread, while I was calling upon God in my own room. The close proximity of your seductive amours of course rendered my spiritual bridegroom impotent. What you did in there with men, Hydrangea, is unforgivable." Then, softening a bit, she asked how things were in the Detention Center.

"Oh, things are generally terrible," said Hydrangea, "and my legs are always sore because of these shoes—notice the veins beginning to mar the backs of my legs—but I am after all innocent, and that helps me in the darker hours."

"No one is innocent," remarked Miss Slough, "who is sent by the regime to the Detention Center. The regime would not punish innocence, would it? That is one of your crimes, that you have never felt guilty."

"I did not do it," said her sister.

"Of course you did. Someone presented secret testimony to the Tribunal which proved that it was you. You have never acknowledged the guilt that makes your soul retarded. You always were a liar, and it was you who prevented me from taking final vows in the nunnery."

"I? How did I do that?" asked Hydrangea, her soft eyes opened wide with puzzlement.

"Your reputation. When what you secretly did for the old regime—*with* the old regime, shall I say?—reached the muffled ears of the Good Sisters, there was of course no hope for me. The veil was torn from my head. My hair began to grow again. Look how long it is now—"

"I can't tell how long it is because it's wrapped so tightly on the back of your head," said Hydrangea.

"Well it is long and disgusting. Like Eve's hair, only darker and shot through with gray. But the worse of it was when the Good Sisters sat me on a studded chair and severely mocked me for my own good as they walked in the spiritual formation known as The Circle. No, I will never forgive you for their mockery and their curses. There are times when I still hear their voices . . ."

That first Friday Miss Slough forgot about the man in light

of having Hydrangea home for the first time since her incarceration. Now the routine was nearly always the same. First she would drive to the station. Next she would have her unsettling encounter with the man. Then she would drive Hydrangea back to the villa and lock her in her altered room.

"Why must you lock me in this room?" asked Hydrangea. "I am handcuffed and could not run away if I wanted to, given the weight of these shoes."

"You are a bona fide criminal, don't forget, and the weight of those shoes should serve to keep you continually aware of that fact. I for one will take no further chances, given what the regime has said you have done already."

"But this isn't my room, this is your room," protested Hydrangea.

"No, you are wrong, miserably wrong. This is your new old room. My old new room is next door. Things had to change. Life is no different from a regime. Now give me the money before I lock you up."

Hydrangea every Friday would clumsily remove a wad of bills from her brassiere and hand it to her sister.

"Do you have to work hard for that money?" asked Miss Slough.

"Yes, terribly hard. Oh, you would not believe what I have to do to get that money."

"Yes, I would, given what you've done already. Your crimes are truly voluptuous and perverted. But if you think there will be men every weekend, think again. They will be denied access entirely. The Cat Patrol is in this sector on Wednesdays and Thursdays only, so give up any idea you may have of miaowing to one of them from your window. The Night Guard also is in a different sector on weekends. This regime has quite changed things, temporarily."

"But what am I to do?" asked Hydrangea.

"I have put a small mirror on the wall with which you may amuse yourself or reflect with remorse upon your state."

"Could I also then have some small pieces of twine, and perhaps also some thimbles?" Hydrangea asked hopefully.

"Will twine and thimbles give you pleasure?" her sister asked in turn.

"Oh yes, very much."

"Then they are out of the question," said Miss Slough. "It seems not unlikely that you would somehow use these materials for an escape. If I were you, I would think hard about my guilt and the disgusting nature of sin."

"I have no sin," said Hydrangea.

"You always were provocative," said Miss Slough angrily. She spread her lips in what could hardly be called a pleasant grin. "In secret, perhaps I am provocative also—but that is for God's eyes alone to know. It may just be that my spiritual bridegroom wishes to make my acquaintance before . . ." She was thinking of the man in the train station, of course, and making wild, possibly heretical speculations before she caught herself. Narrowing her eyes, which looked as though the sheen had been scrubbed from them, she regarded Hydrangea with cold passion.

"I am very pleased to be home," said Hydrangea, "even under a new regime. Perhaps when a newer regime takes over my innocence will be proved, and then we will be as once we were."

"We will never be as once we were!" cried Miss Slough. "And you will never again do with men what you once did. And because of you it may be that I will never again be able to do with God what I once could sometimes do. It was you, Hydrangea, who made me a widow!"

Any exchange between the sisters would end momentarily

Donald S. Olson

while Miss Slough prodded Hydrangea into the room with a pointed stick and locked the door.

After the first time, when the man tenderly stroked Miss Slough's nose in the train station, he became increasingly more unpredictable in his appearances, and generally less tender in what she assumed to be his advances. Having known no men except for God, and having known God as God and never as a man, Miss Slough's perceptions in this area of romantic hypothesis were perhaps understandably askew. She wondered at times if these unpredictable ravishments, first of her soul, and now of her person, were how men and God made themselves known to desirable women.

The second Friday she was in the train station she had almost entirely forgotten about her first encounter with the man. She was standing near the currency exchange windows and the person standing beside her was reading a newspaper. Suddenly she was aware, without directly looking aside, that the person had lowered the paper and was staring at her over the top of it. She took one cautious step sideways, meaning to leave the area, when suddenly the newspaper reader stepped in front of her, blocking her exit. His eyes were very dark and familiar somehow, and seemed to rummage in the privacy of her soul as if invited to do so.

"Yes—what is it?" she asked breathlessly.

"Your eyes," he said, slowly moving the newspaper down to reveal his face.

Miss Slough, frightened, excited, was unable to move. "Yes, what about them?" she asked hesitantly.

"They are the mirrors of your soul," said the man slowly, making her wait for each word.

328

"Of what concern are the mirrors of my soul to you?" she asked, unable to look away from him.

Instead of answering her, the man put out two fingers and moved them slowly, inexorably, towards her face. Miss Slough thought that perhaps he was going to stroke her eyelids, but she was too afraid to close her eyes to allow him to do so.

"Do you see how close my fingers are to your eyes?" he whispered.

"Yes, oh yes. They look odd and dangerous—hypnotic—like the Heavenly Digits," she breathed.

"If you aren't careful," explained the man, "my fingers will suddenly dart forward and poke you in the distorted mirrors of your soul."

"If God did that I would not mind my mystically altered vision," she heard herself saying as she watched his fingers looming closer and closer, "but if only a man did that, I would lose my sight entirely."

"The regime would not blame me," said the man.

"What must I do?" she asked, terrified.

"Blink rapidly several times."

This she did, and when she opened her eyes after blinking as he had said, the man was gone. Dazed, gasping, she pushed her way through the bribing throngs towards Track Thirteen.

"What was it you did with men, exactly?" she asked Hydrangea through the locked door later that evening.

"I told you that I was innocent," said Hydrangea.

"Did you watch as their fingers moved towards your eyes, and wonder if they were going to blind you?" Miss Slough asked. "Did you wonder if these men were God?"

"I never look at men," answered Hydrangea.

"Are there men in the Detention Center who comment on your eyes and nose?" persisted Miss Slough. "Is this a courtship ritual of the new regime?"

"There are no men in the Detention Center. The Detention Center is not unlike this villa before I was arrested and sent away by the regime: hot, mysterious, and no men allowed."

"That must be why you always snuck them up to your old room with its pink frilly curtains and bedspread and full-length mirror," said Miss Slough.

"There were never any men on my bedspread or in my mirror," insisted Hydrangea.

"Yes, and I never wanted to be a nun," said Miss Slough bitterly.

"Is what men do the same as what God does?" Hydrangea asked from behind her door.

"Don't you remember anything the Good Sisters chanted into our ears day after day as children?" asked Miss Slough in an accusing voice.

"No," said Hydrangea, "I retain very little, which is why I am innocent and hopeful."

"I suppose you think that your sins slide off your soul like water off a duck's back." Aggravated, Miss Slough stood back and took a deep breath. "I suppose that it never occurs to you that you are locked in your soul with all its filth and that only God has the key and the broom. I suppose that you have always confused God with men, and what they do to women." Now, trembling with all the weight of her repression, concomitant excitement, and furious remorse for the past, she began a furious tirade that backed Hydrangea into a corner. "I suppose that you have never in all your lewd escapades been driven crazy by God, the chastest of bridegrooms, and also the most passionate. I suppose you were perverted enough to believe a mere man's coarse love can approximate the love of God! It was with God, not mere men, that I once did things in secret. It was God who stoked my being and kept me in hot suspense over his arrival times. It was for God that I made my soul attractive by wearing a tight veil and scouring away my personality and brutalizing my flesh." She raised her hand suddenly, and Hydrangea made a sharp movement, as though a blow had actually fallen on her. "And then, after all that, because of my sister's reputation, He went off and left me no better than a barren widow, with lonely, scarred flesh."

Hydrangea clumped as quickly as she could to her broken piece of discolored mirror and held it up to her face. "I am real," she said. "My sins are not. The regime framed me with those sins."

"The regime or possibly someone else," said Miss Slough insinuatingly.

"You! My own sister! My own blood!"

Miss Slough unleashed another outburst. "I suppose you think you are like me! I suppose that you were once in a nunnery, and expelled from it. And I suppose that as time went by and you waited in pain for your Holy Love to return you never suspected what your imagination was capable of, or how exposed your senses one day would become to men—ordinary, mortal, brutish men. I suppose that you, having once allowed God to take the most excessive of liberties with you, were then incapable of rearranging the furniture of your soul in order to be on a pink frilly bedspread with some man who could manipulate your physical senses only. I suppose, Hydrangea," shouted Miss Slough, choking on her passion, "that the bribery of all experience has never occurred to you. Nothing is free!

331

When it comes to the regimes of this place, nothing is free! Only God exacts no bribery and never devalues the currency, as I have discovered to my humiliation. You can't bribe God to love you. He takes you where and when He wants."

"I pity you," said Hydrangea. "But my own soul is a mirror wherein God is always to be seen smiling and combing His hair."

"That is not fair," cried Miss Slough, stiffening, "and so it is not true! God would not be reflected in anything so dirty and distorted as your soul, He wouldn't comb His hair in your soul even if you bribed Him. I've done nothing, and He won't even give me the correct time of day, while you who have done what you've wished all these many years and been sent finally to the Detention Center for it don't even suffer?" She was about to threaten that she would not allow Hydrangea home for the next weekend, but remembering the man in the train station she held her parched tongue as though a Communion wafer sat on it.

Every Friday afternoon now Miss Slough was in the train station a few minutes early, always filled with tense expectation, never knowing how the man would appear, who he was, or what he would do. Perhaps she should follow him. Perhaps he would lead her somewhere. Perhaps he was . . .

After their unsettling encounter, she would meet Hydrangea's train, drive her home to the hot villa, lock her in her room, and then go into her own room now filled with what had belonged to Hydrangea. Miss Slough would stand in front of Hydrangea's confiscated full-length mirror and wonder how close she was to it. There were times when she was certain that she was standing all the way on the other side of the room—

yet when she reached out her hand, her fingers touched the mirror, and she realized that she was standing only inches away from it. Deeply disturbed, she would move closer, as she thought, only to put her hand out once more and find that she was back in some far corner. Her soul and senses were in turmoil; her internal vision and her rendering of "reality" locked in bruising conflict. Was she not seeing what was actually in the mirror? Or was the mirror, in the manner of God, seeing her differently from the way she saw herself? Whose vision could she trust? What was she to believe?

Something in the man's attitude and appearance suggested increasing danger, but what this danger was Miss Slough could not guess. With so many changes of regime, a person could never be exactly certain what was dangerous and what was merely insane. The man never directly threatened her, but always after their encounter she would walk away, her knees weak, with a queerly heightened sense that she was very close to something—some mystical revelation—and that this revelation would also be terrifying. Yet what if this were all a secular game of the regime? The man could, after all, be a spy. She could be doing something wrong and not even know it. Perhaps in a smoke-filled office somewhere there was a List, and her name, as a former novitiate in the nunnery, was on it.

Slowly she came to realize that she was longing for something, had perhaps always been longing for something. And never had she felt so close to things, so much a part of the hot, giddy, disjointed world around her. The physical world, even after all these years away from the nunnery, still puzzled and disgusted her, but there was also a florid spirituality to be found among its degradations. You had, however, to be rather cock-eyed to find it.

And fear, there was fear. One Friday afternoon, out of a corner of her eye, she thought she saw the man walking down towards the humid restrooms of ill repute. Amazed at herself, she followed out of some hungry compulsion. The stench filled her nostrils as she descended. It was said that down in these parts anything could happen, and even the Patrols avoided them.

Miss Slough's heart was burning and stamping a native dance as down she went. A small crowd of hideous-looking people watched as she stepped off the bottom stair and stiffly made her way to the restrooms. Once inside the door, she gasped and quickly removed a handkerchief which she used to cover her nose and mouth.

"How many?" the bent old woman in charge asked.

After a moment's consideration, Miss Slough put up one pale, candle-like finger.

"This way."

She followed the old woman and entered the stall indicated.

"You have ten minutes," said the old woman. "I am not responsible. Your sins are your own."

Miss Slough, sweating profusely, nodded and quickly locked the stall door behind her. She stood and waited, the suspense mounting, the handkerchief still held to her nose and mouth. What kind of a lovers' assignation was this?

Soon she heard a faint tapping on the wall of the stall. She flushed with fear, but then tapped back. "Yes, what is it?" she whispered through her handkerchief.

There was no answer.

From her handbag she removed a small pocket mirror and dropped it to the floor between the two stalls. Looking down into it, she saw something that made her lose her courage.

Screaming, she ran back upstairs, followed by the machine-gun laughter of the old crone behind her.

And then one Friday the man did not appear. This was difficult to believe—as difficult to believe as his appearances. Miss Slough was even more upset by his absence than she was by his sudden appearances and arcane utterances. His appearance and her resultant heightened perceptions were, or had become, her one reality. Now this rupture! Just as with the nunnery. She felt very alone with her strained senses, like a harmonica waiting for a pair of lips.

"What is the matter today?" asked Hydrangea as they were walking out through the nave of the train station.

Miss Slough pretended to be looking straight ahead, but really she was taking in everything she could peripherally. Now at last she had been made to see everything around her, but she could not see the reason for her seeing. Her vision, she felt, was degraded and banal, the vision of a whore. "Those men you were always doing things with on your frilly bedspread," said Miss Slough intensely, "did they sometimes not appear when you thought they would? How did you do what you did if they were there with you?"

"There never were any men on my pink frilly bedspread," answered Hydrangea.

"This week it's going to cost you double to come back to the villa," said Miss Slough, her voice hoarse and desperate as they approached the station doors.

Later that evening when Hydrangea was amusing herself with the small mirror, she saw in it not only the reflection of herself, but the reflection of her bedroom window. The hot sun

Donald S. Olson

was beating the guilty reflection of the iron grille onto the stiff canvas curtains, and there was another shadow there besides. Hydrangea crossed the room as quickly as her weighted shoes would allow. Handcuffed, she could not part both curtains at once, and so she lifted aside only one.

Outside, in a fierce dazzle of light, was Miss Slough, standing on the top rung on an extension ladder. She was peering into Hydrangea's room with the queer, inverted, intense eyes of a saint or a madwoman.

"What are you doing out there?" asked Hydrangea.

"I suppose you thought I was from the Cat Patrol, come to miaow in your window. I'm checking!" said Miss Slough fiercely. "Checking to be certain that there are no men in your room. Move aside so that I can look carefully. Now go and open your closet door. Now lift one side of the cot so that I can see underneath."

When Hydrangea had done all of this, and Miss Slough had looked as carefully as she could into the room, she climbed back down the ladder. She then came up to talk to Hydrangea through the locked door.

"Did they enter your room on that ladder?" she asked.

"I am innocent," said Hydrangea.

"When they did not appear as you had planned and schemed, what did you do, and how did you do it?" demanded her sister.

"I never did anything."

"Once they did not appear, did you give up hope or did you leave the ladder under your window in case they appeared later on?"

Hydrangea said nothing.

Late that same night Miss Slough lay sweating under Hydrangea's pink frilly bedspread. Carousing revelers could be heard tooting and screaming in the next sector. The new regime was hammering up platforms in the main square. Since changes of regime had come to be regarded as holidays, the superstitious, as on holiday eves, stacked piles of the old currency in front of mirrors before they went to bed, hoping that by the old magic formula and prayers they would wake to find in new currency twice the amount they had set down.

Miss Slough, restless, anxious, bereft, got up to look into Hydrangea's confiscated mirror. She put out her forlorn, trembling hand expecting to touch the mirror's surface, but discovered that she was standing across the room from it.

The mirror reflected the unbarred and open window behind her, and the hot, passionate darkness of the night. Miss Slough, backed up against the wall, feared for her soul. Without God, without the nunnery, she saw nothing but distortions, filth and bribery. She had invited Him back, unbarred her window, lain virginally on Hydrangea's pink frilly bedspread . . . all to no avail. Her awakened senses could not sleep or rest without His embrace, without His eyes upon her. Sweating with torment, Miss Slough moaned. And then, looking again into the mirror, she saw appear the top of a head, and then a head entire. He had climbed up the ladder!

She perked with a kind of weary hope. "Yes, what is it?"

"No, do not turn around. Continue to look into the mirror," said the head, whose voice was familiar, compelling.

"You were not there today. It was Friday," said Miss Slough.

"From now on I will not appear on Fridays."

Miss Slough cried out unabashedly, "But why not?"

"You have seen too much of me, and it has become danger-

Donald S. Olson

ous for you," said the man in the mirror. "You have come too near."

"No, no, never near enough!" she pleaded. "Never close enough."

"It is too dangerous. The regime has again changed."

"Nothing could have been as dangerous as the restroom!" said Miss Slough.

"From now on I will appear only in the mirror," said the man.

"All of you, or just your head? Will it be on Friday nights? What will you do to me from the mirror? If you are in the mirror, I can do nothing to you—nothing, nothing. You may seem close but you will not be. What will you do to me from the mirror?" sobbed Miss Slough.

"Only Hydrangea can answer that," said the man, "and she will not because she is innocent."

"Does that make me guilty?" asked Miss Slough. It was a question she now found herself asking every Friday night as, peering anxiously into the mirror that was Hydrangea's, she waited for the reappearance in one form or another of the voice that was the man Whom she hoped was God.

Notes on Contributors

Walter Abish's most recent novel, *How German Is It* (New Directions), won the PEN/Faulkner award for fiction in 1980. He is also the author of several other books of fiction and poetry, including *Alphabetical Africa*, *Minds Meet*, and *Duel Site*. With his wife, the artist Cecille Abish, he lives in New York City.

Among **Tom Ahern**'s fictions are *A Movie Starring the Late Cary Grant*, *The Capture of Trieste*, *The Strangulation of Dreams*, and *Transcript*. A book of his tales, *Hecatombs of Lake*, will be published by Sun & Moon Press in 1983. He also edits *Diana's BiMonthly* in Providence, Rhode Island.

Roberta Allen, a visual artist, has incorporated language into her art for the past eleven years. Recently, she has begun to write short fictions, which have appeared in *Shantih* and elsewhere.

Editor of the magazine and press, *Unmuzzled Ox*, **Michael Andre** has published *Letters Home* and *Studying the Ground for Hozes*. Most recently, he edited *The Poets' Encyclopedia*.

Winner of the Pulitzer Prize and the National Book Award for *Self-Portrait in a Convex Mirror*, **John Ashbery** has also published *Houseboat Days*, *Some Trees*, *The Tennis Court Oath*, *The Double Dream of Spring*, *Three Poems*, and other books of poetry. He also has written numerous plays and essays, and is co-author, with James Schuyler, of the novel, *A Nest of Ninnies*. He currently teaches at Brooklyn College in New York.

Trailerpark is **Russell Banks'** most recent book of fiction; previously he published *Family Life, Searching for Survivors, The New World, The Book of Jamaica,* and *Hamilton Stark.* He has been awarded the St. Lawrence Award, and his fiction has appeared in The O. Henry and Best American Short Story anthologies. His novel, *The Relation of My Imprisonment,* will be published by Sun & Moon Press in 1983.

Michael Brownstein's *Oracle Night,* a love poem, was published by Sun & Moon Press in 1982. He also is the author of *Brainstorms, Highway to the Sky* (winner of the Frank O'Hara Award), *Three American Tantrums,* and the novel, *Country Cousins.* He divides his time between Boulder, Colorado and New York City.

Norma Jean Deak lives in Solana Beach, California, and has performed her dialogues and other performance pieces at the Whitney Museum of American Art, Artists Space, and Franklin Furnace in New York City, at the Galleria Communale d'Arte Moderna in Bologna, Italy, at the Performance Art Festival in Brussels, and elsewhere.

Laura Ferguson, writer of fiction, poetry, and filmscripts, graduated from Berkeley, where she studied with Ishmael Reed. Currently, she is studying film in Paris.

Harrison Fisher, who recently moved from Providence to Albany, New York, is the author of several books of poetry and fiction, including *Curtains for You, The Text's Boyfriend, Blank Like Me, Six Poems that Made Me Rich and Famous, The Gravity,* and *UHFO.*

Editor of *Crawl Out Your Window,* **Melvyn Freilicher** has published several books and pamphlets of fiction, and is currently at work on a novel, *Stories from Real Life*. He lives and teaches in San Diego.

Steve Katz is the author of *The Exaggerations of Peter Prince*, *Moving Parts*, and other books of fiction. His most recent work, *Wier & Pouce*, will be published by Sun & Moon Press in 1983. He teaches at the University of Colorado in Boulder.

Donald S. Olson has published stories and articles in magazines here and abroad. His novel, *The Secrets of Mabel Eastlake*, was printed by A & W Publishers in 1982.

Toby Olson has published numerous books of poetry, the most recent of which are *Aesthetics* and *The Florence Poems*. His two novels, *The Life of Jesus* (1976) and *Seaview* (1982), were both published by New Directions. In the '60s, he was co-founder and Associate Director of the Aspen Writer's Workshop, and in 1974 he received a CAPS award fellowship grant in poetry. He currently lives in Philadelphia, where he teaches at Temple University.

Born in Saskatoon, Saskatchewan, Canada, and raised in Florida, **Richard Padget** currently lives in New York City. He recently completed two short stories, "Angle of Reflection" and "The Light Is Subtracted; The Space Is Divided."

As an art critic, fiction writer, and poet, **John Perreault** has published widely. Among his books are *Luck* (1969) and *Harry* (1974). Recent fictions include *Hotel Death* and "The Missing Letter."

Joe Ashby Porter's novel, *Eelgrass*, was published by New Directions in 1977; his collection of short fiction, *The Kentucky Stories*, will be printed by Johns Hopkins Press in 1983. His short fiction has appeared in many magazines and anthologies, including *The Pushcart Prize: Best of the Small Presses* and *Best American Short Stories*.

Corinne Robins, an art critic, fiction writer, and poet, lives in New York City. She is currently at work on a new book of poetry, *First*, which will be published early in 1983 by the Pratt Institute of Art.

Mark Sacharoff has written fiction, plays, and short stories. Among his works are a one-act play, "The Front Door," and a full-length drama, *Tempest in Turdyba*. He presently is at work on a comic novel titled, *Alive and Wicked in Greenwich Village*. He teaches at Temple University in Philadelphia.

Leslie Scalapino is widely published in various magazines. Her books of poetry/fiction include *O and Other Poems*, *This eating and walking at the same time is associated all right*, *Instead of an Animal*, and *The Woman Who Could Read the Minds of Dogs*. She has traveled in Asia, Africa, and Europe, and resides in Berkeley, California.

Author of *Mulligan Stew* and *Aberration of Starlight*, **Gilbert Sorrentino** teaches at Stanford University in California. His other books of poetry and fiction include, *The Perfect Fiction*, *White Sail*, *The Orangery*, *The Sky Changes*, *Steelwork*, and *Imaginative Qualities of Actual Things*. North Point Press will publish his *Blue Pastoral* in 1983.

Jeff Weinstein writes for *The Village Voice*, and has published fiction in several magazines, including *Crawl Out Your Window*, *Intermedia*, and *Ear Magazine*. His long fiction, *Life in San Diego*, will be published by Sun & Moon Press in 1983.

Paul Witherington teaches at South Dakota State University in Brookings. He has published fiction in several journals, including *Mississippi Review*, *Wisconsin Review*, *Florida Quarterly*, and *Great River Review*.

This book was set in Goudy type by Barbara Shaw at The Writer's Center, 4800 Sangamore Rd., Bethesda, Maryland.

Printed by McNaughton & Gunn, Ann Arbor, Michigan.

Margaret Horn, Sandra Switkay, and Matthew Logan worked as interns in the editing and production of the book.

Publication has been made possible, in part, by matching grants from the National Endowment for the Arts and the Coordinating Council of Literary Magazines (CCLM).